HADES

Also by Mark Knowles

Blades of Bronze series
Argo
Jason

Other novels
The Consul's Daughter

HADES

MARK KNOWLES

An Aries Book

First published in the UK in 2023 by Head of Zeus,
part of Bloomsbury Publishing Plc

9 7 5 3 1 2 4 6 8

A catalogue record for this book is available from the British Library.

ISBN (PB): 9781801102766
ISBN (E): 9781801102759

Map design: Jeff Edwards

Printed and bound in Great Britain by
CPI Group (UK) Ltd, Croydon CR0 4YY

Head of Zeus Ltd
First Floor East
5–8 Hardwick Street
London EC1R 4RG

WWW.HEADOFZEUS.COM

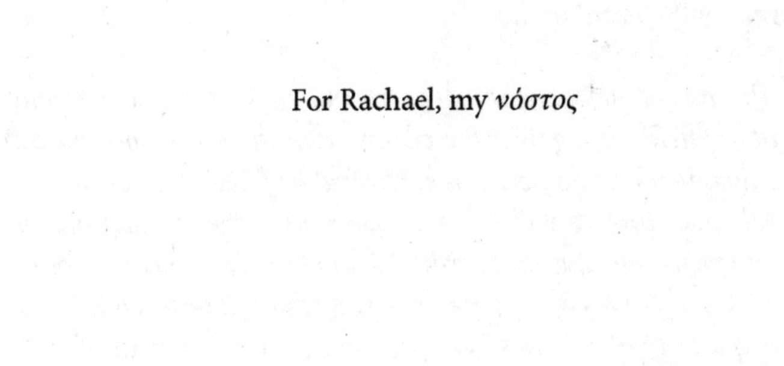

For Rachael, my *νόστος*

By command of the wanax *of Pylos, Great King Nestor, and his* lawagetas *Peisistratus, consider the orders of my followers as if delivered by the hand of the king:*

- *All coastal defences must be mobilised in both lower and upper fiefdoms against the enemy from the sea – 800 coastal watchmen and 600 oarsmen. Drafted by force, if necessary.*
- *All spare bronze will be requisitioned for the making of tips for spears, javelins and arrows. Scrap bronze to include votive gifts and grave goods, if necessary. By force, if necessary.*
- *A quantity of gold has been set aside for the payment of local chiefs and officials in enacting the above.*

In addition:

- *One golden cup and two women (to be drafted) as offerings for Potnia Hera.*
- *One golden cup and one man (to be drafted) as offerings for Hermes.*
- *One golden cup and one boy (drafted) as offerings for Zeus.*

Adapted from Pylos Linear B tablet archive

It may be that the gulfs will wash us down:
It may be we shall touch the Happy Isles,
And see the great Achilles, whom we knew.
Tho' much is taken, much abides; and tho'
We are not now that strength which in old days
Moved earth and heaven, that which we are, we are;
One equal temper of heroic hearts,
Made weak by time and fate, but strong in will
To strive, to seek, to find, and not to yield.

From 'Ulysses' (1842) by Alfred,
Lord Tennyson (1809-1892)

CONTENTS

Dramatis Personae

Lemnos

Alektruon warrior and member of the council
Auge Hypsipyle's handmaid
Euneus *wanax* (king) and son of Jason, leader of the Argonauts
Ekhinos son of Plouteos
Hektor warrior and member of the council
Hilarion member of the council
Hypsipyle mother of Euneus and former queen of Lemnos
Khalkeus warrior son of Idas of Arene (an Argonaut)
Moxos warrior son of Meleager, prince of Calydon (an Argonaut)
Plouteos *nomarch* (leader) of Moudros
Teodora proud young woman from Moudros
Xandros son of Euneus

Surviving Argonauts

Acastus *wanax* of Iolkos
Ancaeus helmsman and carpenter, formerly of Samos
Butes warrior of Athens
Castor and Pollux exiled twins of Sparta
Jason former *wanax* of Iolkos
Idas spearman of Arene
Meleager prince of Calydon
Orpheus the bard
Peleus leader of the Myrmidons of Phthia; father of Achilles
Telamon brother of Peleus

Crew of the *Salamander*

Elissos an archer
Glaux a young lookout

Additional Characters

Acamas *wanax* of Athens
Atukhos Ancaeus' young apprentice
Caeneus mercenary from Argos, son of Argonaut Polyphemus
Creoboros a fierce and loyal dog
Demophon brother of Acamas
Eriopis daughter of Medea
Huliat a warrior of the Peleset tribe
Medea princess of Colchis, formerly wife of Jason
Orestes *wanax* of Mycenae

HADES
N
Samothrace
Troy
Lemnos
Iolkos
Dimini
Sporades Islands
Perachora
Athens
Corinth
Mycenae
Nemea
Argos
Spetses
Pylos
Gytheon
THE ARCHIPELAGOS
Megalonisi
Route of the *Salamander*
0 100 200 300 miles
0 100 200 300 400 500 km

PROLOGUE

I, Orpheus

Stranger, answer me this.

Imagine you are dying of thirst in a sun-baked wasteland, and you see a spring suddenly burble through the dust ten feet in front of you. Could you will yourself to make it to the spring? The answer, I would say, is yes.

But what if the spring emerged from the ground one hundred feet away. Could you will yourself to live then? What about one thousand feet? What about ten thousand?

At some point, your will to live would be broken by the reality of the task set before you, so that it would be easier for you just to lie down and die. At the point of our birth, the thread of our fate has already been spun. At the point of our birth, the limit of our will to reach that spring has already been ordained. I have toiled alongside men and women whose strength of will appeared inexhaustible so that it seemed inconceivable that they should ever fall, yet fall they did.

Then came an age of darkness.

The world had changed. Drought and hunger stripped whole towns and villages of all but the strongest. Western vassal states engaged in frequent rebellions against the Hittite heartland, which started a tidal wave of migration, war and piracy that swept through Anatolia. Confederations of marauding pirates laid waste to those Achaian states that did not tear themselves apart first.

Imagine, if you will, witnessing your loved ones slain or enslaved and your homes razed to the ground. Imagine, at the tip of a sword, shunning death or destitution and groping instead for that spring, that sweet trickle of life-giving water.

We speak so much of memory these days because there is so little of it left. What little remains bards must gather, like precious shells on the shore when the tide of living memory has receded.

I am Orpheus the Thracian bard, custodian of memory and keeper of traditions. Much has already been told about me: only some of it is true. It has been my fate to live a long and eventful life. I have loved; I have lost. I once teetered above the fetid precipice of Hades, minded to jump, but I held my nerve. I rowed with the men of *Argo* to the ends of the earth and back. I lived through the Eastern War and have turned men into heroes and even gods. There are some who say I was born of a muse and a god. Some men are fools.

In my twilight years, it was my misfortune to witness the slide of man into the abyss but heed me when I say that there is light even in its deepest blackness: light cast by the memory of what once was and by the hope of what is to come.

Memory is life, stranger. I have always worshipped the goddess who protects it, for she has been kind. Be kind once more, divine Mnemosyne, and I will ask no more of you before I set down this lyre at your altar, as I once laid down my bow. Grant me the voice; grant me the nimble fingers to take these strands and weave them whilst the thread of Fate – and my waning power – still allows.

It starts with Jason, as many stories do.

BOOK ONE

THE BEGINNING OF THE END

Part One

A gathering

I

The Isthmus of Corinth, 1212 BC

The crack was sharp, rattling the heavens, the shutters and the careworn man who now groaned beneath them.

Curse thunder and the god who wields it. Curse them all, the dogs.

It had heralded his birth and, doubtless, it would herald his end.

But that would not be today. Perhaps, if he prayed for life – and made the fiction convincing – they might deliver the opposite. That was how they worked, these Olympians. At least, it was how they had worked for him.

Jason buried his head in the sweat-sour pillow and sighed. Sleep had been close to claiming him but the storm had dragged him back from the void, and now he was awake.

He pushed himself upright and listened to the steady hiss of rain on the thatch above. All of the oil lamps had fizzled out save one. He watched the plucky little flame cast a disc of light around the scoop of clay as if protecting the precious oil within. It felt like a seed of hope, which he had no mind to entertain, and he flopped back upon the bed.

Had it been worth it?

He looked about him in distaste. A converted byre in a lonely farmstead off the Corinth road. This was where life had led him. From a frescoed palace and a blazing hearth; the patter of soft feet across the hall; the giggling; the warmth of two children's smiles and their ready embraces. The innocent cast of one's own face beaming back, as yet unstained by fault or sin…

I bore you love's – life's! – greatest gift, twice over. You kicked my sweet agonies aside like… like dirt from your shoe!

He clutched his face, nails digging into his eyelids. *No! No! No! NO!*

He felt the grief crush his chest and he struggled to breathe as panic flooded the breach, as it did most nights, when wine or a woman had not patched it up.

You are Midas, but his gold is your pestilence!

His head thrashed about on the pillow. *Enough! Get out of my head! Out! OUT!*

Kicking aside the dirty coverlets, he threw himself from the bed, landing on the cold, compacted earth. The shock of the dull pain silenced the voices. In the darkness, his throat felt raw but he couldn't be sure the screams had ever left his head. He staggered to his feet and fumbled for the ewer of water.

No pain, no grief on earth could have prepared him for the passage of the past three years. His heart and mind had waded through Hades, scorched and tormented, and only his softening, ageing body had reminded him of his continued existence above the ground. No matter where he had roamed, no matter how he had punished his body through exhaustion or drink, his memories trailed behind him with his shadow and, whenever he closed his eyes, they pounced. He was cursed. Medea had done her work and she had done it well.

He felt a sudden rush of bile in his stomach as her voice returned.

Did her moans make you feel more of a man? Just as I made you, you filthy coward, so will I break you!

He made it to the door, falling against it with a clatter as the meagre contents of his stomach spattered onto the cool earth outside.

Dawn took her time in arriving. Once, when they were close, Medea had told Jason about the rumours of Helios being her grandfather, and how useful it was for common folk to believe this. He had to accept, given the pain of waking each morning, that there was some truth to it.

After bathing in a nearby stream, he gathered up his belongings and joined the road, full of misgivings. He walked for a mile, during which time the sun had begun to melt the hazy clouds and sweeten the earth after the previous night's storm. To all of nature's beauty, Jason was oblivious. At some point before midday, when his pace had slowed and his feet ached, he stopped and looked around him. Swifts swooped and chirped above a grove shelving towards the sea to the left while, to the right, the white hills of the central isthmus shone bright. The world was alive and people were waiting yet he had never felt so detached from it all.

He crested a rise and looked out westwards towards the remote, rocky peninsula of Perachora, spearing into the Corinthian Gulf. It would take him another evening and a morning before he would see its rocky waves diminishing towards the tip of that desolate triangle. Its very remoteness from an otherwise central region of Hellas, which had long since shaped its appeal for him, was now polluted. Yet it was here that the dwindling band of men would be gathering.

But his heart wasn't in it; not this year, just as it hadn't been for the last, nor the one before that. He took out a gourd of water and drank deep whilst he made a decision. Sated, he set off once more, resigned to follow whichever path his feet instinctively took him down.

II

Perachora peninsula (Isthmus of Corinth)

The big man removed his straw hat and ran his fingers through his shaggy greying hair. The lake opened up before him and he craved to immerse himself in it. He picked his way down the stony hillside and removed his damp tunic, balling it up and throwing it into the shallows. All around him, cicadas screeched and, in front, the sun dazzled his eyes as it glittered upon the water. He waded into the lake and then plunged in. He took a deep breath and spreadeagled himself on the surface, enjoying the feeling of weightlessness and the warmth of the sun on his face. Floating like that, occasionally splashing his face with water to cool it, he lost track of time until his eyes snapped open and he realised he was not alone.

He dipped his head under the surface and then emerged, his senses sharper as he waded ashore and scanned the rocks.

'You're getting fat, steersman,' came a deep, familiar voice.

'It helps me float.'

'Glad to see you, Ancaeus.'

'Always knew you had a soft spot for me. Been watching me for a while, have you?'

Meleager grinned and the pair embraced warmly. 'Gods above, man,' said Ancaeus, drying himself naked, 'look how grey you've gotten! Burden of ruling, is it?'

Meleager chuckled and looked away. 'Something like that.'

Ancaeus noticed how his friend's smile faded a touch. He slapped him on the shoulder. 'Come on. Seen any of the others on your travels?'

'Not yet.'

They gathered up their kit and made their way up the rocks to the path. Meleager frowned at Ancaeus. 'Are you going to wear that or just let your pharaoh burn?'

'Neither. I want to dry.'

'You've been living near Sparta too long, you animal. What about our *dioskouroi* down there?'

'Nothing.' They shared a worried look. 'Been a good few years now, hasn't it?'

The blood feud between Castor and Pollux and the House of Atreus, they all knew, still held despite the turmoil and the bloodshed of the intervening years. Menelaus had been a brash young prince when he had laid hands on their sister Helen, and Pollux – already a champion boxer – had not pulled his punches in response.

Menelaus' jaw had knitted itself back together and he now ruled Sparta whilst his brother Agamemnon lorded it over the Argolid. It mattered not a whit that the twins had sailed aboard *Argo* to the ends of the earth. Their glory had merely bloated the price on their heads, and it didn't bode well that they had seemingly disappeared from the face of the earth.

They passed along the narrow mule track threading between the bay and the scrub-covered slopes of the headland, talking and asking questions. Ancaeus' year – like most, of late – was less eventful than Meleager's, and it seemed to Ancaeus that the Calydonian was withholding something. By the estimation of most of the Argonauts, Meleager had emerged from the mission to retrieve the golden fleeces from distant Colchis with his reputation as a warrior the most enhanced, though plenty of others had run him close in cementing their *kleos*. Not that he ever spoke of it: he was also the man most likely to brush such things off.

They emerged from a canopy of pine trees and fell into an expectant silence as they walked. Maddened by the heat, cicadas sawed in chorus with the dry rustle of thistle bushes. Here, where a natural track descended towards a secluded bay, they stopped and shielded their eyes. On a plateau of powdery earth, sacred to Hera, was a pair of tents. Ancaeus and Meleager exchanged a look of satisfaction – tinged with relief – and set off to greet whoever was inside them.

As they were halfway towards the tents, three heads popped out from under the canopies in quick succession, like chicks at feeding time, and then a fourth. One of them wolf-whistled at the naked Ancaeus.

'I once owned an old mutt with hair on its chest like that!' shouted one of them emerging from his tent. He, too, was quite naked but, whereas Ancaeus' barrel chest was indeed covered with a pelt of black and grey hairs, his was whip-thin and hairless, albeit marked by impressive battle scars.

'Idas of Arene!' growled Ancaeus. 'Are you cold? You look cold!'

'No,' he replied, thumbing over his shoulder. 'Butes, Telamon and Peleus here have been keeping me company at night. They still snore like hogs.'

"They *look* like hogs! I was going to ask where the others were but, great gods, man! It looks like Telamon's eaten them!'

'I hope you have some wine down there that's cooler than mine.'

'Nought wrong with some warm wine, Lord Meleager, but I won't be touching *his*,' wheezed Telamon, scratching his belly, 'dangling next to his arse crack for the past few miles.'

There was a bleat from somewhere nearby and Ancaeus turned towards it, feeling his mouth watering.

'Bartered a pair of goats on the way in,' said Peleus, tipping his coppery head back. 'Supposed it was my turn this year.'

'Was your turn last year,' muttered Idas, sucking his sharp teeth. '*And* the year before.'

III

One of the goats had been roasting for several hours and there was a second fire blazing as the sun was about to touch the horizon. They rose at the same time, without the need for words. With a finger of wine in their cups, they found the ancient path that led through a patch of scrub to a little stone enclosure, overgrown and silent. There was no conversation now as their minds turned towards those who had rowed with them and not returned.

The grey stone bearing the form of Hera was weathered and chipped but there it still was on its plinth. They all entered the enclosure and bowed their heads before it, murmuring the prayer of thanks and deliverance before pouring the libation.

A breath of cool air made the brushwood rustle, and the Argonauts shuddered. What little superstition nature had allowed them, their lives had all but quashed, yet the sudden response to their prayers unsettled them. They left the enclosure in silence and it wasn't until they were halfway back to their camp that Ancaeus spoke.

'What about Jason's boys?'

Idas shook his head. 'Not yet.'

'Good. I have something for them.'

They all took a little detour towards the tip of the peninsula, stopping before twin cairns. Ancaeus felt the presence of something unseen in the encroaching shadows and, when a gecko scuttled along the earth a few strides in front of him, it made him start. There were no words of derision; just a strong hand on his shoulder which he knew, without the need to look back, would be Meleager's.

Once more, their quiet conversations fell silent. Ancaeus stepped forwards and brushed some twigs and leaves from the stones before removing the offerings from his leather bag. He set one down at the foot of each cairn: olivewood boats carved with graceful keels and bows that curled above their decks like scorpion tails. He heard the Argonauts' murmurs of approval behind him.

Ancaeus had long realised that his skills lay in his hands not his words, but the prayers he whispered were brief and heartfelt. When he rose, feeling his eyes sting in a way he never expected, Peleus inclined his head back towards the path. 'Come on, old man. That goat'll have crisped nicely. My brother brought some herbs.' He turned to Telamon as they walked. 'Tell me you remembered.'

'Remembered what?' he growled.

'The fennel? The oregano? You picked the stuff! You found it!'

'Oh. I think… I think I left it in that hollow.'

'*Ma Dia*, what is *wrong* with you, man? You've got the memory of an infant!'

IV

'It was bugging me,' said Butes, scratching his misshapen wrestler's ears, 'seeing Ancaeus earlier, naked as the day he was born, what it reminded me of.' He pointed his knife at *Argo*'s helmsman. 'But I've got it now.'

Ancaeus rolled his eyes. 'Go on.'

'The land of those Hut-Dwellers… When we first arrived: remember? Those natives going at it in full view without a care in the world, hairy as bears.'

They burst out laughing as Ancaeus stopped eating and glanced down at his chest with a frown.

As the fires crackled and the breakers rattled the pebbles a short distance away, the Argonauts ate and drank in great contentment. The meeting under the full moon during the Month of the Grape Harvest had become one of the most important events of their year. A chance to reminisce and exchange stories, to share tales about former crewmates. It was inevitable that some had drifted further than others but none resented it: the bonds were too strong for that. Sadder was the news whenever one of them had died in the intervening months. No such news had reached their ears this year, for which they thanked the gods, particularly the Great Mother, whom they had adopted as their tutelary deity.

'Anything from Jason?' asked Ancaeus.

They exchanged pregnant glances and shook their heads.

Idas spat to the side. 'Not since that witch did him in.'

'A bad business,' muttered Meleager, hoping the subject might pass. He got to his feet on knees that clicked. 'More wine?'

Ancaeus nodded and held out his cup. 'Does it still bother you?'

'Does what still bother me?'

The steersman caught the sharp glance from Butes. 'That Jason's sons are here.'

'Them? No, not really.' Meleager shrugged his great shoulders as he poured. 'They were just boys.'

Idas tutted. 'It's that witch. She knew what she was doing, bringing them here, polluting the one patch of earth and rock that was ours. Jason should have put a stop to it and he didn't. That's all there is to it.'

'We came back too proud and now our kin hate us. None more than him.' Ancaeus noticed that Meleager was looking out over the sea with his jaw set and he realised he had made a mistake, curdling the atmosphere with his poking. He took a deep breath and asked brightly, 'Anyway, the man himself should be here. What's that, three years now? Four?'

'Three.'

They all snapped their heads up to the voice from the darkness of the coastal path. Ancaeus swept up his axe. 'Who's that? Show yourself.'

'Gladly,' said the stocky figure, bounding down the hill despite the ankle-cracking stones littering the slope.

The man lowered the hood of his cloak, revealing thick curls, gold and grey in the firelight.

'Theseus!' cried Ancaeus, dropping his axe to embrace him. The rest of the Argonauts jumped to their feet to greet him, for it had been a couple of years since he himself had last trekked to the Heraion.

Idas presented him with a cup of wine whilst Telamon sliced him some meat and he sat down, cross-legged, talking as if he had only seen them the previous week. As he spoke, Ancaeus noticed a slight change in him. Aboard *Argo* he had earned the nickname 'Happy' because his demeanour had been anything but. It wasn't until the return leg that he had even disclosed his real name. The sullen, proud youth had gone on to become an adventurer and hero in his own right, purging the lawless Isthmus of bandits and footpads. Their own yearly pilgrimages to the remote tip of Perachora had been made much safer because of his vigorous efforts to stamp out brigandage. Now Theseus was king of Athens and, as Ancaeus watched him holding forth, his handsome features animated in the dancing flames, he could see Theseus didn't wear it lightly.

When there was a momentary lull in the conversation, Ancaeus cleared his throat. 'So then, Theseus. Seems you've kept company with many great names, united Attica, founded games and courted all the known gods, but how on earth do you keep them all happy?'

'Oh, I'm sure I don't but I live a charmed life.'

'Will you be paying your respects here tomorrow?'

Theseus sipped his wine and gave him a shrewd look. 'Now that *would* offend my lady Athena, and you know what these goddesses are like. Very testy!'

The firewood crackled and little glances crossed the half-light like migrating swifts. 'We know what *this* one's like,' said Ancaeus quietly, 'and she's been pretty good, on balance.'

The king of Athens waved his hands vaguely and it seemed to Ancaeus the wine had gone to his head early. 'Ah, maybe I'll sprinkle some barley before I leave—'

'As you wish.'

'—so Pirithous and I, once we'd grieved for our women, decided it'd be a boon to go on a little adventure up-country...'

At some point after they had finally lain down to sleep, a gentle breeze had picked up, carrying the tendrils of smoke from the embers of the fire away up the slope. Ancaeus heard a faint grating of rocks and then a *clack*, like a pebble dropping onto a ledge. His eyes snapped open and he peered up into the stolid darkness of the hillside. Nearby, Butes farted and Telamon sputtered but turned on his side and muttered in his sleep. Seeing nothing, hearing nothing, Ancaeus rested upon his elbows and, a few minutes later, was himself snoring.

The following morning, whilst the others breakfasted on hard bread, cheese and artichokes, Ancaeus stretched and, quite without knowing why, found himself following the path to the sanctuary.

The walls still held; the image of Hera was sat where it had always been. He tipped his head in respect to the goddess and made his way back down the slope. There was a gentle splash from the bay and, a moment later, Theseus' head appeared. He threw back his hair and rubbed the water from his face. A dip in the water appealed to him and his foot made for the slope but the other held, reluctant. Ancaeus turned right and brushed aside the ferns that concealed the path of beaten earth. In a few moments, he reached the cairns raised above the ashes of Jason's young boys.

He noticed it at once. The right-hand mound was as he had left it, with his wooden carving at its foot. The topmost stone of the left cairn, however, had been dislodged and, in its fall, had crushed the olivewood boat. Ancaeus replaced the stone and checked the cairn, testing it for stability. He had helped raise it and it was tightly assembled, with no loose rocks.

The boat was irreparable. It saddened him not on account of the hours he had spent in carving it but because he had liked both lads on the occasions he had met them. He sighed and placed it alongside the other, moving them both between the cairns. When he stood, a chill breeze brushed his skin, making the hair on his nape stand on end. Eyes flaring, he backed out of the cool sanctuary and into the morning light.

Part Two

An arrival

LEMNOS, 1211 BC

Future generations will be quick to judge one of the women who next makes an appearance and, invariably, those judgements will fall wide of the mark. I should know because I spent months in her company, in fair weather and foul. I might even have called her a friend.

Her warmth of feeling, which caused her to love freely and fiercely, grew from the same shoot as unbridled passion, which swayed her towards violence and bitterness. Jason might have spared himself the latter emotions had he only nurtured the former. But, like a temple priest tallying his offerings, his could be a calculating mind.

Her arrival took Queen Hypsipyle by surprise. Alongside her maidens, the queen had spent the morning threshing flax with hackles in the dusty square of Myrine, but the heat – even in the shade – had become too fierce, and she had dismissed the girls whilst she rested in the cool of her hall. This was the summer that she had begun to feel her fifty years in the aching of her bones or, rather, heed them whenever they grumbled.

Now she was alone, with a cup of lemon water and her memories. She didn't hear the approaching footsteps and it made her start when the black-clad figure appeared alongside her chair. Still, she was a queen respected for her self-control, and it was not within her character to show fear. The woman did not seem to be armed but the intensity of her presence suggested she was not to be trifled with.

'Are you a Thracian?'

The woman stared at her, unblinking, and Hypsipyle's blood turned to water. 'No.'

The queen blinked. 'Then who are you and what do you want?'

The visitor cocked her head to the side and, though her green eyes fixed her, Hypsipyle got the distinct impression she was being weighed up. 'To warn you.'

Hypsipyle's eyes darted around the hall and the stranger's lips straightened. 'There is no one here. I met your sons: they were heading the opposite way. They are so handsome, aren't they?'

'To warn me of *what*?'

The smile faded. 'Of hard times, queen. Of death and of grief.'

'Get out of my home.'

The woman tutted. 'When I am gone – a long time from now – you will regret you lacked the courage to ask the questions beating within your heart.'

'Who are you?' Noticing the curious drawl in the woman's accent, she glanced again at the astral tattoos on her cheek, and added, 'Where are you from?'

'You are doing better but surely you showed Jason more *xenia* when he and his pirates first arrived, no? Or is guest-friendship in Lemnos dying along with her soil?'

The mention of Jason's name broke the last strands that reined in Hypsipyle's calm. She felt her jaw go slack. 'You are the w… you are the… the one from Colchis, aren't you? That he took back to Thessaly with him.'

'The witch?'

'Yes.' She paused. 'Medea. This is you, isn't it?'

'I am no witch.'

'They say you murdered your children.' Hypsipyle lowered her voice. 'Is this true?'

Once more that enigmatic smile. 'Would you like it to be true? Would this make it easier to hate me? To fear me?'

'Is it *true*?'

'It isn't true!' The ferocity of Medea's hiss made Hypsipyle flinch.

'Rumour is persistent.'

'Because I killed his beloved *princess*,' Medea spat the word in distaste. 'And rumour did the rest.'

'From beauty soured,
By age devoured,
Do love and lust vie in flight.'

Medea gave Hypsipyle a curious look and then she broke out into tinkling laughter. 'This is the lot of all women, isn't it?'

'So it would seem.'

'If only a man realised, if only he could *feel* – just for a heartbeat – the agonies a woman knows when she brings new life into the world, perhaps then he would look upon her with kinder eyes. This is the field of battle for us women, don't you think? One from which there is less hope of leaving alive.' Her eyes hardened and she pulled her dress tighter. 'I would thrice rather stand in line with shield and spear than give birth just once.'

For a moment, neither spoke, thoughts fencing in the heavy silence. Medea's was a beguiling face and Hypsipyle couldn't help but wonder what she might have looked like in her youth, before age and bitterness had hardened it.

'The unburied souls down there,' said Medea, tipping her head towards the coast, 'are restless. I felt them tugging at my hem even as I passed them. Do not consider that trouble finished just because sand covers their bones.'

Hypsipyle swallowed hard and reached for her cup. Medea watched her sip the lemon water with hands that now shook. 'And this is what you came to warn me of, is it?'

'No.'

'What then?' she said, feeling the cold fingers of dread stroke her innards. Hypsipyle had long since come to terms with the killing of the menfolk for the shame and dishonour they had inflicted upon their wives: for vaunting their Thracian whores. This she could have dealt with.

'It was Jason who killed his sons, not me – no, spare me that look and just listen – Jason it was who abandoned them, much as he professed to love them. There are some who say he had already seeded his little hussy, and wanted us out of the way. That he could have countenanced his sons and their mother begging beside the road. An inconvenience for a future king, don't you think? Jason pushed the first rock that started the fall.'

'And you killed his betrothed.'

'Just as you killed yours. As all your women did. Perhaps, before you judge me, you should understand we have trodden the same path.'

There were faint voices from the courtyard. Young and vigorous. Hypsipyle glanced towards the door. When she looked up again, Medea was staring at her.

'A mob killed my sons. In cold blood. For what I had done to their princess. To Glauke.'

Hypsipyle began to shake but there was no time to answer. Her sons entered the hall, bright-eyed and clean-limbed, they slowed when they saw the visitor.

'Oh, you again. Can I…?'

'Leave us, Euneus. We were just… Please.'

A faint frown crossed the boy's features but he nodded. 'Come on, Thoas. Back outside.'

'But…'

'Out!'

Hypsipyle watched them leave, feeling her stomach crawl with misgivings.

'What lovely boys. They share your looks fairly, wouldn't you say? Perhaps more of his father in that taller one. Euneus, isn't it?'

'Would you care for water?' The queen cleared her throat. 'Something to eat?'

Medea's face twitched. 'I came to warn you and, I confess, to see what sort of woman you were. But I have no further interest in the exchanging of pleasantries with you.'

'Then be done with it. *Speak!*'

'Upon you, I have no particular desire to bring harm, since you have never offended me. But Hekate is angry and I revere her. *She* has been the one constant in my life, despite the promises I broke and the things I have done.' Medea readjusted her *himation* at the shoulder, checking her anger. 'Jason's line is doomed. As it was for me, so is it your fate to bury two boys whilst you still draw breath. Hold them close, while time allows. These are the words of the goddess and they are true.'

Hypsipyle raised her chin. She felt the blood drain from her body and a chill seep through her bones, making her shudder. 'You have said your piece,' she whispered, 'and now you will leave. But mark these words. If you ever return to these shores, my sons will vie with each other for the honour of killing you first.'

'This would not be possible, even if I was to return. Remember what I said, Queen Hypsipyle. Your life is a reflection of my own.'

Hypsipyle watched Medea's black dress glide along the floor as she left. She held in her emotions for as long as she could – long enough, at least, for Medea to have left the village square – before her resistance crumbled and she buried her head in her hands and sobbed.

Part Three

A return

VALLEY OF NEMEA, 1205 BC

'*Shh!*' Euneus shook the water from his traveller's cape and turned to the horses. When he placed his finger on his lips, they whickered and fell quiet. They had been concealed in the maquis of the ridge for several hours, during which time the hissing downpour had soon overcome the chirring of cicadas.

'It's this rain,' whispered his twin Thoas, peering across the valley through the concealment of the cypresses. 'He hates it.'

The other muttered to himself as he wiped his face. 'Not the only one.'

'There! You see her?'

'I see her.' Thoas' hand sought the reassurance of the sword's pommel. He loved Euneus, and Thoas' years of resentment towards the unfair allotment of accomplishments – and looks – had long faded.

Thoas watched the woman bustle about the sanctuary, more than a hundred yards distant. She was attending to her duties with as much dignity as she could, though it was clear to both of them that she wanted to be back inside, out of the rain.

And this posed a problem.

Euneus glanced up at the sky. It was difficult to tell whether the light was fading or the brewing storm was concealing it. Either way, they would have to move quickly. 'Those buildings to the left.' He pointed and waited until his brother acknowledged them. 'I think they're stables. We shouldn't cross them in case the animals become restive...'

'But that way lies the road.'

'Then we take the long way round.'

Thoas frowned and looked into his brother's intense blue eyes. They exuded a confidence he himself didn't feel. 'And where do you think Lykourgos lives? The *wanax*?'

Euneus scanned the valley again, wiping the rain from the hair plastered to his brow. He shrugged but it was a fair question. The sanctuary itself was nothing grand but neither were any of the other buildings scattered about. He was still for a moment.

'Now. We go now.'

His sudden urgency took Thoas by surprise but he twitched into life. The brothers slung their packs around their shoulders and swung onto the horses with some difficulty, for their chestnut flanks were slippery.

They picked their way downhill through the cypresses and patches of wild garlic, taking care not to rush the mounts. A slip now would undermine the months of plotting that had brought them to this very spot, after a week of travel at sea and on land. When they reached the valley floor, they skirted around rows of vines, heading for the sanctuary's main building at an oblique angle, blocking the woman's view of the brothers. She would have no reason for thinking the intentions of two armed men on horseback good and therefore couldn't be expected to stay put.

Crossing the open ground, Euneus and Thoas were now grateful for the rain and the clouds: nobody was outside. They reached the sanctuary's low walls in under a minute and dismounted, stroking the horses' withers as they approached the eaves, pressing themselves against the dirty lime plaster. Rainwater drilled from the roof onto the compacted earth, spattering their shins as they sidled around the building, taking care to duck under the closed shutters.

Voices rooted them to the spot. They were unhurried, unstressed: a youth and, briefly, a mature woman. Thoas looked at Euneus, wide-eyed, but his brother was frowning, listening intently. After a few moments, he held up two fingers and pointed round the corner of the building. A final sweep of the valley then he drew his sword and hurried around the front of the building, Thoas close behind.

A boy with his back to them was at that moment leaning against the cruciform posts that held up the porch. Beyond him, warming herself next to the hearth stones, her damp, hooded cloak clinging to her spare frame, was the woman they had come for.

The boy heard the hurried footsteps and turned on his heels. He had seen twelve or thirteen winters and, there and then, the blood drained from his doughy face.

'*Don't* scream!' hissed Thoas, pointing his sword at his throat. 'It's her we want, not you.'

The boy's eyes darted between the brothers and he nodded, stepping behind the porch column. 'Ah, ah!' said Thoas, beckoning him with his blade. 'Inside, come on.'

The woman, deep in thought and staring into the flames, registered their arrival a few moments later. She gave a little gasp of fear and tugged down her hood as Euneus strode into the sparsely furnished hall and sheathed his sword. Confusion flickered through her fear.

'Mother,' declared Euneus. 'We've come to take you home.'

'No!' she whispered. 'It can't be!'

Euneus turned to the boy, raising the tip of his sword to his heart. 'You don't move; you don't talk.'

'My boys?' When Euneus was stood alongside his brother, she stepped forwards and her eyes ranged all over their faces. They shared her long slender nose and fine features, though their eyes couldn't have been more different.

'Euneus?' she tentatively reached out and ran her fingers down his face. His resemblance to the man who had turned her life upside down all those years ago stole the breath from her lungs. It was as if Jason had just stepped out of her past.

'Thoas... The gods, it is you!' Her voice became hoarse as emotion began to grip her throat. 'What miracle brought you both here?'

'Later, Mother. We have to go.'

From the corner of his eye, Euneus saw the boy slip from the hall and sprint across the sanctuary towards the cluster of buildings opposite. *'Help!'* he screamed. *'They've come for Priestess Hypsipyle!'*

Thoas cursed and the twins took their mother by the arm, hurrying her towards the door. As they cleared the porch, the boy looked over his shoulder. He was splay-footed and cumbersome but his voice carried through the downpour.

'There are others here?'

Hypsipyle nodded.

The brothers shared a look and Thoas was certain he saw a flash of irritation in Euneus' eyes. *Should he have remained with the boy, or bound him up?*

They hurried around the corner, half expecting to see the horses in the distance, for they had not been tethered. Both of them had sought the dubious shelter of the eaves and looked thoroughly miserable. Euneus' stallion bobbed his head, eager to be on the move, and Euneus helped his mother up.

'Can you ride?'

'No!'

'Just hold on to me then. Thoas?'

Thoas helped him up before clambering onto his own mount. They dug in their heels and, heads bent forwards, set off at a gallop around the building away from the cluster opposite. When they emerged on the opposite side, cutting towards the Corinth road, they caught a glimpse of three men, long-haired and capable, barking orders at the boy.

'Hold tight!' shouted Euneus. He felt the arms around his waist tense and, a moment later, they cleared the low sanctuary wall, and the horse skittered a little as it readjusted to the damp ground. He heard Thoas grunt as his horse leaped across from the compacted earth to the softer terrain of the valley floor, checking the speed of both. Thoas looked behind him and regretted it instantly. Three greys were being bustled out of the stable and the boy was shoved aside. The pursuit was on.

A couple of lengths ahead, Euneus pressed his mount's flank with his heel, dismayed by the spongy earth and the scrub bushes that hindered its hooves. Cutting back towards the road reduced the gap to the pursuers but he hoped the firmer surface would compensate. After a few more strides, the horse picked up the pace and he risked a look behind. Thoas had fallen further back but, more worrying still, three men were chasing them down, hair streaming behind them. Ahead lay the road of fifteen or more miles of beaten earth towards the coast, a low ridge to the left and maquis all around, with only scrub and, occasionally, patches of fruit trees for concealment.

They could never outrun the furious Nemeans. He glanced over his shoulder again, desperate to see the pursuers stumble or falling away. Instead they were gaining.

His eyes met Thoas' and, in that fleeting moment, he knew his brother was going to do something reckless.

'Get her home!' shouted Thoas.

Euneus pulled back on the reins. *'Thoas!'*

'No!' Hypsipyle's scream made Euneus' ears ring. *'Come back!'*

Euneus felt her try to dismount and he half-turned, gripping her by the wrist.

'Go, brother!' shouted Thoas. *'Return to your son!'*

The Nemeans were almost upon him.

'No!'

Thoas withdrew his sword, turned his horse in a perfect pirouette and slashed at the oncoming riders. He could not miss. The foremost of them had no time to react and was almost beheaded. Blades flashed and Thoas was dragged to the ground. Euneus looked on in horror. Behind him, Hypsipyle was trembling, babbling in grief and shock. Euneus leaned forwards, willing his body to drive his horse back to the fray.

But it would not respond. Some stubborn sensibility told him to flee, whilst he still could. To save his mother. To fight another day.

Thoas was no longer moving but two horsemen lay still alongside him. The third now stared at Euneus and whipped his reins. Euneus wheeled his horse, his sodden clothes clinging to his skin, and urged his mother to hold tight.

He tried to steer the horse between the ruts left by a passing chariot but most of the track was now blotted with puddles and treacherous slicks of mud. Euneus blinked through the rain and scanned the unchanging landscape for the right location. Foam flew from his mount's teeth and he could feel the heat from his flanks as he began to tire. The horse was as spirited as any he had ever ridden but the time had come. He slowed to a canter and stroked its withers.

'You must get down now.'

Her face was white with shock.

'Get down, Mother! Get off the road!'

'She was right.' Hypsipyle slithered awkwardly off the horse's back. 'The witch.' She turned to him and he frowned at her. The thump of approaching hooves made him look up. The Nemean was fifty paces away and closing fast.

'End this,' she whispered, pulling her hood over her head as she bustled over the mud into a cluster of olive trees. Euneus wiped his hands on his tunic and worked his fingers before withdrawing his cold sword from the scabbard on the horse's back.

He took a deep breath and, at thirty paces, urged his horse to a canter. The Nemean was right-handed and brandishing a club, longer than his own sword. At twenty paces, he dug in his heels and crossed the path of the oncoming charge, forcing the Nemean to swing his club across his body. At ten paces, Euneus lunged at him, ducking low as he sensed the club swinging towards him. He felt his blade punch into a solid mass before brilliant light and pain detonated inside his skull. For a scintilla of a second, he was aware he was free-falling but, of his heavy landing, he felt nothing.

He came to with a pained gasp, shivering violently. Blurred through the film of rainwater came the outline of olive trees and cypresses lining the road. He blinked and, recalling the danger, snapped his head to the side, inducing a gasp of pain.

Euneus forced his pain-racked body to sit up. The Nemean was lying on his side, a few yards away. There was a faint streak of blood in the puddle beside him but the sickening twist of his neck made it immaterial. His grey was beside him, raising its hooves impatiently.

A stone's throw away, he saw his mother, rocking to and fro over the broken corpse of Thoas. He could hear her sobs through the gentle hiss of rain.

'Mother!' he croaked. 'We must go.'

Hypsipyle now saw him. She hurried over and, murmuring

prayers of thanks, smothered his forehead in kisses. She cleared the hair from his face. Euneus flinched. 'The horse…' she began.

'It's still here. *You're* still here, praise the gods!'

'The rider, we…'

'No.'

'Can you stand, my love? Careful!' she said, helping him to his feet. Euneus grimaced as pain lanced through his shoulder and hip.

'We need to take Thoas and go.' He gritted his teeth and filled his lungs, willing himself not to faint. 'I can't lift him on my own. Can you help me?'

She wiped the tears from her face but the rain could not conceal the raw grief. She nodded. 'I can help.'

Stranger, we must leave Euneus and Hypsipyle in Nemea, from where they will return in safety to the island of Lemnos, and turn our eyes towards another island and another boy. All I have learned about him, from the lips of those who know, I now pass to you…

Part Four

An awakening

AT THE SAME TIME, ON MEGALONISI

The boy flinched and pressed his palms tighter against his ears.

It was no use.

He could not unhear the screams, the shattering of whole shelves of pots, the thud of metal on wood. The *terror.*

It was them, no doubt. One moment, he had been carving a figurine in the yard, trying not to cut the muzzle of the goat that would not be dissuaded from trying to nibble the wood. The next, villagers came tearing up the track shouting in abject panic and his father had grabbed him and carried him indoors.

In the previous few months, he had begun to experience a vague sense of unease that had exacerbated his headaches but, like a brief rain shower upon parched earth, the effect was fleeting. Whispered conversations overheard upon entering his parents' room and their sudden, worried looks. The frequent meeting of the menfolk and their murmured conversations beneath the oak tree. His friends, pretending to fight off raiders with sticks whittled from olive wood in the dusty track beyond the village.

Then one day, his parents had sat down with him to eat. He could see their faces were hollowed with hunger and fatigue. The strained silence broken only by the clack of wooden spoons against bowls of gruel: a thin paste of ground acorns and leather boiled in water that at least had the effect of softening the stale bread.

'Listen to me, Huliat, put down your stick and listen to your parents,' his father had said, tugging at his dark beard. It was the end of the previous summer and the leaves were beginning to fall, golden and brittle. 'If men ever come to this village, you do not try to be brave, you just hide; are you listening?' He had nodded solemnly, not meeting his father's eyes. It worried him to see such a big man looking fearful.

'Nothing brave, Huliat!' his mother had added, wagging her finger at him.

'Look what I have made,' said his father, lowering his voice and leading him into one of the rooms adjoining the living quarters. The one in which, during exceptionally cold weather, the goats would sometimes huddle, adding the sweet smell of dung to the smoke, fat and sweat already thick in the house. 'Look at this. See?' he said, clearing away a fresh coating of straw to reveal a little ring of rope attached to a slatted door. 'It pulls up. There will always be a little water in there. Wheaten biscuits too, if I can find a way of keeping the rats away.'

Huliat looked at it with grudging curiosity. He was very large for a boy of just five winters. 'Will I be…?'

'Of course you will fit! I made it myself.'

The assertion was supposed to reassure him but his father's skills lay not in carpentry. He was a hunter, and a good one, and one of the best spearmen in the west of Megalonisi, so he had once heard. Huliat had heard his father busy at work during the previous days but had assumed he was repairing the partition for the animals.

'You could always try, if…'

'No!' declared Huliat. He glanced once more at the trapdoor and at his mother, wringing her hands, then went back outside to play.

As it proved, he did fit into that airless cavity, even after another half year's growth. It took his dad to pick him up bodily and shove him inside, hissing at him to do as he was told, before he finally acquiesced and the hatch clattered into place above him.

The noises had faded now. The isolated crack of a pot and a shout – impossible to tell what language – and the odd bleat of goat and sheep becoming restive. As Huliat's veins pounded in fear, he stared unblinking through the thin gaps between the slats. This proved painful. One of his terrible headaches had begun to jab at his skull, making his vision swim. Screwing his eyes shut was the best way to soothe it. He rocked backwards and forwards, repeating his father's advice.

Nothing brave, Huliat, nothing brave...

His father had swiped straw across the trapdoor before he had picked up his spear from the rack and left: some of it had fallen onto his face. He hoped he wouldn't sneeze.

When nothing happened after a few minutes, he dared open his eyes. Bars of sun from the shuttered windows in the living quarters illuminated fat flies and motes of dust. Through the few gaps not obscured by straw, he could make out the lintel of the doorway and the top few inches of door, still firmly closed. In some ways, the sounds of violence and destruction were less terrifying than the menacing silence that followed.

Long moments passed and the pounding in his temples eased. A few times, he heard the soft tread of feet nearby and what sounded like the *dink* of a stone against the mud-brick walls of the house.

What on earth was happening? Where were his parents?

If the raiders had been repulsed – and he began to allow himself to believe this – then his parents would hurry back to free him. But if they had been killed, how would he know when it was safe to emerge? Or if? A dreadful thought drifted into his head like the wisp of dust drifting above the slats.

If these raiders were to torch the house, he wouldn't know about it until it was too late.

A ball of nausea formed in his throat with the quickening of his heart and he wiped an unbidden tear from the corner of his eye. He felt the panic brimming within him and he sat up a little straighter, so that the crown of his head touched the underside of the floor above.

Better to risk fleeing across the open fields than be burnt to a cinder. He reached for the trapdoor at the very moment the front door burst open, clattering against the wall. Huliat sank back into the musty half-light, hearing the blood pulsing around his skull. He couldn't see who had entered but the steps were heavy and slow. The hope that his father had returned slipped through his fingers like water. He would surely have called his name immediately.

He heard the creak of leather and a sniff then, a moment later, an unstoppered bung and the glug of water being swallowed, or wine. Wine made men violent, even his otherwise-loving father. He detested wine.

Huliat clenched his eyes shut as the footsteps approached the partitioned room. There was nothing of any value in here – nothing worth stealing. The house was set back a little from the main village. It was tidy, sturdy but anonymous. Surely, he repeated over and over in his head, whoever was above would soon lose interest and leave.

The footsteps came nearer and he saw the bare legs of a man, thick and matted with fair hair. Not his father. A scabbard hung from a leather baldrick but he couldn't see any more.

Dust began to tickle his nose and he slowly moved his hand to cover his face. The feet ground the straw and grit of the floor as they turned away and made for the door, but it was too late. He stifled the sneeze but there was no stopping the little guttural noise in its stead. The footsteps froze then approached quickly. The straw was kicked aside and fierce green eyes glared at him through the slats. Huliat tried to turn the moment of surprise in his favour and heaved the hatch open. It hit the raider's knee, making him grunt. When Huliat scrambled up, a bark of command – and a sharp sword tip, inches from his nose – turned him statue-still.

'Up! Up!'

He knew what the words meant even though the voice shouting them was unusual. A powerful hand grabbed him by the tunic and yanked him with difficulty out of the cavity. Calloused fingers clamped his head, turning it this way and that, as if he were livestock at a market. The face was craggy and an unhealthy shade of yellow, and Huliat could see the same fascination and disgust that he always saw in the eyes of someone looking at him for the first time. Huliat noticed liver spots on the man's arms: he had once been fascinated by blemishes like freckles and warts, but there was no question of tracing these with his finger like he'd done when he was little.

So he was unwell. But, by the Skyfather, the man still had raw strength. Apparently satisfied, he shoved Huliat towards the door.

He swallowed the sudden urge to run: he would only want to return to find his mother and father. Better to learn their fate now, even though some dark feeling lurking in the pit of his stomach told him he already knew.

There were other raiders in the village. Most had removed their helmets, revealing dirty blond hair, darkened by sweat or filth. One still wore his. Huliat had never seen the likes before. Curved horns joined by a metal disc.

He felt a shove in his back, making him stumble. There was no reason for it because he wasn't dawdling. The man did it just because he felt like it. He turned and shot the man a glare but he was looking elsewhere, wiping his nose. Huliat felt his eyes stinging. They descended a shallow decline and passed through a gap in some thorn bushes towards the little rill, on either side of which lay most of the houses. One of them was on fire: the smoke rising from the hearth was thick and black, and he could hear the crackling as he passed.

There were sounds of a desperate struggle and a woman's fearful shriek. He stopped and peered around a doorway to see a man's white buttocks pumping back and forth whilst his hands gripped the hair of a woman struggling to escape. Cold terror coursed through his veins and he felt his limbs go weak. He wanted to look to make sure it wasn't his mother but also wanted to wash the raw image from his mind altogether.

Behind him, the raider chuckled and Huliat turned to him, fists clenched. The chuckle faded and the man's lips curled into a snarl, waving him on. Huliat stumbled forwards. Everywhere he looked now, in the fly-blown alleys or out in the open, he saw visions of Hades. Fellow villagers sprawled in attitudes of desperate fight or flight, unmoving. Some streaked in blood. Here, older folk pleading for their lives – or the lives of others; there, pirates kicking villagers or emerging from homes with armfuls of worthless trinkets.

'Momma!' Huliat cried out. 'Pappa!'

The man behind him half-heartedly tried to silence him.

'Momma! Where are you?'

'No, you quiet!'

It was the realisation they spoke some of their own tongue rather than the words themselves that quieted him. As he took in the hellish scenes, he felt a sudden, crushing yearning to cling to his parents. He felt his legs buckle and his body began to quiver uncontrollably.

They had reached the main square. Under the tall date palms were huddled some wretched figures. He stumbled over to them, recognising in the sorrowful faces neighbours and acquaintances.

'Have... Have you seen my momma? Or my pappa?'

They raised their pale faces and looked through him, hollow-eyed. He moved on, past the stares of a sea rover knocking back wine from a clay flagon. He wore the same helmet: horns, the disk.

'Momma?' Tears streamed freely down his face now and his chest convulsed with shock. 'Pappa?'

The boy's raw grief stirred enough pity for some to shake their head. One old woman even tried to offer a sad smile but her wrinkled lips barely straightened.

'Huliat!'

The boy turned to the familiar voice. An uncle, his father's side, grey hair streaked with blood from a nasty gash above his eye. He reached for him and the boy allowed himself to be hugged. 'I'm sorry, my lad.'

'Where are they?'

He shook his head. 'I'm sorry,' he whispered.

'No.' Huliat pushed the man away: his uncle looked surprised by the boy's strength.

'Huliat, stay here. *Listen to me: stay...*'

'No! No! No!' he raved, thrashing his arms this way and that.

Others in the group tutted or blinked at him, uncomprehending. Huliat felt something break, deep within.

The raider hung his flagon on a branch and stalked over to him, hand resting on the pommel of his sword. Huliat gritted his teeth and lowered his head, feeling every sinew in his body clench. His world shrank to just him and the other: the embodiment of his anguish.

He watched the hilt of the weapon being slid from its sheath and he sprang at the man wielding it.

*

When he came to, an hour or so later, his hands were tightly bound and the back of his skull buzzed with pain. He was lying upon a fleece, staring at the buskins of a deep-chested man sat on a stool. His back was aglow with heat and the low crackle told him there was a hearth fire behind him.

The legs of the stool creaked as the man sat upon it leaned forwards.

'Look at me.'

The accent was thick. Huliat had to tip his head back to see the man's face. He had a large, crooked nose, and a bushy moustache bristled above thick pink lips. Dark eyes weighed him up, reflecting the amber flames. To his surprise, they were not unkind.

'By the Almighty One, you are ugly.' He chuckled. 'Just like me!'

The man glanced up and nodded. Another man seized his wrist – Huliat could smell him before seeing him – and there was a painful tug before the thongs were cut loose. Huliat sat upright, rubbing his wrists.

'Good?' The man's eyes crinkled as he framed the question.

Huliat said nothing. Now that the oblivion of his unconsciousness had passed, the misery of his life returned with the crash of a winter wave.

'Drink? Water? Food?'

After a moment, the boy shook his head and focused upon a frayed tassel of the rug in front of him. It dawned upon him that he was in the house of the elder *seren*, wherever he now was.

The stool's legs creaked again as the man sat back. Huliat was vaguely aware of the man making a gesture but he didn't look at him. His head had begun to pound and he wished he had accepted the water. Stubborn pride and hatred would not allow it, however.

'How old you are?'

Huliat didn't answer. His tongue felt like it was glued to the roof of his mouth and it was easier to maintain silence.

'You are Uliat?'

The boy clenched his jaw. 'Huliat.'

'Good, Huliat, good.' He leaned forwards and slammed a

clenched fist into his palm, making Huliat flinch. 'You strong boy. You hurt him, those guard.' The man chuckled again and pointed to his side. 'Here.'

Huliat shrugged sullenly. He couldn't recall doing so, if it was true, and it changed nothing.

Slanting light made the room glow as the door shivered open. The very tip of the sun's rays came to rest upon his filthy knee in the shape of an arrowhead.

'Huliat!'

The boy's head snapped around at the familiar voice. *'Momma!'*

He jumped up and threw himself at her, clinging so tightly to his mother that she gave a little gasp. Her own embrace was briefer, almost guarded, but he didn't care. When she tried to release him, he refused to let go and his sobbing soaked the front of her torn dress. It was only when he finally disentangled himself and gazed at her that he noticed, through his swimming vision, the same haunted cast of her eyes that he had seen on the face of every other villager.

BOOK TWO

REPRISAL

I

Orpheus

Indulge me, stranger, as I take you – many years after the events of this story – to a small town on a well-known island off the coast of Attica. I withhold details not because it lacked distinction (it had charm enough) but rather to avoid confusing you with yet more names, which have no import for this tale.

Why, then, do I mention this episode now?

Because it was at the same moment I broke off my tale to you just now – as Huliat looked once more upon his careworn mother – that something happened in that town I had hitherto never believed possible.

I paused and looked about me. Shadows were beginning to stretch across the dusty square. Clay-bricked houses glowed, and olive and cypress trees were gold-fringed in the dying sun. Somewhere out of sight, goat bells clanked and babies cried. I had heard such sounds in many towns and villages, up and down country, on both sides of the Archipelagos. The hour when children are made ready for bed and livestock are herded back into their pens, when more people join than leave the gathering and are content to sit back and listen rather than chatter and exchange the day's gossip. For bards, this hour is golden.

I had their attention, old and young, man and woman alike. Some were thinking, '*The old bard's forgotten his lines.*' Most believed it was deliberate. At the edge of the crowd, always at the edge, sat the elders. Their lined faces fixed me with their inscrutable gazes. There would soon come a time when every face in the square, wherever I found myself, would have seen out fewer winters than me. At that moment, my lyre must fall silent for the last time.

My epiphany.

That there comes a time when we become the worst judge of our own selves. I hadn't understood quite how vain I was until that moment. As a youth, dark-haired, dark-eyed, naturally reserved, I had never wanted for attention from women and men alike. The one girl whose attention I, in turn, had craved had been the one I had loved, married and lost within one sundown of the ceremony's end. Eurydice had been my lodestar, a dream become flesh and feeling.

Shortly after her death, I had prepared myself to die. It seemed inconceivable for Orpheus to go on drawing breath above ground whilst Eurydice lay cold beneath it. Our names rolled together as naturally as fire and smoke, earth and water; so I determined to join her in Hades. I cannot say why I drew back. Perhaps I was just a coward. Perhaps this is why: when Jason called for volunteers to crew *Argo* on her impossible voyage, I answered at once. Death or glory awaited. Either outcome suited me.

But Eurydice's death also stirred something else deep within. I had always nurtured a gift for singing and music but my grief now found expression and a passion that burned coals in the pit of my stomach. Those months with Jason and his misfit heroes – misfits with whom we forged a brotherhood of bronze – provided experiences that breathed over those coals and started an inferno.

I began training in earnest as a bard – and I mean heart and soul, not just to nourish my voice as a singer of wedding songs, hymns and shanties – progressing with ease from principal beginner to bard's assistant with a speed that astonished all. Within the first year, I had committed twenty stories to memory. By the fourth, I could compose one hundred on the spot, though none would surpass my *Argonautica*. I never formally completed my training. Didn't need to. There was – it became clear – nothing more that any man alive could teach me.

There was something else, too. I found nights the hardest, when the shadow of solitude fell upon me like a heavy woollen blanket. With the unfathomable loss of Eurydice now conspired hellish visions of the voyage to Colchis and back. The shrieks of friends being hacked apart, crying for their mothers, reaching for us just beyond their fingertips; flashing blades and twitching bodies and enraged foemen, teeth gritted, blood-spattered. Constant tensions and fraying nerves, frenzied attacks bursting forth from the darkness, shattering the heavy silence; poison, sorcery... even the ceaseless rocking of waves against the hull. I found that I could only achieve peace by imagining that we fought beasts instead of men, gods instead of cruel nature. And, gradually, through the power of my song, those dreams became fact.

Not wanting to be alone with my memories, I travelled. I travelled all over the known world, singing for king and commoner alike. I devoured new languages as I devoured their bread and wine. I watched empires rise and fall. I was feted as a god for my talent; for my *hubris*, I was even threatened with death. I was, in short, a force of nature.

And then, older than I knew, I reached that island. The unnamed one. My reputation always preceded me. Every man or woman listening, boy or girl, old or young, would know me and believe me the greatest bard ever to grace the Archipelagos. Or so I thought.

And, that evening, my memory failed me.

Thinking partly of the grandson of Jason, called Xandros (around whom the rest of the tale will grow), partly of the struggles that followed, partly – I suspect – of the food and shelter that awaited, the words simply dried up. I had always been able to perform with even one-quarter of my mind on the verse but, that day, sensing an unfamiliar fallibility as one senses a malevolent presence in a darkened room, I turned my entire soul upon the performance. I turned out every foot soldier I could muster to fight the enemy. To no avail. I suddenly felt old and tired.

I *was* old and tired.

Many years after being given it, I still had a document of great significance in my possession – a reminder, if you will, of the fate that awaits us all. I had been entertained by Ammurapi, the nervous young king of the once mighty realm of Ugarit on the far eastern shores of the Middle Sea. Even as we spoke by the hearth of his palace one evening, once the affairs of state had been concluded, we were interrupted by a breathless messenger and I knew at once that my stay would be cut short. And so it proved. The king apologised and rose to hear the news in private. A council of war was called and, unwilling to outstay my welcome, I prepared to take my leave.

Just as I had set foot outside the city gate, I was stopped by a captain of the horse. He had a copy of a clay tablet, so fresh it had barely begun to harden, and pressed it into my hands with the distant look of a man about to meet his fate. I was to convey it to the coast and thence to the island of Cyprus for the attention of the king, asking for his urgent assistance. Several riders were presented with the same and they now scattered over the rolling plains of Ugarit, leaving me in their dust.

I never got the chance to deliver it.

Even as I waited in the harbour to board the merchant vessel that had been requisitioned for the purpose – it was like a bees' nest that had been kicked, only those poor people were panic-stricken, not angry – I was intercepted by a second messenger. The matter was already settled and my host, and his entire army, had fallen.

In the fading light of the village square, my fingers came to rest upon that clay tablet and its tiny, wedge-shaped impressions, long since fired and baked hard to preserve it. I fancied I could trace them all and reproduce every one, if so challenged. I took it out now, explaining briefly its provenance. I read it with my eyes closed (my memory had, at least, not faltered here!) and tried to recall my feelings the moment I first looked upon it.

To the king of Cyprus, my father.

I fall at my father's feet. Greetings to your house, your wives, your troops, to all that belongs to the King of Cyprus: many, many greetings.

My father, the enemy ships are already here. They have set fire to my towns and have done very great damage in the country. My father, did you not know that all my troops were stationed in the Hittite country, and that all my ships are still stationed in Lycia and have not yet returned? The country is abandoned to itself... Consider this, my father. There are seven enemy ships that have come and done very great damage. Now if there are more enemy ships to come, tell me about them so that I can know the worst. Please send such help as you can to a beloved son.

When I opened my eyes again, I caught the looks that those villagers exchanged. Uncomprehending... mocking, even. I realised that the man they saw before them was not the famed Orpheus but some old grey-head losing his faculties.

Those looks stung my heart as surely as a scorpion. Concentrating upon that love of father for son – and the consequences of its absence – I drew upon reserves of energy that I did not realise I possessed and continued as, stranger, I will continue for you.

The name of that town, for what it is worth, I give to you. Lefkandi, and the island Euboea. In Lefkandi, through the dust of its destruction, grew green shoots of new life. And what is this if not a beacon of hope for our own times?

II

LEMNOS, 1190 BC

The Month of Roses

The threads of our story draw together as tightly as a sailor's knot fifteen years later as we return to that plucky little island to the north-east of the Archipelagos. I know more about Lemnos than most for reasons that may already be clear. If not, they will certainly become so.

Xandros stood and stretched, setting runnels of sweat down his lean back as he threw aside the heavy oaken shovel and pushed back his long hair. Not quite twenty but within sight of his most vigorous years, the work was nonetheless taxing. In his estimation, it was also beneath him. He sluiced his face and neck with water from the stone basin outside the stables, squinting in the full glare of the sun. Closing his eyes, he allowed the water to dry upon his skin before ducking back into the cooler shadows, where one of the cows – his favourite – looked at him guiltily.

'What is it, Whitefoot?' He scratched her under the chin and she snorted in appreciation. 'Too hot for you outside?'

She licked his hand and he wrinkled his nose and gently pushed her head aside. Unbidden, a song entered his head – a few verses he had overheard an itinerant trader sing about some hero or other, striving to hold back time – and he began to hum it, tutting when the lines evaporated from his memory. He noticed the girl by the door that led to the barn; caught the look in her eye.

'Melli. How long have you been there?'

Aglow with her own labour, she blew the few dark hairs that

had slipped from her headscarf. 'Long enough. I didn't know you could sing.' She wafted away a fly and put her hands on her hips. 'So what have you done this time?'

He frowned and retrieved his shovel. 'What do you mean?'

'This. Mucking out after the donkeys in the lower village. Not very princely, is it?'

'I don't know.' He scooped some filthy hay from the floor and deposited it on the pile he had made. 'People respect anybody prepared to get their hands dirty, don't they?'

'Oh, I do.' She pointed to herself and ran her finger down her chest, exposing the scoop of her breasts. 'Those strong hands, especially.'

Xandros swallowed hard. 'No, Melli.'

'Why not? In this very corner, wasn't it?' Her large, dark eyes were full of the memory, he could see. His mind certainly was. 'In the hay, as the light was fading.'

'That was wrong. You could have fallen pregnant.'

She shook her head. 'No, I couldn't. I know my moon, Xandros.'

'And anyway, the Cyprian has smiled upon me.'

'And she was scowling at you with me, is that it?' She raised a defiant chin. 'So Aphrodite favours the House of Myrine, does she? Ha!'

'That isn't it, Melli.'

Her proud stare forced him to look away. 'Well. Who is she?'

He considered telling her to keep her own business but could see he had offended her enough already. 'She's called Teodora. I met her at the *Hephaistia*.' The mere mention of her name set his pulse racing, and he almost told her where she was from but caught himself.

'Dancing by torchlight. How romantic.'

There was a burst of laughter and they both turned to see a pair of youths smirking at them on the little paddock in front of the stable.

The taller, black-haired one raised a hand. 'Don't stop! We're enjoying this!'

'Hey, Melli, if the handsome prince doesn't want you, I'll have you.'

'You know them?'

'Unfortunately. Go away, Loukios.'

Their faces fell as Xandros and Melli stared at them. Xandros added a little scampering gesture with two fingers.

'What about "no"?'

Feeling his temper fraying, Xandros hefted the shovel and strode towards them.

'There you are,' sneered Loukios. 'What I said. Without his spear, he's a nobody. Is that why your father has you sweeping up the shit and the piss?'

Xandros closed the gap, tossed the shovel aside and drove his fist into the boy's nose. He felt the septum crumple, surprised by the quantity of dark blood that it unleashed. Unsighted, enjoying the way Loukios slumped to the floor, clutching his face, Xandros didn't see the other youth launch himself at him, driving him to the dusty earth. As he tried to scramble to his feet, throwing the youth off him, he caught sight of a few other farmhands watching him, beckoning others over.

The youth was up first and stamped the ground where Xandros' head was a moment earlier, allowing Xandros to grasp his calf and yank him off balance. As he tumbled, Xandros drove his knee into his stomach and slammed his fist into his nose. He drew back his arm and would have repeated the dose but heard Melli shouting at him.

He forced himself to his feet, winded. 'My first act as king,' he wheezed, 'will be to kill you both.'

Loukios was sat upright, examining his hands, through which dark blood was trickling. He helped up his friend and turned to Xandros. 'This isn't over!'

The way he hissed, like the quenching of a heated blade, and the cold fury in his eyes told Xandros he'd know about it, soon enough. He picked up the shovel and watched the youths stagger away. Melli joined him.

'Are you hurt?'

'No.'

'It wasn't worth what's coming, Xandros.'

'More time in the stables? Let him.'

She tutted. 'No. Loukios' father thinks he's a big noise in the hills. He won't stand for that.'

'And I won't stand for them!' he snapped. Seeing her flinch, he added, 'Sorry.'

Aware that they were the centre of attention on the farmstead, Melli turned on her heels and bustled away, leaving Xandros to glare at them.

'Get back to work, peasants.'

A few days later, the men of Myrine had assembled in what passed for the *palaestra*, a patch of dusty earth, strewn with pine needles from trees that provided only a thin bar of shade. As they warmed up with running laps of the area, Xandros noticed Loukios and his friend. Loukios sported black eyes and a swollen nose though, from what he could see, his friend hadn't been marked so badly. They pointedly ignored him but, when the instructor spoke, he noticed them put their heads together and grin until they were seen and barked at.

Xandros had never enjoyed the spear drills, though he was one of the more capable men in the town and surrounding fields. As the sun steepled and the training intensified, so too did the sweat flow, and the gasps and grunts filled the *palaestra*. During the break, there was a rush for the shady pines and Xandros sat cross-legged, a little distance apart from the others beneath a lone plane tree. He heard the buzz of interest but remained deep in thought, staring into the distance.

'All rise for King Euneus!' snapped the drill instructor.

'No, stay seated. You have earned your rest, gentlemen.'

Xandros looked up to see that his father had entered the exercise ground with a pair of guards, one of whom was also his closest friend. Euneus seemed much older than his forty years. His long hair was streaked grey and his face was drawn and webbed with fine worry lines. Sometimes, his old injuries flared with arthritis, causing him great discomfort, and Xandros could tell whenever he was trying to disguise his slight limp. 'A bruised hip' was all he would say about it, waving the matter away. 'Many have suffered much worse.'

Euneus' jaw was clamped tight and he looked pale. Xandros got up and joined the group, catching the ghost of a frown on his father's face.

'As you know I am proud Lemnos has a fine tradition of breeding warriors. Men *and* women!' Euneus waited for the ripple of laughter to subside. 'And I would prefer that we could meet and train like this more often but, you are also aware, it is never an easy task to assemble so many people, especially in tough times when we are all working so hard. So,' he said, brightly, 'enjoy your hard-earned water, though not *too* much. We have nearly bled the wells dry for you lot and, unlike Herakles, I cannot divert a river!'

Euneus mingled amongst well-wishers and petitioners alike. Xandros took a swig from his gourd and sat back down, watching his father work the crowd, when he suddenly felt a presence at his side.

'Hello, Xandros. M-mind if I sit?'

Xandros recalled his nickname, which meant 'Red'. *God-touched*, was what the few understanding islanders called him when they saw him.

'I prefer my own company.'

'Oh.'

Xandros immediately regretted his sharp tone but the instructor clapped his hands.

'Back up!' he barked.

The men were assigned numbers for the gruelling one-on-one and one-on-two sessions. Xandros tutted when he saw Loukios and his friend approaching the same group. Now they looked him in the eye and he knew that there was trouble afoot.

The instructor was a wiry older man with a downturned mouth and white hair with not a scrap of spare flesh upon him. He was also as tough as old leather, which was what his skin resembled. After a demonstration with his staff – real spears were set aside for this drill – and oaken shield, he selected the first pair. They lunged and parried, and their staffs clacked hard and cleanly enough against each other and the shield boards, until a third man joined the group and the outnumbered defender had his work cut out to fend them off for as long as he could.

After a short while, he sustained a painful blow on his right arm, making him draw breath in pain.

'*Stop!* Not bad. You might have given ground there but not bad. Next, you… and you.'

As Loukios took up his staff and shield, Xandros groaned inwardly. They stepped into the circle scratched in the dust, tapping weapons. Then Loukios thrust the butt end straight at Xandros' face. He suspected it was coming but barely had time to lean aside and his own weapon wasn't raised nearly high enough to counter. He stepped back and raised his shield, levelling his staff at Loukios. They prowled in a circle for a moment and Loukios' eyes blazed like a zealot's. He adjusted his grip and took a wild swipe at Xandros' midriff. Xandros twisted his staff and blocked it, though the force of it made his hands buzz and go numb.

'*Stop!* Stop! What in the gods' name are you doing, boy?' The instructor rapped Loukios' arm with his reed. 'Aggression is useless without control. You'll do more harm to your comrades than him.'

From the corner of his eye, Xandros caught Euneus strolling over, folding his arms.

'You, join him. Perhaps you'll fight better as a pair.'

Loukios' friend now stepped forwards, and Xandros felt his blood run cold. He knew with certainty that it had been prearranged but the only question was by whom.

'*Begin!*'

Loukios' friend winked at him and dropped to a crouch.

Xandros knew he had to take the offensive or be beaten black and blue. He took one step backwards before driving between them, feinting to the left and plunging his staff overarm at Loukios on the right. Loukios stepped aside as he knew he would do, enabling Xandros to whip his staff towards his friend, blind. It cracked into the youth's forearm as he raised it ineffectually, making him cry out. The moment of triumph was brief as Xandros felt a searing pain to his triceps. He dropped to his knees in agony but had the presence of mind to roll and raise his shield against the second blow that now clattered against it.

'*Stop!*'

Loukios' weapon was raised for another strike and his chest heaved with the rush of anger but he lowered the staff slowly.

'What was that?' snapped the instructor. 'Worth your life, was it, for a cheap shot at the enemy?'

Xandros held the man's eye but didn't respond. When the instructor had turned to select another pair, Xandros got to his feet.

'A cheap shot that disarmed him.'

The instructor went rigid and turned slowly to face him. 'What did you say?'

'I said…' Xandros felt the hum of blood in his ears. 'Forget about it.'

'*What?*'

There were a few sniggers in the group and, sensing trouble, other men had turned to see what was happening.

'I will deal with this.'

They all turned to King Euneus who unfolded his arms and approached his son, his face dark with rage. He clapped his hands. 'As you were, the rest of you!' The men returned reluctantly to their drills, glancing over their shoulders in hope of catching some of the drama.

'You shame yourself and you shame the family,' rumbled Euneus.

'For speaking the truth? That was set up to shame me!' He lowered his voice. 'The two worthless *thetes* I fought to defend one of the stable girls!'

Euneus' stare unsettled Xandros and he looked down.

'I heard about this. It seems you learned *nothing!* What were you thinking in the first place? The instructor was right. *A cheap shot!* Is that all your mind can think of? Where is the honour in it?' Euneus coughed alarmingly but recovered his composure. 'Get back in line. If you can't even clean stables without embarrassing yourself, maybe some time with the fishermen will teach you a lesson. Start some trouble with them and let's see where it takes you!' The reprimand was done but Xandros knew the matter was far from over. Euneus jerked his head towards the men training before beckoning over his guards.

His face burning with indignation, Xandros couldn't look

any of the men in the eye. *How many more times would he have to come out on the wrong side of his father's judgement before he exceeded his limits?* He took a deep breath and allowed his thoughts to drift towards Teodora, wondering when he would next get the opportunity to see her. The way her eyes narrowed and creased as she laughed. The whispered promises. How her neck flushed as he kissed it and slid her dress from her shoulder. The tenderness of her skin and her fingers interlacing with his…

Thinking of her acted like a balm upon his troubled mind, and the clack of staffs and shields, the grunts of effort faded into the background. In his reverie, he noticed that one of the boys from Myrine was in the circle, a quiet and unassuming lad called Erythros. His opponent struck him twice before the instructor called a stop to it.

'Try using your shield, idiot.'

Erythros rubbed his bruised arm and Xandros was sure he saw tears gathering in the boy's eyes.

The instructor pointed to a second youth, who now hefted his weapon. He was not tall but his arms were all sinew. Xandros had noticed him earlier, swinging his staff recklessly and with glee.

'Fight!'

Erythros blocked the first strike with his shield but collected a wicked blow high on his arm, making him gasp in pain. He swung wildly, fending off another hit but taking his eyes from the wiry boy, who now took aim beneath the rim of his shield, striking him in the thigh. Erythros buckled and now his opponents rained blows upon him, only some of which he could fend off.

Xandros looked at the instructor with a frown. The old man had his arms crossed.

'Enough,' muttered Xandros, as Erythros yelped in pain, struggling to stay on his feet. A few of the onlookers exchanged uncomfortable glances, and Xandros now glared openly at the instructor. He was unmoved, even when Erythros was felled. One of the blows glanced off the shield and caught him in the face.

'Well? You're the k-king's son,' said Red quietly.

'What of it?' Xandros muttered. 'Didn't I say I wanted to be left alone?'

'Yes but... Are you g-going to stand for that?'

Xandros felt his temper snap. *'Enough!'* he roared, running at the sinewy youth and barrelling him aside. Off balance, he snatched at the tunic of the second opponent, whose arm was raised for another blow. As he stumbled, he dragged the man down with him and they ended up in a pile on the dusty ground. Confused and winded, the man swore, aiming his elbow at Xandros' face.

Then there was pandemonium.

Xandros scrambled to his knees but was tugged aside, and flailing arms caught him in the ribs. He felt the shadows of others looming over him. He threw clumsy punches and connected with some before heavy hands yanked him from the ground and the men were separated, breathing hard through gritted teeth.

'You, boy, are a *disgrace*!'

The instructor jabbed his finger at him. From the corner of his eye, Xandros saw Erythros struggling to his feet, wheezing and dabbing the blood leaking from a cut to his cheek. Nobody seemed to notice. Xandros turned back to the instructor and spat in his face.

He heard the collective intake of breath, the shock. What did he care? The wretch had it coming.

The stinging blow to his face took him by surprise. There was venom behind it and it hurt. It made his eyes water. Then Euneus was stalking away from the *palaestra*, followed by one of his guards. 'Give him the lash and be done with it!'

The training was over; that much was clear. The incident would be the source of gossip in Myrine for weeks.

'Where are you all going?' snapped the instructor. 'I didn't dismiss you. You can all watch this first.'

Xandros looked around him. By the looks on their faces, most wanted to be elsewhere but some, more than a few, looked like they would enjoy what was coming. He saw Loukios and his friend, grinning broadly. He would not give them the pleasure of showing any pain, come what may.

'Over there!' The instructor was pointing to an ancient pine, the lowest branches of which were above the height of Xandros' head. 'Go and hug that tree.'

Xandros ignored him. A gentle breeze picked up, making the leaves sigh all along the side of the *palaestra*. Xandros filled his lungs and closed his eyes, enjoying the warm and fragrant scent of the pine's sap. For a moment, he could ignore the furious pounding of his heart.

'Now let's hear you squeal, you little shit.'

Xandros looked over his shoulder at him. 'You'd enjoy that, wouldn't you? Is that what your dreams are made of?'

The smirk turned to a rictus. 'Prepare for ten.'

'The penalty's five.'

Xandros turned to the dissenter. He was a big-shouldered man, with a mane of greying hair atop a bluff face. He crossed his arms and, though his eyes were calm, his presence was enough to unsettle the stoutest of hearts. The instructor narrowed his eyes at him.

'He'll get five. Then five more for spitting.' The instructor turned back to one of the boys and clicked his fingers. 'Ten's the least he deserves. Bring me the lash.'

In the heavy silence, leaves soughed in an incipient breeze. Xandros looked at the big man, who winked at him. His name was Moxos, son of a famous prince from Calydon on the mainland by the name of Meleager, and he was one of King Euneus' most trusted friends. His arms remained crossed even as the lash was brought over.

The instructor licked his lips, ran the rope through his fingers before setting himself. He flicked back the rope and tried to whip it forwards, grunting when his arm froze. It took him a moment to realise that Moxos had gripped the end of it and was staring at him.

'Five.'

Some of the crowd chuckled at the look on the instructor's face. His lips twitched but, after a moment, he inclined his head a fraction.

Good old Moxos, thought Xandros, tensing his body.

The whipcrack heralded the most intense pain he had ever experienced, like he had been branded. His eyes filled with water and, for a moment, he thought he might pass out. He heard the tail of the rope scraping against pine needles before being jerked backwards. The second lash was less effective, though no less painful. The old man's aim was unerringly good, however. It struck the same stretch of skin, just below his shoulder blade. A sensation of air against his skin told him his tunic had torn.

The third lash made his teeth clench so tightly he thought they might splinter. His fingernails clawed the pine bark.

The fourth made his legs buckle and tremble. With an almighty effort, he straightened them. He heard the rasp of the instructor's breath. He knew the last would be the most spiteful.

It was.

He couldn't contain the gasp of pain. He felt his forehead strike the tree and his kneecaps brush the earth. It felt like molten bronze had been poured down his back. The searing pain took an age to fade, the humming in his ears even longer. He dug in his nails and hauled himself upright, aware now of the trickling down his spine. It would not be sweat.

'That's enough,' announced the instructor, dry-throated. 'Now go to your homes.'

Above him, the trees sighed and Xandros tried to fill his lungs once more, not daring to move in case his body might betray him. He heard the crunching of pine needles and felt the presence of a big man close by.

'You took it well.'

Xandros could only nod. The sensation of his shredded tunic brushing his welts was creating an agony of its own.

'You'd better take that off. We'll dress those at yours.'

'Not here,' he gasped. 'How do they look?'

'A few angry scratches; they'll heal. Come on.'

Xandros took a deep breath and pushed himself away from the trunk of the pine. He ignored the throngs of Lemnians milling about, clamping his jaw. The murmurs weren't quite pitying but he sensed a change in the mood. That was enough.

'S-sorry you had to g-go through that.'

'If you just kept your mouth shut, I—' Xandros noticed one of the men now dabbing Erythros' face. The boy's face was smeared with blood from a gash to his cheek that would surely leave him with a scar. Nevertheless, he managed a wan smile at Xandros.

'Just save your energy, lad,' said Moxos. 'Nothing gained in blaming yourself.'

III

Lemnos, three weeks later

Many thoughts were swilling inside Xandros' mind and not one of them was about pilchards. He blamed the relentless sun and the gentle sea, rocking the boat like a tired mother. It was making him drowsy.

He shook his head, snapping himself from his reverie, and took a long swig of water, pouring a little over his face for good measure. The burnished sea dazzled him and he pulled down the broad-brimmed straw hat. Beneath his feet, the fishing boat was almost still. The stifling heat had becalmed the water as it had the crew. They dozed beneath the canopy or tucked themselves against the hull, where a strip of shade offered a thin hope of respite from the heat. One of the men groaned and cursed, tugging a linen coverlet over his head. The very planks of the boat were becoming uncomfortably hot. Lemnos had become a furnace. He had never experienced heat like this on the island, not in nineteen summers. Small wonder crops had failed on three occasions in that time. If it didn't rain soon, there would certainly be a fourth.

His father's gruff voice drifted through his thoughts. *Remember this, boy: the wealth of an island depends upon the depth of its topsoil.* The topsoil of Lemnos, such as it was, barely propped up the crops. This job was thankless but it was important and there were worse punishments.

Xandros leaned overboard, dangling the tips of his fingers in the sea. It was only in the last couple of days that he could stretch his arms without the lacerations along his back causing any discomfort. They had healed well enough, but they would certainly leave his skin permanently ridged. As Moxos reminded him, however, a man without a few scars was a man without a story.

From the corner of his eye, he saw another two fishing boats from Myrine's little fleet, a few hundred yards apart. They also appeared motionless, as if their hulls were stuck in mud. It was odd when the gulls were silent. Not a single one circled the boats, another sure sign the islanders would return empty-handed. A half-mile distant lay the shore of Myrine, quivering in the heat haze. Perched high on a bluff overlooking the Archipelagos was the huer's hut where a lookout kept watch for tell-tale shadows beneath the water's surface. Xandros had spent time in there, trying to keep his eyes open long enough to catch a glimpse of the pilchards swarming into the bay, rusty brown becoming silver as they neared the surface. If those stupid little fish could just get on with the business of rushing to their deaths, he might be able to get back to the village, and then to Teodora for a few hours. He had neither seen (how could he?) nor heard from her whilst his wounds healed and it worried him.

The hut stared the sun full in the face all day as it blazed along its timeless arc and he knew how suffocating it could become in there. Even with the doors and windows latched open, and a canopy erected outside, the air could be thick and still. He narrowed his eyes but couldn't see any movement. The huer was probably asleep. Though the punishments were severe, he could hardly blame him on a day like this.

'Where's that bloody h-huer?'

Xandros could only shrug at Red's question, which sent a trickle of sweat down his back. Earlier that morning, as they loaded their nets, he heard one of Myrine's most experienced fishermen grousing to another about how far from land they might have to row, where the cooler waters were more attractive to fish. The fishing having been forgotten, it was now more a question of surviving until the cool evening. The problem was that they had drifted, on an imperceptible current, closer to the headland. Beneath the eternal murmur of the sea, he could hear the faint screech of cicadas: the heat seemed to madden them.

Xandros tutted and rubbed his eyes and, even with an economy of movement, he felt his nape prickling with sweat. Red had a point. *What was the huer up to?*

A signal – any signal – was long overdue.

Another fisherman joined him, stifling a yawn. 'Any…?'

The question was cut short by the appearance of a little figure on the headland, raising a gorse bush in either hand. They both watched him describe two slow circles before rattling the bushes.

'What the fuck does that mean?' growled the fisherman.

Xandros shrugged. 'That he's had a good look round and can't see anything?'

The fisherman harrumphed and pushed himself from the rail. He prodded the man slumbering under the linen coverlet, and he snorted like a basking pig. 'Hey, Hilarion! Poli! *Poli!* Get up! We're wasting our time out here. We head back.'

Thank the gods! thought Xandros. His heart quickened at the prospects of seeing Teodora when darkness fell. *This would be the evening,* he had decided. He would have to be careful – and very fast – because the nights were short.

He was about to take an oar when he caught a glimpse of movement atop the headland. The huer, levelling both gorse bushes from high above his head towards the horizon. Xandros turned on his heels and looked in the direction he was indicating.

He noticed something breaking the contours of the distant south-western horizon. When he tried to focus upon it, he lost it altogether and he muttered a curse. He looked to the side of where he thought he had glimpsed it, recalling the old hunters' adage that this was often the best way to detect movement.

Then he saw it. Faint, at the very limit of his sight: unmistakable, nevertheless. Ships under sail.

'What is it?'

Xandros turned to see Hilarion scratching his belly. The man was shaven-headed, and corpulent, with a lazy eye that would follow you around the village square whilst the other could remain quite fixed. Despite this, Xandros had always liked him for his quick wits and his stories, particularly when he was animated by wine, which was often. He had the ability to raise anybody's spirits when they were at their lowest ebb. Xandros was about to say 'ships' but thought better of it. He turned back and, though he strained his eyes, he could see nothing. *Had it been a trick of the light?*

He tipped back his hat and glanced up at the huer's hut. The huer must have gone back in.

'Just the heat haze, I think.'

'Pfft.' Hilarion waved the matter away. He flopped onto a bench and wiped the sweat from his glistening brow. Xandros joined him after scanning the horizon once more. The ships – or, at least, their spectre – had vanished.

It took them a few clunky strokes before the boat roused itself from its torpor. The oarsmen gasped with the initial effort under the relentless sun before finding their rhythm.

'Gambled with Old Spiro last night,' said the skipper, heaving back on his oar. 'He was thick-skulled enough to tell me... he has a few flagons of red he's stashed away for the summer... He lost, so we head for his at sundown, ah? This... is the price you pay!'

There was a chorus of approval, though Xandros plied his oar in silence. He had other plans and he was already thinking about how to carry them out.

IV

Megalonisi

There is venom in Huliat's eyes and vengeance has freshly flooded his heart. His fingers are clenched into fists but he has not entirely lost his control. Within the past hour, he has lost his mother, worked to death weaving flax and keeping the home of the chieftain who had raised the boy in his own household.

In a deeper sense, the day the prows of the raiders first ploughed the shores of Megalonisi fifteen years earlier was the day she had been taken from him, along with his beloved father. What was left had been a shell of his warm, caring mother. She had in effect died twice and, on her deathbed, she had whispered something in his ear as he clutched her hands, and her words had made his heart froth.

And now he is stood before the chieftain's guards.

'He is occupied.'

Huliat takes a deep breath and nods. 'I know but he will want to hear this.' His mastery of the westlanders' language is so complete that he now thinks and dreams in it.

The guards look to one another. Huliat is a head taller than them, yet they have been selected for their size. His prominent brow, which creases the skin above his deep-set eyes into a permanent frown, always exerts an unsettling effect upon them.

'Want to hear what?'

Huliat leans over them, and whispers, 'Conspiracy. And if you don't step aside, I will assume that both of you are part of it.'

They share a look of alarm and step aside. Huliat tugs open the door and enters. The air is thick inside, and warm. There is a scent of oil and leather and stale sweat. The chieftain looks up at him as he enters, and his bushy grey moustache bristles in annoyance. He puts his wine goblet down. There is an elder with him, a trusted adviser.

'Why are *you* here?'

Huliat clenches his jaw and tries to control his breathing. He knows well how crafty and suspicious the man is. 'An important message, lord. It cannot wait.'

'That is my decision to make, not yours!'

Huliat raises his large hands, which also shows he is unarmed. 'I understand, lord, but this cannot wait. Your guards understand, too. Can I trust this man?'

The chieftain's eyes slide to his adviser with a frown. 'What do you think?'

'Good.' Huliat strides towards them. 'Time is short so I will be brief.'

'Go on!'

He knows the king is armed with a knife and, though he has seen out more than fifty winters, is very capable with it. He conceals it inside his robe: to the left of the golden brooch shaped like a bull, if he's not mistaken. The elder is not obviously carrying, which poses a minor difficulty. 'It concerns a conspiracy against your life.'

The chieftain is too canny to react at once. Instead, his disarmingly kind eyes look into Huliat's own, reading his thoughts. The corner of his lips curl a little and Huliat feels ice trickle down his spine.

'We both know this is impossible. I have every man watched. I would know of it.'

'Then you must be rid of your spies.' He leans over the marble table and tips his head in the direction of the elder, then picks up the silver goblet. The chieftain's brow furrows at the liberties Huliat is taking and the elder makes a gasp of shock. He would have to be quick. He sniffs the wine and levels a finger at one of them. 'And start with that poisoner!'

'What…?'

His ruse has bought him a second, no more. It is all he needs. He throws the dregs of wine into the elder's face before swiping him hard across the temple with it, opening up a nasty gash above his eye. He drops to the floor clutching his face, half stunned. The king is on his feet in a flash, eyes flaring, hand reaching for the knife. Huliat is too fast and drives his fist hard into the man's belly, making him double over, winded. He catches him, wheezing, before he clatters onto the table and drags him towards an embroidered throw. Quick as a snake, Huliat has the chieftain's dagger in his grip. Its workmanlike design impresses him: function over form. The blade is soon pressing a sharp crease in the chieftain's throat and he goes rigid.

He glances towards the door. Remarkably, the scuffle has not alerted the guards. Huliat feels his heart launching itself against his ribs as the moment arrives.

'Did you kill my father?'

Huliat watches the chieftain's eyes as they blink in confusion and terror. The old man betrays no obvious signs – he has long since learned to conceal his thoughts. He glances towards the door. *If he knows he is about to die, he will surely shout for help?*

Huliat hears a sharp intake of breath and he is suddenly toppling to the side. The old man has heaved him over and gripped the forearm bearing the knife. The chieftain turns to the door and bellows for help. In the sliver of a second his eyes slide away, Huliat slaps the hilt of the knife with his free hand and drives it into the windpipe of the old man, making his eyes bulge in shock. The pop of cartilage is both gratifying and gruesome. He watches the gnarled hands clasping the blade, trying to tug it free, dribbling with dark blood. As the door bursts open, Huliat heaves the chieftain aside and rips free the blade.

He is on his feet, breathing heavily as the guards hurry inside and then stop, taking in the scene of chaos, the blood pooling by the guttering chieftain and the droplets spattered up the far wall. The adviser is groaning and clutching his face.

'You'll die for this,' says the elder guard, backing towards the door. The younger is just staring, incredulous.

'He killed my father. He lied to me.' The guard's eyes fall upon the chieftain, whose leg twitches and is still. Huliat knows why the guard doesn't want to attack him there and then; why he is backing towards the safety of the door. He fears him. He thinks most of the king's guard – the *former* king's guard – probably do.

'Choose another ruler and I will follow him. A *just* one.'

'What?'

'I killed him because he killed my father, not because I want his throne. As would you, or *you*,' he adds, nodding to the younger guard. Seizing upon the guard's moment of hesitation, Huliat tosses the knife in the air and catches it by the tip, then throws it at the door lintel. It is already reverberating by the time the guards flinch at it.

'See?'

They stare at him as if he has taken leave of his senses.

'I will wait for you here.'

To their astonishment, Huliat sits cross-legged upon the floor. The guards glance at each other and duck outside the room.

V

Lemnos

Xandros had trudged up the slope to the citadel to find King Euneus in a filthy mood. His father possessed an unnerving knack of knowing when Xandros was making plans and creating plausible reasons for scuppering them. Twice before Teodora had disguised herself as a shepherd and ventured, at considerable risk to her safety, to the grove sacred to the Great Mother. Twice she had waited all night for a visit that never came but he was determined not to let that happen today. He hurried out of the citadel and made his way down the path towards the coastal road, passing old Manolis – as he often did – sat astride his donkey, which was plodding its well-worn path into the foothills.

In all his years of living in Myrine, Xandros had never passed more than a few words with Manolis but the exchange had become so baked into the daily ritual of his life that there was no question of either developing it or dispensing with it altogether.

A tip of Manolis' hat – a pinch between his gnarled fingers. 'Good day, young man,' he would growl.

'And to you, Manolis. How is she today?'

'She grumbles but she's steady,' he said, slapping the donkey's rump. Its ears were forever twitching in a timeless war with flies.

'Gathering wood or fruit?'

'Wood today. And tending the vine terrace. A good day to you.'

'To you, too. When will I hear about the Eastern War?'

'Later, young man!' He cackled. 'After I have returned.' Then he swatted the donkey's swaying rump with his reed and the animal shook its lugubrious head as it bestirred itself.

Many years later, the stories about the wars remained stubbornly embedded in the old man's head. Manolis was as constant a presence as the citadel's walls or the sparkling waters of the bay.

Until he wasn't.

'He's quite mad, you do know that?' said Poli the fisherman, overhearing the conversation and rasping his beard as he passed Xandros. 'He's never left the island, let alone fought at Troy!'

Xandros wasn't so sure, though wondered if he just wanted them to be true. Stories of war in far-flung lands, god-born heroes battling hand to hand, watched by sighing women in high-walled cities. It was true that most villagers had no appetite to travel far, nor the resources even if they could. Many had barely moved beyond their own fields or the stand of pines or stony field they owned. If there was one thing Xandros *was* sure of, it was that he would not be one of these people. The prospect of spending his entire life on Lemnos left him cold.

He had reached the path that led down to his shaded cove, a tricky scramble down some rocks, where he could avoid his father's judgemental glare for a while. He reached the bottom and heard the echo of breathy panting behind him. He wasn't surprised that Red had joined him. Ever since Xandros had engaged with him at the spear drills, Red had barely left him alone. Xandros rolled his eyes and hurled a pebble at a rock, striking it with a satisfying *dink*.

'Your f-f-father... wants to see you.'

'Why do you think I'm here? I saw him already. He was angry. I left.' Xandros glanced up at the slope and frowned. 'It's not that steep. Why do you sound so out of shape.'

'So he t-told you about the raid?'

'I heard about it.'

'B-but he didn't tell you, no? To your face?'

Xandros' eyes widened. *Might they sail into the path of the ships he had seen?*

He had always been overlooked for raids, despite his age and despite his father's status. It had been another source of shame for him: the son of the king should be foremost amongst the chosen warriors. It seemed a suspicious coincidence that the night he planned to see Teodora fell on the same afternoon he was to be included in a raid. He looked out over the sea, wondering in which direction he would be sailing, feeling his heart pound with exhilaration and fear. Fear over letting Teodora down – again – and of the unknown.

'Where are we going?'

Red paused a beat then shrugged.

Xandros' mind drifted back to the events of the morning. 'What do you think the huer meant by that first signal?'

'The circles?'

'Those.'

'That his b-balls were on fire. He must have been melting in there!'

'Idiot,' said Xandros, feeling his lips being tugged into a smile. 'And the second?'

'He didn't make a s-second s-signal. He went back inside.'

'What? He pointed towards the horizon.'

'No, h-he didn't.'

'I saw…' Xandros felt a ripple of unease pass down his spine and his words were lost to the lapping of the waves.

'You saw what?'

'Boats! I saw boats when he pointed to the horizon!'

'Has the s… Did the sun fry your brain? He didn't point to the horizon, I've told you! Did anyone else see it?'

'No.' Xandros sighed and let the matter drop. The heat was intense out on the bay – it had knocked the rest of them out – and it was a fleeting glimpse, after all. 'A raid, then.'

The two were quiet for a while as they watched the sun sparkling upon the sea.

Red dared ask, 'Why do you look so m-miserable?'

'*What?*'

'You said you were sick of getting over… overlooked.'

'Did I? I don't think I did; at least, not to you.'

'You're n-never in the raiding… parties. Are you?'

Xandros felt his temper smouldering. 'You would know.'

'Small wonder you have no f-friends.'

Incredulous, Xandros sought some trace of humour in his words. There was none. 'You really are a halfwit. Aren't you?'

'So they s-s-say.'

Years of being ground down or ignored, Xandros could tell, had toughened the boy's skin but that did not make him impervious to hurt. Red's affliction – one of them, at any rate – was that he spoke his mind. Or had no control over his thoughts, which was much the same thing. And what was that, if not a form of bravery?

Xandros hurled his last pebble out to sea, got up and scrambled back up the rocks without looking back.

VI

Moudros. They were actually going to raid Moudros.

Whilst the spearmen prepared themselves and stashed their few provisions for the march inland – wheat biscuits, water, a few hard pears – trying to fire themselves for the undertaking, Xandros staggered about as if in a waking nightmare…

Orpheus

I had their attention now, I thought. *Even the most dim-witted villager knows that all raids are a reckoning. Many amongst the crowd had likely been victims of one.*

First, there is an estimation of risk against reward. Risk of immediate injury or death against the value of the spoils. Any *wanax* of a town or village must show his willing and his ability, for none but a fool will bow their heads to a coward. Every season, his people – especially his warriors – must see metal or livestock being brought in or else they will vote for somebody else to secure it for them.

Then there is the retribution.

In our lands, since time immemorial it has never been wise to scrump from a neighbour's orchard. It is tacit law that you do not raid other *poleis* on the same island – unless, of course, the island is so large that you might get away with it, and Lemnos was not such an island. This was not only an act of hubris but also one of short-sighted stupidity, for the retaliation would be swift and savage, and blood feuds long outlived generations of men. *Sea between the enemy and thee.* That was one of the first things any Hellene learned, alongside his numbers.

But those were hard times. In the wilting heat, springs ran dry, and twice in that intervening decade did crops fail entirely. Although Euneus was resourceful and careful with stocks, people starved. Xandros would see him some evenings, utterly spent, with his head in his hands. Grey hairs had replaced fair. Euneus would make a point of eating outdoors with Xandros, whilst Hypsipyle remained in the dappled shadows of her courtyard, as if to make it clear that they shared the same hardships as everyone else.

Euneus must have made his reckoning. He must have determined that it was worth the risk of the Moudrians crossing the hills seeking revenge, some day or other. Meetings of the council were sometimes fraught but, ultimately, none disputed Euneus was doing his best. We can only imagine tempers ran high during the discussion before this latest raid, a discussion to which Xandros was not privy. Even those present will not have heard all that was on Euneus' mind. Would it have been coloured by the fact Xandros was his only surviving child? I think it must.

Even as Euneus fretted and planned, did he know – I often wonder – that there was a far greater threat heading for his shores than a few score of angry Moudrians? For an unholy coalition of those very raiders that did for King Ammurapi, long before they rampaged through Ugarit, would first visit their devastation upon the island kingdoms of the Archipelagos.

They were the Sea Peoples.

Xandros knew the venture was a great risk: revenge frequently bit more viciously than the initial slight that prompted it. But, for him and him alone, the raid posed an even greater threat.

Teodora, his love, lived in Moudros.

He felt himself choking with frustration. In one cruel blow, his hopes of one day marrying her were permanently, irrevocably quashed. It was one thing to be a citizen of the offending Myrine; it was quite another to take part in the raid itself. And all to secure meat for a festival! Any lingering doubt that his father had, somehow, read his mind and yet again thwarted him evaporated like early morning mist.

Xandros was the last to arrive. There would be ten of them in the party, plus a mule to carry their provisions. Some of the other men acknowledged him with a grunt; one or two just stared at him for a few moments and looked away. Even his father strode past him down the path from the citadel, armed with spear and sword.

No limp, today, thought Xandros. *He's feeling good about this.* He felt a pulse of hatred towards him.

Euneus did a quick head count and then tipped his head towards the east. All discussion about the tactics they would employ had, it seemed, taken place before Xandros arrived, making him feel even more glum.

The walk took several hours in the soul-sapping heat and Xandros naturally found himself lumbered with the mule, trudging a stone's throw from the column of men. They stopped only once to refill their waterskins and cool off in a stream. It was a stream in which he and Teodora had drunk in recent months and on whose banks they had lain, watching the clouds drift over them. His stomach knotted as they passed more familiar landmarks: an ancient olive tree in which he had carved a symbol; a pile of rocks, the topmost still charred with burnt offerings. As they approached the bay of Moudros, however, they followed a less-used track that threaded through a scree-strewn valley, where they were unlikely to be seen.

The track began to rise and, through a gap in the rocks, they saw that they were close to cresting the hill. The last before Moudros. All chatter had long since stopped and they drank from their gourds and skins in tense silence.

Though the water was cold and sweet, it sat heavy in the pit of Xandros' stomach. He looked around him, suddenly aware of how sharply he was registering everything that was happening.

There, leaning against a boulder, with a stalk of wild grass drooping from his lips, was suave Alektruon. Whilst the rest of the group squinted or tipped forwards their wide-brimmed hats, Alektruon seemed unperturbed by the fierce sun. To Xandros, he possessed the face of one who had tried every daring thing in life, physical or emotional, and found all of them underwhelming. It was widely accepted that he had murdered at least two islanders following some private feud or other but he merely shrugged whenever the subject arose. He was, in short, an ideal man for this sort of job.

Sat in the shade of an overhanging outcrop was Hilarion, tighter-lipped than usual. He was one of the king's favourites – one of the most popular figures in Myrine, in fact – but Xandros knew nothing of his skills in a skirmish, if it came to it. At that moment, his cheeks were red and his forehead glistening with sweat.

Just in front of him was Hektor, wiping his brow and putting one hand on his hips. With the other, he drove a spear, butt-first, into the dusty track. His face was a chestnut brown, tough and clean-lined, and was dominated by a bushy moustache. Xandros now noticed the sweat staining his tunic above his belt and the faint tang of his body as the heat radiated from it. That and his snow-white crown of hair.

Only one of the company was missing and Xandros felt his absence keenly.

Moxos.

Like Euneus, Moxos was also the son of an Argonaut.

Then there was Euneus himself, *wanax* of Myrine. Tall and wiry, with the physique of an athlete rather than a warrior. In the harsh winter months, he would drape a fleece and two winter cloaks around his shoulders, and the additional bulk would transform him, lending him presence and authority. This day, however, he was bare-chested and lean. Much leaner, in fact, than Xandros had ever seen him.

He noticed a pair of dragonflies hovering over the water and their iridescent colour transfixed him. The whisper of a song fluttered into his mind, and when Euneus ordered the group to move on, Xandros didn't hear him. He barked at his son, making him flinch.

They continued up the track. Even the hardiest of weeds had dried and grown brittle as they poked out from between rocks, and they crunched underfoot. A light wind had picked up from the arid, stony hillside behind them. Xandros watched Alektruon flicking his grass stalk into it and his slight swagger instilled confidence. Perhaps they could be done with the whole affair before the Moudrians were even aware of their presence.

Euneus held out his arm and they stopped. They had crested the ridge now and, crabbing forwards, could see into the bay below. The village of Moudros shimmered white in the heat haze to the left whilst, below, the hills were parched brown. The bleating of goats drifted up towards them and the prospect of the succulent meat roasting over a spit made Xandros' mouth water.

Euneus turned to them now and reached inside his leather bag for some tethers. He handed them out with some words of reassurance to each man. Xandros, alone, didn't receive one.

'And remember, spare their blood, do you hear me Alek?' Euneus gave Alektruon an intense look. It was only when the rest of the band turned to him that he tipped his head in reluctant agreement. Euneus finished by warning the men off harming the Moudrian children, even if they intervened. This, he added sharply, was a point of honour and he wouldn't hesitate to execute any man of Myrine for disobeying it.

'If we have to run, we leave the mule. Last thing. You, Xandros, are our lookout. Don't get involved, understood?'

The words slapped him across the face. Xandros was as good as any his age, in his own estimation at least, with a spear. Plenty younger than him had taken an active part in raids, so why was he now to be given such an insulting role? Just when he thought the situation couldn't get any worse, his father had proved him wrong. All of this risk; all of this... this *damage* and he was only to be a *lookout*?

'Well, are you listening?'

He felt his throat burn and his cheeks flush with embarrassment and rage. He could only glare at his father. If he tried to utter a single word, he knew it would emerge choked with indignation so he chose silence, barely nodding his head. He felt the eyes of the other Myrinians watching him. Alektruon's hard stare betrayed nothing of his own thoughts. Hektor glanced over his shoulder at him and winked in pity, making his moustache twitch. Xandros didn't want their pity: he wanted their respect. No, tell it straight. He didn't want to be here at all.

Euneus crept to the ridge, shielding his eyes as he surveyed the hillside. At one point, his head became still for a moment before it resumed its sweep of the terrain. Then he shuffled back between the rocks.

'Goatherd's hut to the left, halfway down, about fifty yards. Couldn't see its owner. We take two each: the best we can lay hands on.' He turned to Xandros, pale blue eyes flashing a warning. 'Remember: watch and warn, yes?' Xandros looked away and Euneus beckoned them out of the shade at a crouch. Under the blazing sun, in plain sight of Moudros, every urge was to run at the goats, tether their horns and heave them back towards the track. Looking on, Xandros knew that would have ended in failure. Even as they approached at a purposeful walk, some of the goats skittered away, bleating in fear. Goats follow the herd and it only takes one to scatter them all. In other circumstances, Xandros might have found it amusing, watching the men being led on a dance by those goats, but every second's delay presented an opportunity for the Moudrians to spot the raiders and arm themselves.

With a great effort, he cut through his frustration and focused upon that ancient goatherd's shelter. There was no sign of life. Then his eyes naturally drifted over towards the rooftops of Moudros itself. He had never been allowed inside Teodora's house, of course, but he knew where it was. He tried to pick out the hyacinths against the whitewashed walls but her family was not the only one to favour those purple blooms.

He wondered what she was doing at that very moment and when – if – he would see her again. Even amidst the euphoria of his recent dalliance with Teodora, her warning not to take her for granted had struck home. She was not like the other girls. She would not be treated like a fool. He was so close to her he could see her home, yet he might just as well have been on the other side of the Middle Sea for all that he couldn't get a message to her. He wanted to bellow in frustration.

He put out his arm, feeling for the warm stone behind him as he sidled along the ridge, struggling to concentrate on what was happening on the slope below. Alektruon and Euneus had each succeeded in capturing a pair of brown goats, though Euneus was having some difficulty in getting his up the slope. Their bleating intensified and, echoing from that stone-strewn hillside, it seemed to Xandros that someone on the furthest crag of the island might have heard them.

A figure jumped down beside him. For a fraction of a second, Xandros' brain assumed it was someone from Myrine, late to join them, but the shadow made a sudden move. Xandros jerked his head to the side to see a furious, leathery face beneath a straw hat about to bring a vine staff down upon his head. He yelped in fear and raised his hands. The staff struck the heel of his thumb before glancing off the back of his head. Bright lights exploded before his eyes.

'*Thieves!*' yelled the goatherd.

Xandros had flailed at the staff but his ears were buzzing and his vision clouded, and he missed it completely. As his attacker raised his arm for a second blow, Xandros plunged at him but he had taken a step backwards and he could only clatter into his knees. He heard the rip of the staff and felt a wicked blow against his backside. Dully, he noticed his hair had smeared his assailant's shins with dark blood. He heard a yell of something like '*Hey!*' and then the goatherd was blasted from the side. He clattered against the rocks like a rag doll. Xandros caught a glimpse of his face, clenched in a grimace of pain and wild strands of grey hair.

His father had arrived first, then Alektruon. The old man never stood a chance. *Spare their blood!* Euneus had ordered, which is all to the good until that blood is one's own. He was already quite dead when Alektruon took out his knife, the blade of which he had honed to a razor edge, and sliced off the man's thumb. He wedged it into the wretch's pulped mouth. There were hurried orders and then someone whistled and the bleats drew nearer. Xandros felt his head swimming and, when he tried to stand, he passed out.

He awoke draped over the back of the mule, flies buzzing about his face. His head was thumping with pain and, when he touched it, he felt the linen bandage tied around it. Hektor batted away his hand.

'Want to sit up?' he growled.

Xandros mumbled, 'Yes,' and Hektor gripped his tunic and helped him upright, slapping him on the back for good measure. Xandros helped himself to some water and looked about him. All ten of the raiders were present and, by the looks of it, unmarked, albeit streaked in dirt and sweat.

'Where's that goatherd?' he croaked.

Hektor turned to Xandros and lowered his voice. 'Bottom of a ravine, cooling off 'neath rocks and brushwood.'

'And no one else came? From Moudros, I mean.'

Hektor shook his head. 'If anything gives him away it'll be the stench of his old body. Or circling carrion birds.'

Xandros watched his bulky shoulders as he moved off to join in some story or other that Hilarion was telling. He rolled his shoulders but his limbs felt utterly drained of strength and the bright sun stung his eyes. He rummaged about in a saddle bag for a pear and some water: the hard fruit did little to restore his spirits so he thought about Teodora instead, glad at least that there had been no hue and cry raised from Moudros. With the mule beginning to tire and drop back, he whispered some words of encouragement into its ears and scratched its flanks.

Because of the way it was spat out in distaste, he heard 'twelve' in response to a question, then something about leftovers. The number of goats they had stolen, he now realised. Given there were nine in that band, not including him, that meant they were six light. A poor return. At that very moment, his father glanced over his shoulder at him, looking angry. He had no doubt that, in coming to rescue him, they must have released at least a few.

Was I at fault? he asked himself. But even the act of thinking made his skull throb. He flopped back down onto the mule with a sigh but, when he closed his eyes, he could only see the goatherd's rictus of pain and the whip of his spidery hair as he fell.

VII

Tense days followed, during which Xandros' skull knitted itself back together without complication.

Almost without.

There was no reprisal. The Moudrians had no idea about the raid, some speculated. Perhaps they had no heart for a fight, suggested others. Xandros, for his part, thought neither of these things, and kept his own counsel whilst he recovered. Even though his recollection of the goatherd's attack was a little foggy, his voice as he shouted for help was loud and shrill. It could not have failed to carry towards Moudros, he thought. He began to hope that it had. At least that way Teodora would have a possible explanation for his absence.

From overhearing faint conversations in his bed within Hypsipyle's halls, Xandros learned that his father had ordered the farmers in the outlying parts of Myrine to keep their flocks within sight of the citadel and sent out watchmen to monitor the hills and passes around the village. Each evening, as the sun melted into the horizon, they would return with shrugs, though the tension lining their faces undermined their nonchalance.

With each passing day, it was as if Myrine began to breathe once more.

He remembered little of the rest of that first afternoon or the next day. Hypsipyle's handmaid – Auge, meaning 'Dawn' – dressed his head injury with nimble fingers and tight-lipped efficiency whilst Hypsipyle leaned on her walking stick, watching them with sharp eyes. Hypsipyle had taken Auge on six years earlier, after her loyal old maid had died suddenly, and Xandros had always felt sorry for her. Auge had stepped into an impossible situation, for the maid had long been a favourite of the island's former queen and Hypsipyle never missed an opportunity to remind Auge of this. She suffered the frequent tirades and occasional grudging praise with equanimity but, it being impossible for a handmaid to answer the haughty matriarch back, she took it out on him instead.

'Well?'

'Knitting together neatly I think, my lady,' Auge answered quietly as she pinned the bandage in place.

Hypsipyle arched an eyebrow at him but Xandros was too groggy to care. Satisfied, the two women shuffled out and closed the door behind them. With barely any through-breeze, the little room soon became stiflingly hot. That and the twitter of martins flitting about the eaves outside made him heavy-lidded and, temporarily restored after a bowl of broth at midday, he fell asleep soon after. He was oblivious to the golden bars of sun creeping up the opposite wall, and the light seeping from the room at dusk. He stirred briefly but, with the room shrouded in shadows and his skull throbbing, sleep engulfed him.

In the darkness, the aching pulse softened to a series of creaks, followed by the soft *plosh* of water. Xandros strained his eyes – and ears – for its source.

Creak... plosh... creak... plosh, came the unhurried rhythm.

Then, materialising out of the darkness, like the new moon rising through a cloud, a figure in a tattered straw hat. Hunched over the oars of a boat so low in the water the merest ripple could breach its gunwales, he saw a ragged old man with his back to him. As he leaned to the catch of each stroke, his tunic stretched across his spare frame. Long strands of hair – as fine as cobwebs – clung to his back.

Creak... plosh... creak... plosh.

Xandros felt his pulse race as the man approached, a stone's throw now, heading directly for him.

Then the oars came to rest upon the water's surface, skimming over them with a soft hiss. The figure straightened a little, and Xandros could almost hear ancient bones grinding in protest. As if suddenly sensing his presence, the head half turned towards him. A feeling of paralysis seized Xandros. His arms froze as stiff as a thick ash spear by his sides. The boat veered a little, so close he could feel it brush his toes. The hideous figure snapped its familiar head towards him. Sightless eyes in deep sockets. Skin translucent to the bone, shrivelled lips opening to voice a silent scream. As its bony, thumbless hand shot out to reach for him, the paralysis broke and Xandros sprang bolt upright, eyes gaping into the darkness.

The room was utterly still. Gradually, the soughing of leaves from the olives beyond the wall filtered through the slats. As his eyes adjusted to the gloom, and the spectre of the goatherd faded from his eyes, his heart began to settle and the dull pulse of pain at the back of his head reminded him that he was very much alive. He wiped the film of sweat from his brow and swung his legs over the bed, grateful that he could still move them.

After a drink of water, he allowed himself to sag back onto the bed in the full knowledge he would get no rest for what remained of the night.

VIII

The moon had waxed and waned after the raid when, one evening, Xandros was eating in the olive-shaded courtyard of Hypsipyle's house with her and Euneus. His father had been cool with him since they had returned, even by his usual standards. Some days would pass in which he wouldn't so much as look at his son. They were eating husks of rock bread and a thin, bland soup with which to soften them. Euneus was speaking in that absent way he sometimes did, as if clearing his mind rather than engaging in conversation with his mother.

'Next year I think we'll have to try sowing spring barley. The wheat yields in the east fields have been so poor.'

'Is wheat not hardier?'

'It is but we can't keep repeating mistakes. Talking of mistakes...' At this point, he turned dispassionate blue eyes upon Xandros and clenched his jaw. Xandros felt his heart sink. 'There is something I have been wanting to ask sooner – as have others, for that matter – but there have been more pressing matters.'

'What is it, Father?'

'How was it that the herdsman was able to attack you like he did? And raise a cry?'

The question stung Xandros as surely as had the goatherd's staff. He sputtered for an answer and looked to Hypsipyle for some support. Her forehead creased in a frown but he could not tell at whom her disapproval was directed. 'I... He... He crept up behind me. I was watching the hut, as you told me to! He just jumped down from out of nowhere!'

Euneus harrumphed. 'Out of nowhere? You mean from behind

you, don't you?' His voice rose. 'You were daydreaming again. You failed to look behind you, didn't you?'

'But we had come from that direction and seen nothing!'

'That was your only role,' he said, speaking over him, 'and yet you—'

'We had seen *nothing*!'

Euneus' eyes and nostrils flared in anger. Xandros thought he might be struck: it wouldn't have been the first time, though not for some years. 'Euneus,' said Hypsipyle softly, 'he paid for his mistake with his own blood. No harm has come of it.'

'No harm has come *yet*. Come the new moon, you'll be taking a turn in the huer's hut. It will give you chance to make amends.'

Xandros looked from one to the other in disbelief. He didn't see any mistakes to make amends for. The man *had* appeared from nowhere. He would have known every rock and stone of those hills like the back of his hand. Xandros had nearly died defending himself and, even if they hadn't come to his aid, might still have overpowered him.

But he had been daydreaming about Teodora. He stood abruptly and stormed out of the courtyard.

No raid came that week.

IX

Megalonisi

It seems to Huliat that he has been imprisoned for weeks. In fact, a mere matter of days has passed following his murder of the chieftain. Through the gaps in the rough-hewn timber walls, he can hear the laughter and cursing of people passing by. Even if he were blind, he would know when darkness had fallen, not by the drop in temperature but by the raised voices and rougher conversation of men fired by strong wine and bravado.

Just last night, he was awoken by the sound of bodies slamming against the wall immediately above the straw on which he lay. He jerked awake, expecting to hear the thud of fists and groans of pain but, instead, he heard the muffled moans and rhythmic creak of copulation. It depressed him and fascinated him in equal parts, reminding him that he had never taken a woman and, given his appearance, likely never would.

In the early hours of this morning, it had been the slurred talk and laughter of two men. He had overheard his own name and what sounded like a taunt, followed by a snort of laughter. The voices had faded and the sounds of the night resumed. The scuttle of tiny feet – rats, most likely – and the hoot of owls in search of a mate. Shortly afterwards, the faint noises of fighting and shouting. Try as he might to find some rest, he found himself thinking of his mother and father. He had loved them and, being an only child, had been loved wholeheartedly. He was no ordinary boy – he had known this himself – and had made few friends: his beetling face and gangling size had done him no favours here, nor had his volatile temper and sudden clumsiness whenever the headaches seized him. The pain was sometimes so extreme that it gave him double vision. Still his parents had encouraged him, cajoled and soothed him when, invariably, he was rejected, or even pelted with stones.

Many years on, he missed his father and the woman his mother had been, before his death. What remained had been a timid shell, and now she, too, was gone. Perhaps violence was the only way. After all, killing the chieftain – king felt too grand a word for the vicious old bully – had felt right; felt *natural* to him. He was, in short, good at it.

Shortly after dawn's light has begun to filter through the timbers, he hears footsteps approaching and the scrape of the heavy bar being lifted.

'Outside. We're ready.'

Huliat swings his long legs from the pallet, dusts his filthy clothes and pulls loose strands of hay from his long hair. He can see that his delay is annoying the guard so he takes his time, towering over the man as he steps past him into the early morning. He fills his lungs with the savour of dawn to replace the cloying musk of dung and absent cattle. The bright light makes him squint after so long cooped up in the gloom of the byre and he finds he can't fully open his eyes for a few minutes. He passes a few villagers who stare at him but none dare insult him now they see he is unshackled. He meets their gaze stony-faced, and plenty turn away. They enter the village square. The crowds are three deep and a hum of speculation rises as he approaches the tribunal of elders, seated upon a crescent of stools.

'Here,' says one of the guards, pointing to a patch of brittle grasses. He notices the earth has a sheen of early morning dew. The sweet smell makes him relax a little. The ground will quickly dry, however, because it has not rained on Megalonisi in weeks.

He doesn't recognise the sour-faced elder, who now stands and raises an impatient hand to demand silence. He doesn't recognise him, he realises, because foreign blood runs in his veins and he is not from this village. It seems they have drafted in a wise head from elsewhere to adjudicate. A wise head but also a warrior, if the impressive sword at his belt is anything to go by. This is highly unusual, for Peleset law is immutable and it strikes him as a little odd. Perhaps, in being forced to pass a death sentence, his fellow villagers are unwilling to pollute their own souls in the act.

Huliat is feeling calm. The explosive temper in the years immediately following his father's death he has learned to channel, though he has not yet mastered stopping it at source. By taking deep breaths, he finds he can calm his racing heart.

The chieftain taught him this. The chieftain took him under his wing. Encouraged him to train with spear and sword. He used him but he didn't love him. He regrets nothing. Nothing beyond not carving him up and...

Calm, Huliat.

He takes another deep breath. The elder is watching him carefully. He is a small man and, even at a distance of ten paces, must raise his head like a bird at feeding time to speak to him.

'You are Uliat, son of Repha?'

'I am Huliat.'

The elder sniffs. Huliat can see the elder thinks the correction is of no consequence but Huliat disagrees. *What are you if you cannot even take pride in your name?* His mother's words, after he had hurt a boy for teasing him.

'You admit killing the lord of this village? In cold blood?'

'I d...' Murmurs of interest arise all around him but he ignores them and stares at the ground, thinking only to steady his voice. Being so deep, any crack sounds particularly strident. This caused him a good deal of upset when his voice first broke as a youth. The question is a loaded one. An unfair one. Delivered in the man's thick accent, it has momentarily foxed him. 'Not in cold blood.'

'No?' The elder raises an eyebrow and looks to the others at the tribunal. These men *are* locals. He catches one tutting softly and shaking his bearded head. 'Explain yourself.'

'I killed him because he killed my father. And my mother. Is there any man here who wouldn't have done the same?' Huliat resists the urge to look around to gauge the reaction. The murmuring fades away.

'I am told your mother died naturally! Only days ago! How, then, could he have killed *her*?'

Huliat raises his head and meets the elder's eyes. 'She died the day my father died: or at least her heart did. The king…' he grits his teeth as he utters the word '…used her like a whore. She died a broken woman.'

'Your father was killed in war, was he not?'

'He was slaughtered in a *raid*! Defending his home. *My* home!' Huliat hears his voice booming across the square. If the elder's purpose is to rile him, to make it seem like Huliat's anger controls him, he is in danger of succeeding.

'And what proof do you have that the king was responsible? Personally responsible, that is.'

Huliat swallows hard. It takes an effort of tremendous willpower to stop him striding over to the man and rattling him until his filthy teeth fall out of his mouth. 'My mother told me on her death bed.'

'Yet she cannot speak to this, can she?'

'There are others here who can.' He turns a dark glare upon the bearded councillor. One of the former king's men. A westlander. He sees his lips twitch in discomfort.

'The king killed your father but held you in a position of some esteem. This doesn't follow, does it?'

'If I was a weakling, he would have done away with me, too.'

The elder sighs and glances at the men of the tribunal. He seems to be losing interest in the trial. Or concealing the fact that the matter was decided the moment the blade entered the king's throat. The men of the tribunal are inscrutable but Huliat can sense their minds working, considering matters not of justice but of self-interest.

'And the adviser of the king? Did you not also maim him?'

'But I did not kill him, though I could have. I have not killed any other man in this village.'

The elder adjusts his robe before turning to the guard. 'You there. You found this man with the knife in his hand, just after the act. Is this so?'

The guard clears his throat. 'I did.'

'The words of a man caught in such a moment tend to speak from the heart, not the mind. What did he say?'

Huliat gives the elder a reappraising look. *Is there more to him than meets the eye?*

'He admitted killing the king. Said that he had lied to him.'

'Well? Was that it?'

'No, sir. He said… He said that he didn't kill him because he wanted the throne. That we should choose a just leader, and he would follow him.'

'What did he do then?'

'Well, he threw the knife he'd used, and it damn near hit me in the face!'

The village square buzzes with dark mutterings at this. The elder tuts and waves his hand impatiently. 'Do you think he meant to kill you too?'

'Well… I…' His eyes slide to Huliat but Huliat is looking at the ground. 'I don't know. It stuck in the door post.'

'Did he follow up and attack you?'

'No. He… He sat down.'

There is a snort of laughter at the guard's rather witless response and Huliat hears some guffaws.

'He sat down,' the elder repeats, 'and awaited his fate.' There is a heavy pause and the elder purses his lips thoughtfully. Huliat closes his eyes and listens to the faint whisper of the sea and the distant caw of a gull. How he longs to be away from this oppressive little place. Perhaps the only freedom for him is death. He is ready for it, if only it is swift.

'Is there anyone else here who wants to speak?'

From the tail of his eyes, Huliat can see heads turn this way and that but he senses no appetite for any more. A rather sullen feeling has settled upon the square.

'Very well. I will now convene with this tribunal. Take him back.'

Huliat allows himself to be led away, eyes downcast though the weight of people's stares is heavy. As he leaves the square, he becomes aware of movement to his left. Someone jostling for position.

'Huliat!'

He looks up to see a familiar face, though it takes him a moment to recognise it. His uncle, an old man now. He has not seen him in years and had assumed he was dead.

'Huliat,' his uncle says in a cracked voice. 'Huliat, you acted with honour; don't let anyone say otherwise. I am proud of you.'

Then he is barged aside and is lost from view. Huliat walks on, feeling some part of his heavy soul lighten.

By the time he is led back out of the byre, Huliat's stomach is rumbling and causing him some discomfort. Apart from some hard bread and olives, he has eaten nothing since midday. Lean harvests have taken their toll upon all folk on Megalonisi but not all islanders have the same frame to fill. His temper is short and he does not know how he will react if – when – the sentence is passed.

The sun is beginning to sink now, halfway towards the last mountain ridge before the sea. He has seen it slide into the Archipelagos many times from atop the Korykos peninsula, with his father.

This is our home now, Huliat. This was one of his earliest and surest memories. *It is beautiful, isn't it?*

The first time, he fell asleep tucked against his father's shoulder and, rather than wake his son, he carried him all the way down before meeting a muleteer. No mean feat for he was heavy even after just five winters.

We will be safer here.

Huliat had been a babe in arms when his family had fled Anatolia. He had no measure of the dangers his parents, his village, had faced. By the same token, he had no real measure of what 'safer' meant, either. Safer from what, exactly? The whole world – as far as he could tell – was riven by fear. Let it burrow deep into other people's stomachs like a parasite: he was done with it. Let other people fear him, instead. Take it from him!

The men are sat back upon the crescent of chairs. He can tell by the looks upon some faces that there has been disagreement, forcefully expressed. Doubtless this is why they have taken so long to arrive at their decision. The bearded councillor looks particularly unhappy. The elder's face is lined with strain. He stands, joints clicking, and waits for the onlookers to come to order. A hush falls upon the square. As Huliat's eyes pass over them, he realises that he does not recognise at least half of the faces. They are outlandish, as are their clothes.

'The debating is finished; the deliberations are over. Three men are for the death of this man; three against. It falls to me to cast the deciding vote.'

Huliat's jaw is clenched tight and his eyes are fixed upon the ground in front of him. His heart is pounding and he feels a little faint from hunger but he will not shame his family. He hears his uncle's words again and again, and they are as a balm for his mind.

I am proud of you...

'He says that he killed in his father's name. In his mother's. Others have said that he served the king loyally before that day. There must have been opportunities – daily opportunities – to take his life but he did not. *Why is that?* I ask myself.' The elder has presence, Huliat must admit. The square is absolutely silent. It is so quiet he can hear the clanging of pots in a nearby kitchen; the bark of a dog. 'Because there was no intent to kill him then. There was no intent to seize the throne for himself afterwards. So, the decision is in fact a simple one. Huliat must forfeit his life or Huliat must devote his life to honouring his words. It is my decision that Huliat will live.'

Huliat raises his head in astonishment. Some amongst the crowd cannot restrain their displeasure though they are quickly silenced. They are – were – the king's people, he now sees as he looks around him with fresh eyes. The men and women who fell upon the town all those years ago. Despite the intermingling of blood since, the lines are still evident.

The elder raises a minatory finger at him. 'You must prove your honour; you must prove your loyalty. To your people. To me. It begins now. The former king was greedy and he did not look after his people. This island can no longer feed itself so we must leave it behind. The islands north of here are green. Men say their soil is black. Others – many others – have already taken to their ships before hunger makes them wither where they stand. The gods have delivered you to me, Huliat. It is they who have given you a second life, not me. Honour them! Honour me, your new king!'

Still reeling from his unexpected reprieve, it takes Huliat a few moments to also register that the man has called himself 'king'. Truly, Huliat has done him a favour, toppling a regime without so much as a droplet of blood touching the new ruler's skin. A coup had not been Huliat's intention, but then what was?

He looks out over the coruscating sea. The freedom he has dreamed of involved him travelling far from here alone, not in some mass exodus. But this way, his head will remain attached to his shoulders. Perhaps he must endure this to keep his dream alive.

'I will honour them, and you. On my life, I will be loyal.'

The trickle of applause becomes a roar of acclamation and Huliat looks on as the king tips back his proud head in approval.

BOOK THREE

THE HELMSMAN AND THE RING

I

Gytheon, region of Messenia

On the opposite side of the Archipelagos to Lemnos, one of the few yards on the southern Peloponnese still crafting boats was about to close for the evening.

'Pine blocks,' growled the big shipwright, wiping his brow. Atukhos, his young apprentice, loaded the leather bucket with the wood and shuffled over with it between his legs.

Atukhos was not his real name. The fever that ravaged Gytheon a few years previously had carried off the boy's mother along with dozens of other villagers. He could still remember the heat that radiated from his mother's writhing body, and the febrile stench of the sodden bedclothes, when he entered her bedroom. And his father yelling at him to get out. His father had survived the ague but his weakened constitution had not sustained the bouts of drinking and melancholia that followed, though not before he had vouchsafed his son to the uncle who then, in the loosest sense of the phrase, looked after him.

All of this was unknown to the shipwright when he first saw the boy. The shipwright was called Ancaeus: he had a past of his own, and very few people alive knew anything about it. His life was his business and, until anybody crossed him, everybody else kept the same custom.

Drawn by the racket of hammering and cursing, the boy had wandered into the boatyard one day, fascinated by the shaggy-haired giant struggling to shape the keel of a boat. When he had finally finished, he had thrown down his adze and wiped the sweat from his brow. Then he had noticed the boy, standing diffidently by the gate.

Ancaeus eyed him as he drained his waterskin. 'What do you want?'

The boy flinched at the man's tone. He managed a little shrug.

'Then run along. This is no place for you.'

The boy was still there as he resumed his work but, when he next stopped and glanced behind him, he had gone.

He was there again the following morning. 'What is it with you?' Ancaeus asked gruffly. 'Have you no friends to play with?'

The boy shook his head and Ancaeus tutted before fitting another strake to his vessel. Eventually, the boy took the hint and left. The same thing happened on the following two mornings. On the second, Ancaeus greeted him as 'Mus' but the boy just blinked at him, giving him a wary frown. Did he call him 'Mouse' to mock him or just because he was quiet?

Mus was conspicuous by his absence on the third and fourth mornings, though the latter coincided with a sacred day in which work was forbidden. The following day, he showed up at the boatyard at midday, his dirty cheeks streaked with tears. Ancaeus had been in a dark mood because the delivery of pine he was expecting had not arrived, meaning he had to concentrate instead on jobs he preferred to tackle at the end of a build. He rolled his eyes as the boy entered, muttering, 'Thought I might have seen the last of you. What's the matter?' He couldn't help but notice how thin he had become, even in the passage of just a few days.

Then he saw the bruising on the boy's temple. He set down his hammer and went over to him. 'Who did this?' he asked with a frown. 'Well?'

When Mus failed to respond, he added, 'Your trouble is you don't answer back. Boys can be cruel…' His words trailed away as he noticed the marks on his neck. He tutted. 'These are finger marks.' He took the boy's chin and tilted his face to him. Fearful brown eyes slid away from him. 'Look at me, boy. *Look at me!* I mean you no harm.'

The boy met his glare. Ancaeus noticed that, behind the fear, lay pain, both of body and spirit. He released his chin. 'Who did this to you?'

Mus shook his head and looked away.

'Wasn't another boy, was it?'

After a few moments, the boy whispered, 'No.'

Despite himself, despite his advancing years and the toll they had taken upon him, despite the lack of any obligation towards the boy, he felt his pulse quicken with anger. He licked his thick lips.

'Well, lucky for you I can't do my work for today. I think I'll go for a walk. You run on home now.'

A cloud of doubt crossed the boy's eyes but then he nodded and trudged out of the yard. Ancaeus followed at a distance.

They crossed the coastal road and entered the dusty streets of the village. It was a straggle of kilns, sheds and mud-brick houses, in which every hint of colour was bleached by the relentless sun. The boy only looked behind him once and his face was full of trepidation but, seeing Ancaeus, he pressed on towards a collection of hovels at the edge of the village. Dirty rags were pinned across doorways and clothes were strung out to dry across the gaps in the houses. Ancaeus ducked under a shapeless tunic, grimacing as his back clicked, and saw the boy enter one of the houses without looking back.

Ancaeus leaned against a wall, enjoying the feeling of heat radiating from it. He closed his eyes against the sun, wafting away the flies that droned past his face. The stultifying heat and lack of a breeze in the narrow street made him drowsy, and the mind of a man in his sixties inevitably looks not towards an uncertain future but backwards. He found himself remembering that moment aboard *Argo* when, so many years before, they had – somehow – weathered a terrifying storm after he had steered them from the treacherous delta of the Phasis in Colchis. When the wind had finally abated, he was pressed against the hull behind the tillers, clawing the wood whilst he waited for Death to swoop in on the next wave. It was the stillness and the heat that had brought him back to his senses.

A dull thud and a scream snapped him from his thoughts and he stared at the house into which the boy had gone. The noise had surely come from there. He pushed himself away from the wall, clenching his fists, just as a ruddy-faced figure emerged bearing a clay wine flagon. Seeing the look upon Ancaeus' grizzled face, he did a double take as he was about to set off in the opposite direction. There was a moment of mutual recognition – nothing more than the flicker of having seen someone several times before in a small village – but it stopped him on his threshold.

'That noise came from in there?'

The man looked Ancaeus up and down. 'What noise?'

'Mus? You fine in there?'

'"Mouse"?' said the man, screwing up his face. 'What are you, some kind of…'

As the question was asked, the boy stumbled towards the door, touching the blood at the corner of his mouth. He seemed surprised to see the shipwright on his doorstep. Ancaeus snatched the flagon from the man's hand. His heart willed him to slam it into the man's face but his mind suggested this would have consequences. Instead, he drove it hard into his belly, making him double over in agony, pawing at the dusty street as he gasped for breath like a beached fish. Ancaeus smashed the flagon onto the wall, making it explode with a *crack* that doused the wall with crimson liquid and brought heads darting out of doorways. Reading the situation, they retreated and nobody emerged to challenge him.

Ancaeus gripped the stricken man's tunic and hauled him half to his feet. 'Next time, that'll be your skull,' he snarled, letting him drop onto the street. 'Come on, boy,' said Ancaeus. 'You don't stay here anymore.'

The boy took his proffered hand without hesitation and he helped him down the step onto the street. As they walked away from the house, Ancaeus turned to him. 'Maybe that wretch was right about "Mus". What *is* your name, anyhow?'

'Myndos.'

'That's a terrible name. Myndos sounds like some bleak island on the other side of the world. From now on, on account of your bad luck, you're "Atukhos", right?'

'A-tukhos… Atukhos.'

'Just so,' said Ancaeus with a wink. 'Get used to it.'

Though Atukhos dared take no such liberties with Ancaeus' name, in his own mind he was 'The Bear' on account of his size and particularly his paw-like hands. Not that he had ever seen a bear.

His father had once told him a story about how he had encountered one whilst roaming the pine forests in the mountains, looking for stocks of wood. He had frozen, as one was supposed to, so he told his son (though the boy suspected, even then, that fear had played its hand), whilst the great brown muzzle sniffed the air and its breath rasped like overworked bellows. He had been lucky, for it had wandered off moments later.

Atukhos grew to love Ancaeus but had learned to stay out of his way when his mood darkened. For now, however, he merely seemed exhausted.

'One more block?'

The boy nodded even though he was dog-tired himself. It wasn't really a question, after all.

'Good. Now let's see you do it.'

The boy looked up at Ancaeus, wide-eyed. The carpenter had a shaggy head, beaded with sweat, and hair as thick as rope. Most of it was grey but there were still streaks of black. His dark eyes still twinkled in good humour and his thick pink lips now turned in a smile. He ruffled the boy's hair with his paw, making it jerk about like a rag doll.

Ancaeus watched the boy stack the wood into the clay-lined kiln. 'There. You're blocking the holes. How can it flow if you cover the holes?'

The boy's cheeks flushed. He made these simple mistakes when he was tired and it annoyed him. He replaced the lid and banked the woodchips around the bronze base of the kiln. The perforated plate through which the resinous liquid flowed was an innovation of which Ancaeus was very proud.

'That's enough. Now the brushwood.'

The boy dutifully overlaid the dried brush, damping it down with a shovel. When he was done, he stepped back and looked to Ancaeus for approval. Ancaeus walked a slow circle around the kiln before grunting in approval.

'I like that you're willing, my lad. Had no intention of lighting it up; I just wanted to see if you grumbled.' The boy's earnest face lit up. 'You're done for the day. I want to finish here.'

The boy watched Ancaeus enter his shed and, hands on hips,

admired his handiwork for a moment longer before turning towards the shack Ancaeus had built him a short distance from the yard. His smile faded.

That was odd, he thought. He blinked, clearing the dirt and sweat from his eyes. When he rubbed them and scanned the water, he saw nothing. Nothing but the shimmering sea and, nearer, the clump of cypress trees. He was about to turn back when he caught sight of them again, gliding into view beyond the foliage, making for the shore. Three distinct shapes. In nearly twelve months labouring for Ancaeus, he had become quite good at appraising boats and galleys. Appreciating the well-made ones, and noticing those that sat a little low in the water, which were badly laden or, more rarely, badly made.

But these galleys were long and slender, and he could not recall having seen the likes before. He watched them, mesmerised for a few moments by their sleek lines and their taut sails.

'You're still here?' asked Ancaeus, emerging from his hut. 'What are...?' His voice trailed away as he followed the boy's finger.

'Are they Greek?'

Ancaeus cursed under his breath. 'Go! Tell the others to flee then take the goat track and never come back. *Now!*'

'What about you? Wh...'

'*Go!*' he roared.

The boy flinched and backed away before skittering through the yard and out of sight. Ancaeus spat upon the ground and pushed his hair from his face, feeling the blood coursing around his old body like he hadn't felt in many years. He went to retrieve his axe.

Gytheon was not a big harbour town. In fact, Ancaeus doubted it was even the tenth largest in the whole of the Archipelagos. But here, on the southern coast of the Peloponnese, it was the only harbour of any note, and that would make it a draw for any marauding ships. They had sailed from beneath the westering sun. He had heard tales of sea rovers and most rumours suggested they had come from the distant island of the Shekelesh.

In that case, it would be a Shekelesh who would be the first to feel Ancaeus' axe cleave him to the bone. He might even manage a second before he was cut down himself. In his prime, he knew, he could have felled half a boatload before his stamina faded. He would not flee. He had devoted most of his life, since returning from the edge of the world, to this boatyard, though it had taken him a few years to purge the voyage from his mind and body. Years spent drinking, in the main, and fighting.

He would not flee.

One of the boats had already dropped anchor and he had noticed that the second was heeling to port. The third was hard on its stern, protecting it as if it was a wounded cub.

Ancaeus felt his heart pounding against his ribs but he kept still, resting both hands upon the pommel of his axe, blades down in the sand. The men from the first boat waded ashore, weapons poised, eyes fixed upon him. They were fifty paces away... sixty maybe... but he could sense their eyes full of interest. He had known since he was young that men who raved and postured were just as likely to be attacked as those who were timid. It was best to look calm and unperturbed, as he was struggling to do now. Most people found it harder to attack men in such an attitude, even warriors like these.

A babble of voices drifted over to him. Even though the words were indistinct, the cadence was somehow familiar. They wore tight kilts, much as Hellenes did, and feathered headdresses, as they did not. They were dark-skinned, like most of his own countrymen from the southern Peloponnese, and lean. Many of the men had cultivated sharply pointed beards. They formed a sort of armed bridgehead, casting lengthy shadows down the beach, as if claiming it as their own. The second boat disgorged its contents and Ancaeus was surprised to see women and children being helped ashore. Such black hair, he noticed. So dark it took on a bluish lustre in the slanting light.

He heard faint sounds behind him. Villagers trying to flee and making a good deal of fuss and noise about it. He tutted at them. Gytheon was supposed to be a Spartan port and he had come to expect better.

Ancaeus waited. He waited until all of the boats were bobbing in the shallows and a leader emerged, shorter than most but deep in the chest. He strode towards him now, an older man with a sour face, flanked by a dozen spearmen – impressive specimens, all – who eyed him without blinking. Their helmets were unlike anything he had ever seen: the tips of curved horns touching a disc. One of them was the tallest man he had ever seen, and Ancaeus had rowed with Herakles and fought the bronzed giant Talos in the old palace of Minos. He knew they suspected trickery; this was not the way their prey should behave.

Then they were stood before him. Though he kept the thought from his face, he rehearsed in his mind how he would attack, if it came to it. He reckoned he would leave three dead before he was felled. Again, his eyes were drawn to the warrior who walked head and shoulders above them all and, by the gods, his face was cruel.

The men stared at him now, trying to intimidate him into saying something. He thought he saw a faint trace of surprise in their expressions, too, respect even for not having fled. Beyond this guard, other spearmen now stalked towards Gytheon. He would soon hear the screams and the crack of pottery and wood. That would be the moment for him to pounce.

'You,' said the chieftain, jabbing a finger at him. 'The boat.' The metallic tang of dried sweat was strong and their skin, he noticed, was caked in brine. They had been at sea for many days. Probably weeks. But it wasn't this that caught his attention; it was the man's voice. It boomed like waves striking a cavern.

'The boat, there. What of it?'

One of the other warriors chattered at him and was answered curtly. Another made the universal sign for breaking. Half of them were now scanning the boatyard; another pointed. He had seen the wood stacks. If any of them was even a half-competent craftsman, Ancaeus would be redundant and slain where he stood. The chieftain beckoned to the throng unloading by the beach, and another man now swaggered across the sand to join them. Ancaeus noticed that he was carrying more weight around his midriff and lacked the definition of the other men. He got the impression he was low in the pecking order.

There was a brief exchange with the chieftain, during which the newcomer didn't take his eyes off Ancaeus. The man nodded.

'You must to repair our boat now.'

'Must I?'

A slow grin played across the man's lips, revealing teeth dark with calculus. 'If you want for to live.'

Ancaeus looked around the warriors and back at the chieftain. As likely as not, they would set upon him after he carried out any repairs but he would at least be ready. He shrugged and made to walk down to the boat.

'No!'

The warriors levelled their spears at him. The chieftain pointed to his axe. 'No,' he said firmly.

'Tell your man that my axe goes wherever I go. Tell him if you want to take it from me, you'll have to prise it from my cold, dead fingers. It's for my protection in case you try something tricksy.'

The man glared at him and, though Ancaeus suspected he hadn't understood every word, he got the gist of his feelings. A piercing scream rent the air: a woman's voice followed by an urgent shout. Ancaeus hefted his axe. *'Call them off! Call them off now!'*

'Hanin! Huliat!' The chieftain jerked his head to the side and a pair of spearmen sprinted off around the boatyard, one of them the giant. The others had dropped to a crouch and Ancaeus was faced with a corona of bronze spear tips, glowing in the evening sun.

'If they touch one of our people, two of your men die.'

After this was translated to him, the chief's face cracked into a grin. There was a commotion and angry voices, followed by the sounds of a scuffle. A few moments later, the spearmen returned, dragging a raider between them, looking groggy and sporting a welt under his eye. They threw him to the sand and turned back to Ancaeus.

'Repair.'

Ancaeus took a deep breath and trudged towards the boat, flanked by the wary guards.

They had been lucky. One portside strake had been damaged at the waterline, with the lightest of scrapes against rocks: anything firmer would have splintered the wood completely, causing the boat to sink in minutes. Nevertheless, they must have been baling for the whole of the day if they had nearly come to grief where he suspected they had: the tip of Cape Matapan, some thirty miles away. It was difficult to say with any certainty, however. The man chosen to translate had become surly and monosyllabic after his imperfect explanation of their voyage.

By the time the sun slipped to the horizon, and the vessel had been dragged ashore, he had only managed to prise a section of the damaged strake free of the other boards. A pair of warriors kept a constant watch upon him as he worked and, before long, their attentions had become so wearisome that he had snapped at the chieftain to get them to help him. To repair the vessel properly would require the removal of the other interlocking strakes above the damaged one, boring out the pins that held the tenon joints together. This would take him many days, working alone, but he had no intention of wasting his time, and valuable wood, on pirates. When it became clear that there was not a single carpenter amongst the crews or that, in their desperation, they had invested blind faith in him, he began to hatch a plan.

'Tell your chieftain,' said Ancaeus, who was now drenched in sweat, 'that I can do no more in the dark. You will have to wait until the morning. And I want some payment.'

The conversation around the fires faded and the raiders all turned dark eyes upon him – more than one hundred of them, he guessed. As the flames popped and spat in the twilight, Ancaeus thought he might have overstepped. In the firelight, the raiders looked tired and drawn. There was an ill-tempered exchange between the chieftain and various others, and much hand-waving. The translator turned to him.

'You stay. Eat here.' His lips twisted into a grin. 'Our payment is for you and the villagers to live. This is generous, yes?'

Ancaeus glanced over his shoulder at the town behind him, shrouded in darkness. He had seen some folk slipping away at dusk. He hoped the boy and one or two other figures he vaguely respected were amongst them but, with a pang of regret, he realised he would miss his lively presence. And his help in the morning.

He tugged his damp tunic away from his chest. Now that the

temperature had dropped, it felt unpleasantly damp. His joints clicked as he lowered himself gingerly to the sand, and he felt the suspicious eyes of the chieftain upon him. The man's mouth made him look sulky even when he was drinking wine. Ancaeus accepted some now and a bowl of the broth that one of the dark-eyed women ladled for him. He was grateful for it but, even with a husk of bread, it barely staved off his hunger. He wanted to stay awake long enough to learn something about them but he felt his eyes grow heavy, and he rubbed his face with a callused hand.

Try as he might, however, he could not follow the conversation beyond the obvious. It seemed some were talking about hunting and he certainly recognised the same words for 'wine', 'water', 'boat' and 'woman'. There were the usual boasts, but the men cut across each other at random. Only the women remained silent. The one nearest him was rocking a very small boy to sleep, swathed in linen blankets, hushing him as he stirred. He was tempted to talk to her but thought better of it; it would likely cause offence. Instead, he waited for a momentary lull in conversation and said, 'This was good,' and pointed to the bowl.

Seeing his comment had barely turned heads, he added, 'Where are you from?' Now they turned unfriendly faces upon him. 'Where. Did. You. Sail. From?'

A few of them exchanged glances and turned back, about to resume their conversations. He was not a thin-skinned man but being ignored in this way made him curiously dejected, reminding him of his great age and his solitude. It had not always been this way… He noticed the outsized man with the beetling brow scowling at him across the fire.

'Peleset. We settled on Megalonisi.'

He looked up but it wasn't the translator speaking. Another man, rounder-faced and older. More than one of them could understand basic Greek; he realised he would have to be more circumspect.

'Peleset,' he repeated softly. 'An island? A region?'

A pause. 'Region, yes.'

'Where… Where are you going?'

The man appraised him with shrewd eyes. He was apparently not one of the chosen warriors but Ancaeus suspected his intelligence had other uses.

'Our land has drought. No food. So we go… wherever we can. The golden fields of Anatolia, perhaps.'

'The Peloponnese… Here… The crops have also failed. All over the Archipelagos.'

The man's eyes hardened. 'Maybe you don't like for us to be here.'

Ancaeus shrugged. 'I am old. What do I care?'

The man stared at him for a moment longer and tipped his head in partial agreement.

He lowered his voice. 'That one, there. The freak giving me the filthy looks. What's his problem?'

The man chuckled coldly. 'You don't want for him to become angry.'

'Seems to me he already is. Why?'

'Who am I to say what is in the mind of another?' He shrugged. 'It could be you have the look like the man who killed his father.'

Ancaeus made a snort of derision. He sensed their interest in him waning rapidly. Other conversations now resumed. 'These three ships. Is this all you have?'

From the corner of his eye, he saw the woman with the baby stop rocking. He sensed the raiders prickling all around him.

'No. We have many.' The first translator turned to the side and spat. 'So do Shekelesh, Sherden, Weshesh, Teresh. Many tribes, many ships. No more boresome questions, you understand?'

He had heard the rumours but, until now, had seen no evidence and paid them little heed. Yes, he understood well enough. The Archipelagos would soon froth with blood.

II

Ancaeus completed the repair inside a couple of days. It was without doubt the worst piece of carpentry he had ever completed and, even though that was exactly the point, it still pricked some part of his conscience. He had managed to shape a new strake into the space left by the damaged one and, at a glance, the hull looked all the better for it. However, the planking had been pinned in the most makeshift way imaginable and he had daubed over the repairs with tar. He hoped the vessel would begin to take on water within half a day of sailing from Gytheon. Far enough, at any rate, for them to be too far away to consider returning.

As he completed his work, the beach behind him began to stir with activity. He made a point of backing away from the hull several times and appraising it with a critical eye. On one of these, he had nearly stepped onto the toes of a woman carrying a baby. He automatically turned with a raised hand and there was a look of mutual recognition: the same mother and child he had sat near on the first evening. The woman smiled at him, manipulating her baby's arm to imitate a wave. The little gesture pleased him more than he wanted to admit but then the woman's smile faded and her face immediately clouded with fear.

Ancaeus turned to find himself face to face – or rather face to chest – with the giant spearman, who now looked down at him with furious contempt. He waved his thick finger past Ancaeus' face and shoved him in the chest. Ancaeus was a big man, even in his twilight years, and had never been a pushover, but the force was irresistible. He stumbled onto his backside, to the great amusement of the bystanders. He noticed the woman turn her face in shame. He noticed the chieftain thunder over to the giant and upbraid him. To Ancaeus' surprise, his spearman took it like a scolded boy and stomped off after giving the carpenter a withering glance.

Ancaeus got to his feet, dusting himself off. With every fibre of his aged body, he wanted to feel his axe severing the warrior's neck but the chieftain was watching him suspiciously and his axe wasn't to hand. The translator alongside the king asked, 'The boat is ready?'

Ancaeus nodded.

The king grunted and turned his back on him without another word whilst orders were issued on his behalf. He heard the word 'boats' but understood nothing more. He was glad they were now some other town's problem but felt the guilt of a man who already knew there was nothing further he could do about it. At least some of them would drown. Perhaps some Hellenes might be spared death at the tips of the doomed men's spears.

Some of them began to embark whilst others formed a huddle around the campfire with their chieftain. He noticed one of them give him a sidelong look. With a few select men, he fancied he could still cut down most of the bodyguards and the chieftain with them. It would be like severing the head of a snake. He imagined how he could inflict maximum injury but then shook his head. It would be a waste of a long life.

At that moment, he watched the mother and child heading for the very boat he had been working on. His pulse quickened. To Hades with the others, but he wouldn't condemn her to a watery grave. Ancaeus made a point of wandering over to inspect the rest of the hull, catching up with her without – so he hoped – making it too obvious.

He rapped his knuckles against the stern section, as if checking for rot. Sensing she was passing, he hissed, *'Listen to me!'*

She stopped and someone muttered something at her for blocking their path. He rapped his knuckles against the hull again. *'This boat. Don't board it, yes?'* He glanced at her and saw the confusion in her dark eyes. *'Don't. Get. On. This. Boat.'* He tipped his head towards one of the others which was, at that very moment, being dragged into the sea. *'That one. Go! Go now!'*

He had drawn attention to himself and he wanted the woman

to walk away. He moved on, checking the boat again at a distance, acting like a man in whose veins a love of carpentry ran thicker than a fear of foreigners. The woman lifted her child higher over her shoulder and cut across the stream of those heading for the trap he had set. As he looked on, he saw others amongst them he wished he could help but he knew it would be folly to risk another conversation. If they were to perish at sea, it would be down to Poseidon, and the Fates. He turned away and noticed the man who had interpreted for him, days previously. He was whispering something to one of the warriors, who now glanced at Ancaeus with a frown. The helmsman felt a pulse of unease and tried to locate his axe. It was lying on the sand where he had tossed it aside earlier.

Unwise. But he was tired, not thinking clearly.

He considered retrieving it but decided it would look too suspicious now. Behind him, a group of raiders had broken away bearing torches, heading back towards the village. Ancaeus watched them until the unease that made his stomach swill registered in his brain.

Torches on a sunny morning?

They were halfway to the gate to his shipyard.

'*No!*' he roared. He made it to his axe on legs that had lost the drive they once had. He swept it up as he ran, stumbling in the yielding sand. He heard the soft thump of heavy feet and saw the huge frame of the chief's spear-bearer lumbering towards him. Ancaeus' axe was gathering speed as he felt a devastating thud that blasted the air from his lungs, and the blade buried itself harmlessly in the sand.

The raider was on top of him now and, even with his wind, he doubted he could have thrown him off. The gods had granted Ancaeus a long life and prodigious strength but he was old. The raider's blunt face was contorted with rage. There was spittle on his trembling lips and sweat beading his brow. Ancaeus gripped him by the wrist, trying to wrench it from his tunic, but his long fingers didn't even meet around the raider's bones.

Ancaeus could see he was drawing back for a punch so he yanked his long hair, making the raider gasp in pain. It was thick and greasy and he had to insinuate his fingers in it to keep a grip. The man's veins stood as proud as ship's cables but he yielded; even the strongest of tables needed three points of contact. Ancaeus gritted his teeth and yanked harder, drawing the man's ear towards his mouth. He would be sure to leave the cur an everlasting memory of his treachery.

The warrior suddenly rolled aside in the direction of the tug revealing another face above him. Behind him, others were hurrying over, shouting and babbling. Ancaeus managed to twist his head to the side, coating his damp cheek with sand. From the corner of his eye, he saw the first tongue of flame leaping into the sky in his yard and then a blow to his head made lights explode in his skull before engulfing him in blackness.

III

Lemnos

The following day was the last before Xandros was due to take a turn in the huer's hut. He had already made the decision to sneak out to Moudros that very evening and, somehow, get Teodora's attention. It would be incredibly dangerous but he felt like his future depended upon it and that, in itself, was intoxicating. He needed distance from his father, he needed excitement, he realised, and he needed adventure. Truth be told, he was also beginning to feel the shadow of a solitude that was cast by something bigger than the wretched huer's hut.

After he had gone through the usual ritual with Manolis and the request, half-hearted today, for his stories about Troy – 'Maybe today; perhaps tomorrow!' – he went about his jobs with no enthusiasm and, after skimming the milk from the goats, abandoned them altogether and decided to go for a walk along the beach. Red joined him after a few minutes. He helped Xandros find a few smooth ones, suitable for skimming. 'There's a bit of s-sea wrack out there, you see it? Bet you can't h-hit it.'

It took Xandros' mind off his father for a time and he was grateful for the distraction. For all of Red's idle prattle, he knew when to keep silence. Considering the angry words of their last conversation he also knew, it seemed, how to forget a grudge.

'Do you ever miss your parents?' Xandros dared to ask.

Red disappeared into his own thoughts. 'Sometimes, when I see the old f-folks around the village, I wish I could talk to them. But...'

Xandros waited, thinking he would finish his sentence. 'But what?'

'But when I s-see the way your father treats you, I think I might be happier without.' When Xandros winced, he added, 'Sorry.'

After a few moments, Xandros muttered, 'Don't be.' He tossed away his last pebble and carried on walking.

When he reached the far end of the bay, he noticed Moxos fishing by himself on a little creaking jetty. Overlooked by pines, the shaded spot was much coveted. Even if a man had just set down his stool, he could almost count on another to appear and complain: 'Have the wooden legs grown roots?' or 'Any chance of you moving this year?'

But never when Moxos was in occupation. People would just shrug and move on. Though gifted with extraordinary strength, his eyes were full of kindness and not a little sorrow. It shamed Xandros to think it, but he wished Moxos was his father instead.

Upon seeing him, Moxos winked. 'Hello, Xandros. How is your head?'

'Healing well. Thank you for sparing me five more lashes, by the way.' Xandros' voice sounded reed-thin compared to his deep, bass rumble. Moxos waved the words away without looking at him and Xandros sidled over to look at his catch. Though he was always genial with him, Xandros never wanted to cross him and stomping over the rickety boards of that jetty, scaring the fish, would have been one way to test his patience. 'Your basket is empty,' he said quietly.

'It's too hot. The fishes are keeping cool in the deeper water.'

He was not wrong. The planks beneath Xandros' bare feet were so warm he had to keep shifting position. Moxos gave him a bemused smile. 'Why don't you stop dancing and cool them in the water?' Xandros did as suggested, idly rippling the water with his toes. The light that shimmered upon it was so dazzling that he was forced to cover his eyes. He pulled the linen headscarf further over his forehead, which already felt like it was burning.

'Do you want a fig?'

Xandros accepted it gladly, for figs were his favourite fruit and they were a precious rarity that year. They fell into a companionable silence whilst the cicadas chattered and the water slapped and gurgled against the stanchions of the jetty. Eventually, it grew too hot for Xandros and he glanced at Moxos, who looked quite unperturbed. 'How can you bear to be out here all day?'

He shrugged. 'My skin is thicker than yours, like leather.'

Xandros chuckled. It was true that he looked weather-beaten. 'Thank you for your company and the fig,' he said as he stood.

He hadn't taken two steps when he heard footsteps slapping along the path and breathless panting behind him. It was Hilarion.

'*Come quickly!*'

'What is it?' Moxos said irritably.

'It's Manolis. He's been set upon!'

'Set upon?'

'By Moudrian bandits! He's half dead!'

Moxos' jaw set and, as he stood, his joints clicked. 'Where is he?'

'In the square. Hurry, yes?'

Euneus was already there: most of the village was, it seemed. Lying in the shade upon a table, stripped of his threadbare clothes, Manolis was all skin and bone. Xandros winced when, between the press of bodies, he glimpsed the bruised and bloodied skin. He could see Manolis trying to move but his tired old body wouldn't allow it, and he groaned pitiably.

'Quiet! *Quiet!* All of you!' Euneus snapped. The chatter dropped to a murmur, which yielded to silence. A red kite keened high above and, with them being carrion birds, it seemed a terrible omen. 'Who did this, Manolis?'

'Ba… bandits,' he whispered.

Euneus tutted. 'I know this, but…'

Manolis' dry old throat clicked as he struggled to speak.

'Take your time,' said Euneus, clasping his hands.

'Three,' he whispered. 'With clubs… The donkey…'

Moxos shared a look with Euneus, shaking his head. 'Bring him some honeyed wine,' said the king. 'Take him indoors and let him rest.'

Some of the younger villagers prised him from the table, struggling not on account of the weight of their burden but because, whichever way they moved him, he wheezed in agony. Xandros watched him go with a leaden ball in his stomach. Old Manolis was part of the fabric of his life and seeing him in such a wretched state tore a great rent in it.

The village square buzzed with doom-laden gossip and, inevitably, claims to have sighted bandits in the hills on previous occasions. The council gathered in its little meeting area, formed by stone benches. Euneus, Moxos and most of the others. Xandros' eyes fell upon one of the men. Khalkeus was the son of a famous spearman from Arene called Idas and must have seen out forty winters by then. He was heavy-browed and his stare had a morose weight to it. He frowned at Xandros now as he tailed after his father.

Euneus followed the look and saw him. 'What are you doing? We're having a meeting.'

Xandros felt his cheeks flushing and looked from one face to the other, finding little sympathy in any of them apart from Moxos.

'Let him stay, Euneus,' said Moxos. 'He needs to learn from you.'

Khalkeus snorted with derision. He was peevish in looks and character, and resented the fact he had no son and heir; only a wayward daughter. But he was an aggressive fighter and unflinchingly honest, though this quality now drew a sharp glare from Euneus.

'Very well,' grumbled Euneus. 'Sit here and be quiet.'

Xandros listened intently to all that followed. 'Who found Manolis?' asked Euneus.

'One of the boys who lives in the hamlet to the south.'

'Was he stripped when he got here?'

'No,' said Khalkeus. 'They took his clothes.'

'And his donkey.'

'And that.'

One of the men spat upon the ground in disgust at the cowardly attack. They were all living hand to mouth: none more so than Manolis.

In the heavy silence that followed, Khalkeus looked around the meeting place. 'Well, must I be the one to state the obvious? They're from Moudros, isn't it clear?'

Moudros. Dark looks crossed the benches. *Was this, at long last, the start of their reprisal?*

'Lower your voice!' Euneus glanced over the square. 'How is it obvious? Tell me that?'

'Because they've driven off our cattle before. Because blood has been spilt with them recently.'

'Not in the passing of nearly two moons.'

'What does that prove?'

Nothing, thought Xandros. *But why would we want to start a war with Moudros?* Khalkeus tried poking the nest a few more times but could see there was no appetite for war. During one of the brief silences that followed, Xandros cleared his throat. 'Can I say something?'

His voice drew a few dark looks. When one of the other men shrugged, Euneus said curtly, 'Be brief.'

'Would anybody want to risk a war for a single donkey?'

'Times are hard.'

'The boy has a point,' said Moxos.

Emboldened, Xandros continued, 'I heard some people talking about seeing bandits in the hills before.'

'Idle gossip. What of it?'

'What if it isn't just gossip?'

Khalkeus snorted with derision.

'I will speak to Manolis' wife myself,' said Euneus, ignoring Xandros' remark altogether. 'We can share what we have.'

'And the festival?' asked Moxos. 'Does it go ahead in a few days?' Expectant eyes turned upon Euneus. 'It goes ahead.'

IV

Gytheon

The sun was sinking fast when the boy Atukhos dared to emerge from the coop in which he had hidden. Most of the citizens of Gytheon had fled to the hills when he had sprinted through the streets, shouting and wildly gesticulating. One or two others had also spotted the ships and they knew what was coming: they had all heard the stories, embellished in the telling, of pirates sweeping through the islands like locusts, leaving no building standing.

Yet the only building they had destroyed belonged to the one man who had helped them, however reluctantly. The sense of injustice fired some burning ember, deep within the boy's soul, and he surveyed the flames not open-mouthed but with his little fists balled. Nothing had been spared. The intensity of the heat had passed its peak as the fuel had been consumed but individual fires still blazed.

On a whim, he darted inside the gate, shielding his face from a bonfire of uncut pine strakes that spat and hissed at him. Across the yard, the roof of Ancaeus' cabin had partially collapsed. He made a dash towards it then checked his steps as something else dropped from the walls with a dull thump, sending up a little cloud of sparks just inside the threshold. There had been shelves inside on which sat an odd collection of artefacts Ancaeus had once dismissed as 'trinkets' from his travels, though it was clear he valued them highly. There was no hope of recovering them.

He stepped back and surveyed the yard, coughing and retching. The heat and smoke were beginning to make his eyes water and he feared he might not be able to find his way back out. If the breeze picked up, the smoke would only intensify. A sudden hacking cough made him drop to his knees and he felt his ears begin to hum. Fearing he might be dying, he scrambled back to his feet and dashed for the gate, stubbing his toes on something hard and sharp. He gasped at the pain and turned to see what had caused it. Ancaeus' leather bag of tools was stretched out on the floor, partially unrolled. The shipwright was obsessive about them and would never leave them lying around, attesting to the panic created by the arrival of the raiders.

There was a rush of scalding air as something toppled just behind him. He bundled the tools under his arm, sprinted for the gate and kept on running until the heat faded from his back. Then he saw the figure spreadeagled on the beach, partially concealed behind a little dune. He dropped the tools and dashed over the sand, fighting against the mounting panic that made his heart leap into his ribs.

It was the hair that he noticed first, matted by sand and drying blood, and then the very stillness of the man. Also, how old he looked. He dropped to his knees. 'No! No! Wake up!' Unsure how to go about it, he resorted to gripping the filthy tunic and yanking it this way and that. 'Wake up, *please*!'

He looked around him in desperation. There was no question of dragging him into the sea to revive him but then he remembered that his own little shack was untouched and that he still had some water. He dashed back inside, amazed that it had not been touched by the raiders, and retrieved a gourd. His own mouth was parched and he drank a little as he ran, grimacing at the taste of dust and soot as he swallowed. He upended it over Ancaeus' face and, leaving no time for a response, slapped his cheek. One of Ancaeus' eyelids sprang open and a noise of shock escaped from his throat, like he'd seen a ghost. Then he flinched, wincing in agony.

For a moment, Ancaeus was convinced he had died and been woken on the banks of the Styx by the water from Charon's punt. The humming in his ears was surely the groaning of restless souls and the spiteful pain lancing from one part of his skull to another some punishment for a life of misdeeds. Then the bright blur morphed into the sun and, nearer to hand, a familiar face.

The boy, whose name was as elusive as fruit from Tantalus' fingers.

Atukhos.

The boy's brown eyes were wide and full of concern that dissolved even as his name registered in his brain. Ancaeus wiped his damp face and looked at the drying blood. Then he remembered the desperate struggle with the raider and he tutted, trying to prop himself upon his elbows.

'Any more of that,' he croaked, 'for my mouth as well as my face?'

'Oh… I… Wait.' The boy sprinted off and returned a few moments later with a waterskin. 'There's not much in it…'

Ancaeus snatched it from him and drank it down. It tasted like nectar. 'The spring. Can you?'

Without a word of complaint, the boy swept up the empty gourd and skin and sprinted off.

When he returned a short while later, he found Ancaeus slumped against the base of a myrtle tree, staring distantly at the flames consuming the last vestiges of wood in the boatyard. For a moment, Atukhos was concerned he had crawled there to die because, as he approached with the water, he appeared not to blink. Then he stirred, murmuring to no one in particular, 'One third of them will die before they touch land. The rest will die after. I swear it.' He reached out for the gourd, took a swig and clawed his way to his feet. The boy dropped the skin and hurried to help him but Ancaeus batted away his hands.

'I'm not an *invalid*!' he snapped and staggered away towards the water to bathe his head.

When he returned, the sun was sinking fast and, with it, Ancaeus' anger had yielded to melancholy. They ate in silence from the few leftovers that Atukhos had stashed in his shack. Husks of bread, half a wheel of hard cheese and a handful of olives each. The boy watched him like a dutiful dog but Ancaeus couldn't tear his eyes from his smouldering boatyard. Just before darkness shrouded the beach, he suddenly rose and made for it. Atukhos knew better than to follow him. He returned half an hour later, his hands empty but smeared in soot. The streak of dirt by his eyes where he had wiped away tears betrayed that his emotions had gotten the better of him.

When he thought sufficient time had passed, the boy gathered the few pieces of scorched wood that were serviceable and banked a decent fire. He swallowed hard and said quietly, 'You haven't lost everything, you know.'

'Don't talk silly, boy. They even took my axe.'

'I know,' he said, getting to his feet. Ancaeus watched him hurry off – the boy seemed never to have lost the toddler's habit of running everywhere – and frowned as he returned more slowly with something tucked under his arm.

'See? You still have these!'

The frown melted and, with it, some of the thunderclouds in his mind. He took the bundle from the boy with trembling hands and unrolled it with that familiar *clank* of metal and wood. Most of the tools were tucked into their allocated slots in the cracked leather – in reuniting them, the boy had not been *that* observant – but the adze alone was worth a number of fat sheep. Atukhos was right: he still had these.

And something else.

'Let me show you something. Close your eyes.' Despite everything, despite the fire, his uncle's beatings and the fact that he was effectively an orphan, the boy's cheeks dimpled as he smiled in anticipation. His optimism was infectious. Ancaeus fished out the little artefact that, in a sense, was the most valuable thing he had ever owned.

'Open them.'

A gallery of expressions crossed the boy's face and Ancaeus was amused to see faint disappointment register last of all. He slipped the ring onto his little finger and turned his hand towards the fire.

'A ring,' said Atukhos. 'Where is your wife?'

'This isn't a wedding ring, you clot!' Ancaeus chuckled. 'Have you heard of the voyage of *Argo*?'

The boy shook his head. Ancaeus was about to grumble about

his ignorance but thought better of it: Gytheon was a backwater so what else could he expect?

'Many years ago, I went on a long voyage: a *very* long voyage, mind.' When he saw that Atukhos was listening intently, he cleared his throat. 'On that boat were some warriors and heroes who have become famous...'

'Like Achilles?'

'Achilles? *No!*' Pain lanced his head and he rubbed his eyes. 'No. Gods, boy, how can you have heard of him but not... Never mind. As a matter of fact, Achilles' father, Peleus, rowed with us.' The boy's eyes glimmered with awe, so he continued. 'We had to steal something valuable, a fleece, a golden one... two actually; the details are complicated,' said Ancaeus, dismissing the question as it was forming on Atukhos' lips, 'from a strange place at the ends of the earth; a dangerous one. Not everyone made it back; the return was even harder, you see. Jason – he was the man who led this voyage – burned one of these fleeces in the hearth of the palace that he had won back. Iolkos, a long way from here, up country. He couldn't have done this without us, you understand, so we all raked the little nuggets from the ashes the next morning. This ring was made from those nuggets but I never wear it when I work for fear of damaging it. Look. I had a ram's head engraved on it.'

Atukhos peered at it with reverence and made a little noise of amazement. 'Some people said you were just a pirate. Can I touch it?'

'Did they now?' This didn't surprise him. Truth be told, he had always kept himself to himself once he had settled in Gytheon. He had outlived many of his age – the last of those in the town who might have known differently – and a newer generation had gradually taken their place. 'You can, but it's never leaving this finger again.'

The boy touched it as if it might scald his skin. 'Is it magical?' he said in awe.

'Magical, ha!' scoffed Ancaeus, adding another section of wood to the fire. But as he thought again about the distance that gold had travelled, all of the blood that had been shed for it, the lives lost and friendships formed, the question did not seem so ludicrous.

And was there not some alchemy, after all, in turning a stinking bit of fleece into the most precious object in the world? He grunted. 'Well, maybe a little.'

The wood spat and popped and Ancaeus let his head fall back against the myrtle tree.

'What will we do now?' asked Atukhos.

'"We"?'

He gave the boy a sidelong scowl and immediately felt bad that he should look so crestfallen. 'Let me think on it,' he replied after a few moments. 'We can't stay here.'

He looked up at the slender sickle of the new moon. In twenty-five nights, more or less, she would fill her horns and shine once more upon a quiet corner of the Isthmus of Corinth. With the passing of the years, he had come to view the Month of the Grape Harvest with increasingly tainted feelings. He feared a day when he would make the long journey to the tip of the Perachora peninsula, drop into the sheltered cove, sacred to Hera, and find himself alone. They had discussed this and they had accepted this. Stubbornly enduring though its surviving members were proving to be, the Brotherhood could not last forever.

He had even contemplated not making the journey this year but Atukhos had found the ring and that was surely a sign. Even if he was the last man standing, he wouldn't be alone. The boy would have to go too.

V

Lemnos

Manolis succumbed to his injuries two days later. With no surviving offspring, his wife led the sorrowful procession down to the beach. It was decided that cremating him anywhere other than the beach would be dangerous, given the earth was as dry as kindling. His old wife worked herself up into such a frenzy of grief that she collapsed on the backshore and had to be revived in the shade of the dunes. Xandros watched the whole thing numb with sorrow. Funerals he had attended before but this one burned deep, though he dared not show emotion in front of his father.

Euneus spoke fittingly if briefly and, as the crowd of mourners made its way back up the slope, Xandros heard dark mutterings about evildoers from Moudros: clearly, Khalkeus had been unable to keep his opinions to himself and Xandros smelled trouble in the air. Dark misgivings made his stomach swill. It was as if Fate was conspiring against his union with Teodora but there was something else in the air, too. The faint beat of Strife.

A few days later, the Festival of the Argonauts was upon them. A single afternoon of torrential rain had restored some colour to the parched hills and the joy and palpable relief with which the rain was received helped assuage the sorrow and anger of the Myrinians following Manolis' funeral. For a few days, the earth smelled sweet and fresh.

It had been forty years since the Argonauts had arrived on the island on their way to Colchis. Most of the Myrinians owed their very existence to that fateful landing but Euneus never talked about it. One winter's evening, many years previously, Xandros had asked him, 'Do you ever think about your father, Papa? About the day grandfather Jason's boat, the *Argo*, arrived?'

They had been sat in a mud-brick hut belonging to one of the Myrinians: Xandros, Hypsipyle, Hilarion, he and Moxos. Euneus leaned forwards and spat the pip of an apple he was eating into the hearth flames. 'Only when you ask me about it, which is too often.' He didn't even look at his son as he said it. Moxos gave the boy a sad, conciliatory sort of smile but dared say nothing in front of him.

'You see, Xandros, it's like dragonflies.' Hilarion settled himself on his stool, oblivious to the sharp look Euneus gave him. 'They mate on the wing and, while the female lays her eggs in a tree, the male just flies off. *Whoosh!*' He made some vague gesture that didn't seem to approximate to the flight of a dragonfly. 'Then he stings some poor, naked fisherman on his rod and gets eaten by a bird soon after.'

Though she was turned aside and affected not to be listening, Hypsipyle made a dismissive grunt and Moxos tactfully steered the conversation towards other matters.

This year, Euneus was in rare good humour and even helped string up the festoons of garlands in the village square, whilst the women did their best with the benches and tables that were still serviceable outside the walls of Hypsipyle's once beautiful halls. A fire had destroyed much of the upper floor many years before, and it had been the former queen herself who put a stop to efforts to restore it whilst so many others on the island suffered through famine.

Eight of the twelve goats taken in the raid had been slaughtered, and the succulent scent of roasted meat drew to the smoke villagers who had, for the previous year, come to regard chickens and ptarmigans as the height of luxury. Perhaps, some said, the gods might now bestow their favours upon the Myrinians after a spell of such meagre offerings. There were others who muttered the gods had long since ignored the savours of charred bones and fat. At the public sacrifice, Xandros overheard Khalkeus, rolling his dark eyes and folding his arms, chuntering that they were all wasting their time. When he turned to him in shock, he did not look away and his scowl did not soften. A villager dug him in the ribs. 'You know,' he growled, 'I sometimes think you must be a Moudros.'

Once the sacrifice had been made and preparations were well underway, the descendants took the track that zigzagged to the beach. Xandros filled his lungs with the briny tang and looked out over the sea sparkling under the afternoon sun. By the time they reached the water's edge, they were all silent. Gulls cawed high above and the breakers hissed against the fine pebbles: for a few moments, none dared break the spell of that moment with idle chatter. Then a young boy near Xandros spoke up. 'I think I can see the Argonauts, Dadda!' Inevitably, the men cast their eyes over the sea but there were no craft beyond the beached fishing boats. His father chuckled, and the nervous edge did not go unnoticed given the desultory reports of pirates attacking vessels at sea.

'Not out there, Dadda, *there*!' he said, pointing along the beach to some high dunes.

His father ruffled his hair. 'I think not, my boy. The Age of Heroes has long passed.'

Then one of the women atop the walls flashed a bronze dish and, as they made their way up the track, the aroma of roasting meat made their stomachs growl. They passed through the gateway and the women made a show of feting them with ribbons and garlands, and there was much singing and dancing as they took their places at the benches. One of them was said to be the very bench at which Jason sat and it was revered like a talisman.

Hypsipyle was sat at its head, in the same place she had all those years ago. As Xandros drew near, he saw her dab the corner of her eyes. Even after the lapse of a generation and more, the occasion never failed to affect her in a way that practically nothing else could. There was so much he wanted her to tell him, so much wisdom and knowledge for her to impart, but it was as if each passing year drove her further into herself. But Xandros knew that her prodigious memory remained as sharp as her dark eyes.

Once everyone was seated, Euneus rose and raised his wine cup. Time had clouded even Hypsipyle's recollection of the exact words spoken during that first exchange between her and Jason.

'To the goddesses who protect this island, please accept this humble offering as a symbol of our thanks.'

He poured the crimson liquid into the earth and, as was the custom, some of it must splash against his toes.

'From which shores and where do you sail?'

'Thessalian Iolkos to Colchis rich in gold.'

'Raider, be seated. We may ask no more questions until your bellies are full.'

Euneus, it was clear, never cared much for the ritual and was glad to sit, whilst Hypsipyle sniffed and regained her composure. Then they all set about the food at the tables like locusts, whilst the other villagers had to make do with stools or woollen throws or spaces on the ground or walls. As the wine began to warm their blood, the dancing and merrymaking began.

As the shadows lengthened, Xandros noticed that the conversation and the gaiety suddenly dropped before a chilly silence fell upon the square. He became half aware of a figure of some presence at the gate. All eyes now turned towards him and, in his wake, the handful of strangers making their way into the square.

Euneus' sword was free of its sheath in a heartbeat and his best men were by his side at once, though one or two – worse the wear for drink – fumbled their weapons. The newcomers were armed, and their own hands twitched towards the pommels of their swords, but the man leading them raised his hands peaceably. He seemed to be enjoying the attention and Xandros noticed his eyes roving the square, the houses, its people. Even at a distance of thirty or so paces, Xandros saw his lips curl. He was tall and statesmanlike, greying in the beard and hair, so trimmed as to disguise its retreat. His tunic was well cut and clean. An imperious youth stood beside him, unmistakably his son.

And then someone else stepped into view. She looked around the square with a quiet intensity, pushing back a tendril of chestnut hair that had escaped from her headscarf. The young man put his arm around her waist and she looked demurely at the ground. Like one observing his own funeral, Xandros' blood turned to ice.

Teodora.

'I apologise for interrupting your… your…' the leader of the newcomers had a mainland accent and now waved his hand vaguely '…what is it we're interrupting, exactly?' His son smirked back at him.

'There had better be a good reason for this disrespect!' Euneus advanced, sword pointing towards the stranger. 'Who are you?'

'Peace, King Euneus, peace! There is no need for a drawn blade. As you can see, my own has not left its sheath. I am Plouteos, Nomarch of Moudros.'

'Moudros?' Now Khalkeus pushed past to get to the newcomer. 'Do you want to die?'

'I come as a messenger, with my son and some councillors. Never a good thing came from killing a messenger, did it?'

'Some of your dogs set upon one of our elders. They beat him, stripped him and stole his donkey. He died, a defenceless old man. His ashes have only now grown cold and you tell me you know nothing of this?'

Plouteos raised an eyebrow. 'I know nothing of this. Indeed, since one of our own has recently disappeared, half of his flock with him, I might counter by accusing you of the same.' His shrewd gaze put the Myrinians on the back foot and the silence that developed was uncomfortable. 'Well? I suspect this isn't news to some of you.'

Euneus said, 'If you are here to make an accusation, out with it.'

'Is this what passes for *xenia* in Myrine? Or do the rules of guest friendship not apply here?'

'There can be no *xenia* between Myrine and Moudros.' Murmurs of agreement greeted this. Even Khalkeus nodded.

'Ah, given the reason for our unheralded visit, this is a grave concern.'

Euneus gave him a sharp look then beckoned him with a jerk of the head towards the meeting place. The nomarch inclined his head and followed. His son took Teodora's hand and kissed it before joining them. Xandros felt a flame of envy scald him and balled his fists. Noticing the sudden change in his demeanour, Red rose from his bench and, just as he reached him, Xandros sidled through the throng. Heart thumping, he approached Teodora whilst most of the onlookers were distracted. He knew she had seen him drawing close by the way she tilted her head a little and stiffened.

'This is a surprise,' he whispered.

Teodora said nothing.

'Didn't take you long to find someone else.'

'He found me, not the other way around. Something you failed to do, three times over.'

'Two of those involved a death, Teodora, the third nearly my own...'

Now she looked at him and there was a flicker of concern in her grey eyes. 'I was ready to cross the island at night but... but things happened. My father...'

She tutted and looked away but he sensed her mind working. 'What was the name of your elder? The one who was killed.'

'Manolis.' Though Euneus had called him an elder, he had never been invited to attend council, as far as Xandros knew. He was sure his father had used the term to inflame the act: from murder to something near sacrilege.

'Manolis,' she repeated. 'I am sorry.'

Not knowing what to say, he added, 'They stole his donkey.'

'I know – they said. Was that all they took?'

Xandros shrugged. 'That I know.'

'I think your father is wrong in blaming Moudros. Would anyone risk walking so many miles for a donkey?'

He felt a crushing wave of sadness as his eyes ranged over her face. He loved her steady gaze. He loved the little curl of her upper lip that offered a glimpse of her white teeth as she spoke, and now her instinctive compassion for the death of a stranger...

Teodora. He used to savour her name upon his lips. *A gift from the gods.*

'Who is he?' What he wanted to say was: *I have missed you more than you could ever know.* He felt like a petulant child.

'His name is Ekhinos.'

'"*Sea Urchin*"! What sort of name is that?' He saw her wince and lowered his voice. 'You prefer a sea urchin to a "defender of men"?'

'Don't get angry, Xandros, not here. I don't like it. I don't like how it makes—'

'So… So that's it then? You're with *him* now? Just like that? What about what happened between us? The promises we made?'

She gave him a look of exasperation. 'You broke them.'

Ekhinos glanced over, giving them a double take. The frown was clear. Plouteos, not a man to miss details, followed his son's glare and his face darkened.

'You have to go,' she whispered. 'They're all looking.'

'Teodora!'

'Go!'

Reading the situation, Euneus beckoned Xandros over and, as he approached, he could see that his father was angry.

'This is my son, Xandros,' he said without much enthusiasm. 'I would like him to hear this.'

Plouteos looked him up and down, though his expression never changed. Xandros could feel Ekhinos' eyes burning through his tunic as he sat down. The nomarch cleared his throat.

'Very well. As I had begun to say, a merchant ship pulled into Moudros harbour seven days ago. Its captain had little to barter other than gossip and he was also conveying several wretched fugitives who had paid passage from the mainland: first-hand witnesses, if you like, of what I am about to tell you.' Plouteos adjusted his clothing, absently fingering the gold chain around his neck. Few in Myrine had such wealth to display.

'The lower Archipelagos, he reported, is infested with marauding rovers. The Kretans on coastal Megalonisi have suffered gravely and have retreated to the fastness of the mountains. The once great kingdom of Minos is no more: it exists only in fragments. The kingdom of the Hittites is threatened at every border. Rhodes is entirely in the control of these pirates, as is most of Cyprus, as are untold other islands. Troy is a shanty town, inhabited by more goats than people.' Plouteos took a deep breath. 'According to the captain, the situation is now so dangerous that plying the sea lanes is nigh impossible. Merchants are demanding outrageous down payments and armed support, which is beyond the reach of most traders. So rumour says, these rovers have even set their sights upon Egypt.'

Whilst the rest of the square murmured in speculation, the

meeting place fell silent. Euneus and Moxos exchanged grim looks. 'We all know the way of rumour. How do we know if any of this is as dire as you say?'

'I thought you might say this,' Plouteos muttered. 'So ask yourself this: why would I choose to make the long walk here otherwise? And if you choose not to believe me, you may ask my son – Ekhinos here. Or even his betrothed – Teodora. They are both witnesses to the conversation with the ship's captain.'

Betrothed? Xandros felt the words like a punch. He thought he might be sick. *Why hadn't she said?*

Ekhinos noticed the look on his face and smirked.

'So why *are* you here, eh? What are you up to?' asked Khalkeus.

'We may not see eye to eye, Moudros and Myrine, but can you not see there are bigger matters at hand?'

'So the lower Archipelagos is afflicted by pirates. To the best of my knowledge, it always has been. What of it?'

'A fair question. Had the news stopped there, I might even agree.' Plouteos coughed and took a sip of wine. 'But it didn't. The fugitives who made it to these shores on the captain's boat did not know where the raiders were from. They spoke in strange tongues, wore foreign garb. Even their weapons were different, so they said. But not all of them. Some of them spoke Greek. They were mainlanders.'

'Hellenes?'

'Yes, Hellenes. As you say, piracy, theft... For us Greeks, this has always been as much a part of life as death itself. But I am not talking about mere cattle raids. Palaces have been fired and razed but not all by foreigners. Poor, starving Hellas is eating itself even as it is eaten, Euneus. Unholy alliances have been formed. Squabbles have been set aside and Hellenes have thrown in their lot with these... barbarians. There is plunder, rapine, murder, the likes of which have never been seen before. United in this common purpose, these Sea Peoples – as some are calling them – are irresistible and it will not be long before their roving eyes fall upon this island, too. Our location will not spare us forever, Euneus. Lemnos and Samothrace, we think, are the only two islands that have not seen their boats; perhaps also Lesbos. But when they come…' Plouteos let the unfinished sentence settle upon the dusty ground.

'"We"? You say "we" like you know these things first-hand. Do you?'

'As good as. I am a man with extensive connections, yes, as are most shipmasters-turned-traders.'

Euneus turned to face the village square. A couple of young girls were gleefully rolling a hoop, decorated with colourful ribbons. Oblivious to the dark tidings, a scattering of others – young and the very old – were going about their business as always. But everyone else was looking at him expectantly. Even if they hadn't overheard every word, it was clear that something was gravely amiss.

'You seek to end our feuds and unite?'

Plouteos' answer was crisp. 'How else can we hope to defend this island?'

Their eyes locked for a moment and Xandros could see his father's suspicious mind working. 'I want to confer with these men.'

Plouteos inclined his head and rose. 'Very well. We will wait.' His party followed him from the meeting place. Xandros didn't glance up at Ekhinos – it wasn't difficult given the dire tidings – but he could feel his eyes scoring his face.

Euneus grimaced as he straightened. 'Your counsel before I give him my decision?'

'I don't like it,' said Alektruon, 'and I don't like him, or his village. I say no.'

'I agree with *him*,' said Khalkeus, raising his chin towards Alektruon, 'but I have heard the rumours of these Sea Peoples myself, and I don't like *them* even more. Doesn't leave much of a choice, does it?'

Hilarion's bloodshot eyes had been switching between Plouteos and Euneus with keen interest as they spoke. He licked his dry lips and scratched his belly. 'I agree. This presents an opportunity.'

A few of the others nodded reluctantly, including wise Hektor. Xandros could sense his father wanted to hear Moxos' opinion and he turned to him now. 'What do you think?'

'The Sea Peoples will come and we must be ready. But he is a snake and I will not fight under his command.'

A hum of mutterings seconded Moxos' comments. It hadn't occurred to Euneus that Plouteos might expect this. 'All in favour of a truce, raise your hands.' Euneus' eyes passed across the group. 'Then it is settled.' He turned to Xandros. 'Bring them back.'

Xandros approached them and Plouteos unfolded his arms as he drew near. His son was leaning against an olive tree and narrowed his eyes at him. 'The council is ready.'

The others moved on graciously enough but Ekhinos gave him a supercilious grin before spitting onto the ground. Xandros' fist twitched, his temper a hair's breadth from fraying.

'We have an answer for you,' said Euneus, when he was sure he had their attention. 'We accept the truce between Myrine and Moudros. But, if there came a time to take up arms, my people would only do so under my command. How you choose to lead your men is up to you.'

'Then there is a truce,' Plouteos replied at once, and Xandros wondered what lay behind the smile.

BOOK FOUR

ATONEMENT

I

Has an alliance more unholy – or more disgraceful or fateful – ever been made in the history of our people? Like a shattered vase, it took me some years before I was able to piece together the sherds and, even then, some eluded me. At such moments, I must fill the gaps as I saw fit, as is the way of the bard, with the benefit of experience and imagination.

I recently heard another bard sing of this alliance on the mainland. He was competent, though no more so than many an Ionian street-corner rhapsode. The chatter and the comings and goings of those at the back of the square was as sure a sign of any of restlessness and inattention. The bard's name has regrettably slipped my memory (and here is another sign) but I do recall the song's name: it was 'Seven against Thebes' and barely a verse – barely a line! – of it was true.

The true story is this.

The Theban House of Cadmus was cursed: few would dispute this. I can vouch that King Oedipus both knowingly and unknowingly committed unspeakable wickedness, though his life is worth a song in its own right. It is also true that a petty dispute between Thebes and the mighty city of Orchomenos over grazing rights on the fertile plains by Lake Kopais blew up into a war that neither city could afford in a time of drought. Orchomenos was sacked and put to the torch. For its hubris, and whilst Thebes was still reeling, other cities in the Peloponnese began to whisper of invasion, for Thebes was ripe for the taking...

Smoke billowed black where the flames had reached sunken jars of olive oil. Constricted by the earth the fat *pithoi* exploded, rending the air like lightning. The heat was so intense it melted the stone flags of the palace into black glass (something I later saw for myself when picking my way through the ruins). The screams had not yet fallen silent – there were some pockets of resistance where families had barricaded themselves indoors or where women and children had been caught hiding in alleyways – but the rumble of flames and falling masonry, and the triumphant yells of armed men were foremost.

Though they shared the plunder, some of the warriors from the Peloponnesian towns gave the barbarians sidelong glances as they ransacked houses, spitting when their backs were turned, muttering in the shade cast by scorched trees. But could they have forced the gates without the ferocity of these pirates in their curiously dandyish feathered helmets? Could they have overpowered the sentries without the bronze-clad titan in their midst? *No,* they conceded. *Not a chance.*

A pair of chariots rattled along the main thoroughfare towards the Kadmeia, setting dust and smoke whirling in their wake. Soldiers stepped aside, inclining their heads respectfully as they passed. The *wanax* stood on the footboard of the first chariot, wearing a helmet made from plates of boars tusk, kept his gaze upon the blazing palace but those close enough could see that his jaw was set in anger. Even as they clattered up the rise, they could feel the heat pulsing from the gates of the *propylon*, which had not yet been consumed by flames. The king waited for his driver to rein in the horses before jumping from the chariot.

'My lord!'

One of the *wanax*'s followers, his bare chest smeared in sweat and dirt, bowed before him.

'The king, Auteson, where is he?'

'He's…' The follower blinked in confusion and glanced back at the palace. 'Well he's dead, my lord! He took up arms!'

'My orders!' The eyes of the *wanax* blazed. 'Those were NOT my orders!'

'My lord, we followed them! It was not us… His wife and children… We spared them at least, my lord; stripped the treasury and the armoury…' The follower raised his hands and looked towards the nobleman in the second chariot. Far from supporting him, the nobleman merely folded his arms and cocked his head to the side, looking faintly amused as he leaned back upon the rail.

The *wanax*'s chest heaved up and down but the prospect of riches seemed to soothe him and the follower leaped upon it. 'I have never seen such a quantity of agate and jasper! Cylinder seals of lapis lazuli...'

The eyes of the *wanax* fell upon a knot of people emerging from another part of the Kadmeia. Their faces were flushed and they sweated freely. In their midst was the champion, who by the estimation of most had turned the tide in their favour. The *wanax* squinted as he looked down from him to the chieftain of the raiders – a small but stocky man who brimmed with energy.

The chieftain raised his arms. 'A great victory!' he said in his thick accent. The *wanax* inclined his head. The raider turned towards his men. 'Then why he look so fucking miserable?'

The *wanax* waited for the roar of laughter to fade. When it did, he scratched his nose and smiled briefly. 'I, in turn, have an amusing question for you. I am told that the dykes to the lake have been destroyed and that the plains are flooded. *Flooded...* You understand this, yes? My question is, *Why?* Why would your men do this?' The chieftain's grin became a rictus. 'Why would they destroy *crops* in times of *famine*? Why would they turn once fertile land into a stagnant and pestilential fen?'

The chieftain snapped his head towards his men but they could only exchange looks of confusion and alarm. 'They would *not*!' he snapped. 'Orchomenos is *ours*!'

'Yes, it is. Whatever wretched patch of dry land remains. I hope your men are good engineers: those dykes took ten years to build.' The *wanax* jerked his head at the nobleman to follow him. '*Ten years!* This is why I look so miserable!'

When they were out of earshot, the nobleman said quietly, 'Well, you convinced me and I knew you were lying!' He glanced over his shoulder to be sure they weren't being followed. 'Do you think they will stay?'

'Some of them. Women, children; the weaker ones. A small garrison, probably.'

The nobleman thought about it. They were by the rear section of the palace and flames were leaping from the roof apertures. *'Load those crates now!'* he yelled. Their men were exhausted and had been caught loitering but at the approach of the pair, they stirred into action and now began to heave the valuables onto a waiting wagon. 'And the rest?'

'What choice do they have? Their hands are forced!'

II

Lemnos

A week or so later, a messenger came haring into Myrine. Xandros had just returned from a boar hunt arranged by Euneus when he heard the short, sharp note of the trumpet announcing his arrival. The council gathered immediately to hear him. 'Go and water his horse, Xandros,' said Euneus when he hurried out into the square. 'It's a grey tethered by the backshore.' The glow of the hunt faded at once. He trudged down the slope from the citadel to the beach with two pitchers of water and a bag of fodder slung over his shoulders. Red noticed him looking deep in thought and joined him. 'You h-have a way with animals,' said Red as the horse set about the food after a vigorous snort and bobbing of its head. Xandros stroked its withers.

'Easier than humans, aren't they?'

'Yes, I s-suppose they are. How was the hunt?'

'Just one pig. Must've been the runt because neither of its parents was around.'

'Know how it f-feels!' said Red with a wry smile. 'Your father's k-keeping you busy.'

'What do you mean?'

'I mean, to take your mind off T-T... off your girlfriend. Shows he cares, no?'

'You don't miss anything, do you?' Xandros huffed. 'Anyway, she's not my girlfriend. She's betrothed to that... that fucking sea urchin.'

'Won't last.'

Xandros shook the fodder bag, whispering encouragement to

the horse. He heard footsteps approaching from upslope and was surprised to see the messenger.

'That was fast,' said Xandros.

The man looked harried but, when he saw the care that had been taken of his horse, muttered his thanks. He swung his travel bag further round his shoulder and prepared to mount.

'I am the king's son,' said Xandros. 'Are we in danger?'

He tugged at his black beard when he turned back to Xandros, looking him up and down. He could tell what he was thinking – *Then why weren't you at council?* – but his eyes registered the resemblance to Euneus. 'Thebes has fallen, and Orchomenos before her. Galleys have been sighted to the south. The men of Moudros are heading here.' He didn't wait for a response before stuffing the tether in his leather bag and wheeling away in a cloud of dust. It was then that Xandros noticed a fire beacon had been lit to the east.

Xandros watched the train of pack animals and warriors from atop the walls of Myrine. As the Moudrians threaded through the valley, the sun broke through the haze of clouds and glinted from the distant tips of spears and bronze helmets. He heard his father grudgingly admit that it was an impressive march – ten miles was no mean distance to cover in that time – and quite an impressive sight. Xandros felt an unfamiliar churning in his stomach and wondered what might have been causing it, scarcely wanting to admit that he would have preferred not to see Teodora again, if it meant enduring her and Ekhinos. Then he heard his father yelling at him for being idle and he pushed himself away from the walls.

The Moudrians arrived a couple of hours later, lathered with sweat and dust.

Though it had only been a matter of days, they and the Myrinians eyed each other with suspicion at first but it soon eased in the face of bigger considerations. Plouteos entered Myrine looking less self-satisfied than the first time, but then Xandros saw Ekhinos. He was bare-chested and straight-backed. It pained him to admit it but the sea urchin was broad in the shoulder and his skin was sun-bronzed. As he issued orders to some men and boys in his charge, his eyes lingered on Xandros for a moment but there was no sneer. It was as if he was so far beneath him that it wasn't worth the expenditure of energy.

All afternoon, the shore bustled with activity as supplies of arrows, spare spears and shields, and skins of water were deposited and men pushed past each other in their haste to ready themselves and form a beachhead. A relay of women ferried food and linen bandages up and down the slopes to the citadel like a line of worker ants. As the sun burned away the few remaining clouds, tempers frayed and there were heated words exchanged, though nobody came to blows. People barely looked ahead as they walked: all eyes were glued upon the glittering sea.

As the sun began to wester and the bay was bathed in golden light, a strange hush descended upon the beach, leaving only the hiss of the breakers lapping the shore. It was as if an unspoken message had percolated through the Lemnians: *The Sea Peoples are near.*

Only they weren't.

A murmur spread along the line that the nearest fire beacon had been extinguished and, within the hour, as the sun shimmered over the horizon, the same bearded messenger returned. Xandros happened to be close by the tree stump at which he had tethered his horse earlier in the day and, as he dismounted, the messenger tossed him the reins. Even as Xandros protested at the insulting gesture, the messenger was loping across the beach, where Euneus was stood with Moxos. Then his eyes fell upon Teodora as she was coming down the path and he wondered how on earth he had missed her. In the warm, slanting light, flushed from bustling about her duties, her skin glowed. She had a water jug perched on one shoulder and cradled it with both hands as she walked. It had the effect of stretching the fabric of her stole, accentuating the depth of her bosom.

She was truly a woman now. Xandros felt his lips forming the words as he watched her. As she noticed him at the foot of the path, he felt his heart sink. How was it possible that the passage of just a few days could have such an effect on someone's appearance? Was it the distance, he wondered, or her new lover?

Xandros felt self-doubts crowding him and tore his eyes away, concentrating on tying up the messenger's horse. She would not see him upset. Instead, he focused upon the conversation taking place a short distance away. The chatter on the beach faded as people sidled nearer.

The messenger had drained his proffered cup of water, splashed his face and now cleared his throat. Euneus raised his hand and the beach once more became quiet.

'Speak out.'

'The galleys I saw with my own eyes earlier today, south of Lemnos, have now passed out of sight, eastwards towards Anatolia. There has been no further sign of them, along any part of the coast. The fire beacons have now been doused and banked up again, in the event they return.'

At that moment, Xandros noticed movement to his left. He looked over his shoulder to see Ekhinos appear behind Teodora, laying a hand upon her shoulder. Seeing the look upon his face, Ekhinos stroked the scoop of skin beneath her jaw and gave him a wink. Teodora, he noticed, closed her eyes at his touch and he did not think it was in pleasure.

A few more words were exchanged with the messenger before he turned once more for his horse, and Xandros moved away. Being treated like a groom was bad enough but, in front of Ekhinos and Teodora, it would have been unbearable. Meantime, people began talking again and Xandros could sense the relief pervade the façade of disappointment. The Moudrians in particular had gone to considerable lengths to march here and were now at something of a loose end. There was a brief conference between Euneus, Plouteos and one or two others before Plouteos took his place on a little dune and appealed for quiet. When he had it, he told the Moudrians that they would camp for the evening on the beach and leave some time the following day, once it was clear the threat had passed.

Ekhinos was at that moment in discussion with another youth. Teodora's eyes briefly met Xandros' and a little green shoot of hope grew in his heart.

III

Early the following morning, under a burning sun, Xandros saw Moxos practising with his sword against a stake driven into the beach. He watched him, rapt. The strikes were not fast but each was delivered with perfect balance, such that the *clack* of sword upon wood seemed to reverberate across the island. Moxos hacked and lunged at the stake for the duration of a song, after which he threw down his blade and laced his fingers behind his head whilst sweat sheeted from his brow. When his breath had returned, he towelled his face and pointed to some practice swords.

His chest was still heaving when he noticed Xandros. 'Do you want to try?'

'I'm better with a spear. And a sling.'

'A sling is a child's toy,' Moxos said with a frown, handing him a weapon. 'I carved these myself from yew, after a new type I once handled and admired.'

Xandros ran his finger down its edge: the sword was smooth and beautifully weighted; like an extension of his arm.

The drills went well enough, for the first few minutes. When he saw the doubt creep into Xandros' eyes and the strain on his face, Moxos said, 'Keep at it, lad. Don't expect to master it so soon.'

For all of that first day, to the sinking of the sun, Xandros jabbed and parried and slashed at the stake and, later, at low-hanging branches of fruit trees that grew near the shore. The more the training absorbed him, the less self-conscious he felt as the Moudrians emerged from their tents and went about their business around him.

They had a break for water, which seemed to pass too quickly and, when he next stood, Xandros felt like his grip was so numb, and his hand so raw with blisters, that even a weak blow from Meleager's weapon would be enough to jar it from his fingers.

'Ready?' he asked.

Xandros could barely stand. 'Do you ever think about your father?' The words came out quickly, before he could think about reining them in.

Moxos' face darkened. 'Now why do you want to know about that?'

'Because my father never talks about Jason. He once promised to tell me about the heroes he met who fought at Troy, when they landed here, but he won't. I don't understand it.'

'He'll tell you when he's good and ready. Not my place to say any more on that.'

'Did you meet them?'

He frowned at Xandros and gave him the strangest of looks. Then he looked away and spoke quietly. 'I did meet them. And to your question, yes, I do sometimes think of my father. His reputation reached these shores when I was growing up but he never returned. None of those Argonauts ever did. I'd say that's the reason why your father doesn't want to talk about them, and it's a good enough reason too.' Moxos rose abruptly. 'Come on, boy. I think the time has passed for training. We can resume tomorrow.'

IV

After Xandros drew water for a bath and treated his blisters with a salve made from burdock leaves, he stepped out into the lengthening shadows of the square, enjoying the warmth of the golden evening sun on his face. When he opened his eyes, his feeling of wellbeing evaporated in a trice.

'What's going on here?'

'It s-seems that sly one from… from Moudros, what's his name, the nomarch—'

'Plouteos.'

'Him. He's decided to k-keep his lot here one more night.'

'There's trouble afoot,' Xandros muttered. 'I can smell it. Like the heavy air before a thunderstorm.' Feeling hunger gnawing at him again, he walked over to the meat that had been carved up on a trestle table, spearing some goat's cheese whilst he was at it.

'I wonder if these M-Moudrians know that they're eating their own g-goats?'

Xandros had taken a swig of wine and nearly spat it out. 'Serves them right.'

From the far end of the square, he looked back upon the scene. One of the Moudrians was, Xandros had to admit, a very decent harper and next to him – in their cups – was a pretty hideous-looking pair, a man and a woman, whose faces suited their voices.

He whispered to Red, 'What is there to celebrate? Galleys of raiders have been skirting Lemnos like vultures yet they're behaving like we've scared them off.'

A little group to his right were in high spirits, laughing and joking. A girl detached herself from them and it took him a moment to realise it was Teodora. She turned to him, her face flushed and, after a moment's hesitation, approached.

'To your health, Xandros,' she said.

He glanced from her clay wine cup, half empty, to her lovely face. 'And yours.'

In the tail of his eye, Xandros glimpsed a black figure gliding past. An overwhelming sense of dread chilled the very marrow of his bones. He took a draught of the wine and glanced about, trying to locate it again. He wondered if the Moudrians had laced the *krater* with pennyroyal.

'Do you not want to speak to me?'

The wine burned as he struggled to swallow it. He wanted to take her by the shoulders and scream *Of course I do!* Instead he murmured, 'I wasn't expecting you to be here.'

'No.'

She tucked her hair over her ears and looked to the ground. He could feel precious seconds slipping through his fingers like fine sand but couldn't find any words. Xandros could sense Red gearing himself up to make a petty remark so he said the first thing in his head to fill the uncomfortable silence. 'Ekhinos,' said Xandros, 'your betrothed, wouldn't like to see this, would he?'

It was like the sun going behind a cloud. 'I will talk to whomever I want.' After a moment she added, 'Are you afraid of him?'

'I don't even know him yet I *hate* him. And his father. They're sly and I don't trust either of them.' He waited until the indignation at her comment had leached from his heart. 'But I'm not afraid of him.'

'Good.' She considered his words and some of the light returned to her eyes. 'Where is your father?'

He swirled the dregs of wine. 'I don't know.'

'It can't be easy for you.' She placed her hand, briefly, on his wrist and he felt his heart flutter. 'It's the other way around for me. I love my mother but she's so…' Teodora's voice dropped to a whisper '…so timid. Like a frightened bird.'

'I don't remember anything about mine. At least you have her.'

'Truth.'

Xandros looked around the square, not seeing what he ought

to have seen. 'I want to leave this island, one day. I want to see something of the world.'

He said it to himself – and he heard Red cough – but the effect upon her was profound. Her eyes brimmed with joy. 'As do I! Whenever I see ships passing by, I wonder what it must be like for them. The view, I mean. Where they're going, what they've seen.'

Xandros raised his chin. 'Here comes the urchin.'

'I'll tell you what *I've* seen,' said Ekhinos, forcing a smile that didn't reach his eyes. 'A gloomy past and a very bright future. Come along: I have a surprise for you.'

He cut Xandros with his eyes as he guided her back to his friends. Xandros watched her go with an ache in his heart and she did not look back, though he sensed she wanted to.

'The answer to your question,' said Red quietly, 'is "she will" but you c-can't force it, I think. Come on. The harper is quite good.'

The harper played until the sun was touching the horizon, when people began to drift away to their homes or the tents on the beach. Xandros passed a small group of young men without paying them any attention, not seeing a pair leave the group. He unbuckled his belt and was just about to piss against a wall in a shaded alley. He felt a rough hand shove him between his shoulder blades, and his forehead cracked against the mud-brick wall. He felt his legs buckle as the impact reverberated around his skull, and an elbow graze the crown of his head. He heard a grunt of pain before realising what was happening. He covered up and stumbled clear, catching a glimpse of two youths. One now grabbed his tunic. Xandros pivoted on his heels and shoved the youth against the wall. Pinning him with his left hand, he drove his right elbow into his belly, driving the wind from him.

His ear hummed as a heavy swipe scored it; the pain sharpened his senses. The face now contorted with aggression he might, or might not, have seen before but it made no odds. The attack was unprovoked. Xandros swung wildly from the hip, like a discus thrower, and his fist cracked into the boy's face with a satisfying *pop*. The other boy was now straightening. Every fibre of Xandros' body fizzed with exhilaration. He grabbed a fistful of the youth's hair and drove his knee into his face. The eager blow only made him stagger to the side so Xandros heaved him to the ground, and drove his fist into his face, once, twice, a third time, until it was clear by the sagging head that he was unconscious.

He got to his feet, his breaths ragged, and dabbed his head, seeing the smear of blood. He looked around him but there was nobody nearby and the voices of people in the square were faint. Somewhere close, a nightbird called and swooped past. He heard the first youth begin to stir. Xandros looked closely at him and now he recognised him: one of Ekhinos' friends. It didn't surprise him. Feeling his blood warm, he grabbed him by the neck of his tunic and hauled him upright, and the youth staggered about like a new-born lamb, mumbling protests and swearing.

'Move!'

Xandros shoved him, realising he would have to be quick before the wretch came to his senses and put up a fight. Close to the square, he went down on all fours but Xandros soon had him upright, balling his tunic in his fist.

There were perhaps thirty people – no more – milling around in the twilight and, at first, they paid Xandros no notice. Then the merriment and singing stopped and people turned to look. He heard a woman scream, glimpsed a few men running over, one of them his father. Xandros shoved the youth to the ground.

His father stared at him with wide, uncomprehending eyes. 'What is this?'

'They attacked me in the dark – him and another.'

There was a babble of voices and protests. 'Be *quiet*!' barked Euneus, draining Xandros' last dregs of triumph. 'The other... Which other? Where?'

'We were just going to piss...' croaked the youth, smearing the blood from his mouth.

'No!' Xandros shouted, *'Lies!* The other's still there. He's one of Ekhinos'—'

'And he fell upon us both when our backs were turned!'

'Enough!' Plouteos pushed past the bystanders. 'Go and look for him!' He waited whilst a pair of his men hurried off into the deepening shadows. 'This boy *is* my son's friend. What of it?

What matters is you attacked a guest-friend, you worthless thug. You've…'

Moxos' sword was free from its sheath and pointed at Plouteos before he could even flinch. The nomarch now stared at its tip, inches from his heart, incredulous.

'No, man, lower your sword!' Euneus pressed down his friend's forearm. Xandros had never seen such a look on Moxos' face. The blade quivered with his indignation and he sheathed it with his jaw clenched.

Plouteos' lips twitched. 'It's true what they say about you. You have lost your mind, haven't you?'

Seeing the murderous look in Moxos' eyes, Euneus stepped forwards with his finger raised. 'Keep speaking, if you want your heart sliced in two. Do I have your attention? Listen, man. Why would my son attack two men? Why would any man here, on such an evening? It makes no sense.'

Plouteos rolled his eyes. 'Oh, by all the gods, are you blind? A girl! It's always over a girl; my son's betrothed! He had designs on her!'

Euneus raised his eyebrows and turned to Xandros. 'Well?'

Xandros had been watching them in mounting disbelief and now sputtered his words. 'Is this… Do I not get a chance to speak? Look at my head – the blood. They shoved me against the wall, when my back was turned, the cowards! Yes, I defended myself. What is the shame in *that*? Well? Would you prefer if they had beaten me senseless or worse? Yes… No, I had no designs on her! I was *with* her.' His eyes swept the square but there was no sign of her, or Ekhinos. 'And… But I had not seen her in a while. Teodora, that is. That's her name. Not since Manolis died and the…' He was about to say 'raid' but caught himself, though his words now dried up. 'But they attacked *me* first! How can you not—'

'This one is barely alive!' They all turned to see Plouteos' men emerge from the gloaming, dragging the second youth with his limp arms draped around their necks. What sympathy Xandros had clawed back vanished in the sharp intake of breath. The boy's face, he now saw, was a mess. He also saw the looks exchanged. *Make the first move,* they seemed to say, *and I will gladly respond.*

Plouteos drew himself up tall. 'What will it be, Euneus? The lash?' Euneus' hand twitched by the pommel of his sword. 'Or the rod? We won't move from here until justice is done.'

'Get your people…' Euneus' voice rumbled with menace '…out of here. Right now.'

'Are you serious?'

'Do it.' Behind him, Khalkeus folded his arms. The tip of a short sword poked a few inches from under his armpit. Alektruon yawned and rapped his blade against his knuckles. More looks passed between the Moudrians.

'Get out!'

Plouteos flinched and, with a jerk of his head for his men to follow, stalked away. His guards set after him, hitching up the semi-conscious youth with some difficulty. When he was near the arch, Plouteos half turned. 'Lines have been crossed this evening, Euneus, you'll see.'

When they were out of sight, Euneus began to cough alarmingly whilst his councillors stood by, uncertain how to respond. When the convulsions subsided, he cleared his throat. 'Make sure they leave. Let me know when they do.' He walked towards Hypsipyle's halls, hawking onto the ground.

Darkness had now fallen and the night held its breath. Khalkeus laid a hand on Moxos' shoulder. 'Come on,' he murmured. 'See them off and then we'll drink.'

The rest of them dispersed leaving only Xandros and Red, who now turned a slow circle, boots scraping on grit. 'Well, I s-suppose you do have a t-talent for making tiresome guests disappear. Are you hurt?' he asked.

Xandros shook his head, feeling like he was in a waking nightmare. He raised his hands, turning them over, watching them tremble as if they were cold. Blood and dirt had combined to leave a dirty smear on his knuckles.

'What have I done?' he whispered to himself.

V

The Messenian coast

The bawdy marching song was based upon a paean to Apollo but the column of men singing it now fell quiet. Instead, they passed the mountain to their left to the creak and rumble of the two wagons they were escorting along the coast road. This section of the route was haunted, so the story went, by the restless souls of a former king's bodyguard, who were massacred in an ambush, long ago. Fringing the road on the right, obscuring the view of the coastline, grove after grove of olives. The westering sun cast their gnarled shadows almost as far as the mountain's lower slopes, cooling the sweat that made their tunics cling to their skin.

Only the two wiry old men – twins, leading the column – were unperturbed. They had seen and experienced too much of the world to be shaken by much, though they wore it lightly. Between them, they might even have killed more men than the massacre that so perturbed travellers.

As the mountain began to recede and the terrain became more level, the conversations resumed.

'Any danger we might stop soon?' came a familiar, grating voice. 'The women need to piss.'

The elder of the twins turned to locate him. 'Meaning *you* need to piss, I presume?' He shared a look with his brother. 'We stop shortly.'

'I'd happily swap the girl for him. The little Grinling makes my flesh crawl.'

'Hera would take grave offence. The man's a halfwit. A runt. Also, a drunkard.' After a few moments, he added, 'Sound familiar?'

'Up yours, Castor.'

The pointed look he received from his brother made his grin evaporate. 'Careful,' he whispered. 'They have eyes and ears everywhere.'

His brother didn't disagree. Small miracle they had managed to evade detection for as many years as they had and that, as senior followers of old King Nestor, they had even managed to thrive, despite the bounty on their heads. Even their long fair hair stubbornly refused total domination by greys, but then stubbornness had always been a trait of Spartans. 'I'm sure people know, by now.'

'Change the subject.'

'Gladly,' he said. 'You think we'd know if Nestor had commissioned new ships, wouldn't you?'

'What are you talking about?'

'...because they are not Messenian galleys, are they?'

The pair looked south, towards the Bay of Pylos, where a flotilla of dark-sailed ships was lying at anchor.

'Smoke!' came the cry from behind them. The hum of speculation became one of despair and the twins looked to where people were pointing. A mile or so inland, a dark smudge sullied the sky. The palace, the settlement, maybe even the fields. All ablaze.

'Raiders!'

The twins shared a look. It had come to pass. They'd warned the king for the past few years and only recently had he begun to take them seriously. By a cruel twist of irony, the very mission they'd been sent upon to avert the threat was the reason why they would survive. Eighteen men, two mules and a wagon bearing scrap metal and a girl. All that would remain.

The twins were joined by one of the junior peers. In their estimation, Myron was one of the more competent courtiers. A capable spearman but a long-haired dandy and sycophant, nevertheless. 'What are your orders, sirs? Abandon the wagons and hurry across country?'

'We have none,' muttered Castor.

'Sorry, sir?'

'He said, "We have none." Clear enough for you?'

The peer screwed up his face. 'But those are our homes! Our families!'

'Yours. Not ours.'

'What he is saying,' said Pollux, giving his brother a cutting look, 'is that anything giving off that much smoke has been burning for a long time. It doesn't make for pleasant viewing.'

Myron looked at him in disbelief but Pollux ignored him. 'Everyone, listen! *Listen!*' When the hubbub faded and their eyes were upon him, he continued. 'You are all hereby dismissed from service, or whatever flim-flam it is that the king is meant to say in the circumstances. Do what you must from here. Salvage what you must. Mourn who you must. And if you are burning with some desperate desire to die, make sure you take a few pirates with you.'

At first, the men of the train just gaped at him. A couple retched. Then they stirred and went about their business with hands that shook in fear and growing rage. The twins watched the column disperse. A few sloped off the way they had come, casting surreptitious glances backwards until they realised they weren't about to be stopped. Most of them – and they admired their bravery – retrieved their weapons and belongings, and cut across the open country towards Pylos, avoiding the road. They wore the haunted looks of those who knew they were going to face death: their own or its grisly work upon others.

'What are *you* two going to do?' Myron was clutching a handful of javelins in addition to his own kit. Likely they had belonged to the deserters. Pollux noticed, too, how he had dropped all terms of respect.

'Nothing you need concern yourself with.'

Myron held Castor's gaze for a moment then shook his head. 'You know, I don't understand you pair. You somehow become favourites of the king yet you repay his loyalty by dismissing his men and *mocking* him! How will you live with yourselves? You had a chance to make a name for yourselves!'

Pollux chuckled without mirth. 'Oh, if only you knew, boy! If only you knew the problems our names have caused.' He raised his chin towards the smoke. 'On your way, now. You're a decent enough fighter but don't be careless with your life. Good fortune to you.'

Myron turned with a huff and hurried to join the others. Pollux watched the line of men snaking inland towards the low hills whilst Castor scanned the coast. There would be no miraculous intervention from any other city but at least there would be no more pirates; not today, at least. He watched the dust settle back upon the road, now clear of men. They had abandoned clothes, towels, bits of unwanted kit and other bric-a-brac that men accumulate upon their travels. Doubtless there would also be some food. One of the mules snorted impatiently. He would go and water them.

He heard a stifled scream and scrabbling of feet. Pollux, too, turned on his heels, and the pair hurried over to its source. Castor glanced beneath the undercarriage of the wagon. Seeing nothing, he drew his short sword, tipping his head to indicate that he was going around the far side of the mules. Arriving at the rear of the wagon at the same moment, they whipped aside the curtain that concealed the rear.

The setting sun framed a grim scene. The captive was on her back, bound arms pinned above her head. The Grinling was straddling her, trying to remove his loincloth with his free hand. Now he snapped his head around, sour with frustration. Seeing the king's followers, he froze. 'Wait your turn, old men.'

They both climbed aboard, and the wagon's platform creaked in tandem with their joints. Castor yanked the man's hair back, presenting his face to Pollux, who swiped his cheek. The blow was satisfyingly hard but he had learned how to temper his fists, and the animal would meet his fate whilst fully conscious, more or less. They dragged him towards the rear of the wagon and flung him off the back step, and he landed with a heavy thump on his back. Whilst Pollux made sure he didn't try to scurry away, Castor cut the girl's bonds and eased her up.

'It seems the gods don't want the old miser's sacrifice after all and I, for one, am glad.'

Her large dark eyes darted about, looking for the next danger but, seeing none, her breathing subsided.

'What happened?' she croaked. 'Where are they?'

'The men have gone to their homes: what's left of them.' He helped her off the wagon. 'Look, over there. You see it?'

She shuddered. 'The Sea Peoples?'

'Probably.'

Now she looked down upon the bloodied Grinling, whose chest was heaving up and down in fear and indignation.

Castor presented her with his sword. 'Have you ever killed a man before?' She looked at it like she had never seen a blade.

'No matter,' said Pollux. 'If you make a bit of a mess of it, you just prolong his death.'

She looked from the bronze to the man on the floor, wide-eyed and terror-struck. But then she saw his loincloth underneath his tunic, partially undone. Seeing what was about to happen, the man jabbered and started to crab away.

'Ah, ah!' said Pollux, stamping him back towards her. 'Die with more nobility than you lived.'

The girl clenched her teeth and lunged at his groin. Pain exploded on his face, stealing the breath from his lungs. He clutched at the ragged wound, leaving his heart and neck exposed.

'Are you sure you're new to this?' asked Pollux with a grimace.

Emboldened, she gritted her teeth and began to jab at him all over his face and chest and legs and he squealed like a piglet until there was barely a square inch of his tunic not saturated with blood. When the Grinling had stopped twitching and the dark fluid was nourishing the earth, Castor gently took back his sword. 'Well done,' he said quietly, as she began to shake. 'He deserved worse.'

'Listen, my girl,' said Pollux. 'Look at me, not him, look at me; that's it. Where we are going, you cannot follow but we all need to get off this road, eat and rest. You will be safe with us for this evening, you hear me? Safe.'

VI

Xandros rose early to avoid his father but, after midday, he became hungry and cursed himself for setting out without his sling or his flint kit. He slipped home unnoticed. The house was quiet and he could hear Auge working in a room to the right of the hall, singing to herself. From the stores, he stuffed a blanket, some bread, wine and cheese into a leather bag and tiptoed back down the corridor to the front gate. At the far end of the square, in the shade of an ancient oak, he saw that his father had now joined a few of the elders. They were seated around a table upon which perched several jugs of wine. The moment he closed the gate behind him, Euneus' eyes fell upon him.

'There he is!'

Euneus beckoned him over and Xandros felt his heart race. The temptation to ignore them as if he'd not heard them rose then died. He could hardly have missed his commanding voice.

As soon as he drew close, he knew it had been a mistake to venture outside. Euneus' face was pallid and drawn and behind the glassiness of his eyes lurked something volatile. Xandros glanced from Hektor to Alektruon and Khalkeus, noticing the space where Moxos should have been. He got the impression his father was deeper in his cups than any of them.

'My son!' He grabbed Xandros' shoulder. 'Well? How are you?'

'Well enough. Thank you.'

'Going somewhere?'

Xandros shrugged. 'Just hunting.'

'Sit. Drink.' He shoved Hektor with a grunt to make space for Xandros, slapping the bench so hard it made him flinch. Alektruon poured him a cup and behind the hard set of his eyes was another look that he couldn't immediately fathom. Xandros took a swig. It was unpleasant and vinegary but he tried not to let it show.

'So, here we are.' Euneus made a vague gesture towards the elders and Xandros caught Alektruon's eye once more. The man was a killer yet he was sure there was a flash of a warning there. *Be ready*, his look hinted.

'Here we are.' Euneus took a long draught and poured some more wine for himself. Not all of it arrived in his cup. 'You must have some questions for us. You always have questions, my lad, don't you?'

He was antagonising him, no question, but also testing him, despite his state. To see how his mind worked, the undeserving heir to the throne of Myrine. Still, he knew he must play the game. 'Will you move against Moudros?'

'What do you think?'

Xandros stuttered but there was no easy response: any course of action might unleash disaster. 'I think… I think whatever… It depends on whether the Sea Peoples return. They pose a bigger threat…'

'In other words, you'd do nothing.' He gave his son a bitter smile. 'Just wait and see, is that it? You see, gentlemen? This is what I have raised! A shitting oracle!'

Xandros had never known shame like it. He felt his jaw slacken and the blood rush to his cheeks as he stared back at him.

The king's insult met a stony silence.

'You go too far, Euneus,' rumbled Hektor.

'Too far,' added Hilarion gravely.

Euneus' eyes flashed. 'It was *his* opinion I asked, not yours! I'll seek your counsel when you're guided by good sense, not wine!'

Hilarion's shoulders sagged and Hektor's grey moustache twitched in disapproval. He looked away.

'What do you suppose these great heroes of old would do, eh?'

Xandros gave him a black look.

'Well? What would the wily Odysseus of Ithaka have done, do you think? Or Agamemnon, hm? Or even,' he added, spitefully, 'my own father, Jason, damn his guts.'

He knew he should have got up and walked away but his feet

were leaden and he resigned himself to whatever was coming. Euneus gave a sardonic laugh and drained his cup. 'He asks lots of questions about these heroes; likes hearing about them, well enough. But he lacks even the smallest spark of what it takes to become one. Don't you, son?'

'He defended himself. Two on one.' Xandros glanced at Alektruon in surprise. 'There's your spark.'

The others murmured in agreement but Euneus sucked his teeth dismissively.

'What were you *thinking*? Are there not enough other girls on this island? And you're supposed to know these stories! Well? Is it not a cautionary tale, that little shit Paris stealing another man's wife? Or is that who you're really trying to follow? I didn't rear a son to be such a fucking stuttering fool!'

Xandros looked him square in the eyes. He could see the turmoil within, like the deepest seas beneath a storm. Resentment... disappointment... stress... fear... and exhaustion. Yes, they were all broiling within him. Xandros stood. Though he tried to keep his voice under control, he heard it quaver.

'You didn't raise a son at all.'

Red, who had witnessed it all, followed him through the gate and down the slope towards the beach. When they reached the sand, Red said, 'I'm glad you said that to him. He d-deserved it.'

'Maybe I did too.'

Red snorted in disagreement. 'He may have been drunk but that... all that was s-so wrong. Even that m... Even that madman Alektruon looked like he didn't want to b-be there. What are you going to do now?'

Xandros frowned as if he was witless. 'I'm going to leave Lemnos.'

They spent the afternoon in an adjacent valley, practising with a sling. Chancing upon a flock of fat wood ptarmigans in the late afternoon, Xandros struck one full in the breast, and the others took to flight in a puff of its feathers. He plucked it and roasted it over a fire then settled into a companionable silence in the dappled light of an ancient oak, listening to the shrill calls of the grass crickets.

When they became restless, they set off again. Cresting the hills, they could see that Lemnos tapered like the body of a fish before flaring out, north and south, like its tailfin. It would take a night in the wild and another day walking, Xandros supposed, before they would reach its eastern shore.

The sun was flirting with the tops of some tall poplars when they decided to stay for the night. As Xandros retrieved the blanket from his bag, there was a loud clap of wings. He turned towards a grassy hillock to the south-east, from where a flock of blackbirds took to sudden flight. Hearing the swishing of dried grass, Xandros reached for his sling as a hooded figure appeared atop the hillock: he had loaded a shot by the time he realised who it was.

'Hello, Xandros,' she said.

'Teodora! What are you doing here?'

She frowned at him. 'The same as you, I suppose.'

He swallowed with difficulty. 'I didn't expect to see you again.'

'Nor I you.' She reached out and touched the angry graze on his forehead, sending a shock through his body.

'I'm sorry!' she said, seeing him flinch. 'Does it still hurt?'

'No.'

'In Moudros, they are saying you got drunk and attacked them, when their backs were turned.'

'They raise such heroes there.'

'Well? Did you?'

'Of course I didn't!' he snapped. 'I'll bet your fiancé was pleased with his day's work, though, wasn't he?'

'He denied he knew anything about it,' she said distantly.

Xandros frowned at this. 'Don't you think it strange he got you out of the way first?'

'We were leaving anyway.'

Xandros tutted. He didn't want to hear any more about Ekhinos so offered her some wine. He liked the way she drank from his cup, unhesitatingly. She settled herself onto the grass with crossed legs.

Sent you out as a spy, did he?

Xandros muttered a rebuke to Red under his breath.

'What was that?' asked Teodora crisply.

Now that the thought had been put into his head, Xandros couldn't ignore it. He tutted. 'It just feels like… you've been dragged into his scheming. Somehow.'

Teodora screwed up her face. 'He knows me better than to try that. Besides, I don't live with him yet.'

The brief glimpse into the intimacies of two lovers burst the little bubble that had begun to swell in Xandros' heart. 'When is the marriage?'

She gave him a knowing look. 'The Month of the Goddess.'

'Ah. Unless the sea-wolves spoil the celebration.'

'What a strange thing to say.'

He is strange, murmured Red. *That's what m-makes him different.* Xandros stood and brushed away the grass. 'I want to walk: the sun's sinking fast. You?'

Teodora looked up at him. He seemed to be wrestling with conflicting emotions. 'Why not?'

They set off through the clearing and plunged down a hillside of heather that brushed their knees, releasing its musky scent, and picked their way over the sudden dips that could easily turn an ankle. Xandros loved watching Teodora's face as she lifted the hem to her stole and skipped over them: concentration and joy.

After half an hour, they began to descend towards the coast and they now saw the dark sea, heaving silently against the shore. The moon hung low and bright, and its light shimmered over the Archipelagos.

Xandros drew up short and held out his arm. He heard Teodora close by, breathing deeply. They had covered a lot of ground.

She asked, 'What is it?'

'Voices.'

They held their breath but heard only the squeak of a bat and the soft buzz of an insect's wings. Then they continued down the hillside, more cautiously now, and the ground dropped away towards a rocky beach. They picked their way down the slope, trying not to make a sound. They were a stone's throw from the backshore when they froze.

Somebody was singing in a voice like woodsmoke and honey

and mellow wine. They caught the last few lines of a verse, and it was only after the words had faded into the hush of the sea that Xandros realised he had been holding his breath. They looked to one another with raised eyebrows and crept down the rise, keeping to the shadows of some carob trees. A campfire was blazing to their left, and two men were stood behind it.

In the light of the flames, Xandros beheld an old man - old but not lacking vigour - and one much younger. The latter, his unruly dark hair bound by a fillet, was holding a beautiful lyre. The elder had thick white hair swept back so that it curled at the nape, lending him the air of an old aristocrat. His skin was as dark as a chestnut and it crinkled around his eyes as he gazed at them.

VII

Orpheus

'You can step into the light,' I said. 'We know you are there.'

I recall the words very well because I am a bard and I was there. I remember the moment I first laid eyes upon them as if it were yesterday. They took a few sullen steps forwards into the fringe of firelight, watching my apprentice and I.

'You needn't be afraid,' said I.

'I'm not.'

I gave a wry smile. He was no arrogant youth; merely honest. In fact, from that moment to his last, I never saw him tell a lie nor coat his words in honey. I don't believe he had the conceit. They weighed us up; I very much doubt we looked particularly threatening but stories of pirates were legion and we could have been merely two of a larger band. Between us, as the seconds stretched uncomfortably, the flames danced.

'We didn't expect to see anyone here.'

'Evidently, yet here we are. Introduce yourselves then.'

He mumbled their names but I could see his eyes moving all about the little bay, absorbing everything. He had quick wits, it was plain to see.

'Where is your boat?' he asked. 'I assume you didn't swim?'

'No indeed. We disembarked here.'

He frowned a little, as if we might be mocking him. 'Why? There's nothing here.'

'Oh, there's plenty here, my lad.' I chuckled. 'Boundless peace and quiet.'

'And who are you?'

'Is it not obvious? We are bards!'

'Bards,' Xandros repeated softly. 'I h-have never met one. Were you singing about Troy?'

'No, I wasn't,' I said, noting his slight stammer. 'I was instructing this man here. This is Phemius, son of Phemius of Ithaka.'

Phemius inclined his head but, ever tetchy and aloof, I could see he was already losing interest in them. He carefully set down his lyre and retrieved a waterskin, gargling at some length before spitting it out and drinking another draught. They watched him in curiosity. 'Merely protecting his throat.'

'And what is your name?' asked Xandros.

'Orpheus. But where are my manners? Please. Sit with us by the fire. We have bread enough to share.'

Xandros looked at me as if he had seen a ghost. '*You* are Orpheus?'

'Indeed I am. Or at least, I think so. Some of the stories I hear about me are most bizarre.'

'But… but you rowed on the *Argo*!'

'We refer to her just as *Argo* but, yes, I did. A lifetime ago.'

Behind me, Phemius sniffed. He could be so sour at times but his was a god-given talent, so I tolerated him. He is not nearly as widely known as I now am but I hear he has become very wealthy. In the half-light, Xandros and his friend mouthed something at each other. I had seen such a reaction many times. 'Come, eat something. We have wine to spare.'

'Thank you,' said Xandros, and now his words tumbled from him. 'My grandfather also rowed aboard *Argo*. His name was…'

'Jason?'

'Yes, Jason. You knew.'

I was thunderstruck. I confess, I was not often at a loss for words but, in that moment… He stepped out of the shadows and it was as if Jason was emerging from the past. The effect stole my breath. The shape of his face; his build; the quiet intensity of his presence, particularly those blue eyes…

'Gods above, let me look at you!' I gripped him by the shoulders, quite taking him aback, I think. I did not often smile so broadly and I have been told I have a rather awkward grin. 'Forgive me!' I said, releasing him. 'Sit, please! Phemius, don't be such poor company!'

I turned to him and he raised an eyebrow, marginally impressed by the turn of events. 'Some wine!'

As they sat, my eyes lingered on Teodora for a moment and she looked away. I did not know just then but I suspect my recognition was coalescing. There was something else I noticed about Xandros; something I had also observed with his grandfather. We call it an *aura*, for it is as insubstantial as the wind but, with some, it is there, all about them.

Phemius presented them with beakers of wine – fortunately, we carried spares for wooden ones do not travel well over seas – and I broke off some sweet flatbread for them. They were famished and I did not want to rush them, so I refrained from asking any more of them, as the laws of hospitality insist. They were of an age where they could have devoured every crumb we had and still not been sated but their manners were good.

Xandros spoke up. 'Have you met Jason? I mean, since you returned?'

'Not for a long time. Before we all parted, we swore that we would meet every year to honour the dead… keep the brotherhood alive…'

'Ah… So when was the last time?'

'Many years… Nineteen? Twenty?'

'Twenty! Why so long?'

I sighed. I had asked myself the same, many times over. 'Well, there comes a point with such things… I had been travelling far and wide and was unable to return for several years, and there comes a point beyond which it becomes awkward to just… expect things to be the same. I regret it.' And I really did. 'Perhaps one day. And you? Have you ever met your grandfather?'

'No,' he said quietly. 'Never.'

This was both sad and a blessing, for it also suggested that he knew nothing of the tragedy that hung over Jason's name like a black cloud. He had become synonymous with both sorrow and great evil though, evidently, an evil that had not reached the shores of Lemnos. Or so I thought.

'And what of your grandmother, Queen Hypsipyle? Does Myrine

thrive?' My eyes passed over Teodora again and recognition took a small step closer.

'She is still very much alive and Myrine... Well, Myrine is Myrine!'

'This *is* good news!' I shook my head and chuckled. 'A remarkable lady...' And she was. My mind cast adrift to that moment, many years previously, when we heaved *Argo* to and waded ashore. We all felt that Lemnos was the last haven before hostile waters. Our reception was unlike anything we had ever experienced before, or would ever since, and of course we had left behind more than just pieces of our hearts when we raised anchor. Once the bitterness and shame of our departure had faded, we had discussed a return – bearing olive branches – but I didn't think it had ever happened. And, as I have already said, there comes a point beyond which... Well, for all I knew at that moment, I could have been the only Argonaut still drawing breath.

It was fully dark now. The stars and the moon glistened silver upon the dark sea, which whispered by the shore a stone's cast beyond our fire.

'Tell me,' I said to Teodora. 'Are you also from Myrine?'

'I'm from Moudros.' With that comment, I assumed I had been mistaken in seeing a glimpse of someone significant. My old mind was playing tricks upon itself.

'You knew my grandfather...' I looked at the girl. Her tone – bold, unaffected – I had heard it before. 'His name was Oileus. Did you know him well?'

If I had ever doubted the existence of the gods, or Fate, whom we call *Moira*, or Providence, they put the issue to bed. I felt my lips move but no words came. I had no idea how it was that they now lived in different towns, or how they had come together, but I could feel the eyes of Fate upon us. No looks passed between Xandros and Teodora, which told me they knew nothing of their grandfathers' bond. I was about to tell them but then I caught myself.

'I knew him very well, my girl, very well indeed. He was a brave man. A tough, loyal man; one of the best of us, without a doubt.'

I watched her nod distantly. She gave the initial impression of one not appearing to be fully listening but, in time, I would see her sharp intellect. She was also a brave-heart in her own right. The resemblance between her and her grandfather was more subtle but, again, it was the eyes – those flint-grey eyes – that should have told me.

I could see Xandros looking from Phemius to me and back. He was a shrewd one, that boy, and I knew what was coming. 'That song you were singing when we interrupted you… It wasn't about Jason's voyage, was it?'

'As a matter of fact, it was.'

'Sing it again… please!'

'No. I had once thought it finished but there is more to be done. Those words will come – they are in the ether waiting to form – but it is not the bard's way to snatch at them.'

He turned to Phemius and I can still see my young accomplice's dark curls as he shook his head dismissively. 'This man,' I added, 'must be the first to learn it: to complete it himself, if necessary, though I hope that will not be the case.'

The light in Xandros' eyes faded a little and, by the Great Mother, had I seen that look before. It gave me a most peculiar feeling. 'I hope you can complete it,' said Xandros quietly. 'And that we will hear it, one day.'

Phemius inclined his head with sufficient grace but looked at me expectantly. In his opinion, it was clear, they were beginning to outstay their welcome. Phemius was on the haughty side of handsome so it took little for him to signal disapproval. I don't know where this bearing came from: it certainly wasn't his father who, for all his talents, was a humble, gracious man.

We finished our bread and wine with some fruit, feeling a little light-headed and heavy-limbed. It was plain to see that young Xandros was brimming with questions but I was becoming tired. He was, I think, unconvinced by my explanation of our arrival but it was true that we had been dropped off by a merchant vessel on the previous day and were expecting another boat to take us to Samothrace in the morning, from where we would head to the coast of Thrace, and – briefly – my home in the mountains of Rhodope. Something occurred to me at that point.

'Tell me, before you leave, how did *you* come to be here?'

It struck me as significant that a question so simple could cause such awkwardness: truly, they were appalling liars! After much stumbling for words, Xandros surprised me.

'I wanted to get away from Myrine…'

'And Moudros…'

'…and Moudros. For a while…' My raised eyebrow told them I wasn't entirely convinced. 'And Lemnos, for that matter.'

'You want to leave the island? Why on earth would you want to do that in such dangerous times?'

'You said yourself you had travelled far and wide. What can anyone know of the world by staying here?'

'I left because I was escaping something, though I won't say what. What is it that *you* are escaping? Are you in some sort of trouble?' The furtive glances told me they were.

'I have caused trouble, yes, and now I want to atone for it.'

'A noble enough thing, whatever your worries. Atone how?'

It was Xandros who looked me in the eye, and once again I saw something of his grandfather, albeit not the Jason at the beginning of our voyage, the rather callow youth. 'I have shamed my family here. My father hates me: he's not alone in this.' Some pregnant look crossed between him and Teodora and he took a deep breath. 'Moudros and Myrine had settled a long-standing quarrel to unite against the Sea Peoples, who most people think will arrive here soon. I… broke that fragile truce, and it can never be repaired, so now we must fight alone.'

'Oh?'

'I didn't break the truce on purpose – it was self-defence – d-despite what people are saying.' Xandros took a deep breath and glanced at Teodora. 'But sometimes, my anger gets the better of me.' It didn't surprise me to hear the boy talking in this way: people often do in my company, perhaps because I prefer to listen than prattle. The readiness with which he opened his heart, however, did.

Xandros paused for a moment. I had expected Phemius, behind me, to tut or shuffle in impatience but he was still. 'It's not who I really am, though. I've even given it a name: "Red". He listens when nobody else ever has.'

His *aura*. Aglow like fire. Truly I had not been wrong.

'There is a time for anger,' I said, 'but it is a powerful weapon that must be used sparingly. Find your voice, young man, and control will follow. Trust me in this.'

He turned to Teodora. 'You probably think me an idiot, now, don't you?'

'No. I only wish you had spoken before about this.' She bit her lip and looked to the ground. 'And because you have been so honest, so must I.'

I could see the look of alarm in Xandros' eyes.

'You said we must fight alone but it's worse than this.'

'How can it be worse?'

'I think the nomarch, Plouteos, has been treating with the raiders.'

'What?' asked Xandros. I even caught Phemius twitch with interest at this. 'What do you mean "treating"?'

'As in striking a deal… negotiating… what else could I mean?'

'You *think*? Or you know?'

'Think… No, I know… Oh, I can't be sure!' she said, throwing her hands in the air. 'I overheard him earlier today, talking to a stranger; someone I've never seen before…'

'About what?'

'If you gave me time to speak, I'd say!' she tutted and, right there, forty years just melted away. I saw Oileus' surliness in every angle of her face; it was extraordinary. 'I was at Ekhinos' house—' the mention of a sea urchin baffled me, I confess '—and I heard an argument. Plouteos was asking why the cost of a guarantee for safe passage had risen so sharply. These were his exact words but footsteps approached the door I was hiding behind, so I had to slip away. This was why I went for a long walk and you found me.'

A heavy silence settled upon that little cove and, in the fire-washed darkness, poor Xandros looked quite crushed. I had never been much interested in the private affairs of individuals I didn't know – and I expected the same courtesy to be extended to me – but this was something different. I scratched the stubble of my chin – it had always irritated me to be unshaven, even aboard *Argo* – and steered them back to something Xandros had said. 'You were about to explain why you were leaving the island. Does this news change that?'

'No,' he declared without hesitation. 'In fact, it makes it more important. Since I am the one to have damaged Myrine's defences, I want to be the one to repair them. I want to bring warriors to Lemnos; to prove that the raiders can be defeated. I just have to go and find them.'

'Err...' Teodora looked at him as if he had taken leave of his senses. 'What? You never told me about *this*, either!'

'That's what I'm doing now.'

Behind me, Phemius made a little snort of derision but I ignored him. 'How...' I scratched my temple as I recast the question. 'Where, exactly, do you expect to find warriors willing to leave behind their own homes to defend foreign shores many miles away over the sea? Unless you have the metal to pay for them, that is?'

'My question exactly,' declared Teodora.

'These men won't need it. Or want it.'

'Who?' we all said in unison, in varying degrees of patience.

'The greatest adventurers and warriors who ever lived. I am going to find the Argonauts.'

Phemius burst out laughing and, this time, my tolerance cracked. I glanced behind me and shot him a look before turning back to Xandros. It was a ludicrous mission for many reasons, even if he could get off the island, and I barely knew where to start, but I had long since learned to keep doubts from my face.

'You do know,' I said, 'that I was one of the youngest on that voyage? And look at me: do you think I could still wield a sword? Or would want to?' I shook my head gravely, for the thought was a truly depressing one. 'I wouldn't be particularly surprised if I was the last of us still alive. Even the sons of us men would probably say they were past their best.'

Teodora nodded in vigorous agreement. I assumed she would

also be part of this hare-brained plan and I didn't want her – either of them – to come to harm for such a whim.

'The Argonauts, their sons, their grandsons… I'd ask them all…'

'What about their daughters and granddaughters? Or do you think we can't hold a shield?'

Xandros flashed her a warm smile. 'I *know* you could. You are right, Orpheus, that nobody would want to leave their homes unless the reasons were strong; *really* strong. But what could be more important than your own children, children they'd never even seen, if only they could be persuaded that they still live, and that they need them more than ever?' His face grew more animated as he found his voice. 'You said yourself that none of the Argonauts had ever returned to Lemnos but that you had all discussed it. Surely their curiosity would be too strong, given a last opportunity to lay eyes on their own flesh and blood?' He looked at each of us, almost pleading. Teodora was frowning. He gave me a certain look, as if he was weighing up the question that I was sure would follow. 'Well? Aren't you even a little curious to see if you have a child in Lemnos?'

I felt a stab of resentment for that boy, I can tell you, stranger. He was overstepping the mark and he knew it, but he had kicked open a box I had long since considered locked. I doubted very much I had left any issue in Myrine, since I hadn't abandoned myself to those women with quite the same vigour as had my friends. It felt too much like a betrayal of Eurydice, even though she had been buried some months earlier.

I answered curtly. 'That is none of your business.' Xandros' face dimmed only a little. 'And, even if you are not wrong on this, the fact remains that the few Argonauts who remain will be old men and you will be unlikely to locate a single one of them. They are not men who have lived like others: theirs were no ordinary lives. If they don't want to be found, they won't be found.' I was thinking in particular of Castor and Pollux with this last comment, who had been fugitives at the time they had first boarded *Argo*, but there were plenty other rogues and misfits amongst them. 'Even Jason, if he still lives and you were to find him, was never a man given to doing something that didn't provide gain for him.'

'But if you never dare to try… You, more than most men alive, Orpheus, you know this.'

I took a deep breath and sighed. Now that the surprise had faded, I was feeling exhausted once more. 'How would you travel to these far-flung cities?'

'Lemnos has a galley and a few fishing craft. I'd persuade one of the skippers; or bribe him. Failing that…' he shrugged '…I'd steal one.'

'Bribe them with what, may I ask?'

'We have some gold and silver. A little.'

'And suppose they refused and simply told your father. What then?'

Xandros looked down. 'I hadn't got that far.'

'Orpheus!' Phemius had had enough. 'We're wasting precious time here.'

I gently waved away his impatience. 'You needn't steal a boat: I very much doubt you've ever sailed beyond these shores and the seas are treacherous, I should know.' I shook my head, barely believing my folly. 'Fine. I will pay for the crew to return after they have deposited me in Thrace—'

'Madness!'

I ignored the comment. The boy had tapped into some vein of mischief or rebelliousness I had long believed exhausted. 'It will be three or four days from now. You must be ready to leave at first light on both mornings.' I raised my finger at Teodora. '*Both* of you. That is my sole condition. To keep an eye on each other and, whenever he attempts something rash, to make him think again; you hear me?'

They stared back at me, wide-eyed for a moment, and I thought that either of them might refuse. Then their faces cracked into broad smiles, warmed by the unheralded prospect of travel and adventure. 'Look out for a black-sailed merchantman. The crew are rough fellows – I suspect trade is only part of their livelihoods – but, as Phemius here can attest, they have never let us down.'

I looked hard at them to make sure I had their attention. They were rapt. 'There is a second condition. If you somehow manage to find any of the Argonauts still alive, I want you to convey a message to them, from me. Tell them… Tell them that… far from forgetting them I have been busy on their behalf and that they will hear all about it soon enough; in this life or the next. Did you hear that? Good. I will instruct the crew myself about where they are to sail. Do you know a place where they can moor away from prying eyes?'

Xandros eagerly described such a place to me. I nodded. 'I will relay this to the crew but, if the sun is a handsbreadth above the horizon and you are not there, they will happily raise anchor without you.'

'Thank you, sir. From the heart, thank you a million times over, Orpheus!'

'You can thank me if you return, and believe me when I say I will soon know of it. Now then, Phemius and I must finish whilst I have the energy and he still has the patience.'

'Of course.'

Xandros looked at me a little like a dog at his master, and I could see his thanks were sincere enough. It was his greenness that concerned me.

Reluctantly, they got up to leave though, by the looks of the pair, they could have easily curled up on that little beach by the fire and gone to sleep right there, to the sound of singing and talking.

'Thank you for the wine,' said Teodora, offering me her hand.

'And you for your company. It was well met.' I rose gingerly, wincing as my joints groaned. There was an awkward silence as Xandros looked poised to walk away but remained rooted to the shingles. 'My grandfather, Jason…'

I raised an impatient eyebrow. 'What of him?'

'Was he… What was he like?' From the corner of my eye, I saw Phemius frown. I could almost hear him groaning. *Begone!*

I closed my eyes and took a deep breath. 'He was… a complicated man. Brave, yes, certainly… And I will say this: he set out on that voyage a boy – not so much bigger than you, in fact – a boy with much to prove. To himself as much as to others, I suspect. He returned a man, and what is this if not a lesson to us all?'

He smiled distantly, my answer barely scratching the surface of his curiosity. Phemius, meanwhile, hurried to retrieve a pair of resin-tipped torches. He lit them and handed them to the two youngsters, hoping it would prompt them to leave, no doubt.

'Farewell,' he said, as they trudged back up the slope.

Farewell, indeed, I whispered as I watched them leave.

VIII

'What you said is madness: pure madness!'

But, as they picked their way inland, Xandros could see the smile tugging at Teodora's disapproving face. 'Can't go back on it now; not after what Orpheus just said.'

'And you expect me just to appear at your every whim but you failed to show for me three times. *Three*, Xandros!'

'I did say I was sorry. There was nothing I could do. Anyway, this is different.'

'Is it? I don't see that it is.'

They walked on, swishing and crunching through the darkness. Even by torchlight, it was impossible to recognise exactly where they were. Teodora's silence was ominous. Eventually she said, 'I don't know about this. What about my mother? If my disappearance didn't hurt her, the shame of it surely would.'

'Then you could tell her. Swear her to secrecy.'

'But the *shame*!'

'The shame of doing nothing, *trying* nothing, when we have been given an opportunity. Isn't it worse? Raiders will come, someday soon; you must know this.'

She said nothing for a few minutes. All around them, the sounds of the night were clear and crisp: bats, owls and other creatures scurrying by, unseen.

'Or is it that you don't want to leave Ekhinos?'

'Xandros…'

'No, forget it. I'm sorry. It's enough you are here with me now.'

It took the better part of two hours before they were able to cross the narrowest stretch of the island and begin the descent into

Moudros. Though he was tired, Xandros insisted upon walking her all the way into the outskirts of the town. Teodora refused.

'They've started setting watches,' she said.

'For the coast, not inland.'

'I wouldn't be so sure. Anyway, I need time to think.' She handed back the torch to Xandros and kissed his cheek, leaving the familiar, fleeting scent of rosemary. 'That was an evening I won't soon forget! Thank you.' He yearned for her embrace but saw the confusion in her eyes and knew better than to say anything. Pulling her cloak about her, she set off down the slope towards the bay. Xandros watched her fade into the night, full of misgivings.

Solitude fell lightly upon him whilst he got his bearings and the island slumbered all around him. He felt charged with responsibility. Talking to Orpheus had lifted a terrible burden from his soul, one that had weighted him down for as long as he could remember.

And now he could see clearly.

The removal of one burden had made way for another, one that he was prepared to shoulder – *wanted* to – for the salvation of the island, and not a soul in Myrine knew of it.

He filled his lungs with the cool, fragrant air and set off. *Do you think she'll show?* he murmured to himself.

Would you still go if she didn't?

Red's voice was fainter and different. It was, he realised with a smile, his own.

Well?

Xandros sighed. *Yes. Yes, I would. But, Red, you're not coming.*

Teodora descended into the outskirts of Moudros lighter on her feet than she had set out, with the trace of illicit adventure still in her veins. She felt like she had learned more about Xandros in the past few hours than in all the days she had known him since the *Hephaistia*. It was not only his father he had been contending with, and his expectations: it was also himself. He had been waiting on an opportunity to discover something of himself and, in the chance encounter with Orpheus, perhaps he now had it. Perhaps she did, too.

She now heard the purr of the sea and, in a gap between houses, she could discern it, restless against the darkness of the bay. She stepped onto the harbour road and saw the figure, outside her mother's house, up-lit in the sickly glow of a lamp. Her heart thudded into her ribs and she tried to step back into the shadows of the path but he had turned to her and it was too late.

'What are you doing out so late, my dove? The watchmen are already set!'

'I'm… I…'

So suddenly, with such clarity did the decision arrive that Teodora considered running but Ekhinos had closed the gap with grace and his fingers clasped her by the arm. She could smell the wine on his breath, sour and hot.

'Are you cold? You feel cold.'

'I am fine.'

'Come to my bed, let me warm you.' He leaned to her and, for a moment, she thought he might force his lips upon her. Instead, he lifted her hair and inhaled it. 'Come to bed, my darling. Woodsmoke suits you and I'm aching to know how it got there.'

IX

Iolkos, the mainland

The king dropped upon his throne and threw down the whip. He closed his eyes whilst his breathing subsided, unaware of the looks that passed between his *lawagetas* and chief scribe. The cold porphyry cooled the sweat of his back in a way that was both gratifying and uncomfortable.

His *lawagetas* rubbed his beard – it irked him that it had not seen any pomade in weeks – and cleared his throat. 'Please be careful, my lord. I do not think that was wise.'

The king opened one eye and closed it again, rubbing the sweat from his brow. The heat in the *megaron*, with no through breeze, was stifling. 'You'd have let him off, would you?' He laughed and, realising how dry his throat was, clicked his fingers at his scribe. Whilst he fetched him a ewer of water, the king added, 'And you have designs on my throne… You have become soft. Like all of my family. All my courtiers.'

The king drained his cup noisily and wiped his mouth with the back of his wrist, making the hairs stick to it. His cousin, his last surviving kin, looked on and tried to keep the resentment from his voice. 'I am not saying I wouldn't have punished him.'

'What then?'

'I would have got someone else to do it. I think a king must distance himself from such things. People are *starving*, my lord.'

The king's eyes snapped open and he jabbed a finger at himself. 'And I am one of them!' He turned to the scribe. 'How many times? How many times has that family not paid its dues?'

'I would have to check the tablets, my lord, but I think this was the first.' The scribe quailed at the look of mounting rage on the king's face. 'Certainly not the first time it has underprovided, however.'

"There.' He settled back upon the throne. 'You see? They are taking liberties. That's what your *distance* does.'

There were raised voices from the far side of the courtyard. Something clattered upon a flagstone. The king tutted. 'See what's going on out there.'

His cousin tipped his head and clicked his fingers at a pair of guards flanking the door, leaving only the scribe hovering by his throne. 'Have you nowhere else to be?'

'Of course, my lord.' The scribe bowed and crossed the *megaron*. Because he had closed his eyes again, the king did not see the look of alarm that seized the man's face. He did not notice the scribe glance at him and then back through the entrance to the hall, making a rapid calculation, nor did he see him scurrying away through a side door, never to be seen again.

X

Iolkos, the mainland

Even though Xandros was shattered after walking almost until dawn, his mind would allow him no rest as it plotted the details of his escape. Shortly after midday, he heard his grandmother calling him. She was stood by the ancient oak tree that grew in her hall, looking out towards the sea. He always imagined what the house might have been like in its heyday, when the old woman with her back to him was in her pomp. As he entered, he could almost hear the tinkling laughter of her maids and see them reaching out over the now charred balustrade that ran around two sides of the hall, idly plucking leaves from the tree as birds fluttered in and out under the eaves. It wasn't difficult to imagine the reaction of Jason and his men, gazing about the sylvan scene when they first entered.

All was silent now: Xandros had to strain his ears even to hear the sawing of cicadas. Hypsipyle stirred when she heard him enter but did not turn.

'Join me, Xandros. Come.'

For a few moments, they gazed down at the sea. The horizon was still clear.

'Did you know,' she said, her voice as dry as baking sand, 'that we were going to kill the Argonauts after they set up camp down there?'

He looked at her in unpleasant surprise.

'Of course you didn't know.' She took a deep breath and closed her eyes. 'You wouldn't be here next to me had we succeeded. We were all standing in the square out there in the dead of night, ready to carry out what we had voted upon.' She chuckled softly and shook her head. 'None of the women who were there that day still draw breath – not one of them – except me.'

'What makes you say this now?'

She ushered him further into the hall. 'Let me give you some advice, Xandros, from a wise head to an impetuous one. It is this: never run from a problem without first looking it in the eye.'

His eyes widened and he turned cold.

'The answer is, Xandros, because you have never learned to conceal your thoughts. And because I noticed a pile of your clothes. And your spear. It looked very much like you were leaving, no? The look on your face only confirms it.'

Despite the passing of the years, and the weakening of her body, her mind remained as keen as an eagle's talon. 'Does Father know?'

She shook her head sadly. 'He is too preoccupied, Xandros, but the news would break his heart. And he would put a stop to it.'

'Will you tell him?'

'You haven't told me anything, have you?'

'No. Not yet.' He wondered why she might be willing to keep her silence but then was she not the only one not wary of Euneus? 'You said you were ready to kill Jason's men: why didn't you?'

Hypsipyle was silent for a moment. He had never seen his grandmother in such a reflective mood. 'Many reasons. I heard one of them singing to a lyre, and it was the most hauntingly beautiful thing I'd ever heard before. Or since. It made me change my mind about them; about their intentions.' She looked at him down that long, slender nose of hers with a knowing smile. 'And because we would die out, otherwise. We would never get such an opportunity again, and so it proved. At the time, it felt like that song was composed for my ears but, of course, this is fanciful nonsense. I only wished someone else in Myrine had heard it. Perhaps they had.'

'Was it Orpheus?'

Her eyes became sharp. 'Have I told you this before?'

'No.'

'Then why are you grinning at me like that?'

'Because I have met him.'

Hypsipyle tutted. 'Don't talk nonsense. You and your imagination...'

'We heard him singing, in a cove a long way from here, with another bard...'

'Enough now, Xandros...'

'Teodora and I, and he promised to help us leave—'

'Enough!'

Xandros felt his frustration brimming but then remembered the words of the very man they were arguing over. He shrugged. 'You will see, soon enough.'

The cold flash of anger in her eyes told him he would be wise to say no more on the matter. Faint from the square came the sound of a conversation and Hypsipyle glanced towards the door. 'Listen now. I wanted to give you some advice, Xandros, before I die.' She tutted as he tried to protest that this wouldn't be any time soon. 'I have lived a long life and that day will soon come.'

'Tell me, then.'

'This girl you nearly started a war over—' Not caring to hear any more about it, he began to protest. 'Are you going to *listen*?'

Her tone brought him up short and he nodded meekly.

'Good,' she said. 'I have heard some of the angry things people have said about it, some of the threats they have made. One of the benefits about reaching my age is that people think I must be deaf. I am not. Or that I have lost my wits. I have not. In fact, there is more wisdom in here than in ten generations of theirs!' She tapped the side of her temple with a crooked finger. 'So you listen to me, and listen well, because I do not say it lightly. Young Teodora is a good woman, and good women – let me tell you – are builders. No, don't give me that look. They can take a ruin and turn it into something respectable, and you are not a ruin! You have something about you, my boy, despite what your father might say.' He wondered what Euneus might have said to her in private but kept his lips straight. Not for her to glaze her words with honey. 'Do you know anything about Teodora's ancestors?'

He did because Orpheus had told him but he clenched his jaw and shook his head.

'Did you even know Teodora's mother grew up here?'

'*Here*? She was from Myrine?'

A triumphant smile crept across her lips. 'Yes, she was. Teodora's mother was born on the same day as your father.'

'We are related?' he asked in horror.

Hypsipyle rolled her eyes. 'No!' she tutted. 'Have we taught you nothing? Most of that next generation were born within a week or two of each other to those Argonauts. Nor was he just any crony of Jason's, though I must admit he looked like one when I first saw him.'

'Who was he?'

'His name was Oileus and Jason was very fond of him.' Whilst this information sank in, she added, 'So, quite apart from her qualities, you see the beauty of the threads the Fates are spinning... Don't give up on her, not for some wretch from Moudros. I can see by the look on your face that you have many questions, my boy. Ask them, then, whilst you can, though I won't promise you answers.'

Xandros' head began to swim. He wished he'd had time to think it over.

'Why does Father hate me so much?'

'Your father doesn't *hate* you.' She blinked at him in surprise. 'Don't say such a thing, Xandros, less still ever think it. I will tell you something – no, don't look away – I will tell you something that you will one day experience and only then will you know. No father who has ever gazed upon his child asleep in his arms has ever hated him. *Never*.'

She pulled her mantle tighter over her shoulders. 'This island's history is unique. Of course, every island in the Archipelagos will say so but none has such a claim to the word. Your father has never had a father – never *known* one – therefore it is hard for him to behave towards you as you want him to behave—'

'Others here have managed it!'

'But no other has also had to lead the *polis* and to lead during times of such hardship. To lead without the comfort of another to love and support him.' She sighed and looked away. 'Sometimes he locks his grief away, such that none would know of it. Sometimes, he drags it behind him like a sack of stones, Xandros. But – no – he doesn't hate you. And if you left this island, he would have nothing: nothing left but me, and my days are surely numbered.'

Xandros was silent for a moment whilst her words sank in. 'What happened to my mother must have tested him. And you.'

'Euneus loved her, it's true. But childbirth is a dangerous time – any fool knows that – especially for someone like her. She was not like some of the broodmares I once knew.'

'What was she like?'

'It was such a long time ago, Xandros.' She waved the question away. 'Different to your father. Euneus used to call her a nymph because she was at her happiest in the fields and meadows. Beautiful, too, so they say… I… such a long time ago.'

He shook his head, thinking he had misheard her. 'What do you mean by that? Did *you* not think so?'

Hypsipyle leaned back in her chair and sighed whilst a songbird trilled in the trees outside the courtyard. 'I never met her.'

'What? Never *met* her?'

'No.' She smiled sadly at his incredulous expression. 'Never. I was away from Lemnos for several years, in Nemea.'

'Why? Where is that?'

'Oh, somewhere on the mainland. I was taken there, Xandros. I was a slave.'

His face fell even further. After a few moments, he whispered, 'I don't understand.'

'I said I wouldn't promise you an answer.'

'But why?'

'I was exiled from this island by the very people I had served for so long. Whom I had protected… I spared my own father when others had lost theirs. They discovered my secret.' She quivered with some long-suppressed emotion. Anger, bitterness, sadness… all of these or none, he couldn't tell. 'Your father and Thoas, his brother, came to rescue me. I barely recognised them when I saw them again, they had grown so much. You knew he had a brother, don't you?'

'But he never mentions him.'

'No, he doesn't. Because Euneus feels responsible for his death when, if the blame must be laid somewhere, I should claim it.'

As he regarded her, Xandros had never felt so adrift. *How could he know so little about his own kin?* He swallowed hard. 'Go on.'

'Thoas died as we escaped from Nemea. He was killed. That's all I'll say on the matter, so don't push me. I raised brave sons: that's it.'

More voices rose and fell, just beyond the courtyard but Hypsipyle seemed lost in a reverie.

'I'm sorry, Grandmother. I knew nothing of any of this.' He wanted to add, *And I will never understand why.*

'I can feel you have more questions, Xandros. Ask them, then.'

'Why did Father not go to fight at Troy, when the other Hellenes came here? Why did nobody from Lemnos go?'

The words were out of his mouth before he could even think about preventing them and Xandros doubted he had ever seen her so wrong-footed. She recoiled and tutted, arching those greying eyebrows. 'You make our men sound like they were scared to go! I have told you we don't raise cowards on this island, Xandros.' Her tone scolded him. She took a deep, rasping breath and composed herself. 'Your father wanted to go off and fight but there were greater considerations closer to home. He had become king here, king of a single, slender generation of men and women, and it proved a wise decision. A small number of men went off to fight: only one returned.'

'Who? Manolis?'

'Manolis didn't fight at Troy.' She tutted. 'It was Moxos.'

Moxos! Now he understood the man's reluctance to talk about those years. 'And… what were they like, the Achaeans who came here?'

'They were just men, Xandros, men of flesh and bone, no different to you and your father. But I expect you want to know about Achilles? And Odysseus, and all the other names that everyone talks about? There were more impressive men amongst them – kind, brave men with more to lose – but nobody ever talks about them, do they?'

He didn't know whether to nod or shake his head. He did neither.

'The whole affair was a vainglorious waste of time. War often is.

Young men with their best years ahead of them lay rotting just to enrich a few greedy tyrants! *Nemesis* bit them hard and true, the fools. Listen well, then, because I will never talk of this again.'

'I'm listening.'

'Only a few of them beached their boats here, and not for long: just to fill their waterskins and take on some food. I can still see them dragging their black-hulled ships ashore one fine morning, thinking they were pirates. We all frantically armed ourselves, prepared to fight to the last, as we had done before, our hearts thumping against our ribs as we heard them trudging up the path to Myrine, singing and laughing. Odysseus was the one I remember clearest, full of mischief and swagger that he was. I can see him now, stopping at the gate and grinning at the spears and cleavers and kitchen knives all pointed at him. "I take it we missed breakfast?" That was what he said. "Can you at least spare us some water?" He was the one who put his arm around your father's shoulder, who took him for a walk along the beach that evening, filling his ears with honeyed poison about booty and slave girls and everlasting glory and who knows what else.' She waved her thin arm dismissively. 'Knowing what we do of the man, small wonder Euneus remained.'

He let Hypsipyle's words work their magic. None on that island devoured the tales of heroes more than him, and Odysseus' name was already a currency all over the Archipelagos. And he had spent time with Xandros' own father, showing him respect…

'What of Achilles?' he asked. 'Did you meet him?'

'Pffft! He left no impression on me at all, or at least nothing favourable. If you had asked me to point out then the man whose name they now sing of as if he were a god, I'd have looked at five or six others before I got to him. He was tall, I'll give you that, tall and fair but I didn't like him. Looked down his nose at us and I'd be surprised if he spoke more than a few words all the time he was here. He could sing as well as you, Xandros, but he had a companion, dark and quick-eyed, who had twice the voice. Now we all remember *him* because he was so different. He didn't look like a warrior at all.'

'Patroclus?'

'Hm?'

'His companion, Patroclus. That was his name.'

Hypsipyle swatted away a fly. 'Yes, it was.'

Xandros heard the creak from the courtyard gate, as if someone was leaning upon it. 'How long did they stay?' he asked, not wanting to be disturbed. Hypsipyle, however, looked like she was tiring of the subject.

'A few days, no more. They exchanged tokens with us, jars of honey, a few other trinkets, but then your father outdid everyone by gifting them half the island's wine, or so it seemed, and they set sail content enough. They were never seen again, though a cargo of bronze and hides arrived soon after, sent by the Atreids themselves, supposedly. But listen. Take a piece of advice from me, Xandros, and never ask that question again, not to me, not to anyone, unless they raise the matter first. The passing of a hundred winters wouldn't be enough to clear the pain of loss; take it from me.' She turned away and gazed out over the sea once more but then ruffled his hair with her cold hands. 'You're a decent young man and I know you'll listen to your grandmother.'

'I understand why father might not want to speak about the Eastern War,' he said, trying not to let his eagerness bundle tact aside. 'But I don't understand why he is so unwilling to talk about his father. Is he ashamed of Jason?'

'Ts! Ts! There's the boy, not yet a man! Look at it the other way: what is there to be proud of? Did Jason ever come back here to check on his issue? Or the mother of his children? Did any of them? And when the first songs about that… that voyage started to drift over the Archipelagos, about Jason the great adventurer, the great hero, defying the odds and avenging his own father, how do you think he was supposed to feel?' Xandros saw the flare of anger in her eyes and pictured her as a proud young queen. She clasped her hands together, as he had often seen her do when composing herself.

'All of that would be hard enough without what followed. Taking a High King's daughter for his wife – a wild *sorceress*, so men say! – and having sons with her. Upon *them* did he lavish his affections!'

This naked insight into her mind left him wide-eyed. How could he have been so short-sighted? Her words curled around his mind like smoke. Hypsipyle looked at him thoughtfully, weighing up the wisdom of what she was about to say.

'Her name was Medea. Did you know this?'

'Yes.'

'Do you know anything else about her?'

He shrugged. 'Nothing more than you have just said.'

Hypsipyle experienced a wisp of cold air breathing through the hall and pulled her shawl about her. 'She came here, years after Jason returned…'

'Medea came *here*?'

'Don't interrupt if you want to hear this. She did. She stood right there. Your father also met her, briefly. He must have been fifteen, maybe sixteen. She warned me I would lose two boys; just like she had done…'

Xandros looked on, thunderstruck.

'Your father fell from his horse when he rescued me, though he had killed the last of the pursuers. I thought I had lost my two sons within minutes of each other. So when he came round, I was overjoyed because I thought that here was proof she was wrong. Her two boys – her sons – had died, but only one of mine had.'

Judging it safe to respond now that she was quiet, Xandros said, 'And here he still is. She *was* wrong!'

Hypsipyle watched his smile fade as her expression didn't change. 'Perhaps. But soon after you were born, and by then rumours about that woman were rife, Euneus came to me, asking about her. I made the mistake of telling him what she had said and then he remembered the woman in black whom he had met. "Two of your boys," he said. "Did she say 'boys' or 'sons'?" I thought about it but her words had never really left me. "Boys". He went pale. His wife had already died in childbirth, remember? Well, here he now was worrying about losing his son as well. His *only* son. Do you see now why he has treated you the way he has? Do you see how he would surely react if he knew you had left?'

Xandros tried to dislodge the lump that had formed in his throat. How could he possibly leave, knowing this; knowing that he would compound his own damage with a harm even more irreparable? But then he considered the opportunity Orpheus had presented to him. And Teodora. If he stayed, he would be a coward. A name without a story. He would be Nobody, the grandson of a hero, who had seen the faintest glimmer of salvation and had ignored it. How could he live with that?

'Is this why Father hates Jason? Because he blames him for everything that has happened?'

'Oh, he was curious once, like you. But, after he heard about Medea, it was easy enough to persuade him that he was better off living in ignorance. You should ask yourself, my boy, why none of the praise-singers have anything good to say about Jason after his return with those wretched fleeces, do they? Or his hussy. No happy homecoming for him! Jason died an unhappy old man.'

'Did he?' Xandros asked crisply. 'I have heard nothing about his death.'

She placed her hand on his. Her skin felt cold and slack over her ancient bones. 'Forget about Jason, Xandros. Jason is dead, and all who sailed with him, save perhaps this Orpheus. Perhaps they were never real in the first place, or not in the sense the bards would have us believe.'

Her stubbornness pricked Xandros but her voice had become drier as she spoke and she looked drained. More voices filled the house now and he knew he had but a minute or two. 'I was the one who ruined our treaty with Moudros and I should be the one to make amends. There is help to be found from outside of this island, I am sure of it. If we do nothing, these sea-wolves will destroy us, island by island. Who better to unite us than the Argonauts, or their descendants: we are their own flesh and blood!'

'So *this* is why you want to leave? To find your *grandfather*?'

'And others! I want to bring men back to Lemnos, to defend it against the raiders.'

He had never seen his grandmother so surprised. He wondered whether a small ember of hope in seeing Jason still glowed – however faint – within her.

'Xandros, you are required outside.'

It was Alektruon. Xandros bit down upon his irritation and turned to walk out of the hall.

'Leave the dead in peace, Xandros. Don't provoke the Fates...'

XI

The mainland

The king had heard enough screams to know. From outside the *megaron*, somewhere in the courtyard, someone had received a mortal wound. Not in the belly – that tended to wind a man – nor the heart, for that was a quick kill. A clumsy, ragged one. He had not heard such a sound in many, many years.

The shouting intensified and another pair of guards – bare-chested, armed with spears – emerged from the little yard by his private apartments. Their grim faces quickened the king's pulse.

'Tell me what's happening out there!'

Neither of them looked at him.

The king wiped the sheen of sweat from his brow and glanced at the far wall and its faded fresco of rearing bulls, scarred by a blade strike. It made him shiver. *Had his life turned its full circle?*

A dark-haired, handsome figure peered over the gallery, yawning and stretching. He propped his arms upon the balustrade and looked down at his father. In the shadows behind him, the king noticed a slender girl – one of his servants – try to sneak past unnoticed, naked from the waist up.

'I have just had the deepest sleep. What is that *racket*?'

'You are whoring when the palace is under *attack*?'

The news wiped the grin from his son's face and he pushed himself away with a snort. He thundered down the stairs a few moments later, bare-footed, armed with a cuirass and spear, and crossed the *megaron* to unhook a shield from the wall. The crash of a heavy pot outside in the courtyard made the king flinch.

'Don't worry, Father. They'll pay for their *hubris*.'

He watched his son hurry out of the hall. He heard him yell

orders – the boy was a more natural warrior than he ever was – and the dull thump of bronze on wood.

The king paced the hallway, wondering why it was that he couldn't bring himself to approach the door and see what was happening for himself.

Never any blood on your *clothes.*

Theseus' words, in the aftermath of that short but brutal encounter with the *Cynocephali* – the 'dog heads' – often tormented him in his quiet moments. They would perhaps sting less had Theseus not gone on to make so great a name for himself but, as it was, the reckoning of such a man was a permanent stain upon the king's character. It didn't matter that there was likely nobody alive to remind him, although rumours persisted.

The slap of heavy footsteps made him freeze. One of his guards, his bare chest heaving, burst into the *megaron*.

The king was about to snap at him but composed himself. The guard was usually reliable and steadfast, and he noticed that his right arm was misted with a spray of dark blood. 'Get your breath, man, and tell me.'

'You need to barricade this hall, King Acastus. It's the people... Your people have risen up against you!'

XII

Lemnos

Xandros wavered for two days, his mind torn about leaving. On the evening of the second day after meeting Orpheus, he fell sick.

He awoke that morning with a lack of appetite but put it down to fraying nerves and apprehension. By mid-afternoon, he felt his limbs grow heavy and his whole body being dragged towards the ground. Shortly afterwards, he begun to shudder and, barely reaching the latrine in time, vomited. Whilst his stomach lurched and twinged, and between every visit to the room to gasp and spit at the bitter taste in his mouth, he cursed his predicament. He entertained visions of the galley rounding the secluded headland in the morning upon a perfect sea. Of Teodora, standing with folded arms by a pile of their possessions, waiting for him in vain. Of the brusque skipper muttering tired curses and, as the sun cleared the horizon, throwing his hands into the air and raising anchor, leaving her on the beach.

Eventually, dismissing the attentions of his father and grandmother, he dragged himself back to his bed in the early hours.

The crow of a cockerel jolted him from a deep sleep. It took him a moment to come to his senses and then he flung aside the sheets and, stumbling towards the shutters on weakened legs, pushed them aside, craning his neck around the frame to locate the sun.

The morning was a brilliant vermillion, suffused with the gold of the sun, already half risen.

Xandros clutched his hair in frustration, frozen by indecision. On a whim, he grabbed his pack and his spear, pulled on his sandals with shaking hands, trying to ignore the faint waves of nausea still swimming inside his belly. Then he crept out of his room into the hallway, flattening himself against the doorjamb when he saw Hypsipyle's handmaid pass by. He cursed under his breath but, unwilling to wait any longer, dashed across the corridor and into the empty hall.

As quietly as he could, he unlatched the door to the courtyard whilst his stomach crawled and eased the door ajar. The courtyard was cool and quiet. He crept across it and out of the front gate. The sun was three-quarters clear of the horizon now. There was nothing for it. He would have to sprint, however nauseous he felt. Gritting his teeth, he ran down the side of the village square towards the arch.

Whilst there was nobody on the winding path to the beach, he was aware of fishermen preparing their boats on the far side of the bay and, behind him, a dark-clad woman astride a mule. Word would quickly get back to his father but he felt himself being propelled headlong towards an uncertain fate.

By the time he reached the coastal road, the sun had cleared the horizon. He pumped his free arm for all he was worth but his legs seemed unable to respond. The track down to the secluded bay was still a hundred yards distant, up a gradual incline, and he felt his legs tying up completely. He wanted to yell for them to wait yet doubts also began to gnaw at him. Was his description good enough, even for an experienced skipper? What if the boat arrived the following morning, instead? Would Teodora even be there? There was scarcely a worse outcome than running away without a further word only to find that the shoreline was empty.

He was halfway up the slope now and panting hard, lungs aflame. Either side of him, cicadas had begun their sawing chorus and the sun was beginning to warm the earth. The faint sound of voices drifted to him from the cove to his left.

'*Wait!*' he shouted, but his lungs were so overworked that his voice emerged as a wheeze. Under the weight of his bag and his spear, his legs had become leaden. He would have to pause for a moment. The sun had cleared the horizon now. The breadth of a hand, Orpheus had said.

That moment had passed.

He retched violently, vomiting a bitter string of cloudy fluid. The suddenness of it made him double over and he fell upon his knees, clawing at the dusty earth in frustration and pain. When the clenching of his stomach had subsided, he staggered to his feet and shuffled onwards. The gap in the rocks that marked the start of his scramble to the shingle of the bay was in touching distance now but it was as if the sun was playing tricks upon him.

How could the sun have risen so far so suddenly?

He stumbled to the rocks, shielding his tired eyes from the light. He imagined a cloaked figure, looking up at him, tugging down his hood. There was no mistaking Red. His friend was angry. '*Waaaaait!*' he screamed.

Even from his vantage point, Xandros couldn't see anything. A little rocky promontory screened the view to the immediate north of the cove. Then he caught sight of a spar and then the mast. He jumped up and down, waving his arms frantically.

It had already raised anchor, and no amount of shouting from where Xandros was standing would ever reach it. He tugged at his damp hair in frustration. Had that boat already cleared the horizon and passed out of view, it would have been easier to accept, but to have come *this* close to meeting it after how hard he had pushed himself?

With a leaden heart, he began to scramble down to the deserted bay.

It was a treacherous descent. Xandros had never experienced the sensation of his legs quivering from being forced so hard. In the shade of the rocks, his feverish sweat soon cooled, making his tunic cling uncomfortably to his skin.

Xandros threw down his bag and spear in disgust, wiping the sweat from his brow. He glanced up at the path. Teodora had been here just once. Though she said she remembered it, how could she be sure? He fell to his knees and pounded the shingle, roaring in frustration. When his knuckles were sore, he staggered to his feet, wondering what to do for the best. Would it be possible to find Orpheus again? He had said he would know, soon enough, when Xandros returned. That being the case, he would have to wait for days – weeks – before the boat returned from wherever it was heading. And, even so, why should he expect to be given a second chance?

He kicked the beach and picked up his kit, glancing over his shoulder as he made his way back to the slope.

The galley was describing a graceful sweep as it began to turn, a couple of bowshots distant. He had to stare at it for a few moments before he could believe his eyes and then jumped up and down, waving his arms, whereupon he realised how dishevelled he looked. And smelt. He stripped off his clothes and ran into the sea, scrubbing his body with his fingers. The bracing water had a revivifying effect upon him: that and the sight of the galley – miraculously – responding to the faint call from land. He watched the prow turn to face him, scrubbed his balled-up clothes once more and waded back ashore.

Did you really believe she'd come? he asked himself.

No.

Liar.

Not for lack of effort – on her part – I'm sure.

The prow began to turn away from the beach and a pair of oars now sprouted from the gunwales, dropping into the water to bring her to a standstill. Xandros glanced back up the path and strained to hear footsteps or laboured breathing. Seeing nothing, hearing nothing, his heart sank.

'What are you fucking waiting for? You're late!' The skipper, or so he presumed, was stripped to the waist and tipped back his straw hat in annoyance. The man looked lean and sun-bronzed and hard, and the gravel in his voice suited him well. Another few men now appeared, furling the sail and then staring overboard, hands on hips.

'Wait a moment!' yelled Xandros, tugging at his hair. *'Please!'*

He ignored the incredulous looks that the crew exchanged. They would be doubly furious, that much was clear, but he was struggling to accept that Teodora hadn't come. However much he had tried to pretend otherwise, deep in his heart he had believed that the Fates had conspired to reunite them, just as they had brought them to Orpheus that same evening. And now even the boat had miraculously turned back. Could the Fates be so cruel?

Xandros looked over the water. The crew looked like they had had enough and were preparing to depart. He cupped his hands and yelled, '*Wait!*'

He picked up a large pebble and hurled it at the slope with a sharp curse then raised his kit above his head and began to wade out to meet the boat. As the water reached his waist, he began to swim with one arm, balancing his kit with the other. He looked behind him. The cove was deserted. *Why had he not gone to find her first?* He hoped she wouldn't be resentful towards him: there would be recriminations enough waiting for him in Myrine, if he ever did return.

With the sailors looking on, equally hard-faced, Xandros struggled towards the vessel. One of them peeled away and returned with a rope ladder, which he draped over the side.

'Pass me your things,' he growled at him. They were snatched from him and strong, calloused hands helped haul him aboard. Xandros could tell by the looks that passed that the men were not impressed. Doubtless they had expected a seasoned warrior, not a youth. He had barely flopped over the rail when the oars were shipped and tossed unceremoniously onto the rowing thwarts.

'Let her down!' ordered the skipper. The sailors stirred and began unfastening the brails from the cleats with practised hands.

'Thank you for turning back,' said Xandros.

The skipper didn't look at him as he checked the tiller fastenings. 'You're lucky.'

'Aye!' called the crew.

The breeze was light and the sail rippled. *Don't provoke the Fates,* his grandmother had warned him. The galley began to cleave the water.

Was his sickness an omen?

Xandros turned towards the shore, one last time. For a fleeting moment, he thought he saw a figure, watching him but it was just a trick of the shadows. He slumped against the hull, full of misgivings.

BOOK FIVE

ACROSS THE SEA

And be there no sad farewells if the sea should part for me.
An eternity is no time for me to spend alone with thee,
Amidst blessed vales and fair valleys deep; and these all trod
In graceful step by many a paired foot of nymph and god.

I

The Archipelagos

'"*Happy is the man who, before dying, has the good fortune to sail the Archipelagos*".' At the helm, the captain snorted, blotting Xandros' happy mood. He shot him a look. 'What? Haven't you ever heard that line before?'

'I've heard it.'

'And?'

The captain spat overboard. 'Whichever fool made it up had never set foot on a boat.'

'How do you know?'

'Because what sailors really say is: "Happy is the man who has the good fortune to sail the Archipelagos without getting smashed to kindling. Or sunk. Or just killed."'

The other crewmembers laughed at the skipper and turned their eyes upon Xandros. He weighed them up before answering. 'So why do you do it?'

The smiles faded. 'Because you can't live on air.'

'Unless you're the son of a king,' added the skipper with a smirk.

Xandros shook his head and looked away. 'You know nothing.'

A wave slapped the hull, sending a spume of misty brine over the gunwale.

'You hear that, lads? "We know nothing". Yet here we are, heading for the mainland on a perfect bearing.'

'You know nothing about *me*!'

As the mast creaked, an unpleasant silence settled upon the boat.

'So what is your complaint?' asked Xandros, unable to let the matter rest. 'Have you not been paid?' When they didn't answer, he added, 'Well?'

'Handsomely,' said the skipper.

'And not by my father, either,' he snapped. 'Am I right?'

One of the crew, the youngest – fair-haired and wiry – pointed to the south. 'Boat.'

They all turned to look. Faint in the rainbow dazzle of sun upon spray, a couple of miles distant, a boat shimmered on the water. The captain shaded his eyes and rolled his golden earring. It was something Xandros had noticed him doing whenever he was deep in thought. 'Black sail. Shake it out, boys!' He winked at the young lad, making him beam. 'Eagle eyes!'

Despite their coldness towards him, Xandros had to admit that they were impressive to watch when they went about their business. There was none of the cursing and shouting of the fishing craft. The galley creaked as the prow veered north, towards a string of islands.

Xandros waited until the sail was bellying and the sheets had been secured before approaching the captain.

'Sea rovers?'

He received a terse nod.

'Will we make the coast today?'

The skipper snorted in response. 'No chance, boy. We're heading for the Sporades, where we stay for the evening.'

The boat was called the *Salamander* on account of the boxwood carving fixed to the bow post. It was clear that the crew adored the vessel but, to Xandros, she looked old and heavy. The prow was sleek enough but it was the snub-nosed stern that spoiled her line. Her hold was only one-third laden with ingots and skins, earthenware jars and amphorae, which did at least mean there was some space, lined with fresh straw, to escape below deck. Xandros, however, found it nigh impossible to rest in this dark and airless cavity. The hull, perpetually creaking several feet beneath the waterline, pressed hard by the brine, threatened to spring open at any second. Almost as bad, he could swear he heard the scraping of little claws.

That evening, the *Salamander* rode at anchor in a sheltered bay in a string of rocky islands. Certainly there were other more amenable places to rest, the shipmaster said in response to Xandros' question, but there was less likelihood of encountering any pirates there, so here they were.

'Who made that lizard?'

The captain tipped back his straw hat and raised an eyebrow at him. There was something compelling about his face: a story etched into every crease and frown and scar. Though he had the decency not to comment upon his stutter, the look he shared with his crew was not kind.

'She's an amphibian.' He threw another branch onto the fire. 'And I carved it, a long time ago.'

'Why a salamander?'

'Why not? They're born survivors. They're cunning… adaptable. Hard to kill. They lose a limb, they grow one back. And, best of all, they keep to their own business.'

Xandros took the hint. It was an uncomfortable first night away from the island that had been home for his whole life but the shipmaster's word was good and they were unmolested. In his loneliness, his thoughts inevitably turned towards Teodora and his heart ached.

There was a favourable breeze the following morning and they breakfasted with bread and eggs. When the sun was at its zenith, they threaded past the island of Skiathos and the Thessalian coast on the right.

'What's the matter with you?' asked the young lookout as Xandros paced up and down the gangway. 'Do you have fleas?'

Xandros looked him up and down. 'I want to get off this boat, that's what.' He stomped over to the captain, who was at that moment in the middle of a conversation. His brows knitted at Xandros when he interrupted him.

'Why are we tacking across the water like this? You said we'd be in Iolkos this evening!'

The men exchanged knowing looks. 'Did I?' said the captain without interest, turning his gaze back over the shimmering sea.

'Yes.'

'I did not. I said we'd be in Thessaly this evening, and so we shall. We rest on Trikeri this evening and, with a fair wind, will be in Iolkos tomorrow.'

II

Xandros' heart fluttered as they drew towards the coast of Iolkos and it began to emerge like a chalky smear from the morning heat haze beneath the indigo sweep of Mount Pelion. Now that they were so close, and despite having been so impatient for this moment, Xandros wanted the captain to slow his boat down so that he could savour it.

At one point, he glanced behind him in frustration and he noticed the skipper's furrowed brow as he scanned the coastline.

'I can't wait for a swim,' murmured Xandros. 'It's stifling on here.'

'You get used to it.'

Xandros turned to the lookout, whose piping voice had begun to grate. 'How old are you?'

'I'll bet I've seen more of the world than you.'

'That wasn't what I asked.'

The boy gave him an insolent look. His eyes, Xandros noticed, were unnaturally bright.

'Glaux is thirteen.' The oldest crewman, whose beard resembled thistledown, now stood beside the boy, chewing mastic. 'And he's right: he has seen more of the world than you.'

'So have most people,' Xandros muttered. 'I presume you call him "owl" because of his sharp sight. Are you all named after birds?'

'No.'

When it became clear that he wasn't going to elaborate, Xandros looked back out over the prow whilst the captain guided them towards a jetty that looked like it might collapse under the weight of anything more than a boy and a goat. 'You did it,' he said to the captain, feeling his heart quicken. 'I'm grateful.'

'We did.'

'So why are you looking so glum?'

The captain shared a look with his crew and rasped his stubble. 'Take a look around you, boy. What do you see?'

Xandros did. 'Calm waters… Trees… No sea rovers.'

'Anything else?'

'No.' He shrugged.

'And that is the point. No boats – unless you call that upturned fishing skiff a boat. No traders. No warships. Nothing.' When Xandros looked blankly at him, he slapped the gunwales of the boat and his crew looked away. 'Were you born in a barn, lad? This place is derelict! There's nothing here!'

Xandros half raised his arm as he was about to point to somebody emerging from the town gate at that very moment but he stopped himself. It was an old herdsman and a few goats. Pretty mean-looking goats at that.

'Do you get it now? There's no trade to be done here. Whatever you feel the need to do, do it now and be done. We leave tomorrow morning.' He tossed a rope onto the jetty in disgust and one of the crew jumped up and eased the *Salamander* over until she touched the stanchions with a soft *dunk*, and it seemed a small miracle the whole assemblage didn't collapse. Xandros snatched up his kit and strode along the jetty towards the crumbling walls of Iolkos.

The prospects of help faded with every step he took, hungrily watching another pair of goats as they were led, bleating, from the gate. Xandros raised his hand at the old herdsman, whose eyes darted to the spear and widened in response.

'Good health to you, citizen.'

After a few moments, the herdsman inclined his head a little.

'Tell me please, who is the king here?'

The man's cheek twitched as if a bird had pecked at it. He clicked his tongue and carried on his way, followed by the goats. He didn't look back.

Xandros felt a stir of apprehension as he watched him rapping his goats with a reed and tried to imagine how the city might have looked in its heyday, when his grandfather first entered its walls. Fresh coats of lime plaster keyed onto the wattled walls; sagging roofs underpinned with newly hewn wood. But what most broke his spirit as he wandered the same streets as Jason had was its people. They looked thin, hungry and cowed, and they eyed him with suspicion. In Lemnos, particularly in the lower village of Myrine and the hills round about, there were some houses in which livestock occupied the ground floor whilst shepherds lived above them. Here in Iolkos, it seemed everybody lived in this way within the very walls of the city. Were they so fearful of losing cattle in raids or was it the Sea Peoples they feared?

He passed a sacred enclosure on the right in which thornbushes clambered all over the stones before passing through a cluster of tumbledown houses, from which the stench of animal dung was pungent. In a square to the left here, at least, were a few men in conversation in well-cut tunics and whose backs straightened as they saw him. From a shaded slum, he felt several pairs of fearful eyes watching him as he passed.

He rounded a bend in the dusty track and there before him, squat upon a low rise, was the palace, set back from gates that were mottled and ancient. He unhitched his waterskin and took a good glug before entering, then backtracked and peered more closely at the stones. The dark discoloration, he now saw, was dried blood. There were patches and droplets all around him, some of which had been scuffed or covered with dust. Inside a little courtyard, a pair of armed guards pushed back from the opposite gate and levelled spears at him.

'What do you want?'

Both men were tall, with tanned skin taut against the bones of their face. They seemed to Xandros on the hungry side of lean. He was about to repeat the words he had rehearsed in his head so many times on the voyage in but something stopped him.

'I need to see the king. About the troubles here, and those to come.'

They looked him up and down. 'And who are *you*?' one of them drawled, brushing a fly from his face.

'His grandson, that's who.'

'His grandson, he says! I say horseshit; you don't look nothing like him.' The grin faded and he jerked his head to the side. 'Piss off.'

'You *know* how testy he is; how quick to temper, especially when he's wronged, don't you? If he repeats what you've said, I will leave, of course. But if you're wrong…' Xandros thought of the drying blood '…especially after what happened here, it would not go well for you both. Or your families. Think on this.' Sensing them wavering, Xandros added, 'Tell him; I'll wait.'

He watched them with his heart pounding, catching the faint snort of livestock from somewhere beyond. His hopes of Jason being still alive and, somehow, *wanax* of Iolkos had vanished but he had come too far not to know who had succeeded him.

One of the men reluctantly left his post and entered the palace whilst the other glared at Xandros, far from convinced about his story. It was clear, however, that their own interests were too important.

The air suddenly tightened around him. His temples began to throb and he experienced a peculiar shifting of weight in his body that made him feel unsteady on his feet. He noticed that the animals within the courtyard beyond the gate had fallen silent. There was no barking of dogs, no birdsong.

Xandros glanced at the remaining guard and it was clear he, too, had sensed something amiss. A low grumble emanated from deep within the earth and the ground quivered for a few seconds.

'Did you feel that?'

The guard gave a curt nod. 'Yesterday the same thing happened. The gods are angry.'

Though the pressure in his head had eased, Xandros realised, even without ever setting foot in its streets, that the city was tense. He had sensed it in the looks he had received as he walked past.

The other guard returned. 'Give me your spear. He will see you briefly.'

Xandros did as he was bidden. He felt the most extraordinary sense of exhilaration walking through the courtyard towards the porch of the palace *megaron*. Here was something much grander than anything on Lemnos: Hypsipyle's house was the largest on the citadel and it would have fitted into the area they now passed, in which pigs snuffled through dried mud and straw. There was a brief conversation with the guardsmen at the porch before they were led inside. Faded frescoes ran around the hall, notably scarred on the far side, and a hearth sat at the centre of the room, bathed in a shaft of sunlight that did nothing to lift the gloom that pervaded the *megaron*, thick as a pall of smoke. Xandros tried – *yearned* – to trace something of his grandfather's presence within the hall. He could not.

A steward, armed with a sword and naked to the waist, intercepted them, nodding curtly at the guards. Over the man's shoulder to the left, seated on his throne, was the *wanax* of Iolkos. Xandros' heart sank. He glimpsed nothing of himself in his face. It was, as he had told himself, folly to expect Jason even to be alive. More than a generation had passed since the return of the Argonauts from Colchis. Had any king in the history of mankind ever ruled any land for so long?

'What is your business, boy?'

'Just bring him over,' the king tutted, beckoning with a hand that fell upon the armrest. And then he was stood before him. Thinning curls crowned his head and a beard flecked with the last vestiges of dark hair. Xandros noticed at once, set within the grey and rigid stillness of his figure, the dark eyes, distant at first but then weighing him up with the ghost of a frown.

'You are?'

'My name is Xandros, son of the *wanax* of Lemnos.'

'Lemnos…' The king's stare became intense, making Xandros' nape prickle. 'And why did you say you were my grandson?'

The look on the man's face! thought Xandros. *Did he actually believe it was possible?*

'Because the history between Iolkos and my island is a strong one, my lord.'

The king smiled sourly. 'What is *my* name, boy? Tell me.'

From the corner of his eye, Xandros could see the steward rest his hand upon his sword pommel. 'The status of king transcends his name.'

'No, I didn't think you could.' He leaned back upon his throne.

'Would you like me to remove him, my lord?' asked the king's man. 'He is a fool and a trickster, and I don't like him.'

To Xandros' great surprise, the king raised his hand. 'Look at me, boy.' Xandros had the uncomfortable feeling of those dark eyes searching deep inside his skull. After a moment or two he gave a satisfied little harrumph. 'Yes, I'm sure of it.' He turned to the steward and chuckled and his eyes glimmered. 'I know who this boy is and I suspect I know his intentions. A trickster he is not. Foolish… naïve… desperate… yes, I think he probably is but, the gods know, we need some levity here. Out with it then: amuse me. Why are you here?'

Xandros ransacked his mind: *was the man bluffing?* 'To seek help and an alliance with the people of Lemnos.'

'Help?'

'Against the Sea Peoples. Their plunder and savagery must have reached your ears? Alone, we have no chance against them. Together we do.'

'We know about them. Tell me this: why might we be remotely interested in your affairs when – if what people say is true – we must look to our own shores first? Are you offering us gold? Silver?'

'We have some, of course.'

'Galleys?'

'One or two.'

'And you have come here, all this way, alone…' The king removed some dirt from a fingernail. 'Does your island have any men?'

Xandros was about to answer but the king seemed to be suppressing a smirk. 'We have good men, yes.'

'How times change!'

A look passed between the king and his steward. A shared joke, perhaps. 'Enough. Tell me straight, boy. Your father's name. What is it?'

'Euneus.'

'*His* father?'

'Jason.'

The old man slapped the arm of the chair and grinned, revealing long teeth. 'I knew it! You have much in common with that man,' he said, drawing a circle around his eyes. 'I hated Jason. I hated him more than I thought it was possible to hate another man.' The sudden hardening of the king's face was alarming. 'I wonder if you would have dared enter these halls had you known what your grandfather did near where you stand? When he murdered a king and exiled his own mother, who was pregnant with that king's heir?'

The king slipped from his throne and circled the visitor like an ancient vulture. Xandros had always wanted to hear more about his family but had mostly been rebuffed. And now here it was. The truth of his ignorance.

'You knew none of this, did you? Xandros, son of a nobody, grandson to a traitor and a coward. Perhaps all your line is as dim-witted as was he.'

'I came here to seek an alliance against an enemy that will soon swallow us all whole.' Xandros felt anger bubbling through his fear and astonishment. 'You, whoever you are, have just spent the years harbouring spite. Well, here I am.' He let his arms fall by his sides. 'Enjoy the moment. Enjoy the insults, for all the bad taste your bitterness will leave.'

The old man threw back his head and laughed. 'This day is a gift that keeps giving! I enjoyed my moment many years ago, you whelp, when I came back here with men of my own and deposed your grandfather whilst he brooded on that very throne. Do you know *anything* about your past? Or did the praise-singers omit the part in which Acastus – this is me – returned after a few years to avenge the cowardly murder of his father, King Pelias?' He tutted as if he was ticking off an errant child. 'That *is* a shame, as it's quite the dramatic ending, wouldn't you say?'

The cold glee in the king's eyes fixed Xandros to the spot. He was once told, and he couldn't remember by whom, that knowledge is power. By that logic, he reasoned, his ignorance left him weaker than a puppy.

'*You* sailed on *Argo*?'

'Is it not obvious?'

'No. That voyage made many names famous throughout a generation: yours is not one of them.'

Acastus craned his neck forwards and bared his long teeth. 'And yet I am the last of them!'

'Forgive me, my lord, I spoke untruthfully. That voyage and *Orpheus*. Did you not know the bard still lives? He will make those names ring forever. I should know because I have heard him sing.'

The king's face was a twisted mask of confusion. In the heavy silence, Xandros could even hear the gentle hiss of the oil lamps dotted around the room.

'Orpheus,' whispered Acastus at last. He shook his head ruefully. 'And an island of no-marks; sons of bastards, sons of whores and traitors.'

'My grandfather was a hero.'

'How can you say that?' Acastus spat the question as if his mouth was full of brine. 'Your grandmother knew him for a week; a week spent on her back! I knew him for years. Jason was a traitor! His life a by-word for failure and misery!'

As if wearied by the heaving of the tide, Acastus shuffled back to the throne. He turned to an unremarkable patch of the floor, one of several sections where the stucco was flaking. 'I watched Jason's man die there, where you stand. He bled out. An unpleasant death, though also a fitting one for another traitor.'

Oileus? Xandros shuddered involuntarily. Perhaps it was at least a small mercy that Teodora wasn't present, if it was true.

Xandros caught the king glance at the wall behind him and close his eyes for a moment. The rearing bull depicted upon it had faded from red to a parched brown and the fresco was scarred by a blade strike. He would never know that the fatal blow in this exchange was still his to land.

There seemed little point remaining in the hall. The only question was whether he would be allowed to leave without a fight which, without his spear, could only end one way. In the flicker of the nearest oil lamp, having retreated inside his thoughts, the king looked lined and worn. Xandros turned to leave but one of the guards gave a little shake of the head in warning.

'Let him go,' said Acastus. His voice, dry and distant, sounded like it had aged a decade. 'He has his answer.'

The guards stepped aside and Xandros passed straight through the courtyard without looking back, never to set eyes on the palace of Iolkos again.

III

Xandros wanted to be free of the city – free of the oppressive fug of animal dung that hung over those streets, free of the dark weight of memories – as quickly as he could. It was mid-afternoon, which left the question of what to do for the rest of the day. He considered returning to the boat, though it would have been an admission of defeat. He wandered instead along the coastal path, away from the *Salamander*, which now rode at anchor, squat and impatient. Beyond it, the waters of the Gulf of Pagasae glittered as far as the horizon. It was a false serenity and he knew it. The earth tremor was a warning, he was sure: the sea-wolves were near.

He had a little to barter – glass beads, twists of copper – and ate some bread and cheese from one of the many goat herders by the waterfront. Despite the warmth of the sun on his back, he could hear the dark wings of loneliness beating in his mind.

Unwilling to succumb, he got up and dusted himself off. He considered walking as far as the slopes of Mount Pelion – he had heard the crew of the *Salamander* talking of wild hillmen, centaurs inhabiting its forested slopes – but continued instead along the path until he came to a cluster of buildings beyond a low spur. Here, too, the roofs were sagging and the plaster was in dire need of repair, exposing the innards of the wall. There being little else to do, he decided to take a look.

Little potsherds, so small it was impossible to say what they once belonged to, crunched underfoot, and Xandros had to duck beneath the bowed lintel of one room: some kind of workshop, he reckoned. A potter's wheel lay on its side. The thick drapes of cobwebs between the spokes suggested it had lain in this attitude for some time. Once-sturdy shelves ran around the room, all empty save for one, immediately above the wheel. On it sat a terracotta figurine. He lifted it down and blew the dust from it.

He wished Teodora was with him. She claimed to know the names of all the gods, great and small, ancient and new. A misshapen female, hands raised, womb swollen. The nose was a little pinch of clay and two holes made little eyes.

He left the workshops and approached a little sanctuary. Like the rest of the complex, it wore its neglect badly. Plaster had crumbled and there was more broken pottery underfoot. Xandros felt a cold breath brush his neck the moment he crossed the threshold. There were pots and cheap votive offerings and some bronze artefacts. He bent to pick up a bronze blade, dull with verdigris, which had been cleaved into two pieces.

He wondered why it had been broken in this way and set it back down. From the corner of his eye, he saw another terracotta of the goddess. Or, rather, pieces of it, since it had been broken. The beady eyes made him uneasy. 'I should go,' he whispered to himself. *The gods have long since abandoned this place.*

Outside, the haze had thickened and a brisk wind was drawing darker clouds from the direction of Mount Pelion. He walked back towards the harbour where the *Salamander* was moored but the crew was nowhere to be seen. Xandros was glad they didn't see him at that point, despondent and low.

He turned to the low promontory behind the jetty that ran into the sea, thick-screened by pines, dried needles from which crunched underfoot. Emerging the other side, Xandros stopped in his tracks. Just beyond a mouldering boatshed, a galley lay on its side.

'More ruins,' he muttered. 'Is this all there is to Thessaly?'

It was clear that the timbers below the waterline had once been black with caulking tar but only streaks of it remained, ashen grey and pockmarked. He walked around the hull and whistled in appreciation. Running his palm over the warm prow he looked into the fading eyes painted upon it by some long-absent hand.

On the starboard side, several planks had crumbled into dust, exposing the sun-bleached ribs like the carcass of some animal stripped by a buzzard. Xandros caressed the ship's sweeping stern. Here, at least, there remained some dignity, where time had been kinder to the pine and it was possible to appreciate some of the high-class workmanship.

There was a gaping hole in the hull by the stern. He clambered inside, next to the mast box, and sat astride a thwart; one of the few that had not been stripped out in years gone by. It was tilted at an angle that made it difficult not to slide along and, when he placed his palm upon it, he felt the ridges of some kind of symbol, scratched there. He peered at it but it was weathered and meant nothing to him.

He tried to imagine the faces of the fishermen or traders who had once manned her, the places they had visited and the sights they had seen. It induced an odd feeling of melancholy when he considered how little of the world he knew.

The sudden, furious, *crack, crack* against the stern made him jump in shock.

'Get out! Get out! Get out!' Between the rotten planks of the hull appeared a gnarled face, contorted in rage.

'Go easy, old man!' Xandros said, raising his arms. The wild look in the man's eyes intensified, so he sidled off the bench and stepped through the gap in the planks. 'I mean no offence nor harm.'

The old man ambled around the stern, gesticulating wildly. 'Disrespectful *wretch*! Go on, clear off!' He raised a knotted stick and Xandros thought he might strike him with it. 'Leave her in peace!'

Xandros lowered his arms slowly, palms down. 'I was only admiring her.'

'You'll break her, young idiot: she's old! Leave her and go!'

Between harangues, Xandros noticed how he muttered away to himself. Between that, his white hair and wild blue eyes, he realised that he was quite mad. Xandros couldn't help but think of Manolis back on Lemnos.

He glanced over his shoulder at the derelict boatshed. 'Did you make her?'

The stranger cocked his head to the side and looked at Xandros as if *he* was the idiot. For a few uncomfortable moments, he said nothing; just stared at him.

'I did *not*!'

Xandros decided he should take his leave. The afternoon would soon yield to evening and he was growing hungry. As he turned to walk away, the old man muttered, 'But she is mine. She will always be mine. We go back a long way.'

'I was thinking she might be as old as the Eastern War.'

'The Eastern War, he says. Pah! Older than *that*!' He squeezed the neckline of his tattered tunic, which hung off him like an old sack.

'*Older?* How old?'

'A generation older! Doesn't know he was sat in *Argo*, does he?'

Xandros wheeled upon the boat as if she had stung him. The painted eye of the prow now seemed to cut him in indignation, and it was as if the essence of a god had pervaded the ancient planks to make his nerves hum in reverence.

'*Argo*...' he whispered. He turned once more to the old stranger and there, under the rags and the slack skin, he caught a glimpse of the man beneath. 'Who *are* you?'

He stood a little taller and that sour old mouth straightened. 'You are talking to Jason, son of King Aeson.'

Manolis had proved him a gullible fool, once, with his claims to have fought at Troy. Xandros wasn't about to let that happen again: not in front of some old lunatic. 'You shouldn't mock the dead like that. Jason is long gone.'

'Yes, I suppose he is,' he said with a laugh as dry as sand. 'I suppose he is. And all that remains is the old man. And his boat.'

From the concealment of some younger pines, a woman now approached them. She had an oilcloth tucked under her arm and slowed when she drew near.

For a fleeting moment, Xandros thought she might run away, or even shout for help. The passing of the years had left her with a handsome face, full of pride, and her dark eyes were full of wariness. She approached the old man, presenting him with the bundle.

'I mean him no harm,' said Xandros.

'Didn't recognise the most famous ship that ever sailed, did he? Young vandal,' he tutted as he unwrapped the cloth. 'Is there an onion in this? I can't see the onion.'

The woman raised her chin. 'Look more carefully.'

The old man began to stuff his face with the bread and cheese as if there was nobody else around him.

'Is he your grandfather?' asked Xandros.

Her frown told him it was a ridiculous question.

'She is merely a kind soul,' the man said with his mouth full, 'taking pity on an old man, and the gods know there aren't so many of those souls anymore. Especially women.'

There followed an uncomfortable few moments, during which time the food was eaten, noisily, and the woman looked like she would rather be anywhere but there.

'Thank you, my dear,' said the old man, handing the oilcloth back with a grin. 'And next time, perhaps you might bring some wine.'

The woman took it and turned to leave.

'Wait,' said Xandros. When she turned, he added, 'Is it true? Who he claims to be?'

'Impudent *wretch*!' snarled the old man.

The question seemed to startle her, and she looked to the old man for guidance. He nodded. 'Who are you?' she asked quietly. 'Why are you asking this?'

'I am Xandros, son of King Euneus of Lemnos.'

The old man fixed him with his blue eyes. 'Lemnos? You said Lemnos?'

'I did.'

He scowled and jabbed his walking stick into the ground. 'You have a look of someone I knew there, once, but it cannot be. Queen Hypsipyle is long dead.'

'She is not. She is my grandmother.'

Mutual recognition struck them both dumb. In Xandros, the unlikely hand of Fate, which had closed two generations and many miles to the length of an arm, stirred within his heart a heady sensation of joy and disbelief, tinged with disappointment in the most unheroic figure before him.

Jason stared at Xandros and, for a moment, it looked like the shock of the moment might make him keel over. Then he gripped Xandros about the shoulders and the ears whilst he gazed into his eyes. 'Yes... Yes, I believe you may be talking truth!' He turned to the woman who had brought him food. 'You see this boy, Agata? He is my grandson! I had a boy! All those years whilst... I endured my life and suffered my misfortunes – oh, my boy, may you never suffer as have I! – all those years in which I wondered, until wondering became too late for action, what had become of my... our child.' Xandros saw that tears were gathering in those eyes which, he surmised, had long been dry. 'Tell me true. Does Hypsipyle still live?'

Xandros freed himself from Jason's cold grip. 'She does. But she has had a hard life, and that is down to you. She, too, has suffered.'

Jason blinked, unsettled by the hardening of the boy's eyes. An image of Hypsipyle's face flashed before him from many years before. She was stood resolute on a golden beach – he remembered the name now; Myrine – surrounded by her hand-picked guard and, as she removed her helmet, her eyes rooted him to the spot. Yes, the boy had inherited something of her intensity. He nodded and looked to the ground. 'I am sorry to hear this. Forgive me and, ah, my friends. I may no longer hold sway here but I have not forgotten how to treat visitors. Stay, you must stay and eat something... Perhaps share some wine.'

Xandros looked about him with a frown. 'Where do you live?'

'A village.' Jason swung his stick to the westering sun. 'Over there. Dimini. All but derelict now. I live amongst ghosts and goats.' He registered Xandros' raised eyebrows and said crisply, 'I am forgotten there and it suits my purpose. I still have more than many – you mark my words.'

Agata turned suddenly towards Iolkos and became tense.

'Is it that time already?' Jason asked with a frown. 'The *wanax*. He's setting his watchmen for the evening but he is early. Come, follow me. Useless though they are, we need to be quick. I have not been spotted here for a long time.'

Xandros heard words of faint conversation and the decision was made. Screened for the first few hundred yards by the trees, they hurried into the lengthening shadows of almond and olive groves. Xandros was surprised by the speed with which Jason moved. His legs were stick-thin but he covered the ground sure-footedly. After a couple of hundred yards, Xandros dared glance over his shoulder.

'Down!' he hissed.

Clumsily, they dropped upon the carpet of dried leaves and soil behind the twisted boughs of ancient olive trees. The concealment was poor but the half-dozen spearmen they now saw heading for the coastal paths had not seen them.

Jason turned to Agata. 'Have you seen them in these numbers before?'

'No. Something has spooked them.'

'I went to the palace this morning. Perhaps it was that.'

Jason gave Xandros a curious look. 'I see we have much to discuss. Agata, are they still there?' He turned to Xandros. 'My eyes aren't what they once were.'

Agata shook her head.

'They have gone. Let's go quickly.'

Xandros entered the crumbling walls of Dimini with a sinking heart. Everything he had seen in this region of Thessaly told him that his efforts to muster support for Lemnos were hopelessly in vain: he could only hope the same wouldn't be true of other places. Jason had told him on the way in that this was where the usurper king Pelias had once lived and where he had exiled Aeson, Xandros' great-grandfather. Whenever Dimini's heyday had been, Xandros thought, no man still living could possibly say. All around him were signs of silent decay. Forlorn mud-brick houses, with roofs as bare as *Argo*'s hull or, at best, sagging badly. A well with a leather bucket covered in dust. The distant bleat of goats. It made him shudder: by comparison, Myrine looked like it was thriving. It made him a little homesick.

They approached the hall in the centre of the settlement. Jason prodded the doors with his stick and they creaked open. The shutters were closed and had contained the dry, musty smell into which they now walked. Bars of early evening sun lit motes of dust swirling around the hearthstones, old storage jars and a battered chest. At the far end of the *megaron*, two doors led to bedchambers and another to an anteroom. It was hard for Xandros to believe that once powerful rulers resided here.

Jason whispered a few words to Agata and she bustled away, leaving Xandros to wonder once more at what drew them together.

'Bring those over, please,' said Jason, pointing to some stools piled in the corner of the room. 'Sit.' He eased himself onto a stone ledge, with a scooped seat, set against the left-hand wall. It was so undistinguished that it took Xandros a moment to realise it passed for the throne of Dimini. Jason straightened his back with a grimace and rested his hands – one atop the other – upon the handle of his stick. He beheld Jason through the dusty light: the king of a time-forgotten village.

IV

The food was basic but welcome – cured meat, artichokes and bread dipped in low-grade olive oil – but Xandros barely registered its taste as he sat, enraptured by Jason's tale of his voyage to Colchis and back. He fired a salvo of questions at his grandfather but he was still thirsting for more when he realised that Jason's eyelids had grown heavy.

'Enough, now. My throat is dry and you have told me nothing. Give me some wine whilst you speak.'

Xandros talked of life on Lemnos and the hardscrabble existence when crops had failed. He talked of Hypsipyle's slavery – Jason shook his head solemnly at this – and the subsequent feud with Moudros. For much of the time that Xandros spoke, Jason's eyes were closed and, whenever he hesitated in case he had fallen asleep, Jason would murmur at him to continue. When he had finished, Jason's eyes blinked open and he gestured at Agata impatiently for the last of the wine.

'And now,' he said after taking a sip, 'you will tell me why you are here.'

There was an abruptness about the question that wrong-footed Xandros. 'I came to the mainland for help. These pirates, the Sea Peoples, have been circling Lemnos and will soon drag their boats ashore—'

'A worry for every town and village—'

'Yes, and they are all working alone! Cowering away, like beaten dogs!' Jason raised an eyebrow at Xandros' testy interruption. 'This morning, in Iolkos, in every house we saw, people had brought their livestock to shelter. Against what: the rain? There were more goats than people within the walls. How can any *polis* protect itself against an enemy like that? A *united* enemy?'

Jason cocked his head to the side. 'Go on.' From the tail of his eye, Xandros saw Agata watching him closely as his voice became impassioned.

'It seems to me there's only one answer. To beat them by the very thing they are doing. We must unite, too!'

Jason's fingers drummed upon his walking stick. 'Unity indeed… Did you know there was an uprising in Iolkos, just a matter of days ago?'

Xandros recalled the dried blood by the entrance to the palace. 'No.'

'A lot of people died hereabouts, women and children, not just men. They say Acastus' own son numbered amongst them.'

'Did you witness it?'

'It occurred during the day: I tend not to visit *Argo* during the day.'

'And today?'

'I saw your ship coming in; I was curious. But listen,' he said, raising a bony finger. 'It is not just raiders that kings of cities are fearing, a threat from some distant sea. It is their own people. There is change in the air, Xandros, the likes of which man has never seen before. Fighting is easy enough – any fool can do that – but *knowing* who your enemy is… Now that, my boy, is a true skill.' A slow smile spread across Jason's lips. 'So… Why are you *here*?'

'People say the Age of Heroes has passed but I do not think they are right. Not yet. There are heroes who still live and breathe; who can inspire other men to come together and copy them. That can provide light in an age of darkness.' Xandros held Jason with an unwavering gaze. 'And one of them is my grandfather.'

The room became still and expectant for a moment. Outside, animals snuffled through the dust and long-discarded refuse. Jason clapped his hands suddenly. 'A fine speech, young man! One I would have been proud of in my day.' He leaned forwards and rapped his stick on the ground. 'But my day has passed, Xandros, and I am old. I am sorry.'

'Orpheus said you might be like this.'

Jason's face twitched. 'Orpheus?'

'Orpheus. He, for one, is still alive and well.'

'You spoke with Orpheus?' Jason's laughter was like the flexing of toughened leather. 'Are you mocking me?'

Xandros described their chance meeting with the bard and the practical help he had offered, hoping it might shame Jason into action. 'I am truly happy that he still lives. Perhaps one day the bards will cherish his name as they must surely forget mine.'

Xandros sagged in deflation. 'Are you afraid of seeing Hypsipyle again?'

Jason chuckled and wagged a bony finger at him. 'Of course I am, as should you be. A fearsome lady still, no doubt. But, no, and don't you try to rile me to get me to change my mind. It is my fate to die here.'

Whilst Jason had spoken animatedly of his adventures with the Argonauts, Xandros could glimpse the hero within, but the downturned mouth was that of a morose old man. He stood, not wanting this to be the abiding memory.

'Did I say I wouldn't help?'

Xandros dropped back onto the stool. 'No.'

'Twenty years ago, I would have joined you.' He settled back upon his throne. 'Twenty years ago, I would have happily… taken advantage of any reason to leave the mainland and throw myself into something – anything – that might have spared me my own company. My own thoughts. But look at me now. I must seem twenty years older than I am, and this is why you will find no mirrors in these rooms. Life has aged me badly. I can feel it well enough but have no wish to *see* it!'

A heavy silence settled upon the *megaron*. Xandros was about to ask him to explain but Jason stirred. 'I was born in the palace of Iolkos, where you have been, on the very day Pelias, my father's own half-brother, invaded it and deposed him. By some… extraordinary trick, or moment of luck, I was spared death only because they thought I was already dead: a still-born. And in that palace, after I returned with two golden fleeces, I had my revenge.

With these very hands, I ran Pelias through and skewered him to the wall.'

Now in the flow of his story, there was something gleeful about the way he said it, and his hands and fingers became rigid as he spoke. It seemed to Xandros that he had revisited that story in his head every day of his life. An image of the deep scar in the frescoed wall entered his mind. He wondered why Acastus had not ordered it filled with fresh plaster.

'In *these* halls, over in one of those rooms, I first laid eyes on my father and mother. Twenty years after my birth. *Twenty!* Can you believe that?'

Xandros wanted to ask: *Had he not been listening when I told him I had never even seen my mother?* His lips twitched but he said nothing.

'And in this very hall, perhaps where you are sat now, my father, King Aeson, fell, slain by Pelias' men.' Xandros glanced at the floor, as if he might yet see traces of his lifeblood. 'So you see, my place is here.'

Agata had slipped from the hall and now returned with a cup of water. Whilst Jason drank, Xandros asked, 'And have you never left Iolkos? I mean, since you returned from Colchis?'

The cup froze at his lips and he lowered it wearily. 'I have.'

To Xandros' surprise, Agata flashed him a look of warning and a shake of the head so faint he might have missed it.

Jason's voice rumbled as if speaking was physically painful. 'I have, and here is another reason against me following you to Lemnos. It pleases me more than you could know to hear about my son reaching manhood, though it grieves me equally to know I lost another son I never knew.' He shook his head sadly. 'Truly, I am cursed. Thoas was not the only son I have lost.' When he looked up, Xandros saw his eyes were swimming in tears. 'Many years ago… my two sons were taken from me. No, say it right… they were murdered. In cold blood. Never a day passes without me regretting I had no chance to say goodbye; to tell them how much they were loved. I was too preoccupied, you see. I looked up and smiled at them as they waved to me and then I looked back down to the document some… worthless scribe had given to me, as if this were more important. As if being heir to the throne of Corinth was more important than my own flesh and blood!' Through the gauzy light of late evening, he appeared to have turned to stone.

'I never saw my boys again. Medea… time was when I swore never to utter her name again because to do so would be to breathe life into her… Medea fled Corinth the day their bodies were found and, naturally enough, she was blamed for their deaths. That she poisoned my betrothed… Well, I don't doubt that but killing our boys as well… No, I think not. We both loved them so dearly. But she laid a bitter curse upon me before she left.'

'Come to Lemnos then, Grandfather. You have a son who still lives!'

'No. I would only disappoint him. It is enough to know I raised a king. I will outlive her… "She who hurts from afar"… Yes, those are the first words we all heard about her, whilst we were travelling to Colchis. Her curse worked but she won't outlive me. Those spiteful gods must grant me that, at least.' Jason's words settled upon the hall like black snow, muting sound and light.

'With every moment you spend alone with your sadness, Medea's curse prevails. Don't you see this?'

Jason stirred but didn't answer.

'Do you believe in the gods, Grandfather? This is the first time you have mentioned them.'

'Pah!' He brushed the question aside. 'They and I have a history that I will not explore. Vindictive! Agata, you know what you must do?'

Unspoken words crossed between her and Jason. Then she bowed slightly and pushed aside the curtains of one of the rooms adjoining the *megaron*.

'You will have your hands full, you and your crew.'

'I know. We sail tomorrow.'

Jason gave an enigmatic grin when Agata returned, struggling under a large bundle. Xandros bounded over to her. 'Let me help you with that.'

'There is more,' said Jason, nodding at Agata. *'Leave it!'* he snapped as Xandros dropped the bundle and reached for it. 'Wait a moment.'

Xandros gaped at what Agata held in her outstretched hands. 'Go on, take it!' Xandros took the sword from her as if he were handling a new-born, twisting it this way and that in one of the shafts of evening light.

Jason tutted. 'Not much use *in* its scabbard, is it? Nearly one hundred years old and not a speck of verdigris. Go on, take it out! The nicks are all my own. It belonged to my father and now it belongs to you but you must earn the right to keep it. That's what I was told once, or something like it...'

Xandros felt an unfamiliar lump in his throat. Gifts – especially ones of such value – were not something he was used to. 'I don't know what to say,' he murmured, sliding it from its sheath. Jason was right: the blade was clean and oiled. Well hafted, too.

Jason uncurled a finger towards the bundle and took a deep breath. 'Now you may open it.'

Xandros felt like he was being buffeted along a river in sudden spate as he untied the leather thongs holding the bundle together. The first unleashed a foul smell of musty air but then the other fastenings slipped free, revealing the contents. He stepped backwards in reverence. The fleece glinted dully, significant but jaded, like the very hall in which they now stood.

'Can I...?' asked Xandros, leaning over it tentatively, as if it might come to life and bite him.

Mesmerised by the fleece, for a moment Jason didn't reply. Then he gestured vaguely towards it. Xandros touched it with the back of his hand. It was matted and cold.

'You must take it with you,' said Jason. 'No, you must. What good would it do here, mouldering and harbouring cobwebs? It would soon be stolen.' He clasped his hand atop the handle of his stick and became pensive. 'I cannot promise you any good will come of your travels, Xandros. I have not seen any of the Argonauts in many years. I don't know what men they lead. Meleager was the last to visit me: Meleager, *wanax* of Calydon. He is a good man – a virtuous man and one of the finest warriors we had. But that was...'

He blew the air from his cheeks. 'Five… six years ago, and age had caught up with him even then.'

Jason fell quiet again and stared into the distance, seeing things only he could see. 'Use the fleece wisely, my boy. Use it to rally men, as you see fit. But always respect the distance it has travelled and its history and the blood that was shed to fetch it.'

'I will. I will guard it with my life!'

Jason's eyes glimmered in the encroaching shadows. 'Then I am right to pass it on. One more thing, before you go. Agata?'

The woman obediently went off to the same room and returned with a smaller oilcloth. 'You have my sword and the fleece, Xandros, but these alone won't sway people. Open it!'

Xandros carefully unwrapped the bundle. Shapeless nuggets of gold, the size of his little finger's pad, made him gasp. 'I have more but must hold some back. Yes, well might you look at me with surprise! Some day you will learn not to judge a man on appearance alone! My life has not been lived entirely in penury and how else do you think I retain Agata's services, hm? She has a good heart but even the kindest of hearts would not tolerate my ways without something to mollify it. Go, now, Xandros. I am tired. If I am to ensure I see you before your ship leaves, I must rest. Tomorrow, I will have more practical help for you but I must think on it.'

Xandros slung the sword over his shoulder and gathered up the fleece, tying the thongs tight. Jason stood gingerly and raised his stick as they left the hall. 'Until tomorrow, then!'

'Until tomorrow.' Agata left with him carrying an oil lamp before gently closing the doors behind her and bustling across the courtyard towards the one house, through whose shutters glowed faint bars of light. She did not look back.

Xandros left in pensive silence. It wasn't until he reached the gates of Dimini that he wondered, curious rather than resentful, why his grandfather hadn't offered him a place to stay for the night. Especially after gifting him a sword, fleece and gold.

Just outside the gate, he stopped in his tracks. He had wanted to tell Jason that his friend Oileus lived on, after a fashion, in Teodora. It suddenly felt important to him; a gift of his own that would surely make him smile.

Xandros hurried back through the gate towards the old palace. He deposited his bundle and opened the doors carefully, so as not to startle Jason. Most of the oil lamps were still aglow but the throne was empty. Xandros was about to call his grandfather's name when he heard a snuffling noise, coming from one of the rooms on the far side of the *megaron*. He approached it, more cautiously now. As he was halfway across, he heard a muffled sob, and a sense of growing guilt made him hesitate.

Was there another reason Jason wanted him to leave so abruptly?

He was about to turn back but, strident through the sobs, came an anguished cry. Xandros continued towards the door, from where faint lamplight flickered. He peered around the doorpost. Jason was hunched on his knees, rocking backwards and forwards. His straggling hair had been pulled wild and he looked like a wretched beggar. Then he noticed that he was clutching something in his hands. Obscured by Jason's swaying body, it took him a few moments to make it out. Some kind of wooden sculpture… A horse on wheels… A child's toy.

There was other bric-a-brac laid out on the floor, just beyond the fringes of lamplight. As Xandros' eyes adjusted to the gloom, he could discern a leather ball and a little sword.

He had seen enough. He regretted having returned and crept back across the hall towards the door, closing it silently behind him, leaving Jason to his solitude and grief.

V

Orpheus

Xandros would later confide that this had been the most heart-wrenching scene of his short life. Such is the eagerness, however, with which the young grasp at superlatives, he would soon revise his opinion. The road to Hades is cobbled with the best of this, the worst of that but, in the end, these are just projections of the same pleasures we all experience. Or pains.

Our eye must turn at this juncture back to Myrine in Lemnos. It was perhaps for the good that Xandros was ignorant of events here.

Lemnos

'*Send him away!*' hissed Euneus through gritted teeth.

'You need to drink this, my lord.' The physician tried to introduce the infusion to Euneus, propped against the pillows, but he shoved it away, causing most of it to spill over the physician's tunic.

'He is trying to *help* you!' protested Hypsipyle. 'He has come a long way!'

'With *poison*?' Euneus wiped his forehead with hands that shook, plastering the hair to his wrist with his sweat.

Stood around his bed was the council: Khalkeus, Alektruon, Hektor. Euneus had been in the grip of a fever for two days and, beforehand, had grumbled about aches and pains that kept him awake at night.

He grasped Hektor by the forearm. 'Tell no one of this!'

Though the wild look in the king's eyes alarmed him, and although Hektor summoned his usual unflappable calm and inclined his head, his bushy moustache twitched in concern.

By late afternoon of that same day, a man dismounted from his horse and walked it through the heat that shimmered from the rocks by the coastal road to Moudros. He was sweating freely and had drained the last drop from his waterskin some time before. Both he and his horse were parched. He wafted aside the flies that buzzed around his mount's chestnut flanks and scratched his forehead in agitation where the straw of his hat had been rubbing it.

The scatter of houses he passed were shuttered against the heat that made the faded paint curl from the slats, but he sensed he was being watched by suspicious eyes. Everyone knew everyone else in Moudros and the latest arrival was not a local; that much was clear. Eventually he crossed paths with a boy returning – empty-handed – from the sea. His little net was empty and, at the end of his line, the bait remained transfixed on its thorn.

'House of the nomarch?'

The boy was bare-footed and raised each leg as the baking earth burnt his skin. 'Over there, mister.'

The stranger followed the line of his finger and grunted at him.

The nomarch's house was set back from the main path and framed by two tamarisks. On its two sides, fragrant pines separated it from other houses, giving it a sense of grandeur and privacy. He hadn't even reached the door before he was intercepted by a pair of burly stewards, who eyed him with suspicion.

The stranger was too shattered to care. 'A message for the nomarch. An urgent one.'

The stewards nodded after looking him up and down for weapons. They took the reins from the horse and tried to chivvy it along but it would not budge. 'He needs water,' said the stranger. 'As I need wine.'

The ill manners of the nomarch, Plouteos, and his haughty son irked the messenger. As they hovered about him in the shaded courtyard, he tried to ignore them whilst he dipped his bread in olive oil and washed it down with water, taking his time. He could feel their impatience emanating towards him so he chased the last few crumbs around his plate with his forefinger and sucked it.

'Delicious,' he said, brushing his hands. 'And now maybe some wine?'

'You said your message was urgent. Nothing about you suggests urgency.'

'I have travelled a long way, in some haste. Would you have me melt here, in your lovely courtyard, before I've even delivered it, yes?' The looks he received made him smile inwardly. 'Very well, to business. The *wanax* of Myrine, Euneus son of Jason, is gravely ill. Some say that the fever, as serious as it is, masks something deadlier still. If one doesn't see him off, the other surely will. That is my message.'

Plouteos worked his jaw up and down whilst his mind raced.

'Father, this changes things! Surely now is the time to act. Surely...' Ekhinos' voice tailed off as his father raised his hand.

'For how long has he been sick?'

The messenger shrugged and scratched his paunch. 'With fever, a couple of days. But, as I said, the other disease – whatever it is – who knows? I know him better than most and hadn't seen any obvious signs.' He thought about it for a few moments. 'Except he has become thinner.'

Plouteos gave him an intense look. The messenger had a lazy eye; both were bloodshot and his face was a florid red. The man was a habitual drunkard – that much was clear. Such people made unreliable witnesses. 'And what of his son? Any news of him?'

'And my Teodora? Some say they left together.'

From the corner of his eye, the messenger saw the anguish on Ekhinos' face. Myrine had been thrown into turmoil when Xandros disappeared. Some said that it was responsible for the steep decline in Euneus' health.

'No,' said the messenger, rubbing his closely shorn head. 'No news. But as for the girl… Impossible.'

'What do you mean?'

'Impossible she left with him, is what I mean. She is in Myrine!'

'Myrine?'

'Yes, she arrived in a bit of a state, I recall. Split lip and a bruised face. We thought she might have been set upon by bandits.' He shrugged. 'But then she probably wouldn't be alive, would she? My lips are suddenly very dry… perhaps some wine now?'

The look on the boy's face was very gratifying but the messenger's pleasure in seeing it was fleeting. In correcting the rumour, he realised he had likely brought Moudros and Myrine nose to nose once more. He cursed his idiocy. *Worthless pig,* he thought. *Dull-witted drunkard.* Euneus was right.

'Father, surely we must act *now*?'

Plouteos turned sharp eyes on his son. *There will be stern words after I have gone,* thought the messenger. He had taken an instant dislike to the boy the moment he had clapped eyes upon him. *What had the handsome brat ever known of hardship?*

'I will summon the council. The moment there is a change in his condition, for better or worse, you must return. Understood?' The messenger nodded, tugging at the loose skin of his throat. Plouteos noticed the gesture and added sourly, 'My stewards will give you the wine on your way out. I hope your panniers are empty.'

VI

Iolkos

The sinking sun had set the sky ablaze and, by the time Xandros returned to the *Salamander*, the sea glowed like molten bronze.

He heard the crew before he saw them. Despite their cool attitude towards him, he was glad for their laughter and crude talk. When Xandros appeared, sheened in sweat with the effort of bearing the fleece on one shoulder, they fell silent. In their midst, a small fire spat and hissed as droplets of fat from a skewered rabbit fell upon it. 'What is that?' asked the skipper, chewing a piece of straw.

'Spare bedding.'

'Bedding, right. And a new blade? Now where did you find that?'

'It's not new.' He lowered his voice. 'And I stole it.'

The captain stopped chewing and gave him a look. 'You *stole* it?'

Xandros shrugged. 'I only had a spear and now I have a sword.'

The captain narrowed his eyes at him then grinned and turned to the other crew. 'Y'hear this? The boy's light-fingered! Who'd have believed it? I could get to like this princeling but, gods above, boy, you'll have the whole town descend upon us.'

The eldest sailor cackled and plunged a knife into the rabbit. 'Have a piece.'

Xandros dropped the fleece and sword in the encroaching shadows and approached the fire, but stumbled to the side as he became suddenly dizzy.

The captain tutted. 'What's the matter with you?'

The sea came to life. From being calm one second, the next it began to heave, and the *Salamander* thumped against the jetty. Breakers curled and seethed a pebble's toss from the campfire.

Xandros dropped to one knee alongside Glaux. The young lookout cried out, 'It's happening again!'

The earth began to quiver and even the captain looked alarmed. The trembling became more violent and there was a faint moan from deep within the earth. A clay lamp rattled across the rock upon which it was perched and shattered upon the pebbles of the beach, snuffing the little flame. The sailors fell to their hands and knees, swearing and groaning and babbling incoherent prayers to Poseidon. Xandros scrambled clear of the campfire and gazed at the walls of Iolkos. He was not surprised to see women and children come sprinting clear and, in their wake, goats and sheep, scuttling through the gates with bleats of confusion and fear.

He felt a peculiar tension in the air but, this time, understood that it was not the earthquake: he had felt it in the heavy stares of the Iolkans earlier in the day. Violence.

There was a muffled crack from the city, like a tree being wrenched from its roots, followed by raised voices and a scream.

Glaux' voice broke as he asked, 'Shall we help?' Gone, Xandros noticed, was his youthful bravado.

'No!' snapped the captain. 'Stay put!'

Xandros' eyes returned to Iolkos. Deep in his gut he had a sense of something imminent and dreadful awakening, and at that very moment a tongue of flame flickered above the city walls. He scrambled to his feet, ignoring the chorus of shouting, drawn to the city as if she was a nymph whispering to him. Dashing low on unsteady feet, he made it to the gates in brief minutes. At least two buildings were ablaze now and hungry flames crackled over the tinder-dry buildings. He stepped aside as a train of panic-stricken townsmen bolted for the safety of the backshore. One of them dragged a handcart, piled high with personal effects that clattered under a blanket.

'Get out!' someone shouted but Xandros didn't know, or care, who it was meant for. He plunged into the main thoroughfare, grasping at a *stele* in the sacred enclosure to keep his balance as another rumble shook the earth, turning his legs to jelly. Ahead, he saw figures screaming at the stricken buildings; yelling for those trapped or missing or consumed by the spreading flames,

he couldn't tell. When the tremor faded, he pressed on, grim-faced, through the terrified bystanders as if through a waking nightmare.

As he passed, he felt a strong tug at his tunic and on instinct he batted the hands away, regretting it at once. A young woman, her dirty face streaked by tears, implored him to help. He saw her lips forming words but the sound was drowned out in the tumult. He turned to the doorway of the house opposite, the lintel of which had sheared, dragging the upper floor with it. He saw – or thought he saw – a pale silhouette in the window, arms raised. He took a step towards the doorway but a violent tremor buckled his knees and he had to scramble backwards as the building gave way in a hideous crack and thump of tumbling wood and masonry that unleashed a choking gale of dust and smoke.

Xandros got to his feet, retching from the depths of his lungs, holding his breath as he blundered through the debris, bumping from one fleeing citizen into another. Then he was clear of the cloud and blinking hard, filling his lungs through the filter of his tunic's hem. When his chest stopped heaving, he looked about him for souls easier to save, driven by some ancient impulse to do something – anything – for the city once ruled by his grandfather Jason.

Through the ash and dust, he barely recognised where he was. To his right, smoke plumed over the rooftops of houses and workshops and, amidst the rising rumble of flames, he could hear coughing and screaming. He dashed to the nearest door and kicked it open with the flat of his sandals.

'Get out! *Get out now!*'

He didn't wait for a response, sensing the impossible weight of the overhanging eaves and imagining them crashing down upon his skull. The adjacent door was already torn from its hinges but, when he kicked open the next a few yards further on – it took several powerful stamps – two spluttering forms fell to their knees. Flames were already consuming a rear wall and, in the billowing smoke, it was clear they had failed to locate the door. He dragged them over the threshold and across the street, and it was only in the faint glow that he saw their contorted faces. The woman was struggling to say something whilst her chest convulsed, pointing back at her house with a trembling hand.

'*What?* What is it?' demanded Xandros. 'Your children?'

Without waiting for an answer, Xandros covered his mouth once more and darted back, encountering a shifting wall of acrid smoke. He caught the pungent whiff of olive oil and burnt animal hair, and that was enough. He glanced back over his shoulder as he rounded the corner, his mouth parched and thick with the foul stench. When he tried to hawk the taste from his mouth, he found he had no saliva and that his search for life had now become a feral craving for water. A knot of men barred the street and he stopped in surprise, blinking hard and shielding his eyes. It was clear by the way they froze that he had disturbed something sinister.

'Get away from here!'

At first, he thought they were guardsmen from the palace but what he had taken to be a spear was a shepherd's staff, and their clothes were homespun and crude.

A tall man, with his face wrapped in a cloth, stepped towards him. He hefted a club onto his shoulder and pointed back down the thoroughfare. '*Go*, man! You've no business here!' Serf or not, his voice carried authority and no mere hint of violence.

They were joined by a few others, emerging from the dilapidated building he had seen earlier in the day. They were all lean and gaunt. Two brandished old blades, rapier-thin. He had not seen the like in many years.

Xandros took a step backwards. He glimpsed, silhouetted against the red sky, the contours of the palace. He knew with absolute clarity what was about to happen and was only glad that the bitter old king Acastus had allowed him to leave. He turned and hurried back down the street.

The seafront was alive with scores of Iolkans, huddled together, tending to forms, lain out on the backshore, some wailing, some talking in low, urgent voices around fires. Skittering through them, goats, sheep and even a pig. As he staggered through the gates, Xandros picked his way towards the jetty and, when his feet encountered yielding sand, he stumbled. He heard a loud cry that he recognised – Glaux' voice was as shrill as his eyes were sharp – and he homed in upon it. The sailors were stood around the fire with weapons drawn and the captain had his hands upon his hips. Xandros collapsed to his knees, coughing and croaking.

'Get him some water!' hissed the captain.

Xandros groped for the waterskin as it came near him but then a hand clamped his wrist. 'Gargle first. Don't swallow, yes?'

The advice was good. Once he had cleared his mouth, he tried to drink but, feeling the contents of his stomach rise, he dropped the skin, ran towards the sea and vomited a black torrent.

'Mad little bastard.' But he was sure the captain had a grin upon his face.

VII

Xandros awoke at dawn from a fitful sleep, tormented by images of death and destruction, with his throat raw and smoke in his nostrils. He jerked upright. The captain was worrying his teeth with a frayed twig, talking quietly to the bearded sailor, and he glanced over at Xandros as he woke before resuming his conversation. Beyond them, a pink sun rose above the waters of the Gulf of Pagasae. Xandros became aware of other forms stirring along the beach.

'There were scavengers in the night. They came near.'

Xandros turned to see Glaux with a short sword, tracing a figure of eight with its tip. 'I stayed awake to keep them away.'

'There's duty…'

'We thought you'd died.'

Xandros swilled his mouth with water and turned aside to spit it out, relieved to see it was more or less clear of dirt. 'Still alive, I'm afraid.'

'Why did you go inside?'

'To help people.' He frowned. 'Why else?'

'But you didn't know them!'

Xandros was about to tell him to keep his own business but, in the boy's mind, the logic was irrefutable. 'No, I didn't know them.'

'You are a crazy bastard.'

'Maybe *you* should wash out your mouth.'

'That's what he kept saying.' Glaux pointed to the skipper. '"*Mad, crazy little bastard*", like that.'

The captain had finished his conversation and now walked over. 'Eat up, ladies. We're sailing.'

They rolled up their tents and ate some bread and water in the shade of the pine trees. The morning was already growing warm and the early haze had soon melted. Xandros went for a swim to clear the filth from his body, and scrubbed his tunic on a rock. Only then did he feel ready to look back at Iolkos.

A cloud of smoke drifted over the smouldering town. A faint but insistent voice told him he had to see the aftermath and, before the crew could object, he was halfway to the gates. He slowed as he approached and stepped inside. The ash lay thick within, like a coating of winter leaves, and there was scarcely a building left with a roof. What the tremors hadn't levelled, the fires had reduced to a few stubborn, charred walls. Save for a few scavengers clambering over the rubble and hauling out pathetic trinkets, Iolkos lay forlorn and derelict; a ghost town.

Xandros crunched along the thoroughfare, filled with melancholy. He passed the house whose lintel had sheared and nearly collapsed upon him; now a formless heap of masonry and timber. He clambered a few metres up but the stones were hot and an evil stench drifted through the fissures and cavities that any man who had ever attended a cremation would recognise. He had seen what he came for and scrambled back down, keen to leave the town for good.

He only needed a glimpse to confirm it. Parts of the palace were still ablaze.

The crew had nearly loaded up and, though they said nothing, he could tell by the set of their faces that they were annoyed with him. He threw his possessions over the gunwales, reminding himself to kick the rolled-up fleece under a thwart, where it would draw less attention.

He went to retrieve his weapons, concerned that there was no sign of Jason. He considered pleading with the captain to delay departure for a few hours so he could hurry to Dimini to see what might have happened to him. Visions of the old man lying half crushed under a roof beam as he still clutched his children's toys began to torment him, to the point he was convinced that this was indeed his fate.

'And that?' snapped the captain. He clicked his fingers and pointed to a discarded bag. 'Whose is it?'

Glaux jumped overboard and hurried along the jetty, and Xandros willed him to walk in order to buy him a few extra moments. The lookout returned with a sheepish look on his face.

'Cast off!'

Xandros' heart began to thump and he felt panic rising in his stomach. One of the crew, a quiet man with a felt cap and green eyes, began to untie the hawsers. Xandros grasped the gunwales until his knuckles turned white, straining his eyes towards Dimini. The tall pines screened his view. Through a single gap in the canopy, he could just discern the track that led towards the almond and olive groves. It was clear.

The deckhand tossed the first rope aboard and made his way to the last, scratching the skin beneath the waist of his kilt, and the man's ignorance of Xandros' plight made him slap the rail in frustration. Glaux, curious, watched him stalk away.

'Who's that wretch?'

It took a moment for Xandros to realise that the skipper was talking to him. He glanced back and saw that he was staring towards the shore, where a wild-haired figure was leaning upon his stick. Xandros was about to exclaim, *It's Jason!* before thinking better of it.

He clambered onto the wharf and went to meet him, ignoring the volley of curses behind him.

'Didn't think I'd make it, did you, boy?'

'I'm glad to see you! I had visions of you crushed by the earthquake. Is the house still standing?'

Jason's face cracked into a grin. 'It is, along with much of Dimini! The gods have a sense of humour.'

'Iolkos is a ruin. I went to help…'

'But?'

'I've seen nothing like it and there was nothing I could do. I met a group of men – armed, angry – who told me to turn back. I think they fired the palace.'

Jason muttered something incoherent, adding sourly: 'No way to die.'

His attitude surprised Xandros but then it dawned upon him that Acastus' life was a double-edged sword. Jason hated Acastus, but hating gave him an incentive to outlive him.

'Get a move on, boy!'

From the corner of his eye, Xandros saw the captain with his hands on his hips.

'I must go. I wanted to thank you, properly, for your generosity. I…'

Jason shook his head. 'Never mind that. I gave your words some thought, so listen well. I have already mentioned Meleager, but Calydon is a long way from here. Instead, you should travel to Athens. My memory is not what it once was but a name occurred to me this morning. Theseus sailed with me and he had a son. Acamas. I met him as a boy, and he was headstrong and capable, just like his father. He is one you must seek, though I cannot be sure he is still alive.' He massaged the bridge of his nose and closed his eyes, as if it were physically painful to dredge his thoughts in this way.

'Grandfather, what about the *dioskouroi*? Didn't you sail with them?'

Jason blinked in surprise before frowning. 'I did but abandon all hopes of finding Castor and Pollux. Some lifelong blood feud had dogged them most of their lives and rumours of their death are already old.'

The news came as a blow: the twins were amongst the first on Xandros' list of warriors.

'Ancaeus, my helmsman and a great bear of a man… Ah, rumour reached me in Corinth he was still alive, but that was many years ago. As for the other Argonauts… I have heard nothing. Time was, we used to meet in a remote part of the isthmus, far from prying eyes, but if even one man other than Orpheus out of those forty still walks the earth… Would I even know if he did?' Xandros saw Jason's eyes become dewy and the old man suddenly clasped his wrist. 'I have neglected the very brotherhood that helped me achieve something impossible. If you meet one, even *one* of these men, remember me to him. Swear upon this! Tell him that Jason still thinks of him and wishes him well, but don't tell them… say nothing of the husk of the man you see now. This is not how I want to be remembered. Can you promise me this?'

Xandros rested his hand on those of his grandfather. 'I promise.'

'And one more thing.' He palmed him a little pouch. 'I have learned to be a good judge of sailors and your men – don't turn around; they are watching – are not helping you from the goodness of their hearts, that much is clear. You will be needing this. Go, my boy. May you fulfil your hopes.'

Xandros gazed at his grandfather with renewed affection. He wanted to embrace him but thought better of it in front of the crew. 'From the heart, thank you.' He was about to leave then added, 'And I will come back to see you!'

Jason gave him a sad smile: the sentiment was genuine but they both knew it would not happen.

'Farewell, my boy,' whispered Jason to Xandros' retreating back. 'And earn it.'

Xandros ignored the skipper's quizzical stare and jumped aboard, being careful to conceal the pouch. The deckhand untied the last hawser and leaped nimbly aboard. While they whistled, busying themselves with unfurling the sail and tightening the cleats, Xandros watched the bay of Iolkos recede from the stern.

Jason cut a forlorn figure, leaning on his stick, with his tunic flapping about his stick-thin legs in the breeze. Xandros gazed at his grandfather until he was a white dot on the golden horizon and only then did he move from the stern.

Even after the ship had passed out of sight, Jason stared out over the horizon, swaying slightly on the spot. His grandson's visit had stirred something dormant, like a breath of air upon the cold ashes of a fire. His tired soul yearned to be free of his past so that it might ease the pain of the present. To see out his remaining days in solitude and find a peace that his heart had denied him throughout his life, save for a few fragments of memory as a shepherd on Mount Pelion. But, deep within, he knew that doing nothing was not the answer. Had Medea's curse not taught him this well enough?

Earn it.

He had never forgotten the words of his dying comrade Oileus. Perhaps that had been the solution for all this time spent navel-gazing. He would have to earn the right to peace and, with the next full moon, came the only glimmer of hope that yet remained in gaining it. He filled his lungs with sea air and closed his eyes, whispering a prayer. Then he turned back for Dimini, hoping Agata's man, whose existence she had so artlessly failed to conceal, might still possess what he needed.

VIII

The coast of Attica

It took five long days to reach Cape Sounion. They encountered no raiders, but something about the *Salamander* sent other merchantmen scuttling for cover upon sighting her. The greatest enemy proved to be the fickle wind which, on occasions, failed altogether, leaving the vessel adrift upon a burnished sea with little cover from the beating sun. Things improved when they rounded the cape and Xandros sensed the tension, which had manifested amongst the crew with fraying tempers and curt orders, easing.

'Attica,' pronounced the skipper, sweeping his hand towards the bays and coves over the starboard rail.

Towards late afternoon, they approached the rocky promontory of Anagyrus, and one of the crew approached the skipper. 'We could make Athens by sundown. Do you want to press on?'

Sat at the helm beneath the shade of his wide-brimmed hat, the captain had been broodingly quiet all day. Now he rasped his stubble whilst he thought about it, taking a look at the benevolent sky. 'We keep going.'

Xandros sensed that the sailors would have preferred to make for shore – it had been a long day at sea, after all – but they accepted the decision without fuss.

They were already threading through the gap between the tip of Anagyrus and its offshore island when they realised the folly of their decision. At first sight, Xandros assumed they were witnessing funeral games: he had heard that powerful kingdoms sometimes paid their respects to rulers with boat races and the like. With the breeze at their backs, the noise of the battle that they had blundered into was carried away towards Athens.

There could be no turning back.

From lolling over the gunwales, the crew jumped into life as if Poseidon himself had appeared on the quarterdeck.

'Ma Dia!' shouted the captain, pushing back his hat. As they cleared the headland, the din of bronze on bronze and wood, screams and bellowed orders reached their ears. To their right, locked together like wasps mating on the wing, two galleys drifted in combat. Further on, dangerously close to the jagged shore, a pair of white-sailed ships were paddling away from a trio of larger vessels.

Glaux shouted, *'Pirates!'* For a moment, even the captain looked conflicted while his right hand gripped the tiller.

His crew stared at him. 'Orders, captain?' demanded another.

They were now a bowshot from the interlocked vessels. Just beyond them, the sea boomed into a cave, sending a plume of mist into the sky. The captain surveyed the scene. The white sails that bore a crude emblem of an owl's eyes and a beak were surely Athenian. He glanced up at his own sail, black and bellying. Xandros could almost see his mind working.

'Captain?'

He turned to Xandros. 'What can you do, boy?'

Xandros gave him a blank look. 'What do you mean?'

'Range weapons!' he yelled. 'Bows?'

'I have a sling.'

The captain gave him an incredulous look and was already turning towards his men. *'Elissos... boys... Arm yourselves! The rest of you, reef her!'*

The pair responded – one of them was the deckhand with the felt cap – unwrapping bows from oilcloths and testing the strings before wedging themselves against the rail. The others heaved upon the brails, checking the *Salamander*'s progress. Xandros went for his bag, rummaging through it for his sling and shot pouch. The captain took them a little nearer the first pair of ships before opening the tiller and bringing them abreast of the aggressor. Men wearing plumed helmets were plunging long spears over the gunwales and at least another pair had boarded. A dozen others manned the benches, and those with free oars port side took little strokes to keep the boat attached to its prey.

One of the Athenians had armed himself with an oar, and was desperately fending off the pirates, crouched ready to pounce with drawn blades. By the way the blade dipped at the end of each swipe, Xandros guessed he was already tiring.

Just then, the steersman of the pirate galley turned towards them in surprise. The skipper raised his fist in greeting and hissed between gritted teeth, *'Let him have it, boys!'*

Xandros' sling was already whirring above his shoulder. Though the *Salamander* had cargo in her belly, she rode high in the water: a couple of feet above the galley alongside them. He reckoned he was a decent shot but the deck on which he now stood was rolling. He took an extra couple of seconds and the pirate hollered at his men, who turned towards the new threat. He would never unleash a finer shot. Though it dipped short, it miraculously skipped off the gangway and slammed into the throat of the rover just as the oar blade swept into his side, tipping him overboard. His next shot was wide but it slapped the bow post, carved like a bird's head, with a sharp report.

The arrows arrived a sliver of a second later. One collected flesh, the other missed but ricocheted off the mast box. Xandros was whirring another shot by the time the pirates responded. The waves had already nudged them closer to their target: too close, Xandros thought. He released his finger from the loop and his shot hummed above the head of one of the pirates as he drew his bow. It had already hit the water by the time he flinched in shock. An arrow purred into the rover's bare chest before he could redraw.

Xandros' heart pumped in glee. At this distance, he could not fail to hit oarsmen. His next shot cracked the skull of a pirate and he slumped to the side, dead before his body slipped from his thwart. He missed with his next – the boat rolled under a strong wave – but struck a pirate in the shoulder with his fourth. Arrows and stones were landing at will.

I suspect trade is only part of their livelihood, had been Orpheus' words. While he retrieved another stone, Glaux and even the bearded crewman had arrows nocked, and they looked like they knew what they were about.

The Athenians responded with a roar, repelling the boarders and pushing the boat away, responding in kind with arrows and javelins. The pirate galley circled helplessly as its oarsmen ducked and flinched, despite the screams of their captain for them to respond. One of them stood and dived into the sea; others followed his lead. Then the captain himself was hit and the yelling stopped.

'Save your arrows!' shouted the *Salamander*'s skipper.

The Athenian galley pulled away. It was difficult to see how many casualties it had sustained but the crew cheered their saviours as they went to help. There was a hideous crack of wood and Xandros saw one of the Athenian vessels foundering on the rocks. The other was now hard against a pirate galley as its crew fought hand to hand.

'Shake it out!' hollered the skipper, slapping his hand on the tiller bar. The sail dropped and filled.

Xandros was pointing at the floundering ship. 'Pick up those men!'

'We'll be picked off. *Elissos, how many?*'

A pause. 'A dozen, more or less!'

He turned to Xandros. 'You?'

'The s-s... the s...' Xandros balled his fist in frustration but, in his excitement, the words would not emerge.

The skipper frowned. 'One more time?'

'Yes!' the crew roared in unison.

Xandros watched the men in the water, desperately clinging onto the splintered vessel as successive waves drove it against the rocks. *'Hold on!'* he hollered. *'We'll return!'* but his words were lost to the waves.

The raiders knew they were in trouble. Even though the numbers were still even, they had allowed themselves to be circled, and their marines darted across the gangway to face off the threat. The first javelin was hurled from the oncoming Athenian ship. It missed the bowman but landed in the lap of a rower, and his high-pitched shriek unmanned his crew. Xandros witnessed the commotion as other crew members hauled in their oars to lay hands upon him, and even then he thrashed in agony until falling limp as he bled out.

'Pin that one!' shouted the skipper. *'Pin that one! Reef now!'*

The crew set about their task manfully, even when an arrow fizzed past them. Elissos responded in kind, dropping a pair of archers as Xandros' shot clattered off the hull, catching a pirate's elbow as he heaved back on his oar. His next shattered another's jaw as he leaned for the catch. The abandoned oar clanked against the others, causing the crew to lose their timing, rowing in antiphase. They were so close they could see the panic on the raiders' faces. The ship in front of the beleaguered vessel heaved away and, for a moment, Xandros thought they would be rammed, so manic were their strokes. But they had spotted a gap and gambled upon taking it.

'Ha ha! Fuck off, kunai!' shouted the skipper. The pirates passed so close to the merchant ship that Xandros might have spat upon them. He selected a shot and whirled the sling for all he was worth. He almost felt guilty – as if he had transgressed the laws of fair fighting – when he watched the stone strike the back of a head. He heard it, too. A sharp *click* as the stone deflected from the bald skull, twenty paces away. The pirate's head sagged forwards and the man at the opposite oar turned to Xandros as he cleared his blade. The rower looked old and grey, and his hair caught in the breeze as he fixed Xandros with his dark eyes. In that moment, Xandros was convinced he had seen him before and it froze his ardour.

'They've surrendered! Would you believe that?' Glaux was flushed with triumph.

'Then they're fools.'

The captain was right. The Athenians' blood was up and they began to empty their quivers into the two boats, which bobbed under the breakers. Xandros had to look away. The pirates' screams and curses, their grunts and wheezing as the bronze tips clattered and thumped into them were sickening. It took the better part of ten minutes to kill them all. Some had seen the hopelessness of the situation and thrown themselves overboard. The first few made it but, when the Athenians saw what was happening, they intensified their firing until the two pirate galleys resembled pin cushions and rivulets of blood streaked the bilge water.

'That first ship,' shouted Xandros, '*please*.'

The captain nodded: even he had seen enough. The pitiable shrieking had faded to a few gurgled calls for mercy until even they fell silent. 'To your benches, everyone.'

IX

The ten Athenians they had rescued, though grateful, were quiet and trembled through delayed shock and cold. They stirred, however, when they saw over the starboard rail the rocky plateau rising from the plain. Outlined like a bruise against the glowing sky, Xandros could see the buildings of the acropolis and, as they drew near, the faintest thread of smoke rising skywards. Somewhere within the halls of those buildings, the *wanax* would be eating, drinking, dispensing justice. Perhaps he might even be looking out over the bay at that very moment, watching the merchant vessel pulling into the harbour. The name of Theseus, sacker of the once mighty kingdom of the Kretes, was familiar enough. It thrilled Xandros that his own grandfather had once known him but something about the way he talked of him and passed over his deeds suggested he had no great love for the man: Jason had spoken of others with readier enthusiasm.

The *Salamander* approached one of the wharves that stretched a short distance into the bay. In the full face of the westering sun, the harbour, the acropolis, even its citizens glowed the colour of run honey. Xandros noticed how few other craft there were, bobbing at anchor. He had expected that their own would have some trouble finding a berth but the bay was vast and swallowed up the ten or eleven other ships. A throng of citizens was watching intently as the three boats drew in. The presence of a black-sailed galley amongst them caused a good deal of chattering and pointing and, as they drew in and moored, Xandros heard the word repeated over and over: *pirates!*

'We are not pirates!' he declared, leaping onto the wharf. 'You hear me?'

Noticing his anger, one of the rescued sailors, limping with a deadened thigh, clasped his shoulder as he shuffled past. He had long dark hair, as thick as rope, and intense green eyes. 'These commoners will soon change their tune, you'll see.'

'Make room for the king's brother!'

Xandros turned to the boat alongside the *Salamander*. Its captain was waving back the Athenians, now four or five deep, with his spear. *'Come on, make way!'*

Xandros asked quietly, 'Who is the king's brother?'

The man with the limp turned back with a wry smile. 'I am.'

The crowd parted with reluctance, allowing him passage. Some of his crew now hurried to his side, helping him onto a little rocky mound. He mounted it with a grimace and silenced the harbour with an impatient wave.

'These strangers – *these* men, whom you see before you – are no pirates. The black sail their vessel bears, though I confess it made us fear we would be overwhelmed, turned the tide. Their bravery, their seamanship, their skill-at-arms, helped us defeat these sea raiders; for now.'

He waited for the cheering to subside. Xandros saw the skipper crack a smile, briefly, when one of his men punched his shoulder.

'But!' He raised a cautionary hand. 'But do not suppose the threat has disappeared. They will return and we must be ready for them when they do. The coastal watch will be doubled, you have my promise, but for now, I want to welcome these strangers!'

The prince gingerly stepped off the rock and placed his hand on his heart. 'I am Demophon, brother of Acamas, *wanax* of Athens, and we are sons of the late King Theseus. And you men whoever you are, will follow me to the palace. I have already dispatched a messenger so you will be expected. Meantime, my men will take your possessions. Please!'

Xandros felt his prospects growing as they entered the outer ring wall and made their way up the path carved into the western escarpment, tired and famished but buoyed by the most unexpected turn of events. In the flickering torchlight, the Lemnians felt like they were ascending Olympus itself, since it seemed impossible that such a structure could be anything other than god-made.

They watched the sun dip into the sea at the very moment they reached the summit of the acropolis, before entering successive gates set within the colossal surrounding walls.

'Surely no attacker has ever gotten close to where we are?' asked the skipper of Demophon. 'It's impregnable!'

The prince had insisted upon walking the few miles from the harbour to the citadel, despite the discomfort of his injury. His teeth were gritted and he looked pale. 'Never,' he confirmed. 'But she's not invulnerable. No citadel is.'

Each guard struck the rock with the butt of his spear as Demophon approached until the last gate was closed behind the little procession. Xandros counted nine and, with no view over the bastion, was quite disorientated when finally they emerged onto the plateau.

The palace complex, flat-roofed and sprawling, dominated the summit, dwarfing the scattering of ancillary buildings nearby. Lamps and torches skirted the perimeter like a flickering necklace, and a wisp of smoke arose from the centre. The prevailing breeze carried the faintest trace of roast meat and his stomach growled in anticipation.

'The view from up there…' said Xandros, pointing to a terrace. He imagined the vista at night. Over the walls, he could see nothing but the infinite vastness of the starlit sky.

They had reached the palace entrance now. Fat wooden pillars, painted red, gave onto a porch and beyond lay a grand courtyard dotted with fruit trees and pots of cyclamen. They could see people passing the upper storey windows along the wings, dimly lit by oil lamps – courtiers or members of Acamas' family, perhaps.

Surely such a powerful city could spare men for the defence of Lemnos? Xandros allowed himself to believe it would be possible.

The doors at the far end of the courtyard were closed but, upon seeing Demophon, the two guards bowed and rapped upon them with their spears. Xandros noticed how the prince straightened his back a little. For all his gratitude at being saved and for the raiders being repulsed, his pride had plainly sustained a bruising along with his leg.

The doors opened upon a *megaron* that would have comfortably fitted two of Queen Hypsipyle's halls with room to spare. Inside, the hearth was ablaze – the temperature had dropped notably on the ascent of the acropolis – casting its fiery glow upon the brightly coloured frescoes of mythical beasts and scenes of hunting. King Acamas rose from his throne to the right, flanked by two aristocratic-looking men; chamberlains or stewards, Xandros thought. There was no mistaking that Acamas and Demophon were related, except that the king was broader and taller. He was an open, bluff-looking man who exuded energy: the scar – half a finger in length – that crossed his cheek also spoke of a man of action. He embraced his brother with a hug that might have winded a frailer man.

'I heard everything,' he said, frowning, and indicating to the men by the throne that he wanted more stools. 'But it was very garbled. The hour is late but you will eat before I ask any more of you. And you, strangers, are most welcome. No, please don't hover there like crane flies! Sit.' He set down the stools that were now being relayed into the hall. 'Warm yourselves. The city hums with gossip about the pirates that saved my fleet, wielding slings and bows like the Thunderer hurls his bolts, and I would not miss this tale for the world.'

X

Peracora, earlier the same day

For the first time in Ancaeus' memory, ominous clouds hung over the peninsula of Perachora. The journey had taken weeks and, with a second mouth to feed, had been the hardest of all his annual expeditions across country. Atukhos had not breathed a word of complaint, suffering his guardian's changes of mood with remarkable equanimity. And now they were stood at the foot of the rocky path that led to the Heraion.

'Listen, now, boy,' said Ancaeus, raising a thick finger. 'There is no place in the entire universe more important or more sacred to me than what lies at the tip of that land, you understand me? Nowhere.'

Atukhos looked along the forbidding headland and solemnly nodded his head.

'And the people we're about to meet, however many there may be, are every bit as important. Never – not once – has any of us brought along someone who didn't row on our boat, *Argo*...'

'...because you want to remember.'

'Right. Because we just want to remember. Together and in peace. So you will respect that peace. You will respect every rock and person standing upon them as if they're sacred, got it?'

'Yes.'

'Good. There's a nice pool at the end of it so let's get moving.'

After an hour of negotiating the difficult path, they were grateful for the cloud cover. Ancaeus could not remember it being so punishing upon his joints, which began to twinge every time he was forced to climb. Eventually, after several hours of trekking, they reached the lake, the surface of which rippled under a light breeze. They set down their possessions and, after a long gulp of water, both stripped off and plunged into the cool water. It had an immediate effect upon Ancaeus' spirits and fired his tired limbs.

Whilst Atukhos whooped and splashed about, Ancaeus floated upon his back, experiencing that same slight frisson of fear as he did every year at this stage of the journey.

One day, one of us will be the only person, the last Argonaut, to set foot upon the Heraion. What will that man do the following year, and the next?

It, and variations upon the theme, had become an increasingly frequent topic of discussion around the campfire with the passing of each summer. As he drifted in a slow circle, Ancaeus came to face the track along which they had passed. From the corner of his eye, he caught a glimpse of a familiar figure stood by the edge of the lake. He splashed water on his face, about to shout a good-natured insult at his closest friend. The track was deserted, and his stomach sank in disappointment. He rubbed his face and turned this way and that, seeing nobody. Atukhos was watching him intently.

'Did you see someone stood there, at the water's edge?'

'When?'

'Now,' he tutted. 'Just now.'

The boy shook his head slowly and Ancaeus huffed, striding out of the water. 'Come on,' he said, and the boy dutifully followed.

It didn't take long before they passed through the pine trees at the track's end and the little bay emerged into view. He was immeasurably relieved to see three tents already pegged out. His heart soared when he saw the bow-legged Idas and heard his strident complaint about something or other. He and Butes the wrestler, as squat as a satyr, turned to look up at him.

'Late again!' grumbled Butes. 'Just as well for you the goat's not ready!'

Ancaeus now caught the faint savour of grilled meat and his stomach growled in anticipation. Now they turned their eyes upon Atukhos and they became still. Just at that moment, Peleus and his brother Telamon crawled from under their tent to see who had arrived. As Ancaeus and Atukhos picked their way down the treacherous path, the four Argonauts stared at them such that, when they reached the bottom, Atukhos stepped instinctively behind his guardian.

For a moment, nobody spoke. Then Idas pointed at him. 'Is the sprog yours?'

'No. And yes.'

Peleus tugged at his beard. Nothing about his leathery face had ever softened, though the man beneath was considerably mellower than in his pomp. 'What in the name of fuckery does that mean?'

'No, he's not mine but, yes, I now look after him. He's had it tough.'

Butes shrugged. 'So long as he keeps his hands to his own stuff.'

The men embraced and slapped shoulders, fencing with the usual bawdy insults before filling their cups. Ancaeus pointed to a spare patch of ground. 'Your time to shine, Atukhos. Let me see you raise that tent.'

Grateful for the distraction, the boy set about it.

'Any sign of Meleager?' The Argonauts became still and ominous looks passed between them. 'Well? Out with it!'

Idas sucked his teeth but couldn't look Ancaeus in the eye. 'Looks like it falls to Idas, then. Meleager is dead. We're all sorry, Ancaeus, but none more than you I suppose.'

'Dead?'

He nodded.

Ancaeus felt his legs grow weak and he groped for the ground to take the weight off them. Butes went away and returned with a wineskin, filling Ancaeus' cup without asking.

'When? How?'

'Early in the Month of Sowing, it seems,' said Peleus. 'A messenger was passing through Phthia. We offered him refreshments and asked him for his news. Amongst the tittle-tattle, he knew of clan rivalries in Calydon reaching a head, and we know Meleager's kingdom has always been a fickle one, but had nothing more to say about it. It was evil news.'

Atukhos watched the men become quiet, fascinated by the way they interacted with each other. As old as Ancaeus was, the two gruff men with the beards looked ancient though no less dangerous, somehow. There was an unguarded ease and affection that he had never witnessed before. He supposed it had something to do with their great age, and that this was how all men behaved who were born in another time.

Ancaeus sagged, murmuring something to himself and after a few moments took himself away to sit on the headland, gazing out to sea. He remained there, lost in his thoughts, for an hour, during which time he didn't see the two heads swimming around the opposite side of the little bay.

By the time he stirred and eased himself back down the rocks, the westering sun had scattered most of the clouds, casting the little bay in golden light.

'Hello, Ancaeus,' said one of the newcomers, towelling himself dry. Lost in thought, Ancaeus blinked at him in confusion, looking from one diminutive man to the other. 'Has it really been that long that you don't recognise us?'

'Great merciful gods!'

Ancaeus fairly swept up Castor and Pollux and crushed them in his embrace. They felt his chest heaving up and down without comment, because they knew something of how he was feeling. When it subsided and he released them, his eyes brimmed with tears and his voice cracked. 'We'd long since given up on seeing you ever again!'

'I know,' said Castor quietly, 'but in our minds we came back here every year.'

'Let me see you both.' Idas had his hands on his hips and looked them up and down. 'Life on the run suits you; some might even say you look better than me!'

'Quite the compliment coming from Idas of Arene!'

'Goat's ready,' came Peleus' voice from a short distance away. The promise of food raised their spirits and the conversation resumed as Idas circulated with the wine.

'When's Idmon coming?' asked Telamon hazily.

'How much have *you* been drinking?' said Pollux in bemusement.

'Did he make it last year? I can't remember.'

Peleus gave the Argonauts a pointed look and their smiles faded. He stabbed the side of the goat with his knife and wiped his hands on a rag as he approached his brother. He put an arm around him and drew him in. 'Not last year, nor the one before, brother. Idmon died a long time ago. With Tiphys.' He looked from Ancaeus to the twins to Idas and Butes and they understood. 'We're all getting old, aren't we? Minds not what they once were.'

'Just so,' said Ancaeus.

'Oh aye,' agreed Butes.

After a moment, Idas added, 'Butes here has begun to wet the bed, isn't that right, old friend?'

'I will do tonight, you *kuna*. All over your face!'

The Argonauts burst out laughing and fetched their knives and bowls.

XI

Athens

The platters of meat and flatbreads had been cleared away and the beakers of wine refilled when Acamas returned, and in his wake came a woman wearing a flounced skirt and a *chiton*. Her face exuded character, and in this she seemed well matched with her husband, though her darker skin, large, dark eyes and the angular cast of her features marked her out as a woman from more distant shores.

To Xandros' surprise, Acamas held her hand as she took her place upon the throne whilst he pulled up a stool alongside his brother. Two young handmaids sat at the queen's feet.

'Another headache, brother?' asked Demophon quietly.

The king inclined his head with the faintest of frowns but didn't reply. 'I trust the food has restored your spirits?'

'Thank you,' said Xandros, wiping his hand upon a napkin.

Acamas accepted a cup of wine and settled back. 'So then! Talk to me.'

Demophon recounted what had happened, the prelude to the Lemnians' arrival being the pirate vessels being spotted early before the Athenians manned the only ships available to head them off. Nine Athenians had perished: three fighting hand to hand and six drowned or maimed upon the sharp rocks. Acamas had been listening to the story with raised eyebrows or low whistles but the tally of dead soldiers clouded his face. He raised his hand to his brother and leaned towards a steward, issuing quiet instructions for silver cups to be given from the treasury to their families.

When Demophon had finished, Acamas turned to Xandros and the crew of the *Salamander*. He let his hands fall upon his knees to emphasise his words. 'Truly, the city of Athens is indebted to you. We will send you on your way with honour and with a full hold of provisions. And some silver, of course.' The captain pressed his hands together and thanked him but Acamas took a long draught of wine and gave Xandros a shrewd look over the rim of his goblet.

'I must ask, however, what such an unusual crew – in a black-sailed galley, no less – is *doing* in Athens. The colour has long since been a harbinger of bad news, when you consider rumours surrounding the death of my grandfather Aegeus, after all.'

The captain turned to Xandros with the faintest of smirks, as if to say, *Good luck because a free supper's all you'll be getting.*

Xandros tried to ignore him. 'Lord Acamas, your father and my grandfather knew each other well. They both sailed on *Argo*, which I think I'm right in saying was King Theseus' first—'

Acamas stopped Xandros with an extended hand. 'Wait. Jason was *your* grandfather?'

'He was.'

Acamas turned to his wife with a look of being impressed though Xandros felt a twinge of misgiving, as if he had already figured this out. 'Then we are doubly honoured, young man. Please, continue!'

'To speak to the point, I have come in search of help from King Jason's former comrades against the threat from the sea. I want to defend my island.' When Acamas blinked at him, he added. 'That is, Lemnos.'

Acamas massaged the bridge of his nose and leaned back. 'Forgive me, are any of the Argonauts even still *alive*?'

'They are. We have already met my grandfather… and Orpheus, the bard, is the one who paid for our boat.'

'Wait now.' The captain raised a hand. 'We haven't met Jason.'

'Yes, we have.'

The captain raised his eyebrows. 'That old man? *That* old man was Jason?'

Acamas turned to his brother. The pair, it seemed to Xandros at that moment, had the faculty of communicating without the need for words. 'And what help has Jason vouchsafed for you?'

'Some weapons, a little gold.' He was about to mention the Golden Fleece but thought better of it.

'But no men?'

'Jason lives alone in a dusty palace. He has no men at his command; not anymore.'

'A shame. It seems the Fates have not smiled upon him since his return.'

'No. But there are others I want to find. Meleager of Calydon. The Spartans Castor and Pollux. Ancaeus, his helmsman.'

Acamas swirled his wine cup before setting it down upon the floor. 'Allow me to be honest, young Xandros. I see two ambitions spurring you on, both noble in their own right. One, you wish to meet some of the heroes of old, kinsmen of your ancestor and, it must be said, a dying breed. Two, you want men to sail to the defence of Lemnos, perhaps to assert your authority as a king-in-waiting. Am I right?'

Xandros opened his mouth to protest but Acamas continued. 'With the former, I happen to think you will have some success. After all, you found Jason, whom I had assumed would be long dead. With the latter, alas, I fear your efforts will be in vain. You have already seen that the city of Athens is hard-pressed enough to defend its own people, and for that reason I can spare you the trouble of asking for help because, with great regret, the answer is no. We need every able-bodied man we have.' Xandros saw how the king's brother Demophon looked to the floor at this. 'Though I can't speak for other kingdoms, you must prepare yourself for similar because the question that must be asked is why any man would want to defend a far-off island before securing his own hearth and home.'

'Lemnos isn't like any other island.' Though Xandros had not meant his tone to bear an edge, his disappointment provided it. 'Lemnos is populated by offspring of the Argonauts; from their stay nearly forty years ago. I am not asking for men to defend strangers: I want them to defend their own kin.'

Acamas clenched his jaw and Xandros divined that the king's mind had already been made up in the hour before the Lemnians had even arrived at the palace. Now it was clear he had been put in an awkward spot.

'I think I see more sense in your voyage. However, I don't see that it changes the game sufficiently. Given the choice, a man would always defend what he knows best. What he has cultivated from the root to the fruit. I am sorry.' Something about his demeanour hardened and he drained his cup. 'Where do you plan to sail next?'

'The Argolid.' Xandros glanced at the captain to gauge his reaction. He gave him a sidelong glance that betrayed nothing.

'I see. Argos... Tiryns... You say you have some gold and there may well be mercenaries willing to take it. A word of advice: be circumspect with whom you ask, and how. Mercenaries are loyal to their purses and their stomachs. In that order. And another thing. Avoid Mycenae, a little inland. I have heard it is not the place it once was. And now, forgive me but I am tired and the business of the palace never ends.' Acamas rose and extended his hand to Xandros and the others. 'Please accept the heartfelt thanks of the city of Athens. We may not be able to offer you men but, as I promised, I have seen to it that your bravery will not go entirely unrewarded. I hope I may see you in the morning, before you leave.'

XII

Argos

Acamas had already left by the time they rose and breakfasted in the *megaron*. Demophon relayed his apologies, explaining that the king had to preside over a trial in an outlying deme, followed by a wedding in another, in which feuding clans might be united. The king's brother moved stiffly about the hall and Xandros could tell by the way he grimaced whenever he stretched his leg that he was in severe discomfort.

'Forgive me. I won't be seeing you off at Phaleron but I have arranged tokens of friendship and gratitude.'

It seemed to Xandros, as the prince embraced them in turn with little eye contact, that there was a good deal more he wanted to say, as if he was experiencing some kind of inner conflict.

They arrived at the harbour of Phaleron an hour later. As they approached, armed guards stood by the *Salamander* nudged each other and stirred. The ranking officer, tall and bull-necked, spoke in a voice as gruff as his appearance.

'The king tasked me with resupplying your ship. You won't be going hungry for a few days.' His thin lips straightened briefly. 'A safe voyage.'

The captain dipped his head in gratitude. 'Are Athenians so hungry you need an armed guard for some food?'

'It's not the food.'

The captain's eyes twinkled. 'I understand.'

Xandros had never seen him board so quickly, nor cast off with such fast hands.

'I don't want any of you going below deck before me,' he said as they raised anchor and pulled away from the coast. He drummed his fingers upon the tiller bars and snapped orders at the crew to pull faster until they were clear of the bay, whereupon he was relieved at the helm and scrambled down the ladders. They heard him a few moments later, whooping with every faint *clink* of embossed silver cup and plate.

The winds were kind and, by the time the *Salamander* scraped ashore at the Bay of Argos just past midday on the second day after leaving the Athenian coast, the sky was blushing.

Xandros cricked his neck and looked about him, beyond the pebbles of the bay to the low mountains, hazed in purple cloud. There were a dozen or so other vessels dragged onto the waterfront, and the *Salamander* was the furthest along the bay, alongside a mid-sized galley with its bow post carved like Aphrodite in repose.

'Lodgings,' he said to himself, tugging his tunic away from his chest. 'Then a bath.'

He set off down the beach, pebbles crunching underfoot. When he realised the captain and his crew weren't following, he turned to them. 'What are you doing?'

'We stay here.'

The bay was amenable, it was true. 'But don't you want at least one night with a roof over your head?'

'Look above you, boy? Have you ever seen a finer ceiling than *that*?'

Xandros had to admit he had a point.

'We leave on the third morning; tomorrow being the first. At dawn.' He rubbed his nose with the back of his hand and added, matter-of-factly, 'If you're not here by first light, we cast off anyway. Understood?'

Xandros nodded and turned to leave.

'And another thing.' Their faces, he noticed, were more serious. 'Listen to what that king said, Acamas: avoid Tiryns. And Mycenae. The man spoke some sense. They've fallen on hard times and some say there's a darkness about Mycenae. In you, they'd see rich pickings—'

'I can look after myself.'

'Against the robber barons and twenty, thirty men? No, I think not. Stick to Argos.' A wolfish grin crept across his face. 'You'll like Argos.'

The captain shared a look with Elissos and, in that moment, Xandros was tempted to do the exact opposite of what he was saying because he thought they were toying with him. He looked east and could see the citadel of Tiryns a few miles distant, shimmering atop a low hill. Argos was just a mile or so away, nestled at the foot of two rocky hills that dominated an otherwise flat, dry plain. He took a deep breath, picked up his weapons and slung his bag over his shoulder.

It took less than an hour to reach Argos. At the crown of the rocky escarpment, he could make out the walls of a citadel, though no smoke rose from it. The sun was beginning to wester as he passed through the mud-brick walls into the lower town. He was directed towards the house of an apprentice wheelwright whose father had died in some sort of a skirmish – the details were vague – which left a dusty, creaking room vacant upstairs. He freshened up with a couple of pails of water in the wheelwright's yard, which still held some of the sun's warmth, before heading out to try to barter some food from an emporium he had seen.

He sidestepped a dirty-faced child and passed a tannery, wrinkling his nose at the pungent odour of urine and animal fat. Street urchins threw stones at broken pots outside huts of clay brick with rags draped over the windows. Here were the poorer quarters of the town, whose streets the prevailing wind would torment with the stench of the dyes.

At one point, he paused and looked behind him, convinced he was being followed. There were a few passers-by but none appeared to be paying him any particular attention. He arrived at the emporium a few minutes later but most of the stalls were being dismantled for the evening. Xandros noticed a man packing up his canopy in an area set back from the square. He looked pinched and tired, and his balding pate was sheened in sweat. He hurried over to him, making him flinch when he looked up.

'Please,' said Xandros, 'before you go. Can you help me?'

'Yes?'

Xandros pointed to the citadel. 'Is the *wanax* in residence, do you know?'

'Not up there he isn't.'

'W-where then?'

'The largest tomb at the foot of Shield Hill. Can't miss it.'

Xandros blinked at him and he rolled his eyes. 'There's been no *wanax* here for many years. Our last was Diomedes.'

'Diomedes, of course!' The hero's name rang like a distant bell in Xandros' mind. 'So who lives up there now?'

'It's abandoned, as far as I know.' The trader pressed thumb and forefinger together to make the apotropaic sign. 'So if you're one of those strange hero-worshippers and it's the great and the good you're looking for, you need to find the cemetery. Go pay your respects there.'

Xandros' shoulders sagged and he looked about him, uncertain about what to do next. Noticing this, the man added, 'The city's fortunes died with Diomedes, I'm sorry to say. Argos is now in the hands of a council, and the council is controlled by Mycenae, more or less.' He nodded and turned to finish his work.

'And does the council provide a city guard? Does Argos have a fleet?'

'A *guard*? There is a militia, of course, but... Why are you asking these questions?'

'I just need some help.'

The merchant wiped his forehead with the back of his hand and looked pointedly at the half-packed stall. 'Look, this won't finish itself so if you want any more answers, you'll give me something in return.'

Xandros had already retrieved a fragment of gold. He showed it in his palm but withdrew it when the man reached out for it. 'I need wine and all the food you can spare. And where might I find mercenaries?'

The man raised his eyebrows, looking from the gold to the pouch around Xandros' neck. '*Mercenaries?* How would I know? Listen, do you want the food or not? I'm leaving now.'

Xandros opened his fist and the man took the gold with eyes full of suspicion. 'Dried fish. Cheese. Oil. Bread. I have some wine, also.' He added pointedly, 'My own. In days gone by, I would be done by midday. Lucky for you.'

He ducked under the half-dissembled canopy and retrieved the food, which he had placed in a sack. 'Bring the wineskin back, when you're done.' Xandros thanked him and turned to leave.

'One moment. Look… I hear there's a house not far from here where men drink; men with influence. It's also a place where men meet women, if you know what I mean. The street of the pines, just outside the city walls. It has a faded blue door, though I know no more about it than what I have said. A word to the wise, my friend.' He pointed to the pouch-shaped bulge beneath Xandros' tunic. 'A sword alone would not be enough to fend off the thieves here. If you must visit that place, be more careful.'

XIII

Perachora

That same evening, the Argonauts were contentedly picking the last of the meat from the bones and swilling the mellow wine in their cups, having paid their respects at the little sanctuary to Hera. Peleus banked the fire with more wood and resumed his seat. Atukhos, whose eyes had been growing heavy for the past few minutes, now slumped against Ancaeus' shoulder, sound asleep. His comrades looked on as Ancaeus managed to clamber to his feet without disturbing him, draped him over his shoulder and carried him to his tent, where he lay him down and pulled his fleece up beneath his chin.

'Ancaeus the doting father,' said Idas, looking impressed. 'I never thought I'd say that.'

'You can't because I'm not.'

Butes growled, 'As good as. Suits you, old friend.'

'Castor, did the pirates settle in Pylos?' asked Ancaeus, changing the subject.

'I don't know but I doubt it. Can't have been much left to settle in.'

'Of the town, no,' added Pollux, 'but they didn't scorch the fields. I think they want the fields.'

Idas spat to the side. 'Pfft, they just want metal, like all raiders. And women.'

'No, I think there's more to it than just this. The seas are infested with them, like nothing ever seen before. Those grievous little signs that the clerks scratched on clay tablets in Pylos; they were apparently full of it. Marauding northmen have driven the

Thracians to the coast. They've joined with Anatolians; who were they?'

'Lykians,' said Castor.

'Lykians, but the whole seaboard is taking to its boats. Or so it seems. Some say the gods have abandoned Olympus and are leaving them to it.'

Idas gave him a bemused look. He had never set much store by the gods. 'And what do you say?'

With all eyes upon him, the Spartan retreated into his thoughts for a moment. 'I say they're starving. Starving men will do desperate things to stretch their bellies.'

'Talking of Thracians, has anyone heard news of our fierce little brother Zetes?' Ancaeus' question was met with a heavy silence and a few shakes of the head. The death of Kalais, Zetes' twin, in the final battle for Iolkos, had torn his heart into pieces. He had fought like a man wanting to die alongside his brother but Fate had decreed otherwise.

'Has he ever returned here?' asked Castor.

'No, never.'

'Pity the poor fool who tries to stop him invading!' said Butes.

'If he still lives.'

'If.'

The clatter of hooves startled the Argonauts and they snapped their heads towards the track, snatching up their weapons. In the gloaming, they didn't see the traveller dismount but they heard his exhausted cursing.

'Step into the light, whoever you are!'

'One moment, please.'

Ancaeus lit a torch from the fire and walked to the foot of the path. 'Whoever you are, tie up your horse. It's a miracle you didn't hobble it.'

They heard the man gasping as he fumbled about in the dark and then a silhouette appeared at the head of the path, clad in a cloak and felt hat. He raised his arms peaceably. 'I come with a message.'

'Then deliver it!' said Idas. 'This is a sacred place and you're profaning it!'

'Not willingly, I assure you.'

'Help the man down,' muttered Butes.

Guided by Ancaeus' torch, the messenger made it to the camp, where he was offered water and a husk of bread moistened with the dripping fat of the goat. Whilst he devoured it, the seven Argonauts weighed him up. He was slight of build and delicate-faced but they were impressed that he had somehow managed to guide a horse over such treacherous ground.

'Can you spare me some for the horse?'

'We can. There's a spring nearby.'

They allowed him to fill a leather bag and he watered his horse, stroking its flanks with soothing words. When it had had its fill, they invited him to sit by the fire.

'By the looks of you,' said Ancaeus, 'you've had a hard ride.'

'I have. Long, hot days on the road and plenty of strange folk about.'

Ancaeus grunted. The messenger seemed honest enough and wouldn't be the first person to look unsettled by the Argonauts but he was in no mood for niceties. 'Well, then. Out with it.'

'I've been sent by someone known to you all, and he is keen to tell you he has you constantly in his thoughts...'

'*Who*, man?' asked Butes.

'His name is Jason. I am betroth...'

'*Jason* is still alive?'

'He is and, as I was saying, he wants to send you his warmest affections...'

'I assume he still has legs? And arms? Why can't he deliver these himself? Where has he been all these years?'

'I don't... he... well he has become too used to his own company, I suppose. As I was saying, I am betrothed to his housekeeper. He chose me because I inherited that horse, up there.'

'Out with your message then,' said Ancaeus, 'we can discuss the rest later.'

'Right. Jason says that he received an unexpected visit from someone from the island of Lemnos...'

'*Lemnos!*'

'Lemnos, yes. His grandson, in fact, a youth called Xandros.

Xandros is the son of the king of Myrine. He sailed to the mainland seeking Jason's help – seeking *your* help – against the Sea Peoples who are ravaging Hellas and who will soon reach Lemnos itself, an island, I am told, you will have a particular interest in protecting.'

The message silenced the Argonauts, as Jason had known it would, and the messenger paused at this juncture, as he was told he must. He regarded the expressions of the old warriors. It was like watching the changing of the seasons distilled into just a few seconds. *Could this handful of greyheads be all that remained of a bygone era?*

'Look at us, boy; take a good, long look.' Despite his age, the shaggy-haired, stooped one who now spoke was still a bear of a man. 'At the moment of your birth, I would still have been ten years past my best fighting days. For some here, it's nearer twenty.'

The messenger took another swig of water, turning down the cup of wine being offered to him.

'Who ever snubbed Dionysus? What's wrong with you, man?' snorted the whip-thin one with protuberant teeth, the one they called Idas.

'I don't take wine. Never have.' He ignored the raised eyebrows and bemused smirks. 'Before he sent me, Jason said that I should be prepared to spend many hours picking my way over these rocks only to find nobody waiting at the end of them.'

'That's the choice we face every year but it's never yet stopped us.'

'Then what this Xandros went on to say may interest you...'

'Go on.'

The messenger saw the flicker of interest in those hard old faces and began to realise that, for his sharp tongue and cantankerous ways, Jason's mind still understood the ways of men. 'The boy, he admits, is a desperate dreamer. He stole out of Lemnos and risked his life because everybody on his island says that they must only look to their own interests. But, he said, what good could come of this? Island after island, *polis* after *polis* has fallen because they are fighting alone. They are even attacking themselves.' The messenger wafted away a crane fly that buzzed him and laughed. 'Imagine if those surviving towns and villages decided to pull together and fight back: what would it take to achieve that?'

The big man took a long pull of wine and set down his cup. 'Is this your question, or his?'

'Oh, the boy's...'

'And that's the end of the message, is it?' The messenger turned to the flint-eyed one with a missing front tooth. He had wild hair of copper and grey, and beads in his beard. 'Something tells me it isn't.'

'Not quite.' Despite his exhaustion, he was beginning to enjoy the role of the messenger, sacred to Hermes. He warmed his palms before the crackling flames. 'Hellene hasn't fought alongside Hellene for many years; not since the Eastern War, and those heroes are all long gone—'

'What we did was bigger than *that*. They were thousands; we were forty. *Forty!*'

'But Jason said that the boy wanted to find warriors like you and they, descendants perhaps, to unite the Hellenes once more. I suppose he must have thought you might be able to ask around, or call favours, since you are likely to know cities of proud men.' The ensuing silence was heavy. 'Well, as I say, the boy sounds like a dreamer and the gods love a dreamer, don't they? I've done what I promised I'd do, and been paid. May I trouble you for some more water before I leave? And perhaps a torch or two for the road; what there is of it.'

'Don't be a fool. You'll not try that path this evening. You might as well just jump off the rocks – you and your horse – and be done with it.' This was the flint-eyed one. The eyes of the man sat next to him, squatter and a little older but similar-looking, were growing heavy and he looked weary. 'You can rest here tonight but mind you don't disturb the boy, over there.'

The messenger thought about it. 'Thank you, I am grateful. If you don't mind, I am weary. Gentlemen.'

He got up and went to relieve himself by the water's edge, listening to the hum of quiet conversation that arose when they thought he was out of earshot. He buckled his belt, feeling the little reassuring crunch of gold stitched into the hidden pocket of his tunic. Jason had offered him the same again, if he returned with proof of the message being delivered. He had done his best but Hellas was truly doomed if these tired old foxes were her last hope.

'What are we supposed to make of all this then?' asked Peleus, tugging distractedly at his beard. 'First, do we even believe him?'

'Of course we do,' tutted his brother. 'I always said Jason was still alive.'

'And you've also begun to say that Idmon and Tiphys still breathe, yet they're forty years dead!'

'I'm glad he's alive but it irks me that he hasn't made an appearance here for so long,' rumbled Ancaeus. 'Even accounting for who's buried up there.'

'Well?' asked Idas. 'To the point, do we go? I'm sore tempted, for one.'

'And me,' added Butes.

Telamon narrowed his eyes at them across the fire. 'Have you both lost your minds? Look at you!'

'Look at yourself first! I'd wager I'm still amongst the best spearmen in the Peloponnese.'

'Aye, amongst men that've seen out more than sixty winters.'

Peleus watched them bicker, worrying the gum where his front tooth once rested with his tongue, as he often did when thoughtful. The punch that dislodged it had been thrown in one of King Aeetes' corridors back when he was one of the most feared warriors in Thessaly. His eyes fell upon Telamon. Hard living and hard drinking had taken its toll on his older brother's mind and his body. For how many more years could they keep making the arduous journey to the Heraion? Is this how his life – whatever was left of it – was to be measured out? It seemed obscene that he should have been granted such a span when his own son, Achilles, and his grandson, Neoptolemus, were long since dead. The gods were either cruel or had a wicked sense of humour: with every passing year, he believed more in the former.

'Well, Peleus?'

He became aware they were all looking at him. 'We could put it to the vote.'

Ancaeus shook his head and glanced over his shoulder at the slumbering Atukhos. The boy lay on his side with his hands clasped tight beneath his chin, as if he was praying. 'I won't do it.' He turned back, looking the Argonauts in the eye. 'I won't leave that boy to fend for himself. He'd have nothing.'

'You could always take him with you?' suggested Pollux.

'To watch his guardian die whilst he's sold into slavery? No, I think not.'

Idas harrumphed. 'I've never sailed anywhere intending to die. I think you miss the point.'

Ancaeus looked through Idas, seeing the huge warrior with the long hair bearing down upon him on the beach of Gytheon. In his long life, he'd never met anyone so strong, apart from Herakles. 'I've seen them first hand, Idas. They've not come to play.'

After a few more minutes of debating, they called over the messenger, who had affected to be sleeping. He rubbed his face and crouched by the fire. In its flickering glow, the Argonauts looked spent. It was remarkable to him that they were here at all. It was the warrior with the missing front tooth who spoke, and he looked dejected.

'We have an answer for you...'

XIV

Argos

Darkness had fallen by the time Xandros left his lodgings and stepped out into the street, looking up at the sky. The moon was veiled behind a festoon of clouds drawing in from the west, and he was grateful for the lamps that glowed through the shutters of the houses they passed. He could tell by the pungent odour when he passed by the tannery and shortly afterwards, without seeing a single soul, he was at the southern gate. A pair of sentries stood guard, spear butts planted upon the ground. They gave him a suspicious look as he approached.

'Will you allow me back when I return?'

The guards, both young, looked like they would rather be anywhere else. 'Where are you going at this hour?'

'Ah, the street of the palms.'

'There's no such street.'

'Pines,' corrected Xandros, 'the street of the pines.'

The gruffer of the pair gave him an odd look. 'We'll be here, if you make it back alive. For you, the password is *Crabs*.' His colleague snickered and drew back the bolt. 'Have fun now.'

Outside the city walls, with the houses being more scattered, Xandros became attuned to the silent vastness of the Argolid plain and the sweetness of its cooling earth. To the left, Shield Hill – he was certain that was it – was a symmetrical blot against the indigo of the night sky. Beyond lay more ridges, anonymous strongholds for small-minded robber barons. That, at least, seemed to him what had become of the lands of once-proud Hellenes.

With no sure directions, Xandros wondered how he might have found the road but he needn't have worried. The few hardy pines growing in a little stand marked it out and, the closer he drew, the buzz of raucous laughter and conversation behind the shuttered windows dispelled any lingering doubts about the colour of the door.

He adjusted his tunic, felt for the reassuring presence of his sword pommel and took a deep breath.

He knocked at the door. For a few long moments, nothing happened and he assumed he hadn't been heard above the noise from within. He shifted on his feet, full of misgivings. He raised his hand to knock one more time when the latch was lifted and the door opened a few inches. A pair of dark eyes set in a young face looked him up and down.

'Yes?'

'Prince Xandros, son of King Euneus of Lemnos,' he announced, squaring his shoulders. 'I would like to speak to the city council.'

The young face frowned. 'We are not expecting Prince... Whoever you said you were.'

'Of course you aren't. I didn't send word.'

Xandros could see that the young eyes were full of suspicion. 'Who, exactly, are you expecting to see? Give me a name.'

'I don't have one. Whoever the senior councillor is – it's important.'

He knew the door was about to be closed in his face until he heard the stomping of impatient feet, and it was yanked open. Even though the newcomer blocked most of the doorway on account of his barrel chest, Xandros felt the heat emanating from the hall beyond. At odds with the man's bulk was the waft of perfume and his pomaded ringlets of dark hair. As he shooed the younger man away, he also smelled the wine on his breath.

'Who are you, what do you want?'

Xandros cleared his throat and repeated the same patter. The man narrowed his eyes but Xandros sensed some light mischief within. 'Safe to say we've never met anyone from Lemnos.' He checked over Xandros' shoulder before stepping aside. 'Come inside. This could be amusing!'

Xandros didn't like what this implied but stepped inside. In the middle of the cavernous hall blazed a hearth fire, which was normal enough but, crowding the space within, it was as if the survivors of an apocalypse had gathered in a single room, determined to make the best of it. Villains mixed with nobility, brightly painted courtesans mingled with aristocratic women, warriors, slaves and everything in between. At the far end, a musician was plucking a seductive air upon a cithara whilst stewards circulated with jars of wine and platters of food. The arrival of the stranger caused the conversation to drop as everyone turned to stare at him.

'Silence, everyone, please!' Two mighty claps were enough, and the host rubbed his hands together when the room fell quiet. 'I promised you entertainment, did I not?' He turned to Xandros. 'You may make your request.'

Xandros whispered urgently, 'I wanted to speak to a councillor, on a private matter.'

'There are no secrets under my roof, boy. This is the only law we keep. *Speak!*'

The uncomfortable silence grew as Xandros glared at the host. He could sense the man's patience fraying. He had, apparently, put his own honour – whatever that was in Argos – on the line by inviting him inside.

Xandros let his eyes sweep the room whilst his pulse raced. His stutter would do him no favours here – that much was clear. 'Very well. I am heir to the throne of Lemnos. I have come here, a long way, to seek help from the people of Argos, albeit help I would have rather sought in private.' From the corner of his eye, Xandros could see the host beaming, as if he had foreseen the absurdity of the request. 'I… We are looking for soldiers to help us defend our island and we are prepared to pay for it.'

The surreptitious glances, looks of mild amusement on some, withering disinterest on others – men and women – caused Xandros to forget exactly what he was going to say next. He felt resentment needling him. *Who are these people to judge? Do these fools know nothing of the world beyond their own walls?* In lieu of stuttering or choosing words in anger, he said nothing.

'Defend Lemnos against what, exactly?'

Xandros turned to the questioner in the crowd. The man's

flushed face and unruly, retreating curls made him look like a satyr. 'Against the Sea Peoples, of course.'

The host scratched his cheek with his little finger and raised an eyebrow. When he turned to his guests, making a face, they burst out laughing. Xandros felt his cheeks glowing with embarrassment and anger.

'Forgive me! I meant no offence... we meant no offence, did we, ah?' He put a reassuring arm around Xandros and guided him into the hall. *'As you were!'* The cithara player struck up a different, breezy air – one that made some of the guests laugh.

Whilst the hum of conversation picked up once more, the host turned to him. 'Again, forgive me, I lied when I said the only law in this house is not to lie, which was my first offence. There is a second law, of course, dear to Almighty Zeus, and he is quick to avenge abuses of *xenia*. I hope some wine and food – last season's grape was filled with nectar, I swear it – will help wipe my offence.' He clicked his fingers and stewards came over at once, bearing cups for the wine and platters of pastries rolled in honey and oats. 'These are also quite delicious, see?' he added, helping himself to one.

The man's insistence left him with little choice, and he followed with reluctance. 'About these Sea Peoples, these pirates,' he said, with his mouth full. 'You aren't the first to express your concern, of course, but you *are* the first to seek help from us and this, I think, was the source of their laughter. Forget about pirates and sea rovers, my young friend. Every sea has them: always has, always will. You can do no more to prevent this than you can stay the chariots of the sun. *You, more wine!*'

Xandros covered his cup. 'This is your opinion. Yes, there have always been pirates but not in these numbers; nor so dangerous. We fought with them off the coast of Athens, just days ago. They were very real. But if Argos doesn't see the need to protect itself, then we can pay its soldiers to defend Lemnos instead. And if we are successful, perhaps the threat from the sea can be forgotten then.' Xandros became aware through the general thrum of conversation and laughter of a few faces turned towards him. The bonhomie of the host faded with the hardening of his eyes. 'We were told that we might find city councillors here. Is this true?'

'It is. You are speaking to one.'

Xandros regretted his tone but, now that the words were out, there was no way to recast them. 'Then, councillor, let me also say this. I am the grandson of King Jason of Iolkos. Many years ago, he led a crew of warriors to the ends of the earth and back, some of whom, no doubt, came from Argos...'

'Leodocus.'

'L... Who?'

'Leodocus, son of Pero was amongst them. We know our history here. He was from Argos. Didn't return, poor fellow.'

'Leodocus... I hadn't heard of him. When we came to the mainland, I wanted to meet Jason's men, or their descendants, to see if... if they might come to the defence of an island populated by their own kin. The Argonauts spent some time on Lemnos.'

The councillor gave him a searching look. 'My curiosity in you deepens by the second. And have you found any?'

'I have.'

'Remarkable! Excuse me.' He turned to his steward, who whispered a question. 'Don't make a fuss about it: just prepare another *krater*; same ratio.' He tutted and turned back to Xandros. 'Aren't they terribly old to be waving spears about, these Argonauts?'

'They are proud men still.' Xandros got the impression the host's attention was wandering. 'I wanted to ask something. I saw several boats riding at anchor in the bay. Does Argos have many galleys?'

'Galleys? Ah, no.' He smiled at another guest and raised his cup. 'We are a mercantile people these days, and good at it. There aren't too many trading stations our ships haven't seen, even beyond the Archipelagos.'

'Merchant craft need good men to protect them, no? Especially these days?'

The host looked him in the eye. 'We seem to have turned full circle, don't we? As I said earlier, the threat from the sea is overegged but then we Hellenes have always been fond of a good story. Allow me to be, regrettably, brief. Argos and Tiryns are under the sway of the king of Mycenae, and matters of war and peace are his domain, not mine. Please, do enjoy your wine before you leave. Now, if you'll forgive me.'

Xandros watched the man work his way through the hall, raising his cup here and extending a warm hand there, and only once did he glance over his shoulder at him.

He felt the hair on his nape prickle and experienced the same sensation of being followed – or watched – as he had earlier in the day. Feeling uncomfortable, knowing nobody and unsettled by the strange atmosphere, he set down his cup and headed for the door.

Outside, he filled his lungs with cool air. A bat flitted past his head, making him duck whilst, further away, a nightjar churred in search of its mate. He retraced his steps towards the city gates in thoughtful silence, wondering what the *Salamander*'s crew were doing at that moment. He reasoned that he would rather be tolerated in their company than mocked by the odd folk of Argos, and the realisation left the door ajar for his loneliness. Thus distracted, Xandros was unaware of the figure lurking in the shadows of the stand of pines.

Xandrosss...

The sibilant hiss cut through his thoughts and he looked up, seeing the shape detach itself from the darkness, he froze then fumbled for his sword. The soft whisper of a blade being withdrawn from its scabbard set his pulse racing.

'The gold.' The voice was cold, muffled by a rag. 'Give it to me.'

'I have none.'

'Lies.' The footpad drew himself to his full height and advanced.

Behind them, the noise of conversation and laughter briefly rose and fell, and a door clicked shut. Xandros heard footsteps.

Now he was surrounded. The warnings had been made and he had not heeded them. *Keep the blade moving*, Moxos had told him. He would be sure to maim one before being set upon.

'On me, boy!'

Xandros turned on his heels to see a tall, slim man slide an old-fashioned rapier from its scabbard. In his other hand he brandished a torch. Ahead, the footpad took a few hesitant steps forward, weighing up the prospect of two blades against his one. He turned quickly and sprinted off into the night, leaving Xandros breathing heavily, round-eyed.

'You must be sure of yourself, stepping out like that. Especially here.'

'A mistake. A bad one.'

The man nodded. 'Let me walk with you.'

Xandros waited for his breathing to settle. 'Thank you.'

They reached the city gate and a sentry's head bobbed briefly above the wall before the gates creaked open. The two guards were still on duty.

'Did you get what you went for?' asked the elder of the pair. His grin faded a touch when he saw the look on Xandros' face.

'Both less and more, I suspect,' said his escort. 'Goodnight, gentlemen.'

They heard a mumbled response before the gate closed behind them, and walked on until the torch began to gutter, and the darkness crowded their little pocket of light.

Xandros stopped and turned to the stranger. 'My lodgings are close by. Again, thank you.'

The man gave him a doubtful look. To Xandros, he had the appearance of a man of wealth and influence fallen upon hard times. His cloak was fashioned from well-combed wool but looked worn. His hair, though long and dark, was beginning to thin. He extended his hand and Xandros took it, and his grip was strong and rough. 'Tell me true now, boy. I overheard you talking to the host and, by the by, whatever name he may have given to you, ignore it. Nobody knows his true name.'

'He didn't give one.'

'Then it's of no consequence. What *is* of interest to me, though, is what you said about looking for fighting men. Promising gold like you did… That was brash, and you are young. Do you really have it?'

So the wolf has been driven away by the jackal, thought Xandros. 'But not here. I'm not so naïve as that.'

'But naïve enough to venture out armed only with an old toothpick.'

Xandros noticed through the man's crooked grin that he was missing one or two teeth. 'Who are you and why are you so interested in gold?'

'Give me a man who isn't interested in gold and I will show you a liar! But, remiss of me not to say, I am Caeneus, son of the late Polyphemus, king of Larissa. If the other thing you said was true, that you are a grandson of Jason of Iolkos, then he and my father were crewmates on *Argo*. At least, they were for a spell. I suppose some of my interest lies here, too.'

'It is true.' This news wrongfooted him and he scrutinised the man for some trace of deception. He could see none. 'You say you are the son of a king... So why might soldiering for gold be so interesting? Do you not have enough already?'

Caeneus gave Xandros an amused look. 'Go on, admit it, boy. You think me vulgar, don't you?'

'I haven't formed an opinion. Yet.'

'I said I was son of the king, as indeed I am. *A* son not *the* son. My father sired three; I am the youngest though by no means the least able. In Larissa we keep the laws of inheritance, though they do me no justice.'

Xandros let the words sink in. They seemed to strike a chord with his appearance and demeanour. He looked around him but the streets were empty and silent. 'Are you interested in sailing to Lemnos, to help us?'

Caeneus sniffed. 'Can you guarantee reward for such a service? A *fitting* one?'

'How many men do you have?'

'How *many*? I answer to myself and only myself!'

'Then what guarantee could we have you wouldn't take the gold and leave without raising a hand?'

'Enough fencing, boy. My word is good, as is my arm. *Very* good. I might even say the finest in Argos; not that the men here fight like their ancestors anymore.'

Xandros thought about it for a moment before extending his hand. 'Ask me for no payment now. Our boat leaves at dawn the day after tomorrow: I will show you some gold then.'

Xandros wasn't sure the noise Caeneus made was a grunt of

assent or a growl of disappointment. Either way, he tipped his head and stalked off into the night.

'A word to the wise.' Caeneus turned back, half-concealed by the deep shadow of overhanging eaves. 'If you want to be sure of *meeting* your own boat, can I suggest you don't venture out again like you did this evening?' He added, coldly, 'Few streets are safe anymore.'

Xandros watched him merge into the darkness like the very thief who might have done for him not a half hour previously.

The host was not happy. His popularity amongst Argives was due in no small measure to his ability to make his guests feel like he was present in conversation, such that his considered opinions were appreciated even if they were not always what a person might want to hear. But, that evening, whilst he heard what his guests were saying, he found it difficult to listen. The young foreigner had slighted him and that just wouldn't do.

Perhaps it was also because, at some level, he knew the boy was right, but he had long since reconciled what was right with what was best for a man in his position. Secure. Wealthy. Safe.

He excused himself from a discussion about which country produced the finest gem-cutters and beckoned his steward into an anteroom just off the main hall. In the lamp-lit room, with the door closed and the conversation from the *megaron* a faint hum, he turned to the steward.

'I need you to deliver a message. A private one.'

The steward nodded. He knew full well what that coda meant. 'Of course, master.'

When he had finished, he got the steward to repeat it back to him, which was done to his satisfaction.

'I assume just before first light, master?'

'Yes.' A pause. 'No, now.'

'Now?'

'Yes, right now!'

The steward bowed, doing his best to keep the irritation from his face. 'Of course.'

XV

Mycenae

Xandros was awoken early the following morning by the clatter of carts and loud voices in the street below. He ate an unhurried breakfast whilst he deliberated over the wisdom of his decision. In the end, he realised he had no choice if he wanted to return to Lemnos with substantive help: quite against the advice of more than one person, he would have to take a chance with Mycenae.

He packed his belongings and descended onto the streets, wrinkling his nose at the pungent smell wafting from the tannery. Once or twice, he glanced over his shoulder, unable to shake the feeling of being followed. A toothless street hawker tried to catch his attention and, taking his eyes from the road for a moment, had to sidestep a woman balancing a water jar on her head, who tutted as she passed.

Once he had passed through the northern gate and picked up the road that led away from the coast, he felt the tension ease in his mind. After an hour's walking, in which he decided that returning to Myrine with five spearmen would be the minimum for his journey to be considered a success, whilst ten would be a boon, he reached the crossroads. The main road stretched away into the distance towards Corinth, where he lost sight of it in the parched valley a few miles ahead. To the right, crouched upon a hill between the two mountains, invisible in the haze of dust, lay the ancient citadel of the great kings of Mycenae.

He encountered few people on the road and those he did meet eyed him in a way that began to make him question what he was doing. He recalled what the captain had said about this region.

There's a darkness about Mycenae.

As he crossed a little stone bridge over a dry riverbed, he had to shade his eyes. Clearly, Xandros thought with a wry smile, the man hadn't been talking of the weather.

The main road ran on ahead but then turned right, where a narrower track snaked away towards the twin mountains that guarded the citadel of Mycenae, presiding over the valley before it. After a few minutes, the path began its inexorable climb towards it. As the slope steepened, he passed tombs cut into the rock by the roadside, partially obscured by dried grasses and, shortly afterwards, he looked down the valley upon a straggle of kilns and sheds, and thousands of mud bricks laid out to dry. Goats were tethered outside a few of the buildings, and their plaintive bleats drifted up to him. The structures here were in a poor state of repair and it became clear that only some of the living quarters had been repurposed for storage or as animal byres. Others were simply exposed to the elements, and he wondered if the Mycenaeans had also felt the anger of the recent earthquake.

He passed a magnificent *tholos* tomb on his left, where mulberry trees grew from the clogged entryways, and Xandros shuddered involuntarily as he drew level with it. Something about the valley made him uneasy. The ground, hollow beneath his feet with the ghost-ridden chambers of long-dead nobility, perhaps. That and the forbidding walls of Mycenae that now reared to his right, beyond the grassy mounds of another pair of tombs.

He stopped in awe of the magnificent gate that stood before him, all pretence at worldliness momentarily forgotten. The bronze faces of a pair of proud lionesses glinted dully above a massive lintel stone. One of the wooden doors to the citadel stood open.

As he moved into the shadows of the bastion wall, a gruff voice startled him. 'Stay still! What do you want?'

Xandros looked up. Several figures had appeared on the walls above him, arms draped over spears wedged behind their necks. Two were bare-chested and the one addressing him had a goatskin jerkin and breeches. To Xandros, they looked more like mountain bandits than royal guards.

'I need to speak to the king.'

A dog started barking from inside the gate. 'Useless mongrel,' muttered one of the men, disappearing from view.

'Expecting you, is he?'

Xandros considered lying but thought better of it. 'No.'

He smirked at one of his men. 'Then you'd better fuck off, hadn't you.'

Xandros stood his ground. 'The king is in grave danger. I need to speak to him.'

The guard rolled his neck and blew the air from his cheeks. 'He's starting to piss me off,' he said with quiet menace. 'What's the king's name?' When Xandros remained quiet, 'Do you even know his name?' One of the other guards laughed.

'Do you know mine?'

'I'd sooner eat my own shit than know what your name is.'

'I'm the son of the king of Lemnos. I have gold here and more on our island. I came here to warn your king, to help him and ask for help in return. I expected to find men of honour.' He turned full circle, addressing the half-dozen men now behind him. 'I expected warriors. This is Mycenae, isn't it? Leader of the Eastern War? Mightiest *polis* on land or sea?' He addressed the main guard again. 'Well? I see men who can fight, no doubt, but I see no honour. Perhaps I can take my gold elsewhere?'

It was a dangerous gamble, leaving no further options if he was jeered and hounded out. Or, worse, set upon. The guard's face had set and they stared down at him resolute in their indifference.

Xandros took a deep breath and exhaled slowly. He tipped his head back down the path, away from the gate, with a calm he did not feel. With this, the latest failure, to add to the litany of failures, the adventure seemed risibly ill-conceived. *What grounds – what possible reason – did he have to expect such a distant town with such a proud history to have any interest in the affairs of a backwater island anyway?* He had been told this – in various ways and at various times – in the last couple of weeks but had been too pig-headed to listen. It was time to cut his losses and return.

Guards emerged from the shadows of the bastion: those in front neither stepped aside nor moved to prevent him. They just stared, hard-faced. He could almost feel the bronze spear tips pointed at his back.

'Wait.'

He turned to see the outspoken guard stood, hands on hips, outside the gate, flanked by a pair of bowmen. Now that he was at his level, Xandros saw he was smaller than average height but broad in the shoulder and exuding immense confidence.

'Where is the gold?'

'On our boat.'

'Describe your boat.'

Xandros shrugged. 'It's nothing special. Forty feet long, maybe a little more. Bow post carved like a goddess: the *Cyprian*.'

The guard fixed him with an intense stare and Xandros felt a trickle of sweat form at the curve of his spine. 'I will have your sword and spear before you see the *wanax*.'

He handed over his weapons to the guard, who beckoned him inside, and passed under the immense lintel stone. Being the object of cold curiosity set his nerves humming – soldiers, guards... Xandros didn't know who they might be but they were armed with a variety of daggers and cudgels as well as spears and swords. One man was crouched by a chariot, examining its wheels, and he glanced up at him before checking the spokes.

There was a low growl and he stepped to the side. Emerging from the shadows of a cubbyhole was a black dog with its lips curled back, revealing sharp yellow teeth.

'Where's your bark, you stupid mutt?' One of the guards feigned hitting it and it cowered with a scared growl.

'He'd bark if you treated him properly,' said Xandros. 'He's so thin!' He retrieved a pear from his bag and, before they could intervene, introduced it gently to the dog.

'Do you want to see the king or do you want to lose your hand?'

Xandros ignored him and bent down, making encouraging noises.

'Are you f—'

The dog lunged from its hole so abruptly that the workman stumbled back upon the chariot. Though Xandros flinched, he kept his eyes upon the dog and, to the astonishment of the guards, it glared at him before backing down. Then it snatched the pear from Xandros' palm and retreated into the cubbyhole. Xandros caught the guard's raised eyebrow as he motioned him to move on and heard the workman swearing behind him.

To the right was an enclosure, embraced by the stone circuit walls of the citadel. A few weathered *stelai* stood at various angles amidst the dried grass and weeds, bearing images of hunters on chariots and symbols of the sea. Beyond it, a cluster of old houses, from one of which rose hearth smoke. Directly ahead was a paved ramp and when they were a few paces up it, the guard half-turned to Xandros.

'The king's name is Orestes. Show him respect when you see him, understand?'

It seemed like an obvious thing to add and Xandros wondered why he mentioned it. *Was he scared of him?* 'I will,' he murmured.

As the steep path zig-zagged uphill, Xandros noticed signs of destruction. Charred stone here; hastily repaired walls there. The flat roofs of some bowed alarmingly in the middle. Either side of the path, fragments of earthenware still poked up out of the accretion of dust and refuse. Lime plaster hung off the sides of buildings or exposed the bricks in patches where it had crumbled away. 'Did you feel the earthquake here, a few days ago?'

'No.' The guard tutted. 'Shoo! Go on, get out of here!'

Xandros was surprised to see the dog had followed them up the path and now wheeled away as his escort aimed a kick at it.

'Leave it alone.'

The guard spat to the side. 'Think you're some kind of dog whisperer now, do you?'

They had stopped before a short flight of stone steps and a gatehouse supported by two columns, one behind the other. They were about to enter when a guardsman appeared from the shadows, waving the butt of his spear at the little group.

The sentinel's eyebrows beetled at Xandros but his escort winked at him and, reluctantly, he stood aside, narrowing his eyes at the newcomer. They breezed through a little courtyard before passing through another porchway and Xandros found himself amid the palace complex. Through the two sets of doors ahead, he caught a glimpse of the king's hearth and the comings and goings of various courtiers. A tall window on the right offered a magnificent view of the parched valley along which he had trekked from Argos. In the distance, mountains retreated in fading hues of purple, a majestic reminder of the freedom with which Xandros was gambling.

The guard had a brief conversation with a courtier. He knew it was about him because of the surreptitious looks in his direction. The courtier went back into the *megaron* with Xandros' sword and spear whilst the guard beckoned him around a tiled courtyard into a little suite of rooms with a washbasin at one end and cots at another. 'The guest quarters. You're lucky there's no one else using them. Stay here until you're summoned.' Without another word, he strode away.

Xandros looked around him. The accommodation was comfortable, if basic, but the thought that now drifted into his mind was that he was in prison.

He watched the shadows lengthen in the valley beyond the window. A servant had brought a tray with some simple fare upon it – bread, cheese, olives – but, when asked about how long he would have to wait, the man would not be drawn. 'The king is not in the palace.'

'Then why was I told before he *is* in residence?'

The man shrugged. 'How can I say what other people mean when they speak?'

At some point in the early afternoon, he heard a flurry of urgent voices and an increase in the footfall outside their quarters but it had faded quickly. When Xandros got up to investigate, an armed guard shook his head slowly at him.

Then, as early evening descended and just as he had resolved a plan to try to escape, a different courtier – one with more polished manners and an unctuous smile – ushered him through the courtyard to a porchway that led to the *megaron*.

A fire had been lit in the hearth. Shadows of the four pillars supporting the roof fell into each corner of the hall and, between them, the glow from the flames illumined cracked and faded frescoes. He heard a quiet flutter of laughter and a servant passed the doorway with a tray bearing a pitcher. Wine, Xandros hoped, destined for him.

The courtier asked him to wait for a moment and disappeared from view. He saw him bow before he returned. 'High King Orestes will see you now.'

With his heart racing, Xandros straightened his back and entered the hall behind the courtier.

'My lord, the Lemnian.'

He was not alone with the king. To the right of the door was a couch, upon which lolled a well-built, narrow-eyed man, whose hair and beard glistened with pomade. Sat next to him was a long-legged woman with hair as dark as night and the most extraordinary eyes of marbled green that he had ever seen. They looked him up and down as they were introduced, and the looks they gave him were on the unfriendly side of neutral.

Twin guards flanked the throne, hand-picked if their strong jaws and deep chests were anything to go by. On the throne himself sat the king, propping his chin upon his hand, one leg languidly draped over the arm.

To Xandros, he was a man of immediate contradiction. The expensive purple cloak and hemmed tunic, the golden ring in his earlobe, the louche manner spoke of a dandy. The deep brown eyes and long face spoke of openness and intelligence. But the firelight also revealed a slight depression above his left eye, like a thumb pressed against warm wax, and a scar across his cheek, demarcating stubble from freshly shaved skin, that had nicked his upper lip and healed badly at some point in the past. His weathered hands looked like they might snap a spear shaft merely by squeezing it.

King Orestes appraised him briefly then brushed back his long hair and stood with sudden grace. He opened his palms. 'You want wine? Pour them some wine, Konsta!' he said, without waiting for an answer. 'Please! Help yourself to a stool, behind that pillar.'

Orestes waited for him to sit before raising a cup of his own – made from rock crystal, Xandros noticed. 'Your health and the health of the kingdom!'

Xandros raised his cup, a little self-consciously, and adjusted himself on the low stool. Orestes clicked his fingers and platters of grilled meat and artichokes were brought in from a door to a private corridor, tucked away to the left of the entrance porch.

'Forgive us. We… My manners… This is my old friend Pylades and, one might say, a rather newer friend, Eriopis. We have already eaten but the rules of hospitality remain! Eat, drink and then you will tell us what brings you here.'

Whilst Xandros eagerly set about the food, not having eaten for several hours, Orestes turned back to Pylades and the enigmatic woman, Eriopis. He resumed his light-hearted observations of the ingratitude of the 'ancient peasantry', as he called them, whose protection he had assured since 'seeing off' the usurper. The guests laughed and Pylades offered some advice: a festival day, perhaps? They tend to make people pliable.

'More livestock to the slaughter?' asked Orestes, feigning shock. 'Would my people see me destitute? The flooding of that wretched lake has squeezed us so hard if I were a lemon, the pips would fly out!'

More polite laughter. A fond memory about fighting… repelling raiders. He had fought like a wild animal that day, mainly because he wanted to get the matter done on account of his loose bowels. Uproarious laughter, making even the guards smirk. Orestes had the assurance of a man nearing his fiftieth summer but, in this light, he might easily have passed for a man half that age.

Beneath the bonhomie, however, and the extravagance of his body language, Xandros noticed the searching glances towards the newcomer in his midst. There felt something faintly artificial about the conversation: about the whole scene, even… He felt a ripple of unease but the mellow wine soon becalmed it.

'The grape,' observed the pomaded guest, Pylades, as if reading his thoughts, 'the king *neglected* to tell you, is from Nemea.' He kissed the tips of his fingers. 'It's quite excellent, isn't it? And from a valley a few hours' walk away.'

'Why else d'you think my drink-sodden ancestors set up here?' offered Orestes, to more laughter. 'It's not just the location. The citadel can be turned,' he said, wagging a finger at Xandros, 'but before you get any ideas, you'd need a crack group of men.'

Orestes' eyes lingered on him for a moment longer than was comfortable. Xandros set aside the tray and cleared his throat. 'Your Highness, this is one of the reasons I am here.'

'Ah!' Orestes set his drink aside. 'And I thought you had just come to pay your respects.' He sat upright. 'To business, then.'

Xandros had been rehearsing his introduction and spoke of Lemnos as a unified island lacking only manpower to protects its shores. The Sea Peoples were coming – had already been sighted off the coast of the island – and were disrupting trade even where they weren't causing devastation.

As Xandros spoke, Orestes and his friend exchanged the odd look but he heard him out with a semblance of respect. 'If the seas are so deadly,' said the king, trying to work a piece of food wedged between his teeth with his tongue, 'how is it that we still thrive? "Mycenae rich-in-gold" is still how the bards describe this city, isn't it? If they ever visit your island, that is.'

Xandros ignored the insult and instead recalled the evidence of fire damage on the way to the palace, and the crumbling plasterwork. 'Aren't you worried this might come to an end, someday soon? Haven't you heard of the threat from the sea?'

'Of course we have!' Orestes laughed without mirth. 'Watchmen have been set, resources prepared.' He waved the matter away and sat up straighter. 'But, two obvious questions. Firstly, why would any *polis* want to send its valuable warriors to defend a far-off island? And secondly, forgive me for being so blunt, why have you come *here*?'

Xandros had been asked the same several times over. He gave the same answers, unembellished but with more fluency and force now. 'I am trying to unite us, so that – together – we can defeat them in one action.'

'The grandson of Jason! Not for you just to bask in another man's *kleos*, is that it? How very noble!'

Orestes chuckled but then raised an apologetic hand. Pylades, Xandros noticed, projected the same air of superiority but Eriopis was watching him with a burning intensity.

'People laughed at them, too, at the time. Until the Argonauts returned with the fleece.' He gave Pylades a sidelong glance. 'Then the laughter stopped. Such a thing has been achieved before and it can be done again.'

'I see...' said Orestes, drumming his fingers against the throne's armrest and absently staring into the hearth flames. 'I see.'

Xandros hadn't intended such a curt tone and it now seemed to him a line had been crossed. The atmosphere within the *megaron* curdled a little.

'Spiro... that is, my chief bodyguard... mentioned you came laden with gold.' He cocked his head to the side. 'Why was this?'

'Proof, I suppose. Evidence of the wealth we have at Lemnos.' Even as he uttered the lie, it tasted bitter on his tongue.

'I thought you said you wanted to appeal to the unity of the Greeks. To... higher ideals. But now you appeal to the baseness of your fellow man. Which is it to be?'

Xandros winced inwardly. A sudden pressure had begun to build within his temples, and his first thought was that the wine had been drugged. 'Some men respond to ideals; some to gold. I came prepared for both.'

Orestes was about to respond when he turned to someone concealed in the shadows of the private doorway and raised a finger an inch or two. In the meagre light, Xandros only saw a hooded outline that slipped back into the corridor. Orestes adjusted his cloak and gave a noncommittal grunt. 'I suppose we have men that respond to both. Whilst I myself like to think I am motivated by higher principles, the likes of Spiro and his bandits... Well, gold speaks like a purring whore to them.'

'They are not your men?'

'They are.' His tone became brisk. 'I find that all men, however, respond to some old-fashioned honesty. Don't you, Xandros?'

'I suppose they do.'

'And, to be frank, you haven't been entirely honest with us, have you?'

The pressure in his skull had eased but Xandros felt his stomach swill. 'I haven't?'

'No.'

'How so?'

'Your boat, with the bow post sculpted like a goddess. It isn't your boat at all, is it?'

Xandros swallowed hard whilst his mind raced about the implications. What had the skipper warned him? *Stay away from Mycenae and Tiryns.*

'I'm told we gave the actual boat owner quite a shock, when he returned to find my men crawling all over it. You owe him an apology, I think!'

'It pays to be cautious.'

'It doesn't pay to waste my time.' Anger flashed in Orestes' eyes. 'I need to monitor everyone who lands on my shores. This is *my* burden of care.'

On the couch, Xandros saw the pomaded Pylades take a sip of wine and dab the corner of his mouth. 'I'd like to know, if I may, whether you are even telling the truth about who you are?' Orestes nodded at the sagacity of his friend's question.

'The sword that was taken from me. My grandfather gave it to me just a few days ago.'

Orestes reached beside him and retrieved the sword and its battered scabbard. He slipped the blade free and turned it over, examining it with the eye of an expert. 'Yes, it is rather an old design, isn't it? Seen some action too. Pretty, though.' He rammed it back in with a loud *clack* that made Xandros flinch. 'But I wouldn't say it proves anything. Beyond you owning an antique.'

'Our boat leaves in two days. I will defend my island, whether you believe anything about me or not. I have wealth back in Lemnos and, if I must, I will pay for warriors to help me. But I didn't come here to be tested.'

'You see, I think this is another untruth. I think you have wealth *here* but not on your little island. Am I right?'

Xandros tried to keep the mounting panic from his face. *Had his men also forced their way aboard his boat? Had they found the Golden Fleece?*

'You are wrong.'

The lambent flames of the hearth glimmered in Orestes' eyes. Xandros had the discomfiting impression the man was sifting through his thoughts. 'Time will tell. In the meantime,' he said brightly, 'you will remain a guest of mine. You may finish your wine here before resting in your quarters.'

'You mean I am under house arrest.'

Orestes and his guest raised their eyebrows in amusement. 'If you insist on calling it that – until I am satisfied with your intentions. But what a prison!' he said, gesturing around him.

Xandros rose first and, maintaining eye contact with him, poured his goblet of wine into the flames. 'And until I am satisfied this is not poisoned.'

Orestes laughed and slapped his armrest, but the humour was brittle and offence had been taken. Xandros saw this just as, in the sizzle of the flames, he thought he heard a hiss of warning: a woman's voice. One he had heard before.

XVI

Xandros watched the drizzle fall in the twilight and approached the window, deep in thought. He pushed open the shutters and peered over the sill. Beyond the wall was a sheer drop into the valley, the floor of which he couldn't even see in the gathering gloom. The building itself, he had to admit, perched on the very edge of a precipice, was a feat of engineering he could scarcely fathom. How many men must have died to satisfy the desire of one warlord?

In short, if the fortress offered any means of escape, this window was not it. A few miles away, on the coastal plain, lay Argos. He could make out the faintest lines of the acropolis if he squinted. Somewhere out there was the crew of his boat. He had heard tales, growing up, of people who could exchange thoughts without speaking – without even being in eyesight of each other. Twins were sometimes said to be gifted in this way. He only wished he could get a message to them by such telepathy, though he doubted there would be much that could be done, even if it were possible.

He wondered what the crew was doing at that moment – whether they'd even been aware of Orestes' bandits searching the other vessel. He guessed they would be. There would be no reason to link it to him and his plight, however. He doubted the skipper had even given him any thought, not whilst there was trade to be done. In short, Xandros was on his own.

He leaned against the sill and closed his eyes.

Xandros...

'Yes?' he said. When he received no response, he looked behind him, sure a woman had entered the room. This wasn't the first time but the voice was so near he could almost feel the breath brushing his ear. He gazed back out of the window, wondering if he might be losing his mind. Perhaps, given the fool's errand upon which he had embarked, he already had. Perhaps he was just tired.

Sleep.

Yes, that was what he needed. He pushed himself away from the window, feeling his legs growing leaden and, when he took a few steps towards the cot, it seemed entirely natural to give himself up to it.

He ignored his name being called and closed his eyes, not waking even when he struck the cold stucco.

At some point whilst he sleeps, he feels himself drifting out of bed. He glides across the floor of the guest quarter and on into the tiled forecourt, feeling almost no weight through his feet. He can hear the crackling of flames in the *megaron* and sees the frescoes on the far wall, framed by the pillars and bathed in moonlight.

He enters the hall, where the hearth fire blazes. He hears the soft hoot of an owl through the gap in the roof where the smoke escapes into the night. Drawn by the seductive dance of the flames, it takes him a moment to realise he is not alone. He turns a full circle and, though he can't see anybody, he knows there is someone close by, aware of his presence. Someone in the darkness – in the corridors or adjoining chambers of the palace – of immense power. A power not possessed in the strength of the arm but in some ancient, elemental force. It has left its trace in the hall, as sure as incense in a sanctuary. He follows it into the corridor, where he caught a glimpse of a cowled figure not long before. Aware of movement behind him, he turns. It startles him to see a warrior gazing into the fire with a goblet of wine in his hand. He is short and stocky, with a dark beard streaked grey, and something is amiss.

It takes Xandros a few moments to realise that he is staring at a *phantasma*. The man is not opaque. He takes a few cautious steps back into the hall, circling the apparition as if he is walking upon eggshells. The skin of the warrior's thick arms and neck, he can see, is sun-darkened. He looks tired and there are rings beneath his eyes. That he cannot see Xandros soon becomes clear.

A man strides into the hall, behind Xandros, making him flinch and step aside. The fear is fleeting, however, for the newcomer cannot see him either. He is a younger man; taller, slimmer. He has long, wavy hair, tied loosely at his nape, and a loose-fitting, richly embroidered tunic. He raises his arms in delight at seeing the older man and, though his lips move, the words are inaudible to Xandros. The grizzled warrior looks unimpressed and raises the goblet to his lips. His face clouds with irritation and perhaps a hint of suspicion, and his lips barely move as he utters a word or two in response: no more. The newcomer lowers his arms and is more diffident now. He flicks a glance over his shoulder and, with that slight twist of his body, Xandros glimpses the curved knife tucked into his belt.

The images of both men shimmer like the heat rising from rocks under the beating sun. There is a nightmarish inevitability to what is about to happen and Xandros' horror is compounded by his powerlessness to prevent it. The guardedness of the older man – a king, it is clear – slips for only a moment. Perhaps he expects, by his cool manner, that the younger will take the hint and leave him. He raises his goblet and turns towards the corridor. He bares his teeth when he shouts.

More wine!

The fluid grace of the younger man takes Xandros by surprise. As he closes upon the king, his fingers wrap around the handle of the dagger. The blade is swinging towards the king's exposed side before he can react.

No! shouts Xandros. Despite himself, he rushes towards the assailant and tries to grab his elbow as it draws back for another strike. His fingers pass through the flesh and bone as if they were woodsmoke.

But the king is no stranger to violence. A tendril of saliva loops from his mouth as he roars in shock and anger and pain. Though he is mortally wounded, he lands a heavy blow to his assailant's face with the goblet, making him stumble backwards.

Xandros looks on, benumbed, as a woman now rushes into the hall. Her head is veiled but her face is grimly set and her eyes glitter with intent. She is clutching a dagger of her own, in hands extended like one putting a venomous snake outside. The king's expression becomes pitiable and he sinks to one knee and reaches out for her with dark blood dribbling through his fingers.

Xandros shouts again. *No!*

He has no heart to witness an execution but he is frozen to the spot. It is a tableau that sears itself upon his mind. The assassin scrambling back to his feet, dazed and bloody-nosed. The woman, hesitating only for a moment; driving the blade through the victim's heart then throwing it to the floor in disgust. The old king, slipping to the floor in front of the throne, twitching once, twice, before becoming still as a dark stain pools around him.

Xandros!

He awoke with a start, finding himself back in the twilight of the guest quarter.

Propping himself up on his elbow, Xandros winced in pain. His right arm was sore; bruised. It took him a moment for his eyes to adjust to the lamp-lit room. A familiar face came into focus.

'He lives!' said the woman, tucking her hair behind her ears. 'Thank the Great Goddess.'

Xandros rubbed his face, trying to clear the fog from his skull, but it only sent a jolt of pain along his arm.

'You fell on your elbow? One of the servants helped me get you onto the bed.'

He looked at Eriopis in surprise. 'I don't know what happened… That wine. It was drugged, wasn't it?'

'We all drank from the same *krater*, I am sure. People can faint for many reasons.' She presented him with a beaker. 'This will help clear your head.'

'What's this?'

'An infusion.'

'You made it?'

Eriopis' face tightened a little. 'I did. It contains no poison if this is what concerns you.'

Xandros sat up and sniffed the drink before sipping it. It tasted bitter but he could also smell the honey and lemon in it.

'The answer to your question is mountain herbs.' Her eyes had the faculty of smiling at him whilst also combing his thoughts. Xandros drank some more and, after a few moments, the throbbing in his elbow faded. 'Do they know you're here?'

'No. But they keep the laws of *xenia*.'

'Even when they drug their guests?' He expected her to take her leave but, when she merely frowned at him, he pointed to a chair. 'I'm getting tired of my own company.'

Eriopis glanced through the door and tipped her head. 'For a few moments.'

'Where are you from?' he asked.

'Oh, across the seas.' He had caught a trace of an accent and guessed she was not a Hellene. 'Nowhere you would have heard of. Tell me something, Xandros. It wasn't your falling I heard, just before I entered this room, but something else.'

'What was it?'

'Did you have a dream? I heard you shouting.'

He looked away.

'Tell me.'

His instinct was to lie, and tell her he had seen nothing, or to keep her own business but the images were very clear and, the truth of it was, he wanted to know what they meant. So he told her, leaving nothing out, though he kept his voice low. He even told her about the vision of the hideous old man rowing towards him. It felt liberating to unburden himself.

Despite her saying she only had a few moments, Eriopis was an attentive listener, only interrupting him once to clarify something. He liked the way she looked at him, with no trace of judgement in her expression, the way her lips pursed slightly when he described the violence. He even liked the way, when he had finished, she seemed to retreat into her thoughts, apparently comfortable with the silence. When she next spoke, her voice was a breathy whisper. 'I have always thought that stones can become the carriers of local memories, especially when those stones are ruins and the memories witnessed are strong. Do you believe this is possible, Xandros?'

Such a thought had never entered his mind and he said so but, not wanting to appear boorish, he quickly added, 'Are you saying the hall out there – I don't know – holds memories of what has passed, like a *pyxis* of jewellery?'

'Perhaps. But a box that will not open for just anyone.' Once more, he felt her eyes searching for something deep within. 'Have you told me everything, Xandros?'

'Everything I saw; and not only within the walls of this palace, remember? Don't you believe me?'

'And what you didn't see?'

He frowned at her. 'A poor witness who makes things up.'

'You know this is not what I asked.'

'The answer remains…' He rubbed his eyes; the truth was his senses still felt sluggish. 'I didn't *see* anything else but I felt it. A presence… and a powerful one.' He looked at her to gauge her reaction.

'Yes?'

'It felt like another woman was nearby but that is all.' He considered it for a moment. 'Although I did catch a glimpse of a figure in a cloak earlier: someone Orestes seemed to gesture towards, concealed in a hallway, but it could have been a slave for all I know.'

Her face brightened, like one who has just resolved a riddle. 'You have a gift, Xandros, but you should open your mind – and your heart – towards it. Not try to explain it away.'

'Well? Is there someone else here? Something powerful?'

'Without a doubt. These walls breathe murder and I think it maddens people who remain too long within them.' Eriopis pulled her shawl around her shoulders. 'What was in your heart when you came to Mycenae, Xandros?'

He blinked at her, thrown by the question. 'If you mean what I wanted, you have already heard this.'

Her face flickered with disappointment. 'This was not what I meant. Did you truly expect help or was it something else?'

He was about to flippantly ask if he hadn't made himself clear enough in the *megaron* but something about her eyes made him think again. And now he grasped it. Her way was to ask questions to which she already knew the answer. 'Both, I think.'

'I would say so, too. You will get more than you came here for,

Xandros, but you should be careful.' There were footsteps just beyond the guest quarters but they faded in the direction of the courtyard. 'I must go. You will sleep well tonight, I think.'

He watched her go and, for the first time, disagreed with her. With her exit, the light in the room seemed to dim and he got up to look out of the window. Night had all but fallen and, down a vista of shadows, he could discern little but the dark contours of the valley. Then, just as he was about to turn for his bed he saw, like a fallen star, a brief twinkle of light in the direction of Argos.

XVII

He breakfasted alone in the guest chambers and was relieved to be told by a servant who returned to take his plates that he was free to roam the public spaces of the citadel with a chaperone but was required to speak to the king later that day. Xandros bridled at being told what he could or could not do but saw there was little choice. Perhaps, he reasoned, Orestes was making preparations for him to take some men back to Lemnos.

He left the palace without being challenged, though he felt the sneering looks of the king's guards, and passed through its courtyards into the steep streets of the high city. The afternoon sun was invisible through the thick plates of grey cloud, which the winds sent scudding across the sky only to be replenished by more of the same. They threatened rain but stopped short of delivering it.

He descended from the summit towards a cluster of buildings. Earthenware and sections of timber hinted at a craftsman's quarter but there was something rather forlorn to it all. The stacks of mouldering wood had been collected in months past and had since remained untroubled by axe or saw. Some of the clay pots had cracked during firing and had not been taken away; some were still wrapped in damp cloth, suggesting potters were at least active here.

Behind him, the chaperone was joined by another man and, between the gusts of wind, he heard snatches of murmured conversation. Xandros stepped onto a little courtyard bounded by the massive northern walls of the citadel. Another man emerged into view up a flight of stone steps to the left, bearing two pails of water. With his drooping moustache and belt dragged down by a large knife, he looked like one of Spiro's cut-throats. He jerked his head to the side as he approached, wanting Xandros to move aside. He let him pass and peered into the darkness, where the steps receded into the bedrock. Some kind of water cistern, he presumed. On the opposite side of the courtyard, where the walls enclosed the northern tip of the citadel, rough-hewn planks of wood leaned against the stone. He had come as far as he could go. He was about to wander over to the planks when he heard someone shouting.

The chaperone was beckoning him impatiently.

The ghost of a thought formed in Xandros' mind then vanished as suddenly as his dream. He tutted and trudged after him.

'Our scouts have yet to fail me. The vermin have emerged from their nests and plan to scurry up our walls this night and against them, boy, *you* can prove your worth. If you do, I promise I will send men to you. Is this agreed?'

Xandros looked closely at Orestes. He reckoned that, if he had at least learned one thing on this voyage, it was a deeper sense of a man's character. On the king's face, he could see no trickery but Orestes was clearly a shrewd individual. Ruthless, too.

'What would you have me do?'

Orestes laughed. 'The spirit of the islanders! Very good. My men say that there is a force of bandits camped a few miles west of here. The valley beyond the track to the citadel is the most popular route of attack yet none of the gallant fools who try their luck ever seem to understand that we always know they are coming.'

Pylades was sat in the same chair as the previous evening, watching him as he sipped his wine. Of Eriopis, however, there was no sign.

'Are you even listening?' asked Orestes.

'I am,' said Xandros, 'but it seems you are well enough prepared without me.'

'Indeed we are! But I want to see you prove your worth. My men won't just follow any chancer. You will join a detachment led by Spiro and will do exactly as he says. He is a seasoned fighter. A dirty one, too, if I am honest, but very effective.'

'The man is a devil,' added Pylades.

'You can learn from him. Just don't let him out of your sight because when he has the scent of blood…'

'When do we prepare?'

'Aha!' Orestes clapped his hands together. 'Now that's what I like to hear. Didn't I say I liked him as soon as I laid eyes on him, old friend?'

'More or less instantly,' said Pylades.

'Then why did you poison my wine?'

He watched the grin slowly fade on the king's face and he blinked in confusion. 'Ah, yes, I did hear of this. Could this have been a reaction to the food as well, no? After all, the rest of us were well enough were we not? Woe betide the man who seeks to harm a guest under *my* roof, Xandros! But now you are ready for some fun, eh?' Orestes reached for Jason's sword, where it was still propped by his throne, and tossed it to Xandros. 'A venerable weapon like that fairly thirsts for some blood! Your spear is in the guest quarters. You leave at sundown.'

XVIII

To Xandros' surprise, Spiro treated him with the sort of crude bonhomie reserved for a ten-year comrade. They left by the Gate of The Lionesses just as the sun was sinking into the very valley for which they were headed, twenty-three strong, all clad in similar dark homespun cloaks. All armed and in possession of torches tipped with pine resin.

'Silence now, lads,' said Spiro. 'Voices carry further in the evening quiet.'

They passed by the grave circle and Spiro muttered a prayer towards its ancient stones. Just before leaving the gate, Xandros heard the guard dog snuffling inside the guards' cubbyhole. Then they filed along a track that threaded down through a fragrant grove of fruit trees. The dry earth crackled underfoot, and Xandros reflected upon the arid soil of Lemnos. Evidently all of Hellas was suffering yet, despite the crumbling buildings of Mycenae, Orestes and his close circle ate and drank like lords. Which made him consider once more just what sort of man it was who had sent him out.

The path took them past an ancient tomb on the left, the roof of which had collapsed, and dried branches from some shrub or other poked out of the top. Then it levelled out and they turned right, all the while scanning the sweep of the valley below. Seeds of light flickered through the shutters of clusters of houses and farmsteads. Further along, threads of smoke from hearth fires told of other families huddled together against the encroaching night.

Spiro beckoned everyone into a huddle. 'For our guest,' he whispered, 'this is the best means of accessing the citadel. There are other tracks but they are narrow and steep, and these are guarded also. Understand so far? Good. In a moment, we disperse along this road and then melt into the shadows of the slope. You, boy, use this…' he tugged the woollen wrap hung around his neck '… to conceal your face. Even though there is excellent cover from the trees and also the tombs of our ancestors, you are very pale.' His eyes hardened at Xandros. 'Respect the tombs, please. When the bandits come, we fall upon them, we kill them. Very simple.' His lips curled into a sly grin. 'Light a torch now, if you must, but save the others. You will know when you need them.' He looked around him and nodded. 'Now go!'

The Mycenaeans scattered without fuss, quickly disappearing in the enveloping shadows. Spiro moved away with a handful of men and then said, over his shoulder, 'I will be a short distance away, keeping an eye on you.'

Xandros watched him merge into the shadows further down the road. All the way along, he could hear the soft crunching of leaves and branches as the men took their positions.

'This is where you hide.'

His voice was muffled by a cloth around his face but Xandros recognised him from the previous day: one of Spiro's most villainous-looking bandits. He pointed two fingers to his eyes and jabbed them at Xandros, making it clear he would be watched. The man swaggered away without looking back.

Xandros breathed a curse and picked his way through the undergrowth that scratched his skin and snagged the cloak he had been given, tutting and gasping as he went, until he emerged into a little clearing. A sombre tomb faced him, built into the hillside. The capstones and a foot or so of the relieving triangle supporting it were visible in what little ambient light there was but the doorway and its entrance were concealed.

'Won't be much of a surprise crashing through those bushes, will it?' he muttered to himself. He removed his leather pack from his shoulder, reassuring himself he had his flints, should he need to light the torch.

For a whole hour, nothing happened. Despite the cloak, despite the cover of the undergrowth, he became cold and his limbs grew stiff. The occasional rustle of leaves told him that there were others nearby but even that had fallen silent.

After another half hour, in which the temperature dropped markedly, he began to doubt he could wield a sword with any force. He moved at a crouch towards the track. He could only see the faint glow from a couple of torches, either side of him, and was sure they would also be extinguished at the first hint of the bandits' approach. The road down the valley was clear and there were fewer lights in the valley below, now. At one point, he thought he heard the faint scrape of feet on the earth but, seeing nothing, assumed it was dried leaves drifting in the breeze. He returned to the small clearing, feeling the first twinge of something amiss.

Once the warmth of the brief exercise had yielded to the ambient cold, reasoning that others had done the same, he decided to drive the torch into the ground and light it. He soon sparked a tongue of flame and introduced it to the pine, which fizzled into life. As his eyes and ears adjusted to the night's ambient noises, he became less jumpy at every scrape of leaves, or fluting of an owl, and he fell into a watchful silence.

Another twenty minutes went by.

He considered cutting his losses and slipping from Mycenae, though he suspected Orestes would have considered and planned for just that possibility.

He wondered where Spiro was.

Though he had said he would be keeping an eye upon him, it seemed in retrospect most unlikely. He bent down to pluck the torch from the ground.

Xandrosss!

A branch rustled nearby, and his hand snatched up his sword instead. His blade was already sweeping a protective arc when he first glimpsed the hooded figure come crashing through the darkness towards him. He caught the dull glimpse of a spearhead. A pale face, swathed in rags. He caught the spear shaft low on his blade, near the guard, deflecting its tip mere inches from his heart, feeling it tear his cloak and score his skin white-hot. The pain fired his senses and, on instinct, his fingers clutched the spear. He heaved it, and his assailant did not let go, making him lurch past like a wild boar. As he stumbled, Xandros whipped his sword arm back, feeling the blade bite into the man's jaw. Painful, his senses told him, but not lethal.

Down the man went, with presence of mind to barge Xandros as he went crashing into the dried leaves and ancient roots. In the guttering torchlight, as Xandros regained his balance, he saw the spearman scramble to his feet, blood dribbling from his face covering. Xandros' own spear lay on the ground, beside the fire. *Better a weapon in hand,* he reasoned, hacking at the man, just as he sprang, lithe as a cat, at Xandros' legs. His blade struck his calf.

Xandros tumbled backwards, his overextended knee sending an intense flash into his brain. The small of his back encountered a concealed stone, making him gasp in a duller pain. He saw murder in the man's dark eyes, as well as surprise. There was no room to swing again. Xandros gripped the naked blade with his left hand, twisted and heaved his right arm across his body. He felt its tip punch into the spearman's throat, spattering his own lips and cheeks with warm blood, making him flinch in revulsion. The man flailed about, gurgling and sputtering, striking Xandros hard once… twice in the jaw. With his weight upon him, he couldn't fight back. It took a few long, sickening moments until the thrashing subsided with one final, long exhalation. Then there was a stillness and, between each heavy thump of Xandros' heart, a soft, steady drip upon dried grass.

With his head ringing, Xandros heaved him aside and clambered to his feet, gritting his teeth against the pain pulsing all over his body. If the man wasn't alone, he knew for sure the next attack would be his last. He turned this way and that, straining his ears against the hiss of the burning torch resin.

Nothing.

He filled his lungs and steeled himself before whipping away his attacker's face covering. It did not surprise him to see one of Spiro's bandits: the one who reminded him he was being watched. He felt shame wash over him. *How could he have been so stupidly naïve? Were they such good actors?*

He wiped the blood from his face and swept up his belongings, plucking the torch from the earth, shuddering in fear and disgust and anger as he plunged through the snagging branches. His side was the most painful and he reached inside his torn cloak to press it. Dark blood smeared his palm: such injuries, he knew, soon turned bad.

He burst onto the road, blind with shock, directly into the path of a party of torchbearers. His sudden appearance – wild-eyed and blood-smeared – made one of them shriek, one of the hooded figures was surely a woman – and even the pair of guards leapt back, raising round shields. One of them was quicker to level his spear than Xandros. It was drawn above his shoulder before Xandros realised he was going to die.

There was a furious pattering and panting along the track. A black dog leaped out of the shadows and clamped its jaws around the guard's wrist. He bellowed in pain, dropping his spear, then his shield, trying to punch its body. Stung, it leaped at his chest before springing onto the second man, frenziedly scrabbling at the face of his shield.

'Stop!' shouted one of the women, stepping forwards. Her face was cowled but she had presence. *'Stop this now!'*

The dog dropped to a crouch in front of Xandros, trembling, lips curled back to reveal its yellow fangs. Between the wheezing and gasping, they weighed each other up. Except, it now occurred to Xandros, these bandits were not clad in similar cloaks; nor had he seen the feathered helmets before.

The second woman stepped forward and removed her hood. 'Xandros, do you recognise me now? What happened to you?'

'Eriopis!' His eyes darted from her to the other woman and back, sensing treachery. 'What are *you* doing here? Are they Orestes' men?'

The torchbearer gripped his wrist and shot him a look of hatred. He bent to pick up his shield and spear but the dog snapped his jaws and pounced, inches from his face.

'Don't!'

Xandros jabbed his spear at the second guard as he was about to attack the dog. 'Don't! I'll kill you, I swear.'

He noticed how both men glanced at Eriopis but it was a brief shake of the other woman's head that dissuaded them. The guard carefully raised the rim of his shield with his toes, not taking his eyes from the dog. 'That beast was all that stopped us killing you, boy.'

The dog directed a low, threatening growl at him.

'Tell me why you are here, Xandros.'

'We need to go, my lady.'

'Go on,' she said, ignoring him.

Xandros explained everything. From the tip of his eye, he felt the stare of the other woman, watching him as still as a statue.

'And how many of Orestes' men did you come down here with?'

Xandros shrugged. 'Twenty or so.'

'Twenty... He toys with the laws of hospitality for sport...'

Just then, the other woman addressed her in a curious language, with a voice as potent as smoke. The conversation became animated, and Xandros was sure he heard the younger woman address her as 'maman'.

The soldiers became restless, shifting the weight on their feet. One of them banged the butt of his spear into the earth but the older woman's hand shot out in defiance.

'You, boy, you have I seen many times before...'

'Me?'

She circled him, like a tigress sizing up a stag, rooting him to the spot. 'Let me look at you.'

She slowly lowered her hood. Beneath unruly curls of grey shot through with auburn, the intensity of her green eyes kindled something deep within him; something dark and terrifying and elemental. Xandros met her gaze and experienced the sensation of an anemone sting. He had a vanishing thought of having met her before but in another life.

'Yes,' she purred, 'I thought as much when I heard your voice in that fool's palace, and now I know.' She stopped and raised his chin, bringing her face close to his. He caught the faintest trace of incense. 'No, open your eyes. I mean you no harm.'

Xandros wasn't even aware that he had closed them. He felt himself teetering on the edge of a precipice but then she stepped back and turned to Eriopis. 'This boy also has the Gift, but he fears it.'

'"The Gift".' Xandros' tongue felt thick in his skull. 'What do you mean?'

'You hear voices, don't you?'

He swallowed with difficulty. 'H-how do you know this?'

Her face curdled. 'Your grandfather saw it as an affliction. Your father I once looked in the eye, when he was young. Though I saw a simple, stubborn soul, there was no second light. In you, it falters like a dying flame.'

Xandros felt himself go light-headed and thought he might pass out. The woman wrapped her cloak tighter about her shoulders. 'Your stammer. You have suffered all your life, yes? People have taken you for a fool?'

He nodded.

'There are some who say this is a symptom of the Gift, and I am one of them. The fool who struts about in that palace on the hill refused to believe you were Jason's grandson. He has sold his soul for wealth and power, and he has grown blind.' She raised her chin and flicked a monitory glance at Eriopis. 'And now he risks letting a golden child slip through his fingers. He is quite some idiot. Tell me, boy: does your father still live?'

'He does, King Euneus.'

'Euneus,' she repeated softly. 'Yes, I remember. You are taller. But I see Jason in both of you.'

'Who *are* you?'

'I am Medea.'

Xandros looked on in astonishment. 'I… I heard…'

'That I was a sorceress? A witch? Or a murderess? Rumour has spawned more facts than a toad.' She pulled the hood back over her head. 'Listen now. Some ancient goddess or other made its presence known, just now, otherwise you would be dead. I have encountered her before and I will not stand in her path. My decision is a sound one.'

Xandros was about to speak but Medea raised a finger and her eyes flared in warning. 'Time is against you and you must listen. By dawn tomorrow, you must leave these shores for the common good: these two men will not stop you, if they value their lives. I feel the passing of an old grievance and I… No. I will say no more. Come.' She beckoned the men to follow and, to Xandros' surprise, they did, albeit reluctantly. Medea walked away, cloak trailing along the road, leaving just Eriopis.

'You will have questions, no doubt. Limit them to one.'

'What if Orestes meant this as a test? Before sending men?'

'Naïveté and forlorn hope mimic each other so well sometimes, and this is not the question I would have asked. My mother is right and you are fortunate to be able to leave with your life. And, it would seem, a faithful dog. For the rest, if Orestes sends men, it will not be to help you. He is sworn to the Sea Peoples now.'

'Why are you with these pirates? Why…'

'Wait now!' Eriopis watched Medea and the guards like a hawk its prey. 'Turn aside.'

Her voice was cold and commanded respect. He did as he was told, and even the dog sidled alongside him, looking up at him expectantly. Xandros caught a glimpse of her extending her arms as if she was about to embrace someone, and now he heard Eriopis whispering urgently in a fluttering voice for a full minute: a hymn, perhaps, or a curse, though he couldn't understand a single word.

The words faded into the chilly night. 'Now. It must be now.'

'What must be?'

She turned to him and, in the torchlight, he saw something in her eyes. In the short time he had known her, he had not seen it before. Fear. 'We must go in silence.'

Xandros watched the little sphere of the torchbearers' light recede until they were once more shrouded in darkness. Then they set off along the road.

XIX

It was out of the question for them to retrace their steps up the track through the fruit trees, so close to the citadel. Instead, they kept to the lower path. By daylight, Xandros was sure the route along the valley would have been easy. As it was, they were walking virtually blind in the general direction of the coast, frequently scraped by overhanging branches unseen in the torchlight.

Eriopis stopped to snuff out the flame of her torch. Xandros saw the sense in it: they would need to preserve the resin. Once or twice they froze whenever the dog tensed and his sharp ears pricked up. Though they listened intently, they could discern nothing beyond the sounds of the night and set off again whenever the dog relaxed, resuming their steps with frayed nerves. Then the ground rose before them and they encountered a thicket.

Eriopis' face softened as she turned to face him. Despite her stately poise, it was clear that many emotions competed beneath. 'The answer to the question you didn't ask is because this is where Fate has led me. Because famine and drought are more compelling enemies than any army. I am betrothed to Pylades but the *miasma* of death in that palace suffocates me, Xandros, and its source is older than you could know. Pylades and Orestes are blood brothers and the bond between them is unbreakable. I would always be beholden to both of them, and I truly care for neither. Now do you understand me?'

He held her gaze. 'Truthfully, no.'

'No?'

'No. How did you – and your mother – come to be here, if it holds so many horrors for you?'

She gave him a sad smile. 'Here is the question I expected you would first ask of me, and I will explain all, I promise, but we must hurry. For now, understand that we fell upon hard times and, in Orestes, my mother saw opportunity. Come, we must hurry, and you must clean your wound.'

'Where are you going?'

'Is it not obvious?' She rested a warm hand upon his shoulder. 'With *you*. I see something in you, Xandros, just as my mother did. Why do you look at me like that?' Her laughter tinkled from her lips and warmed his heart, despite the sharp situation. 'And I have sideritis leaves in this bag: the same leaves I used to prepare your tisane and you awoke the next day, did you not?'

He nodded but her words startled him. *She would follow him as, what, a warrior? A friend? A lover?*

He heard the dog licking his lips. It was sat patiently watching them talk with its head cocked to one side. Xandros reached inside his bag. 'For you,' he said, tentatively presenting another prickly pear to the dog. His sharp ears perked up and he sniffed at it suspiciously before delicately taking it from his hands and then savaging it upon the floor.

'What will we call him?' whispered Eriopis, scratching him behind his ears.

'"*Creoboros*".'

'"*Flesh-Eater*".' She laughed. 'I like it, so long as it's never *ours*.' She reached for his hand and clasped it briefly. 'Come on. My deceit will not last long.'

'Your deceit?'

'I will explain later. *Go*, Xandros!'

The torchbearers breezed through the Gate of The Lionesses and heard it being closed and barred behind their backs. Medea turned to the figure gliding beside her.

'You have been very quiet. Are you ill?'

When Eriopis didn't reply, Medea tutted and looked away. 'In company so sour, is it any surprise he calls upon you less?'

They were at the foot of the ramp now. Lights glowed through the shutters in the house of the king's *lawagetas*, just beyond the grave circle. It had been one of Orestes' first acts to put them at Pylades' disposal but, tonight, there would be a ritual opening of another cask at the palace instead. They passed a pair of freshly prepared torches, set in brackets on the walls and Medea, deep in thought, watched her shadow lengthen before her along the cobbles. One of the guards glanced at her as he replaced his spent torch with a fresh one, then his eyes snapped towards Eriopis. Both he and Medea noticed in the same moment that Eriopis herself cast no shadow. The girl walked on for a few more steps before fading and disappearing altogether.

The guard looked terror-stricken. 'My lady?'

'She cast an *eidolon*! She tricked me!' She shuddered with emotion and stretched her neck to scream. *'She. Tricked. Me!'*

Xandros and Eriopis were breathing hard when they finally emerged from the dense hillside bushes. Only Creoboros could weave through them with no difficulty and he looked back at them, struggling and grimacing, with his head cocked to the side. Occasionally he would pick up the scent of another creature and threatened to go off in pursuit but, every time Xandros hissed at him, he would trudge back with his ears flattened.

The ground levelled and they crested the ridge. On the opposite side of the valley, several hundred yards away, atop the rocky escarpment, the lamps of the palace winked at them.

'We're too close,' said Xandros.

'Give me your torch and keep walking,' hissed Eriopis.

'Why? What are you...'

'Go!'

She took it from him and held it at arm's length, and began once more to incant the mysterious words he had heard earlier. Xandros turned away and clicked his tongue, and Creoboros set off after him.

On the roof of the palace, draped in heavy cloaks against the cold breeze, two watchmen stiffened.

'Did you see that?' The words clung to the mist of his breath.

After a moment, the other replied gruffly, 'I did.'

'I will tell the king.'

'Wait. Just wait. We don't know... That could be anyone.'

The piercing scream from the lower citadel made them dash across the roof to see what was happening.

They looked at each other in confusion. 'Something's up. If we're attacked and he's not told... We're dead men.'

The other man inclined his head towards the staircase. 'Do it.'

XX

The going was much easier once they had returned to the main path, propelled by a deepening sense of imminent pursuit. By the time they reached the junction with the Corinth road, the waxing moon had become visible, and the pale light and the absolute silence made them feel terribly exposed.

'We can't rest for long,' whispered Eriopis. 'When they see the inland paths are clear, they will soon know it was the same trick and there won't be a third time. Do you have any water left, Xandros?'

They shared what little remained whilst the dog's eager eyes followed their hands, hoping for a handout. 'When we get back to the boat, Creo,' said Xandros soothingly, 'I promise. Ready?'

'Look at me.'

Xandros did so.

'You look pale: you have lost a lot of blood. Can you make it?'

'We have no choice.'

They pressed on, until they reached the outskirts of Argos, and they followed the wide, gravelly bed of the Inachos river, giving the city as wide a berth as they could. A mile or so to their left, the lights of Tiryns twinkled but the experiences of the past couple of days had drained the appeal of the Argolid cities to their very dregs.

Two hours after they had last stopped for water at the crossroads, they glimpsed the sea, rippling silver under the moon, and they filled their lungs with its salty air. A good distance from each other, a couple of campfires had been lit and one or two dark figures passed in front of them.

Xandros put out a restraining arm and they slowed their pace.

His mouth was dry and his throat burned as fiercely as the wound made by the spear. As waves of exhaustion washed over him, he almost felt seasick.

'What is it?'

He said nothing but scanned the coastline. More boats had been dragged ashore than when he had first arrived, and there was a handful bobbing at anchor in the bay.

'I can't see it.' Xandros clenched his jaw in mounting panic. The *Salamander* had been beached furthest from the others, to the right as they looked towards the sea. Though it wasn't the most distinctive of boats, he was sure he would recognise it. 'It's not here.'

They hurried to the furthest boat, squinting into the darkness, not daring to venture nearer than a stone's cast for fear of being spotted. A fishing skiff. Next to it, a sleek longboat. A pirate galley, perhaps. Xandros thought, *How fitting if they were to be kidnapped on the very point of abandoning the failed quest.*

'Xandros.'

'Wait.'

'Look!'

'What?'

'Behind us.'

Xandros tore his eyes from the boats and followed the line of Eriopis' finger. After a moment, he asked, 'What am I supposed to be looking at?'

'There, coming along the valley. Lights!'

He saw them. Pricks of flickering light. His eyes had begun to feel feverishly heavy but now they rounded when he realised what those lights signified. Even at a mile – perhaps more – he could see they were on the move. 'Chariots. We only have a short time and if they're not here, we hide. *Go!*'

All pretence of concealment was now cast aside: anybody even half awake would surely notice the dark figures dashing about beyond the backshore. Quite probably, they would arm themselves and then they would be hopelessly trapped. Putting aside such gloomy thoughts, he hurried past the boats, craning his head forwards as he looked for tell-tale shapes.

Merchantmen… skiffs… galleys…

He was drawing towards the first of the campfires now so retreated further into the darkness. Glancing to the left, he could see the lights were growing, and he fancied he could hear them thundering towards him.

He heard a faint peal of laughter from the campfire and turned towards it. There was something familiar about its pitch and he took a few tentative steps forwards. Four or five men, passing a wineskin amongst themselves. They spotted him at forty paces. He could tell by the way the first froze and the others looked in his direction that they were going to take up arms but then he remembered he had concealed his face and he had a rangy black dog bounding alongside him. One of them shook a slumbering figure and he sputtered a curse. He only recognised the young archer when he had scrambled to retrieve an arrow.

Xandros unwound the scarf as he shouted, *'It's me! Put it down!'* At twenty paces, the arrow was nocked and swinging towards him. *'Elissos, no!'*

Even as he heard the creak of the bow being drawn, it occurred to Xandros that its bearer might be drunk: so insensibly drunk as to recognise neither the face nor the voice. He was, after all, little more than an acquaintance to him.

Xandros stood rooted to the shingle and Creoboros began to bark.

'Down, Creo!'

'No!' A hand darted out and dragged the bow to the ground. 'It's him!'

Glaux.

They hadn't sailed away. Their word was good. Xandros closed the distance and felt his dry tongue click as he spoke.

'We need to go, right now! They're after us!'

He was met with hard looks. 'What are you talking about?'

'Look over there…'

'I see nothing.'

'*Then stand up!* Look!'

Glaux and Elissos alone stood, reluctantly.

'You see them? Those lights? They're coming for us. They're king's men, from Mycenae.'

Elissos looked him up and down and his eyes blazed at him. 'What the *fuck* have you been doing there?' Creoboros snarled at his tone and the archer gave him a sidelong look. 'Tell me you didn't go all the way there just to steal a dog?'

'And a woman.'

The sailor turned to the lookout. 'What?'

'This is Eriopis. She's coming with us.'

The men turned to her, and their eyes lingered on her for a moment. 'He did steal a woman,' muttered Elissos. 'Of course he did. The mad little *kuna*'s going to start another war.'

'I'll explain but we need to go! *Now!*'

'We can't...'

'What do you mean?'

'The skipper's drunk.'

Xandros glanced down at the snoring figure, wrapped in a fleece.

'Then *wake* him! Can't you navigate yourselves?'

The twin torch flames were as bright as the dog star Sirius now. Xandros guessed the pursuers were already halfway towards Argos, perhaps where the road crossed the River Inachos.

The crew looked at each other uncertainly, waiting for someone else to make a decision. Xandros growled in frustration and picked up a skin.

'*Don't* do that!'

He removed the bung and took a slug of wine. It was warm and vinegary and did nothing for his thirst. 'Well?'

Elissos snatched the skin from his hand and knelt down to shake the captain. 'Help them slide her in!' he snapped.

They all turned to the sound of panting and hurried footsteps. A wild-haired man flung down a kit bag and weapons, clattering onto the shingles, making them all start. 'Let me lend you a hand.'

'*Hey, hey!* Who is this, boy? Zeus' ball bag, who are you?'

Xandros turned to the stranger in surprise. Even by the firelight, it took him a moment to place him. 'Caeneus! What are you doing here?'

'You said you were leaving at first light, yes?' He grinned maniacally and Xandros suspected he had also been drinking.

'Well? Did I not tell you to stay away? And now I hear you are in trouble.' He looked at Eriopis and bowed. 'Now I *see* you are!'

'You owe us for this, boy! Skipper... *skipper!*' hissed Elissos, squeezing the captain's limp shoulders. *'By Zeus you have to get up, man!'* For good measure, he slapped his cheeks. The captain jerked awake, taking a swipe at the blurred figure he now saw looming over him. Elissos shoved the arm aside. *'Get up!* Well...? What are you waiting for, boy? Slide. Her. In!'

Xandros ran to the prow. 'Leave the oars!' barked Elissos. 'Do you want to snap the thole pins? You all push when I say!'

Elissos sprinted out of view, shingle crunching underfoot. After a moment, Xandros heard, *'Now!'*

Xandros splayed his fingers along the sleek hull, struggling to get any purchase, grunting with the effort of trying to budge the *Salamander*. Caeneus, Eriopis and the rest of the crew heaved and, with a reluctant scrape, the hull inched forwards.

The additional pairs of hands tipped the balance in their favour. The hull hissed through the foreshore and cold water slapped against their feet as the keel scythed through the final few feet of shingle.

When the boat was floating in the shallows, the crew dashed back to retrieve their kit. At the very moment Xandros grabbed his bag and weapons, Creoboros snarled and snapped, ears pinned back.

'Shush, now, Creo! What is it?'

He heard the distant rattle and thump before he saw the amber tips of the torches swing into view, burnt through to the wood. Four hundred yards and closing fast, describing an arc along the last curve of the riverbed. Two boxy shapes, fronted by maned heads bobbing up and down. Faint on the breeze came the drivers' commands, giving the horses their head, and then the jingle of their harnesses.

'Go! *Go!*' yelled Elissos, appearing from Xandros' side and shoving him towards the boat. He spun around and clutched at his side, dazed by panic and pain and exhaustion, as he looked for Eriopis. She was knee-deep in the water, beckoning him by the steering oars. 'Clean your wound, Xandros. I will do the rest.'

'Great gods, woman! There's no time for that!'

Creoboros had already leapt aboard and now he was barking at Xandros with his forepaws against the *Salamander*'s rail. Xandros felt himself become light-headed, as if he might pass out.

'Go!'

The last shove had him stumbling along the beach. He hurled his bag and weapons aboard and helped Eriopis clamber up the rope ladder.

'Now help the men with the skipper!'

Xandros glanced towards the riverbed. All along the waterfront, other figures were watching the chariots rumbling towards them, and the commotion he had caused. They were only a bowshot distant now. Perhaps there was an arrow being trained upon him at that very moment...

The captain was muttering under his breath – Xandros could smell the stale wine upon his lips – but he could at least stand without support.

One of the sailors was shouting at him – *'Get up! Get up!'* – whilst the crew were reaching overboard. *'Go on, man!'*

From somewhere nearby, a seabird cried and there was a skitter of sharp metal on pebbles.

'The gods, they've found their range! *Haul the bastard up!*'

Gritting their teeth, Xandros and Elissos shoved him by the backside and he flopped onto the boat with a painful thump. Elissos clambered up the ladder in seconds and the oars were already cleaving the water as Xandros groped for the knot, missing it altogether as the boat slid away from the beach. He saw the first pair of horses bearing down upon him, sixty, maybe fifty yards away. The wheels clattered onto the shingle and men were calling out... warning, threatening, he didn't know. Thigh-deep in cold water, he hauled himself, hand over hand, up the rope before being grabbed by the hem of his tunic and dragged over the gunwale. He flopped onto the deck, utterly spent, hearing his panting reverberate from the hull. The thump of oar looms against thole pins. A chatter of speculation. Relieved laughter. He found himself grinning up at Eriopis and, though her face was taut, she managed a distant smile. 'I will prepare the sideritis herb.'

When he finally dragged himself to his feet, he risked a look back towards the shore. Fading into the darkness were two pairs of horses, stood like black sentinels and, behind them, the silhouettes of three men. Xandros could almost feel the glowering of familiar eyes scoring his own. He turned away and sagged against the *Salamander*'s stern, mouthing a silent prayer to a nameless god for his deliverance.

BOOK SIX

A TIME FOR ANGER

'Fool, who would fain wed Delight to Anger! Go
With blind eyes clothe thee in purple: don this for show
And set the pink-veined marble 'neath thy throne
Then on its golden cushions forever sit alone!'

I

Lemnos

The shipmaster's hangover left him sour-faced for much of the morning and afternoon. He stomped up and down the gangway snapping and snarling at the crew and passengers, it seemed, even for breathing.

Several hours after midday, when they were approaching the island of Spetses, he dropped onto a thwart and took a long pull of wine from his skin. He glowered at Xandros for a moment before speaking. 'Had I known how little you'd respect my advice, I'd have demanded double the payment from your friend Orpheus. In fact, I'd have refused.'

'Yet I'm told the wise king of Athens, Acamas, rewarded you handsomely.'

They all turned to Caeneus in surprise. He was sat amidships with his back to them. 'You keep out of this.'

Caeneus shrugged slowly. 'It's the bare truth. He didn't listen to me, either.' He half turned to them. 'Yet he made it out of that robber baron's lair, somehow. He's young, skipper. Don't tell me you didn't want a piece of adventure when you were his age.'

'Some spies came the evening you left,' he continued, ignoring Caeneus. 'Claimed they were the king's men. Orestes sent them, they said. They climbed all over the boat next to us, looking for something, the one with that goddess ornament. No further questions asked, no permission given. They just... shoved the crew aside and turned the boat upside down, then left in dudgeon, empty-handed.' The shipmaster shook his head. 'I heard the captain protesting *"But we didn't bring anybody from Lemnos,"* giving me the side eye. He didn't sing though; I was grateful for that.' He leaned forwards and gritted his teeth. 'We did a brisk trade, but *you* could have got us all hauled off. And our goods, you damned fool!'

'Is that why you sailed away?'

'What?'

'The *Salamander* wasn't where we'd dragged it ashore.'

The captain sat back. 'Yes, it is why. While the dust settled.'

Eriopis had retreated into herself since their narrow escape. Xandros had hoped he might have had some moment of quiet to talk to her and learn more about her but the additional passengers made privacy nigh impossible. She was sat on her haunches a short distance away, grinding herbs, and now she returned with a pestle of salve. 'You make him sound like he was a child who had wandered off…'

'Not far from the truth, then!'

'But he risked his life for his island, his home. He spilled his own blood for it. Look – this may hurt, Xandros – look at this. How many can ever say they have done this?'

'We all have our scars, lady.' She ignored the skipper whilst she applied the paste, making Xandros gasp. 'Not all of them can be seen.'

'Ready for land!'

The call came from Glaux and they were all grateful for it. The skipper rose without another word and mounted the steering deck, leaving Xandros to blow the air from his cheeks.

'Ignore him,' said Caeneus quietly. He got up and ambled towards them, grabbing the rigging as the *Salamander* creaked into a turn. 'These shipmasters: they're all the same. Full of their own self-importance and… and stories of fronting up to the Earth-Shaker and living to tell the tale. But when it comes down to it, they're more cautious than lambs wandering from their mammy's teats.'

He dropped onto the thwart that the captain had just vacated and rubbed his hands together. 'Now you've been patched up, about my down payment…'

Creoboros padded along the gangway and bared his teeth at the mercenary.

'You know, I'm beginning to think your dog doesn't like me.'

II

That evening, after bringing down a goat – Xandros had to admire the way the crew worked to corner it, ready for Elissos' arrow – they ate in quiet contemplation of what lay ahead, and the conversation was minimal. Though he hadn't been up to hunting, Xandros had bathed and it had revived him. After applying more salve, he felt that the heat had been drawn from his wound and that it would heal cleanly. As the sky started to blush with the sinking of the sun, Xandros finally found himself alone with Eriopis on a little shingled bay overlooked by a fringe of carob trees.

'You promised to explain to me about the spells you cast in Mycenae. I'd like to hear about them.'

She laughed and shook her head. 'Witches and spells... Men can be so ignorant.' Aware by the look on his face she had caused offence, she touched his arm, adding, 'I am sorry – that was unfair. I am not feeling myself.'

'I understand.'

She gazed out over the sea and was quiet for a few moments. 'I learned many things from my mother, Xandros, and not all of them I am proud of. Herbs and potions, these are things that any healer, any person can learn, given the time and dedication. But those incantations were not spells; not in the way you understand them, at least.'

'What, then?'

There was a crunching of shingle below them and Caeneus emerged into view, looking up at them with a wink. Xandros hoped he wouldn't disturb them and was grateful when he ambled by, apparently satisfied with his down payment of twin nuggets of gold.

'I don't really know how to explain it, Xandros. The power of suggestion… Convincing another they are seeing something they want to see. This is possible because when people are wilfully blind to some other possibility, the ancient forces that used to unite humans with nature and allow them to see the world, to *sense* it, in the same way as other animals fade. And weak forces can be… manipulated.' She gave him a knowing look and refused his offer of more wine. 'People are unwilling to see things they don't want to see, even when they are clear to another. Even my mother, Medea, can be deceived now she is older, though this is not easy. Do you understand me now?'

He nodded. 'Are we related, you and I?'

Her eyes crinkled and she laughed.

'I mean through Jason!'

'I know, and I am sorry. No, Xandros, we are not related. I am not Jason's daughter.'

'Whose, then?'

She was about to answer but then waved the question away and her tone precluded any further question. 'My father was nobody you would have heard of.'

He looked away over the shimmering sea and filled his lungs with the fragrant air but something still pricked his momentary contentment. He sensed that Eriopis might even want to be alone. 'Why do you think Orestes sent me to die with so many men yet only one came for me?'

Eriopis was also gazing over the horizon but he noticed a tendon in her cheek twitch. It took her a few moments to respond. 'Even Orestes wouldn't dare kill a guest within his own halls, Xandros.'

'Or poison one?'

'It wasn't poison. You came to no harm.'

'So that was *you*?'

'No… Yes, I added some herbs to your drink, at his suggestion. He likes to know what is in a man's heart and, on this, we had a common purpose. No, don't look at me like that, Xandros. You don't understand—'

'No, I don't! You and Orestes, and his crony… You are all as bad as each other!'

He could see by the way she recoiled that he had wounded her. He wasn't sorry to see it.

'You understand *nothing*. We saved your life!'

Xandros laughed. 'Oh, *that's* what you were doing! And who is "we"?'

She turned weary eyes upon him. 'We – that is my mother and I – persuaded him that his plan was against all laws of nature.'

'You *knew* about that, too?'

'My mother overheard him and Pylades whispering, and she told me. We both spoke to him. She can be very persuasive.'

The revelation left him open-mouthed. 'Not very persuasive!' He tugged his tunic where it covered his wound. 'He still sent an assassin. I nearly died!'

She reached out to him and he allowed her arm to rest only briefly on his shoulder before steering it aside. The gesture hardened her expression. 'But you didn't. Sometimes we need to fight, Xandros, to earn our freedom. To earn respect. Besides, you had a warning. Didn't you?'

He recalled hearing his name hissed just before he was attacked. 'Are you saying she *helped* me?'

'For someone with the Gift, you can be very slow.' Her lips curled into an enigmatic smile. 'But that was an exhausting escape and you were wounded.'

He closed his eyes and let out a long breath whilst his mind reeled. Had he not claimed to be a good judge of character? That notion had been destroyed in just under a minute.

'You won't be coming to Lemnos after all, will you?'

She sighed. 'No, Xandros.'

'And I am just another weak force that you have manipulated.'

'No!' She clasped his wrist in her long fingers. 'Don't ever think this!'

The sincerity in her voice matched the intensity in her eyes. He expected her to release her grip. Instead, she drew him towards her and kissed him and his lips melted against hers before she pulled away. She shook her head.

'No. No, it would not be right.'

The heady rush of passion and confusion made his heart pound. 'What will you do?'

'Are you worried about me?'

It confused him, given the circumstances, given she had just kissed him, that her eyes smiled back at him. *Was this all just a game to her?*

'Of course: a little.'

'Have you learned nothing about me?' She laughed. 'And am I not older than you?'

'And Medea?'

'I suppose you are wondering why she might want to help you? Why a woman with her reputation – a woman whom Jason had slighted so badly – might risk so much for his grandson? You do know she once came to your island, don't you?'

'My grandmother told me she came with threats.'

'She came not to *threaten* her, Xandros! She came to *warn* her. Would you like me to tell you why she might do that? In her own words?'

'I would.'

'Even though she showed Jason much love and little wisdom, for which he treated her not like a wife but as plunder, she sees which way the wind blows, and how. Hellas is in grave danger – you know this – and though her bitterness towards Jason runs deep, it ends at the root, as Hekate has intimated it must.'

Xandros rubbed his face. 'Gift or no gift, I have no head for riddles. Speak plainly, please.' He saw her green eyes flash with irritation and, for an uncomfortably long time, Eriopis seemed to weigh him up. 'Very well. I have been sparing with the truth in some of what I said to you. In Mycenae. For your own good. We did not seek out Orestes solely because we needed help. We were guided to the Gate of The Lionesses by Hekate, with which godhead my mother has never broken faith.'

The tranquillity of sunset was settling upon Spetses and, in its hush, her eyes passed over the purpling bay, checking if they were being overheard. They could both hear the laughter of men around the campfire, very faint. Still, she lowered her voice. 'There is a common saying in these lands – you must have heard it: *nothing in excess.* In his greed for power and riches and revenge upon his mother and kinsmen, Orestes has exceeded all limits. He has turned Hellene upon Hellene. He has made a pact with the enemy from the sea and yet he has duped even them. He revels in control. He thinks he sees everything and yet he is blind to all. He has yoked himself to a beast over which he has no control. Nature, Xandros, is a kindly mother one day and a monster the next. She bares her teeth and crops fail and rivers run dry and men become desperate. Who does he think he is?' Eriopis made a curious flicking gesture with her fingers. 'Who can control those things if not a god?'

Eriopis became quiet for a moment. 'Even though my mother did not foresee your coming, she knew that it had to mean something. It was not your fate to be slain in the dark by some worthless brigand of his. Perhaps she even saw something of her own sons in you. And you *survived.* You encountered us. To what end, who can say? But can you now see beyond the rumour and beyond the lies, Xandros? *Medea, who stabbed her own sons! Medea, the witch!* Do you now see why my mother became so embittered being treated like a pariah in whatever village and town her reputation preceded her? How hard it must have been to be cursed and shunned in front of her daughter, how often she had to cover my ears and shield me from stones? People are so cruel. So small-minded.'

'I see it.' Xandros pursed his lips and looked to the ground. 'I see it now. Where will Medea go? Isn't she in danger?'

Eriopis' face brightened a little. 'She has spent most of her life in danger. She always used to say to me, "One day, when the time is right, my girl, we will turn our back upon the setting sun." That time is now. We will meet again very soon.'

Scraping together the last dregs of his resolve, Xandros took a deep breath, dusted himself off and stood. His knee was still sore and his face twitched in pain. I know you will be well, wherever you go, but you will always be welcome in Lemnos.'

He walked away.

'You are disappointed in me? Angry?'

'No.' He held her gaze for a moment and felt the lie burning his cheeks. 'In case I don't see you in the morning… I hope you find peace and happiness, wherever you travel.'

'Xandros!'

He turned back.

'I thank you. Truly. And may your journey be a long one.'

Xandros felt a knot in his stomach. He still wanted to know more about her; about the places – and the people – she had seen. He liked talking to her. She was beautiful; she interested him; she was a gatekeeper to another world for him. But, despite her protest to the contrary, he felt used and he had learned enough to know not to invest his emotions in something doomed to fail. And, most of all, she was not Teodora.

He knew he would never lay eyes upon her again.

When he returned to the campfire a few minutes later, the crew of the *Salamander* stopped their conversation and gave him an enquiring look.

'Where is your girlfriend?' asked Glaux with a mischievous gleam in his eye.

The skipper's eyes slid from Xandros' glare to the young lookout and he tutted. 'Must you learn the hard way, little owl, not to poke a hornet's nest? Leave him be. Come on, boy, sit by the fire. Fill your cup.' He tapped the side of his head and lowered his voice. Xandros noticed his words were slurred. 'I knew the minute I saw her what she was about.'

The branches popped and spat in the flames as his words sank in. The old sailor scratched his beard. 'Was that when you were legless or when'd you sobered up?'

'Ach!' The skipper lobbed a pebble at him and it bounced off the old man's skull with a satisfying *dink*. The noise made Creoboros' ear twitch as he slept, and he grumbled in irritation.

III

They were another three days at sea, only one of which was without incident. The *Salamander* gave the widest of berths to every ship they caught sight of, causing Xandros to reflect upon Caeneus' description of the shipmaster. It seemed that caution was the only way, however, that they could avoid being set upon by pirates, even if it did add many hours to their voyage.

Despite the thawing of the ice on Spetses, the captain was taciturn with Xandros the following morning and barely exchanged a word with him thereafter, save for the evenings, when they would have to cooperate to capture their food once the supplies had run out. This suited Xandros fine. The nearer they drew to Lemnos, the more he would find himself gazing out over the rail across the sparkling sea, contemplating what he might return to.

'Land ho!' called Glaux.

He broke off his conversation with Caeneus. On the eastern horizon, wreathed at the waterline by mist, the distant, rugged hills of Lemnos were violet against the flawless sky. Xandros had hoped the sight would fill his heart but he felt oddly empty; dejected. Of one thing he was certain: he didn't want to make land at nightfall. His journey had been a failure. Empty words and dubious promises, scorn, doubt, mockery, and these had been the relative successes. He had also been tricked and held hostage inside a once powerful citadel that was now a lair for bandits, then sent to his death by their host, who also happened to be in league with the very people against whom he sought help in the first place. He had allied with and promptly lost Eriopis, retained a single mercenary (of questionable intent), an ancient relic and a dog. In short, when he gave his report to the council, explaining his absence and the turmoil it had caused, he would be ridiculed.

But it wouldn't do to slink back into Myrine like a thief in the night.

He would look his people in the eye and King Euneus would at least respect that. He had dared to try whilst others sat and scoffed. Orpheus, too, would understand, and he felt sure he would see the bard again. He felt an unfamiliar sensation securely lodged in his heart and recognised it was pride.

IV

Lemnos

'What are they doing here?' growled Khalkeus.

The councillors turned towards the citadel gate. All stood save Alektruon, who had been rasping a whetstone across his sword blade. He now pointed it towards the newcomers and blew the fine layer of dust from the bronze. 'Vultures.'

Plouteos now strode towards the meeting place with his retinue. 'Gentlemen,' he said, extending his hand towards Hektor, who looked down at it and folded his arms. The nomarch's lips twitched. 'I have merely come to pay my respects to Euneus. Is he receiving visitors?'

'Save your respects until he's dead, many years from now,' said Hektor. 'And he *is* receiving visitors. Chosen ones. I'll pass on your respects, when I see him.'

'And I can save you the trouble of waiting for a response,' said Khalkeus, turning to the side and spitting. 'He'll tell you to stick them up your arse.'

Plouteos raised his chin. 'I doubt he would.'

'You have some gall, strutting in here.'

They turned to Alektruon. He had removed a rag and was now polishing the blade. 'Given how you were sent packing here weeks ago, a man might easily take offence. Your men are armed. Expecting trouble, are they?'

The men around Plouteos bristled and looked to each other. 'Oh, I think we are beyond a point of offence now, don't you?'

'The point where your dogs set upon the king's son whilst his back was turned, do you mean?' Khalkeus took a step forwards. 'I don't think we are even close to that point.'

'The king's son who tried to elope with *my* son's fiancée.'

Alektruon flicked a glance at Ekhinos, whose cheeks had reddened in shame and anger. 'He should have kept her better.'

'Father! Let me...'

'*Enough!* Enough of this. You can be forgiven your ill temper, given your concerns for your king, but understand we have our limits. You will allow us, I presume, to camp on the beach for a night or two. This island needs direction and I would like to speak to Euneus myself, tomorrow, after he has recovered. And then we would see Teodora, before we return to Moudros with her. My people are becoming restive. Gentlemen.'

Without waiting for a response, the nomarch turned on his heels and beckoned for his men to follow. Ekhinos' eyes cut the Myrinians as he left.

When they had gone, the councillors sat down with fists clenched. It took a moment for their tempers to settle. Hektor flattened his white moustache with thumb and forefinger. 'I smell trouble whenever I see that man. I think he means to press his claim.'

'Of course he does!' snapped Khalkeus. 'The question is how we respond! If Euneus does succumb then who succeeds him?'

'Xandros!'

The ensuing silence spoke eloquently enough but Khalkeus murmured, 'We don't even know where he is.'

'Hypsipyle, then. Well? What do you think, Alek?'

He shook his head briefly and slid his blade back into its sheath. 'We're all children of Time, much as we sometimes want to kill our father. The old dame served well enough but it's forwards we need to look, not back.'

Hektor nodded. 'I agree.'

'Who then? One of us?'

'Where's Hilarion? It's been days.'

'Surely not him?' Khalkeus snorted.

'His voice should be heard.'

'Then his absence is damning!'

'I'll say it, then,' said Alektruon dispassionately. 'It wasn't only his son Euneus drove away whilst drunk and morose. You ask where Hilarion is? He's chasing the bottom of a wine jar, someplace. Forget him.' He rose and strapped his sword to his belt. 'The answer is Moxos. Perhaps it always was.'

They watched him saunter away, unable to find words to suit their surprise.

'Perhaps this will be by the by,' said Hektor quietly. 'Euneus is stubborn; we all know this. He might pull through.'

V

The *Salamander* dropped anchor at the same little cove at which it had picked up Xandros, weeks earlier. The sun had disappeared behind a bank of clouds that had rolled in from the south and the shipmaster looked up at them dubiously as his passengers disembarked. Caeneus went first, holding the rolled-up fleece and his own bag and weapons above his head as he waded ashore.

'You can stay here if you want, in the palace. If you're worried about the weather.'

The captain looked like he was entertaining the idea for a moment but then shook his head. 'We have a southerly. We should be back in Samothrace before the clouds break. You have everything? I won't be turning back this time.'

Xandros glanced at the shore. Creoboros was already shaking the water from his body. 'We do. And thank you. You were every bit as good as your word.'

He recalled the way the crew had stared at him, hard-faced and silent, as he had first embarked. Whilst they hardly gushed with emotion now, there was a difference – a small one – in the way they were regarding him. He was sure he saw a trace of respect. He saluted them and, though they said nothing, raised hands and straightened lips were enough. Only Glaux waved, and the bearded deckhand scrubbed his head affectionately.

'Farewell, little owl!' said Xandros, adding something he had once heard an old Myrinian say. 'A long life and the good sense to live it.'

The captain made a little noncommittal grunt and nodded. 'Go well, boy.' Then he turned away. *'Raise the stone. We leave now!'*

Xandros had come to expect little more from the taciturn man and it occurred to him as he clambered overboard and made for the bay that he might even miss the sailors of the *Salamander*.

Minutes later, they were rounding the coastal road when Xandros drew up short. He pointed to a little encampment halfway around the bay. 'Do you see those?'

Caeneus squinted as he followed the line of his finger. 'Do you want to explain why a few tents bothers you so?'

As they walked, Xandros gave Caeneus an abbreviated history of the conflict between Myrine and Moudros. He was glad for the distraction and the Larissan was quick to assess the implications. 'Then you'd better be on your toes.' He added with his crooked smile, 'It happens up and down country, Thessaly no less than anywhere. My middle brother, for instance. Now *he* would be a Moudrian; is that how you say it?'

The first person Xandros saw was Hypsipyle's handmaid. She was sweeping the courtyard and gave him a startled double take when he entered the gate.

'Hello, Auge,' he said.

She stared at him in her brazen way and looked like she wanted to say something but thought better of it. She rested her broom against a bench and hurried inside. Caeneus raised his eyebrows at the servant's impudence. 'She's always been this way,' Xandros said with a shrug. 'Come inside.'

They heard the slow *clack* of Hypsipyle's walking stick over the flagstones before she entered the *megaron*. When she saw Xandros, she touched her heart and pressed thumb and forefinger together, whispering a prayer to the Great Goddess. Then her sharp eyes passed over Caeneus before resting upon Creoboros with a faint frown. The dog sat down obediently and licked his lips.

Xandros raised his arms and let them fall. 'I told you we'd return, Nanna.' Then he gently kissed both cheeks and introduced her to Caeneus and Creoboros. The Larissan prince bowed nobly and Xandros was grateful that the rogue had at least retained some courtly manners.

'So you knew Jason too, did you?'

Caeneus shook his head. 'My father did, my lady. I never got the chance.'

She gave him an indulgent smile but it was as Hypsipyle turned to Auge that Xandros noticed her slight palsy. It was also not like his grandmother to miss such a detail as a person's lineage. 'Could you light the hearth, my girl? I feel a cold wind rising. Please, take a seat.' She pointed to the stools lining the wall, next to which were stacked embroidered cushions. 'Then you can fetch some refreshments.'

'Please,' said Caeneus. 'Let me help.'

'You'll do no such thing! Sit!'

'I can easily see a spear where now there's a stick!'

'Caeneus…'

Hypsipyle raised an eyebrow at the Larissan's presumptuousness but then a ghost of a smile crossed her lips. 'And you wouldn't be wrong.'

They made small talk until Auge returned with a plate of honey cakes and some spiced wine and only then did Xandros ask the question that had been smouldering since the retreat from Argos.

'Where is Father?'

Auge was stood a few paces behind Hypsipyle, and Xandros knew by the way her eyes darted to her mistress that the news would be grave. He had sensed as much the moment he entered the *megaron* and breathed the heavy, sombre air.

'Beyond the help of any physician, but not yet the succour of a god.'

Xandros felt his stomach swill. 'Can I see him?'

'Later, of course. He is resting now.'

'Is it a fever?'

'Something more stubborn than a fever.' He caught the minatory flash in her dark eyes. 'Will you tell me about your travels?'

The flames from the hearth began to rise, casting early shadows against the walls of the *megaron*. Outside, the sun had disappeared behind lowering clouds and a fine drizzle made the fire hiss and flicker. Whilst Xandros spoke, he thought of the *Salamander*, fighting against roughening waves and of the lands they'd visited, a long way away across that very sea. Embraced by the familiarity of his surroundings, the cities of Thessaly and the Argolid seemed a distant mirage.

Xandros had the impression that Hypsipyle's attention drifted sometimes as he spoke but the moment he mentioned Medea's name, she stiffened and her eyes kindled with rapt interest.

'Deep in my bones, I knew we weren't rid of that witch. Her name is a curse upon this house!'

'The feud is over. She said as much.'

'When vengeance is delivered, Xandros, altruism is cheap.' He caught Caeneus' inquisitive look in the tail of his eye. 'Now continue.'

When he had finished, Hypsipyle pursed her thin, wrinkled lips and became distant.

'What did the Moudrians want, Nanna?'

The question shook her from her reverie. 'That wretched man wanted to pay his respects and now he hovers over Myrine like a carrion bird.'

She clasped her hands over her walking stick and rose gingerly. 'I will have baths and rooms prepared for you all but I want to rest now. We are glad you are back, Xandros; so very glad. Tomorrow will be busy, I think, so don't you stay up too late.' She turned back as she was halfway out of the hall. 'I nearly forgot. There is someone else who would like to see you.'

'Who?'

'Oh, you will see, soon enough.'

They all stood respectfully until she had left them alone by the crackling flames of the hearth.

Caeneus cleared his throat. 'Now then, my boy. Any danger of some wine?'

A light rain was falling, fighting an angry battle with the hearth flames, and Xandros and Caeneus were drinking wine after bathing when Teodora entered the *megaron*.

Caeneus was still for a moment and then rose respectfully: it was all Xandros could do not to drop his cup.

'Teodora...'

Creoboros stirred and stood protectively by his new master. There was a moment's hesitation in which neither knew who might make the first move but then she dashed across the hall and into his arms.

'Tell me *you're* not a phantom!'

She held him at arm's length and laughed. 'Not for a long time, I hope!'

VI

Unable to sleep, Xandros lit a pair of oil lamps and listened to the nightjar in full voice somewhere close to his shutters. The rain had passed and he could smell the sweetness of the earth. He wondered for how many more such evenings Myrine might stand.

A curse, Hypsipyle had decried Medea. But, however uncomfortable the notion, however treacherous the thought, the woman had creaked open a door for him.

The Gift.

He wanted to know more. He had not forgotten the strange episode inside the palace at Mycenae, when he had witnessed the *phantasma* of the old warrior being cut down. Was this a warning? Was it relevant to him? If he had indeed been bestowed a gift how could Medea possibly know of it and when might he have been aware of it?

Whichever way he cut it, it all seemed to come back to the raid, in which his skull had been cracked by the angry goatherd. That was when he first had the vision of the cadaverous man rowing towards him…

The faintest patter of footsteps in the corridor caught his attention. On the floor next to the bed, Creoboros stirred and Xandros sat upright. His door opened and Teodora's head peered around it.

'Can't sleep either?' Xandros' voice felt oddly constricted.

She shook her head and in the weak glow from the twin lamps he thought he caught a certain look in her eye. She was wearing just a linen nightgown which rode up her thighs as she sat on his bed. 'There's something in the air,' she whispered. 'Change… danger… I can't work it out but it's close.'

'I feel it too.'

Teodora bit her lip. 'Queen Hypsipyle would think less of me for being here.'

'She has plenty else on her mind and she's grown forgetful.'

'Can I get in?'

Xandros made space for her and they embraced tightly. It was the first time they had shared a bed and the intimate secrecy of it quickened his heart. He could feel her chest fluttering like a young bird taking to flight. He brushed a tendril of hair away from his nose, catching the vanishing scent of rosemary.

'I'm sorry,' he whispered. 'I'm so sorry about what happened to you.'

'*Time brings great opportunity, though opportunity bears no great time.* You were right to go and I am proud you did.'

They looked into each other's eyes for a moment then kissed tenderly. Feeling each other's need in the brush of their tongues, they slipped out of their clothes with thickened breaths and melted into one. It was only as Teodora rocked above Xandros, hands clasped either side of his head, that she caught the inquisitive face of Creoboros, stood on his forepaws and watching their every move.

She gave a little gasp of surprise and covered her breasts, laughing at the absurdity of it all.

Xandros hissed, '*Creo! Shoo!*'

'He's clever but he can't open doors, my love.'

Tutting with frustration, Xandros unlatched the door and beckoned him out, but the dog stared back at him, resolute. 'Then we'll do this the hard way.'

He was heavy and mewled in protest like a baby but he did not resist. Replacing the latch behind him, Xandros hurried across the cold flagstones to the warmth of the bed and the woman he loved.

VII

Xandros was awoken at dawn, as he usually was, by the familiar crow of the cockerel and the golden light of the morning sun filtering through the slats of the shutters. Teodora had slipped back to her own room whilst it was still dark. All was right with the world.

As soon as he was dressed, however, he noticed it. Teodora had called it a change but to him it was a tense expectation, and he felt it in his chest. Caeneus was already up, pacing the *megaron*.

'Ready for the day, young man?'

Xandros nodded, noting the old rapier sheathed at his belt.

They breakfasted whilst Xandros outlined his plans. He would speak to the council of Myrine before they both faced Plouteos and his son. Before that, however, Xandros would see his father, alone. Caeneus was free to do as he chose.

When they had finished, Teodora squeezed his hand and he went to find his father. He could hear him talking in a low voice to Hypsipyle along the corridor and, as he drew near the door, though the windows were open, he smelled the stale, unhealthy air.

He took a deep breath and knocked and the conversation fell quiet. Without being asked to enter, he pushed the door open. Xandros barely recognised the sallow figure sat in bed against the far wall.

'So you came back.' Euneus winced with pain as he propped himself up. 'Did you find what you were looking for?'

At any other time in his life, the words would have been laced with scorn or anger, but not now. Xandros approached the bed and the miasma of sickness hung heavy around it.

'Father, what is it?'

'No, step back, Xandros.'

He looked to Hypsipyle in alarm and she nodded gravely.

The pained expression on his father's face eased a little. 'Some *phthisis* or other. It's best...' He coughed and the rattle was unlike anything that Xandros had ever heard. Euneus looked like he was being jabbed with needles. 'It's best,' he croaked, 'people stay away.'

'But... the Moudrians are here. They want to speak to you, as do I!'

'And they will! But not like this, in my bed. Your grandmother is ever the cheese-parer with information so I want you to tell me where you have been. Speak to me.'

He had been brief with Hypsipyle on the previous evening but the words now flowed from him and he wondered what had brought down the barricades, and why they had ever been raised in the first place. Euneus raised an eyebrow at the encounter with Medea, as had Hypsipyle but, despite his illness, his years as king had taught him to dissemble his true feelings. Until the end. When he had finished, the sight of a single tear breaching his eyelid – quickly wiped away – formed a lump in Xandros' throat. Euneus was quiet for a few long moments.

'You spoke of "failure" twice, Xandros. Never use that word again, d'you hear me? What you did was rash and impulsive...' He coughed but managed to control the waves of pain. 'But it was... but it was also brave. To honour any of the gallant promises men have made these past months, none has dared raise a finger, except you. And do you think I can't see when a man is trying to disguise an injury? Your left side: I can see how you protect it. A glancing blow, no doubt, but a painful one, I can see.' He chuckled and it made Xandros' eyes sting.

'Who knows what may come of this, Xandros? It only takes the fall of a pebble to start a landslide. Leave me now to dress, my son. I will need the energy for these Moudrians.'

'Yes, Father.' He turned for the door and caught Hypsipyle wink. She had never done so before and it showed.

'And Xandros?'

'Father?'

'I am glad you met Jason. That he still lives is a small miracle;

no less that he gave you the fleece. I will see it later. It shows how proud you must have made the old fool. But not as proud as you have made me.'

Fighting against the tears, Xandros smiled and closed the door behind him, dashing into a room further down the corridor, where he fell to his knees and wept.

VIII

Xandros dried his eyes and filled his lungs before stepping back into the *megaron*. Teodora was waiting for him and it was clear by the look on her face that something had happened.

'How was he?' asked Teodora.

'He's… awake and talking but…'

Teodora smiled briefly. 'There's people here…'

'They'll have to wait until he's dressed and ready. He…'

'No, I mean a ship has arrived.'

'Jason's men?'

'No, Xandros. From Gioura, an island.'

'Gioura?'

Teodora said, 'I'd never heard of it.'

'Me neither.'

'I have.' Caeneus entered the *megaron* with some breakfast wine and swilled his cup before draining it. 'It's in the Sporades. Very small, just a few fishing villages.'

'How do you know this?' asked Xandros with a frown.

'Because I just spoke to one of them out there, wanting to see the *wanax*. Your first refugee, it seems.'

Xandros was about to ask what on earth he was supposed to do about it but a voice – a woman's, soft and calm – breathed into his ear.

Earn it, Xandros.

He met Caeneus' eyes, saw the savvy glint and, in that moment, a new shoot of understanding broke ground. Upon Xandros' response would the Larissan have his measure. 'I will speak to them.'

Caeneus tipped his head. 'Good. They need some reassurance,

I think. You can speak to your Moudrian brethren whilst you're at it.'

'They're here? Already?'

'Looks like it.'

Teodora gave him an encouraging smile as he headed for the door. There were men gathering beyond the courtyard but he could see they weren't all Moudrians. He took a deep breath and opened the gate. The agitated conversation stopped at once and twenty faces or more turned to him in complete surprise. He saw one or two pairs of eyes glance down at the ancient sword strapped to his belt. There was Plouteos and his son Ekhinos, and their expressions fell in a trice; here Khalkeus, Alektruon and Hektor, who all looked at him in astonishment. Just beyond the retinue of Moudrians, Xandros noticed some unfamiliar faces, strained and travel-worn.

'Good morning,' Xandros said brightly. 'King Euneus will soon be ready. Meantime, I must speak to the council.' He stepped aside to let the Myrinians through, being sure to make eye contact with Ekhinos before he turned back. Teodora's fiancé – if such he still was – looked murderous.

'Young man,' said Hektor, once they were in the courtyard. 'When did *you* return?'

'Yesterday, in the evening.' Xandros caught the looks that passed between Alektruon and Khalkeus and resolved to unpick them later. 'We can speak indoors.' They passed through the fruit trees in silence before entering the *megaron*. 'It seems you have already met Prince Caeneus of Larissa – his father, Polyphemus, son of Elatus, rowed with Jason on *Argo*. The other needs no introduction. Please, sit…'

'I can g—'

'You'll stay, Teodora.'

Though her eyes smiled at Xandros, she was canny enough to keep the surprise from her face.

'Refreshments?'

Khalkeus shook his head and adjusted his cloak, then became as still as a rock when a rangy black dog padded into the hall, sniffing the newcomers in turn. Satisfied, he sat next to Xandros with a look that said: *Raise a hand against him at your peril.*

'This is Creoboros – he earned his name, believe me – when we escaped from the palace at Mycenae. Prince Caeneus here has vowed his sword for us, and we are much the better for it.'

This information put them on the back foot and they were silent for a moment.

'So…' Khalkeus scratched his temple. 'You have acquired a man, a dog and some attitude on your travels. Anything else that might help us?'

'And the Golden Fleece. I confess, we didn't sail as far as Jason to acquire it but far enough to see the situation for what it is…'

'Which is?'

'Which is that every *polis* not already in the raiders' power, or tearing itself into pieces, has resolved to fight for itself, with no men to spare…'

'Predictable enough! Was it worth disappearing and doubling your father's troubles just for this?'

'Perhaps. It only takes the fall of a pebble to start a landslide. Merely bickering amongst ourselves would never dislodge that pebble though, would it?'

Xandros could see the flash of anger – and surprise – in the man's eyes but he didn't look away. 'Are you sure you wouldn't take a drink? The day will be warm, I think.'

'No.'

'The fleece.' Hektor's bushy moustache twitched with interest. 'May we see it?'

Caeneus rubbed his hands and looked to Xandros and, seeing the slight tilt of his chin, went to fetch it. When he returned and Xandros took it from him, he caught the musty waft and hoped it hadn't deteriorated on the boat. He untied the leather wraps and let it unravel with a flick of his wrists. As he hoped would happen, caught in the shaft of sunlight from the *megaron*'s aperture, it glittered with ancient promise.

Hektor and, to Xandros' surprise, Alektruon, left their seats to take a closer look. 'Magnificent,' murmured Hektor, stroking the fibres with the back of his hand. 'A thing of legend and here it is. Come, Khalkeus, take a look! Your own father earned his name on this!'

'Later. So you retrieved a relic, boy, or stole it, who knows. And how does this help us?'

'Because it represents something greater than its appearance. Because the men who won it were mocked for sailing to their deaths. It was a myth. It couldn't be found, they said. An impossible voyage.' From the corner of his eye, he saw Alektruon giving him a curious look. 'The many, on all counts, were proven wrong by the few. It is more than just a sheepskin, Khalkeus. It is a thing of hope and unity and brotherhood. With these things, we might prevail. Without them, we will surely fail.'

The *megaron* fell silent. Faint, beyond the twitter of birds in the courtyard, drifted the hum of conversation.

'The boy speaks sense.' Alektruon looked impressed. Just then, one of Euneus' servants appeared from the corridor. 'King Euneus will join you,' he announced quietly. They all rose, even though it was not something they were accustomed to doing, such were the times.

Though his hair had been brushed and he wore clean clothes, the stoop of his thin body was unmistakable, and no amount of powder could disguise the pallor of his cheeks as he lowered himself to his seat. Still, his eyes were alert and met the Myrinians in order of seniority.

'You must be the son of one of my father's former comrades?'

Caeneus bowed. 'Just so, king.'

'Here to fight for us?'

There was a pause, during which Xandros suspected he might reply, *For payment.*

'I am.'

'Then we extend our gratitude to you and consider you our friend.'

Caeneus gave him an enigmatic smile and bowed again.

'So then, Hektor,' continued Euneus, suppressing a cough, 'you three were in a hurry to see me yesterday. I'm sorry I was indisposed. Let me hear it before we see our callers.'

Hektor hesitated, turning to Alektruon and Khalkeus. 'That matter has passed.'

'Has it?'

'I think it has, Khalkeus, for now. What do you say, Alek?'

Alektruon looked at Xandros, his hard face inscrutable. 'Agreed.'

Euneus frowned. 'Where is Hilarion?'

More loaded looks crossed the hall. 'We don't know,' replied Hektor. 'Hasn't been seen in a while.'

'Have you visited his house?'

'It's empty.'

'Then I want a search party.' Euneus shifted upon his seat, divining much that was unsaid by his councillors. He cleared his throat. 'Well then. Shall we see them?'

He gestured to his servant who crossed the *megaron* to the courtyard. Xandros had been watching the councillors and suspected that, had he returned to Lemnos even a day later, the balance of power might have tipped further from the House of Euneus. It suddenly struck him as the Moudrians strode into the room that the councillors might even be in league with them.

Despite the bright sun and the birdsong, the atmosphere within the hall immediately curdled. Ekhinos glowered at Xandros and his blazing eyes fell upon Teodora for a moment before turning away. Xandros squeezed her hand and let it fall.

Euneus' hands fell onto the armrests. 'Here you are,' he declared with no great enthusiasm. 'The question is why.'

Plouteos looked about the *megaron* and sniffed. 'Merely to pay our respects. We heard you were sick, Euneus.'

'A fever. It will pass.'

'I see.' Plouteos looked him up and down, though his expression didn't change. 'Whilst waiting for you, I have spoken to some foreigners, from Gioura, and… forgive me; do you know where that is?'

'I do.'

The nomarch's smirk suggested he didn't believe him. 'They were driven from their homes by the pirates and the word on people's lips is that the northerly islands of the Archipelagos – here, Samothrace – will be receiving an influx of refugees. My question is, are you… shall I say, are you feeling strong enough to respond?'

Euneus' fingers curled around the armrest. Unable to hold his anger, he began to cough. It wasn't the alarming hack that had upset Xandros the night before but enough to give the lie to his passing fever. Xandros caught the look that flitted between the nomarch and his son. *Triumph.*

'Excuse us, if you'd like us to come back?'

Euneus raised a hand whilst the coughing subsided, leaving his face a shade of puce. The gesture of restraint Xandros now saw, wasn't to keep the Moudrians from leaving: it was to keep Hektor and Khalkeus from attacking them.

'And my question… And my question to you, Plouteos, is why you are *really* here?'

'Why I am *here*? Have I not made myself clear…? To pay my respects… For the mutual interest…'

'Horseshit.' They all turned to Alektruon in astonishment. 'Forgive me, Euneus, but I smell horseshit…'

'Alek…'

'We all see you for what you are. You are vultures and I say go find your carrion elsewhere.'

'Alek!'

Euneus' sharp tone threatened to unleash another bout of coughing. He swallowed it back with great discomfort. 'I will answer your question. *We* are strong enough to respond and respond we will. *You* can do as you please.' He levelled a finger at him. 'But question our resolve again and you won't find us so tolerant a second time.'

The nomarch rocked upon his heels. He was about to respond when Ekhinos, who had been growing agitated, raised his voice. 'What are you going to do about *him*, then? Well? Would you stand by if one of us stole his betrothed? Of course not!'

'Not now,' hissed Plouteos between gritted teeth. *'Not here.'*

'I gave no such consent!' protested Teodora. 'Never!'

Creoboros bared his yellow teeth and his growl checked Ekhinos.

'If you want to settle that score,' said Xandros, rising slowly from his stool, 'it can be settled here. Unlike you, a coward, I don't need my dogs to finish my work.'

'Coward?' Ekhinos glared at him for a moment before balling

his fist, whereupon Creoboros sprang at him, snarling and snapping his jaws. Ekhinos jumped backwards with a groan of terror.

'Enough!' Euneus was on his feet. 'Leave this house before blood is spilt. Go!'

Eyes blazing at Xandros, the nomarch and his son stormed from the hall and the heavy air cleared a little. Caeneus, alone, looked like he had enjoyed the spectacle.

'Well,' he said, blowing the air from his cheeks, 'who needs a bard when you have entertainment like *that*? Now I see why you came to Argos, my lad!'

'Xandros,' said Euneus with a frown. 'Speak to the newcomers. Ensure they are settled and do what you can. I want to speak to these men about Hilarion.'

'Yes, Father.' He tipped his head towards the door and Teodora and Caeneus followed him outside, Creoboros weaving his way between them.

IX

The following morning, Xandros wanted to be alone on the palace's farm while his thoughts swirled. The sweet, earthy smell of the sheepfold in the lower village always took his mind from his problems for a few welcome minutes. He leaned on his shovel and watched the sheep fussing and bleating. One of them stopped and turned to face him, the largest ewe of the fold. Her ear was perpetually twitching, harassed by flies. *What I wouldn't give,* but then he laughed at the thought, *for this to be the extent of my problems.*

But then, did they not stare down the same fate, even if they were blithely unaware of it? How many head of livestock would be left once the Giourans – and who knew how many other refugees – set about the stores of Lemnos?

The thought even occurred to him to arrange another secretive raid but, as he shovelled filthy hay, he quickly dismissed the idea. After Ekhinos and Plouteos' bitter departure the previous day, the Moudrians would be cool enough at their backs, and provoking them further would leave them surrounded by enemies.

Arrangements needed to be made. Defence... provisions and equipment... water... tents... more fighting men. For this, he would have to dispatch messengers into the hills and fields. And what about the smaller details, such as bandages and salves for the inevitable injuries? And deaths.

'Much on your mind, young man?'

Xandros turned in surprise to see a familiar figure leaning on a fence post across the paddock. 'I... What... You are back, Moxos!'

'I might say the same for you.'

'So you heard.'

'I did. Alek told me.'

'Alektruon?'

'He alone knew where I'd been keeping.'

Xandros threw down the shovel and went to shake the man's hand but Moxos looked at it scornfully and embraced him. 'I saw those tents on the beach and spoke to our new friends. I think it's time to bury former grievances, don't you?'

'We need you, Moxos. More than ever.'

Moxos tipped his head noncommittally. 'How is your father?' He caught the cloud that passed Xandros' eyes. 'Is he well enough to receive a visitor?'

'Others, no, but you'd be welcomed there any time. You know that.'

Moxos seemed to think about it for a moment. 'Then I will.' He smiled briefly and moved on but then turned a few paces later. 'And I'll tell the others that you've summoned the council this evening.'

X

In the late afternoon torpor, when the people of Myrine were looking to their own affairs after some respite from the beating sun, and Caeneus and Creoboros were sleeping, and after he had checked upon his father, who appeared to have improved a little, Xandros and Teodora managed to steal an hour together. They lay alongside each other whilst their breathing returned to normal in the afterglow of lovemaking. There had been a hunger about it, as if they were both aware of what Time might deny them in the future. He propped himself on his elbow and ran a finger along the contours of her skin, making her squirm with laughter.

'When will you return to Moudros?'

Her smile faded. 'Maybe today, before it gets dark.'

'There's danger under the sun, too, Teodora. Remember what happened to Manolis?'

'He couldn't defend himself.'

He looked at her but kept the doubts from his mind. She was spirited and more capable than she looked but against two bandits?

'Why don't we just send a messenger?'

She thought about it for a moment before shaking her head. 'I want to see my mother.'

Xandros took a deep breath. He had skirted the matter for too long. 'And Ekhinos?'

'What about him?'

'He still thinks you're betrothed, that's what! How do you know what he'd do if he knew you were back in Moudros?' Her grey eyes held him and he knew at such moments that her mind was working hard. 'Well? *Are* you still betrothed?'

'You *know* we are, Xandros. When has it ever been the lot of women to make such decisions?'

The nausea in his stomach erased the last of the afternoon's pleasure. He sat upright and slipped out of bed.

'What are you doing?'

'I'm getting dressed.'

She rolled her eyes. 'I can *see* that. I mean why did you get up so suddenly?'

'What more is there to say about it? If you want to bow your head to the yoke, that is your decision to make.'

'You asked me a question; I answered it,' she said icily. 'I did not say I wanted it or accepted it. Don't you know me better than this?'

Xandros didn't answer as he belted his tunic. 'In all the time we were away, though I wanted to, I never asked if he hurt you or was gentle with you. I never asked because I didn't want to know the answer...'

'Nor because it is any business of yours!'

Now Teodora threw aside the coverlets and began to dress. Xandros winced inwardly, knowing he had crossed a boundary. *She is a good woman,* Hypsipyle had said. *And good women are builders.* Why, then, his appetite for destruction?

'I didn't like it,' she said distantly.

'I know. I'm sorry I spoke...'

'No, I mean I didn't like it when he took me. It was just once and I made him stop before he finished.'

He clenched his fists in disbelief and anger. 'And? Did he?'

'I forced him off me, though he said he would have stopped anyway as it's not his way to break a filly.'

He had no words for this. He just stood there with his fingers clenching and unclenching.

'So you see I can look after myself.' She sat on the edge of his bed while she tied the sandal straps around her slender ankles. 'I will go back to Moudros now. I want to see my mother.'

XI

That evening, under a westering sun, the council – plus several others Xandros had invited, including one of the Giouran refugees – sat in the meeting place. He had been feeling irritable since Teodora had left and now the small-mindedness of Khalkeus in particular, who scowled at the newcomers to the council with arms folded, was tugging at his fraying temper.

Yes, said Poli the fisherman, *of course the fish could be dried and salted, but it must take a lot of work, gutting and cleaning their innards, rubbing them with salt and spreading them out to dry for a few days.* 'But for such numbers, even the laying of dry matting... and catching enough fish in the first place... Every fishing skiff in Myrine would have to be turned out for this!'

He threw his hands in the air in his dramatic way, and the tutting of Khalkeus made Poli screw up his face. He was about to counter with an acerbic word but then Caeneus approached, looking like he had been running.

'Another boat, gentlemen. This one's from Halonnesus.'

Xandros dropped his hands onto the table with a loud thud. 'Send them up. Tell them to be quick.'

Caeneus made a face. 'Yes, master.'

Hektor shook his head. 'Is there a single rock in the sea these pig-fuckers haven't set foot on?'

'How much food do these wretched people think we have? Send them away!'

Xandros shot Khalkeus a look. 'To do what?' he snapped. 'To drown? To join the pirates and bloat their numbers? To tell our brother and sister Hellenes that we turned our backs upon them, to our eternal shame? *No!*'

The meeting place fell silent whilst Xandros and Khalkeus glared at each other. Xandros could see the surprise at the way in which the elder was being addressed: perhaps even a stubborn shred of respect. Khalkeus broke eye contact first, looking to the floor.

The Giouran spoke up. 'I had not realised, until now, the inconvenience our arrival had caused,' he said quietly. 'But I assure you all of this: we will earn every morsel of bread we eat by standing with you and fighting as well as any warrior in the Archipelagos. Shoulder to shoulder. To the last.'

'I never doubted it.' Xandros offered him a sad smile. He could see Khalkeus had wounded his pride. 'We might yet see how you claim that honour.'

Xandros finished outlining his plan – one hatched in the smouldering ruins of Iolkos – without further interruption but he was aware of the dubious looks that crossed the floor. 'We will need more wood than we've ever gathered, and on this the dry summer might actually help us. And oil. Even if it means stripping the fruit off every last tree. That is my suggestion. If anyone else has something to say, now would be the time to speak.'

Their heads turned towards the gate to the citadel. A straggle of people was at that moment making its way into the square, downcast, defeated. A bandy-legged man, top heavy, with a ruff of dark hair, looking exhausted by the climb up the path to the citadel. A woman with him, thin, wringing her hands but gamely meeting the stares. A gangly youth wearing what looked like a sack. An assortment of others, old and very young. Whilst the Myrinians looked upon them with mixed thoughts – some in pity, some with folded arms, some angered by the prospects of dwindling rations being shared ever thinner – the eyes of Xandros and the council ranged amongst them, searching for fighters and finding only broken fugitives.

Xandros could sense Khalkeus shaking his head behind him. The councillors exchanging looks not of despair now but inevitability. Xandros beckoned the most capable over and his rolling gait made someone behind him tut.

'Your name?'

'Laodon,' he answered in a low, gruff voice. 'A fisherman from Halonnesus.' Xandros glanced at the man's raw hands, roughened by decades of scaling fish and hauling nets. He could have guessed his profession without being told.

'And these people?' Xandros glanced towards the newcomers. One of the Myrinian women was pouring water for them into clay cups. 'Also from Halonnesus?'

'They are. Family, some friends. It's a small island.'

Xandros nodded distantly. Halonnesus was the sort of place mentioned once and soon forgotten. A little island creased with valleys and ridges, so small it could almost fit within the bay of Moudros, with little to offer apart from fish. Fish and secluded, rocky coves. He doubted it was home to more than a few dozen souls. The island was a humble stepping stone to virtually anywhere within the northern waters of the Archipelagos. In short, an ideal stronghold for pirates, if only a temporary one.

Xandros became aware of the stillness in the square. A little breeze had picked up, shivering the silvery leaves of the ancient olive tree. High above, oblivious to the worries of men, a kite circled and gave a shrill cry. People began to drift over to the council, wanting to be in earshot of the news.

'And you have fled here before the pirates might arrive?'

A fleeting look of confusion crossed Laodon's face. 'No, young sir. They arrived.'

Laodon made no attempt to lower his voice and now his words whipped across the square. There was a cacophony of crying and shouting, and a shrill prayer.

'Be quiet, all of you!' Xandros stood. 'This is *not* the time! Let the council hear this man!' Xandros turned back to him and allowed the anger and panic to drain from his voice. 'Tell us.'

Laodon rasped his stubble and, taking the hint, spoke more quietly. 'There were seven galleys – long, black-hulled boats. They… We had no choice. My brother… These people are all I could gather on my boat… My brother was in the next harbour around the headland. I had to leave.' Laodon stopped abruptly as his voice cracked. 'I'm sorry, this is difficult.'

'There is no rush,' said Xandros.

Laodon took a deep breath and settled himself. 'I left my brother and his family to their fate. The raiders were approaching from the south, where his village is. Had I sailed there first…'

Xandros glanced at the councillors and, for a moment, saw the pity in their drawn faces. Khalkeus' morose look was gone, replaced by a trace of shame.

'I'm sorry…' Laodon wiped his eyes with the back of his hand. 'Their ships noticed us leave – must have done – but last we saw of them, they were just slipping into the harbour where we had been not an hour before.' He looked Xandros square in the eyes. 'There's nothing to keep them there, not for more than a few days. Once they've set down their women and children, and gorged themselves on what little we had, they'll raise their sails again.'

And attack Lemnos.

If the rumours were true, Thasos had already fallen. A sizeable island, close to the mainland, just two days to the north west with a favourable wind. There were some who said that the rocks of Thasos were shot through with veins of silver, though whether the sea raiders knew that was anybody's guess. Either way, it apparently wasn't tempting enough to draw the rest of their ships. To the south-west, the Sporades were also under their sway. They had even taken Samothrace, to the north, and now Halonnesus, just a few hours at most to the south. That left Lemnos, possibly also Lesbos, as the last ripe ears of corn amidst a darkening cloud of locusts.

Xandros turned to the councillors. 'We need to get down to the beach and prepare. All of us. Right now.'

Until sunset, the beach was alive with activity. The islanders kept glancing out over the waters of the bay, where a sea mist was drifting towards the shore. Some of the more superstitious amongst them made the sign to ward off evil spirits. Xandros had posted a watchman atop the headland in the old huer's hut, equipping him with a war trumpet. The hut itself now floated above a haze and he doubted the watchman would know anything about any boat, not even a whole fleet, until it was directly beneath him.

They worked until the light failed altogether, and the clouds had thickened to obscure the moon and stars. Xandros gazed out over the sea, heaving dark into the bay. There would be no attack tonight. It would be an act of madness.

'Let's have the huer back in,' he said, before standing them all down.

XII

Xandros preoccupied himself the following morning with helping the throngs of people stripping wood from the pines all along the backshore while others lugged it over the sand and bound it up into thick hurdles. He gave encouragement as he passed, carrying some of the wood himself. Creoboros tailed after him, turning this way and that at the myriad noises and smells. At first, Xandros didn't even realise that he was walking alongside his old adversary Loukios, since his face was concealed by the load he carried. Their eyes met when they deposited the branches on the beach and it was clear that Loukios still bore him a grudge.

Whereas it would have once needled him, Xandros shrugged it off as he walked away. In a shaded little clearing, a trio of bronzesmiths was busy pumping the leather bags to fire the portable pot bellows. Two of them were brothers – immensely strong, deep-chested fellows – and they were all working up a sweat in the shade of some poplars.

There was a pair of olive presses in the citadel of Myrine and, to supplement it, a few Myrinians had cleared away the gorse and dried grasses from ancient contraptions that had been abandoned in disused plots. These were now busy squeezing the mush from stone wheels driven by overworked donkeys from the palace farmstead.

Xandros overheard one elderly lady complain to another in a little group, as they carried baskets of pulped fruit, that it was sacrilege to waste the first-pressed oil in the way 'that wayward son of Euneus' was planning. He noticed Melli amongst them and her cheeks flushed with embarrassment when she saw him. Noticing this, the old lady turned in shock to Xandros, touching her heart and apologising profusely.

'The gods will still have their libation if you keep two hands on your basket,' he said to her with a wink, 'and fill me that jar by sundown.'

At the far end of the beach were a dozen boys and young men. It warmed Xandros' heart to see them whirring their slings and he could hear the faint noises of surprise and amazement that followed each *dink* of someone's pebbles striking the trunk of a pine.

The day was hot and shortly after midday they stopped to rest and water, though Xandros himself walked the length of the beach and back again, checking the work with Creoboros trotting alongside him. He raised his hand in acknowledgement at the groups of workers as they rested, dropping a word of praise here and some gentle advice there, trying to project a semblance of calm he did not feel. He caught some whispers as he passed and he could tell by the looks on certain faces that he was being reckoned upon and that, in the minds of some, his authority was not filled with deeds.

Hypsipyle's words drifted through his head and he clung fast to them. *It's seldom the critic who counts, Xandros.*

She was right. *What should he care for the opinions of the few who dare not look Danger square in the eye and see Failure in its tail?*

He gave them an hour. He didn't need to clap his hands or sound a whistle. The sight of the first few drifting back to their tasks prompted the rest and, before long, the beach was once more alive with activity.

By late afternoon, the eerie mist returned, bringing with it the grave cold of the night sea. As it rolled towards the bay it seemed to silence the waves and amplify the ambient chatter. Xandros glanced towards the huer's hut. Once more, it floated above the headland as if upon a cloud. The watchman was invisible. Xandros experienced a tightening within his head that was not unfamiliar and he was not surprised to hear the warning note of a trumpet.

Someone shouted, *'Ships! I see ships!'*

They emerged from the fog like spectres. Two vessels under silent oars, several spear casts distant.

'Sound the horn!' Xandros yelled. One of the Moudrians fetched it – it was hanging by a nail on a tree – and the whole beach came alive at the mournful note, like an ants' nest poked by children. Moxos came running along the waterfront where the sand was firmer, rallying people and snapping orders. His actions wrenched Xandros from a moment of fear-born paralysis.

'Xandros, with me!' shouted Moxos. When Xandros joined him, he whispered, 'There's no shame in it – we all feel it the first time – but men will be taking their lead from you.' Seeing the wide-eyed look in Xandros' face, he leaned closer. 'Women and children: order it now.'

Xandros glanced at the sweeping prows, mesmerised. For pirate galleys, there was something very odd about them. He filled his lungs and was about to shout the order when, at the very moment another sharp-eyed islander yelled the warning, he saw it himself.

'Stay your arrows!'

A white flag. The vessel was also listing to port.

It wasn't being waved with any vigour – as one might imagine a man carving the air in fear of immediate death – but in a languid, almost lazy, sweep. Xandros called the beach to silence and hundreds of pairs of eyes now focused upon the ships gliding a bowshot from the beach. Laodon had described the pirates' hulls as black: it was, in fact, the only word he'd used, suggesting the colour was visible even at a distance. The paint and tar of these ships might once have been black, but their hulls were so old and battered none could tell.

Melli joined Xandros and she wiped her brow with the back of her hand. He glanced at her with a frown but made no complaint about her presumption: she had a tongue as sharp as any sailor. She asked, 'Do you think it's a trick?'

'We'll soon know,' he murmured, 'but I think not.'

'Why?'

He turned to her. 'Because everything we've learned about them says they land and they fight like dogs, not foxes.'

'I agree,' said Moxos, 'but I want to see for myself.'

'Archers!' shouted Xandros. A handful were stood on a nearby dune and raised their hands. 'Cover us!'

He and Moxos pulled down their helmets and approached the shoreline. They could make out the faces of some crewmen now. Alert but unstressed. Though the oars had all been pulled in, it didn't look like there were many passengers. At least, Xandros reflected, there were no bows being raised towards him.

In the moment of tension, the opportunity to exchange a greeting came and went. Then the prow of the first ran aground with a hiss; the other was still fifty yards offshore. Perhaps that was the reason why nobody jumped into the shallows: the crew had disappeared. The moments stretched into a full minute, during which Xandros and Moxos exchanged bemused looks, laced with suspicion. Perhaps a trap was being hatched at that very moment.

Then there was a stir of activity aboard the first as the other drew alongside it. A shape dropped awkwardly into the water and a gruff curse accompanied the soft *splosh*.

'Kuna!'

Xandros and Moxos looked on in astonishment as one of the most extraordinary men they had ever seen waded stiffly towards them, eyes sweeping the beach with a contemptuous scowl. He had bristling grey hair receding from a beetling brow and his ears were lumpen and misshapen, like a wrestler's. A battered sword hung on a cracked leather baldrick and his tunic was grey with age. When he reached the shore, he shook the water off each leg like a dog cocking itself to piss. Xandros and Moxos were stood barely twenty feet from him yet he looked right through them.

'Come on then, woman, show yourself!'

There were a few snickers from behind the hurdles of wood and most of the islanders now emerged for a closer look.

'Butes of Athens said he'd return! Here he is!'

Xandros watched the stranger's grizzled face slump with disappointment. He cleared his throat and removed his helmet. 'Welcome to Lemnos, friend. Can...'

'I *know* where I am, laddie!' he snapped. 'I was here long before you were a twitch in your... in...' The gravel in his voice faded and he approached Xandros with narrowed eyes. Xandros didn't know how to react when Butes gripped his chin and began to tip his head this way and that, scrutinising him like a cow at a market, chuntering away in apparent surprise.

This was too much for Creoboros. His lips curled back and he snarled at Butes but the old man seemed unperturbed.

'This is the son of the *wanax* of Lemnos!' hissed Moxos. 'Show some respect in front of these people!'

Butes released Xandros' face and scowled at Moxos. Other men had started to disembark from the first boat now, none apparently hostile, but he could sense the Lemnians bristling with caution.

'It's the other way round, man.'

'What?'

'I said it should be the other way round.' Butes tipped his head behind him and his lips cracked into a broad grin. 'You are in the presence of great men. Take off your lid.'

To humour the old man, who was quite obviously mad, Moxos removed his helmet and pushed back his thick hair. Butes grunted and did a double take, eyes darting to Xandros. He took a step backwards in shock. *'Ma Dia!'* he growled. 'It cannot be!'

There were a dozen or so men on the beach by then, some of them even older than Butes. They stood there, swaying slightly as they met the faces ranged against them, oblivious to their feet sinking into the oozing sand. One or two leaned heavily upon ash spears, planted into the beach. As the gentle breeze picked up, their cloaks fluttered about their bodies, outlining spare frames, sword sheaths, spindly legs and pot bellies, though some were deep in the chest. The Lemnians looked at them and began to smirk. A barely suppressed snicker from one induced belly laughs in others.

Now that the threat appeared to have passed, Loukios had appeared. He smirked and sauntered along the backshore, muttering loud enough for anyone he passed to hear, 'We've had the fishermen; now it's their grandfathers.' Encouraged by the chuckles, he added, 'What's next? Exhuming the dead and arming them?'

There were guffaws as the foreshore filled with the occupants of the galleys. Xandros turned to them, feeling a crushing sense of shame and embarrassment, though the newcomers were, it was true, a motley – and elderly – assortment of waifs and strays.

'Welcome, all of you,' said Xandros quickly. 'We can offer you a little, if you come with nothing. Then, perhaps, you can tell us where you have sailed from.'

A few – those unarmed and in the most obvious need – drifted forwards and some of the more considerate Myrinians came to meet them. But the one called Butes and several others seemed curiously stand-offish, bristling at the offence they had been given. Another man joined Butes, tall and whip-thin. He had a protuberant mouth, giving his face a vulpine outline. He turned to the side and spat onto the sand, shrugging off his cloak. For an old man, he was all knotted sinew. He levelled his spear at Loukios.

'You, boy, over here!'

Loukios pointed to himself. 'You're talking to me?'

'The loudmouth, yes. Get over here.'

One of Loukios' friends shoved him and he jogged forwards, raising his hands to accept the cheers. As he approached the man, Loukios looked him up and down. Xandros saw his eyes pass over the scars lining his wrinkled torso and a flicker of doubt made his smirk fade. The wolf-faced man sucked his top teeth and stared at Loukios until the youth looked away.

'I thought so,' he said, leaning closer. 'A puffed-up little newt. *Give him a spear!*'

Xandros stepped forwards, sensing trouble. 'Excuse him, friend. His mouth runs away with…'

The other man waved him away without looking at him whilst a spear was relayed to the front of the beach. 'Try hit me with it.'

'What?' said Loukios. 'Why would I want to harm an old man?'

There was a succession of heavy splashes and Xandros turned to see the first passengers of the second boat now wading ashore, and these men were a different proposition altogether. They had packs slung over their shoulders and raised their shields and spears above their heads. The lower halves of their tunics, sodden by brine, clung to powerful thighs. Xandros counted twenty spears, planted in the sand. His eyes were drawn to the designs painted red and bold upon their circular shields. Ants. The newcomers surveyed the defences with the cool eye of a professional soldier whilst two grizzled, unkempt-looking men walked stiffly behind them towards the older folk who had disembarked from the first ship.

'What's this?' asked the one with a pot belly, tugging at the beads in his greying beard. 'Causing trouble already, are we?'

'Wound him up, have we, Butes?' chuckled another. 'Well, come on then! You have your audience; get on with it. I have a thirst!'

The men began to form a circle around Loukios and his old challenger, and Xandros backed out of it. *They've done this before,* he thought.

Looking about him and seeing himself the centre of attention, Loukios picked up the spear. He twirled it this way and that, warming his limbs. The smirk reappeared. 'Which end do you want me to strike you with?'

A few of his friends burst out laughing but the old man gave him a peevish sneer. 'Choose either, you little *kuna*. It makes no odds.'

Slapped by the insult, Loukios hefted the spear, paused for a moment then lunged at the old man. He stepped aside with a tut and the blade flashed past, no more than a hand's breadth from his skin.

'Do it *properly*!' he snapped.

Loukios took a few steps backwards, changing his angle. This time, he tucked it under his armpit, feinting a lunge then swiping forehand at the man's torso. With astonishing speed, the old man flicked his own spear at the incoming spearhead, deflecting it wide, then twisted and struck the meat of Loukios' thigh with a report like a whip-crack. Loukios screamed in agony and dropped like a felled tree.

The stunned silence that fell upon the beach was only broken by the cackles of the men in the circle. The one with beads in his beard looked like a wandering old drunkard. His whole body shook with wheezing laughter until he was quite red in the face.

Butes grunted in satisfaction. 'And *now* we'll take you up on that drink.'

Xandros watched the spearman bend down gingerly to retrieve

his cloak whilst Butes slapped him on the shoulder and they embraced warmly. 'One of these days, Idas, you might challenge the wrong man.'

'He doesn't exist.'

Xandros' heart slammed into his chest.

Idas of Arene!

He gazed at them, wide-eyed. They walked right past him, straightening their backs as the islanders looked on in wonder. The rumour of their arrival swept along the beach and up the winding path into Myrine, and there was now clapping from the walls. Xandros heard footsteps thumping over the sand and turned to see Caeneus hurrying over.

'Is it true?' Xandros had never seen the mercenary so animated. 'Have they come?'

The newcomers were on the lower slope now, looking up at the enthused faces competing to get a view of them, and the slanting light of the evening cast their shadows long against the rockface. Xandros wondered what they were thinking. It had been forty years since they had last trudged up that very path and only his grandmother still lived to share the memory. He wouldn't miss this for anything: not even an invasion of raiders.

'I can't believe it... I don't...' He turned to Caeneus with a beaming smile. 'They've come: the Argonauts!'

One man remained on the second boat. He had been watching the events on the beach with a nagging sense of misgiving. It was one thing to reminisce every year in a remote corner of the mainland, away from the eyes of others, but it was another thing altogether to revisit the past like this and stir its dregs. The prospect of wandering through a cemetery of memories left Ancaeus feeling cold.

The boat creaked and rocked gently beneath his feet. For all the fears of running the gauntlet through pirate-infested waters, it had been the calmest passage he could remember, and this was another reason for his unease. He felt a tension in the air: an unnatural stillness of the sort that often precedes an earthquake.

He glanced down at the boy, slumbering on a pile of fleeces. He had been lulled to sleep by the heat, the waves and the cadence of conversation for the past hour of the last leg, and if he didn't wake him now, he would never go to bed this evening.

Ancaeus bent down on knees that clicked and laid a heavy hand upon the boy's chest. 'Come on, my lad, it's time to get up.' He glanced at the citadel, shimmering in a heat haze atop the hill. 'This is your new home.'

XIII

Dusk was falling. It was a balmy evening. Rush lights and oil lamps had been lit all around the square and people spoke to each other in warm voices. Xandros cradled his dish of wine and looked around him. Over there, Laodon, the fisherman from Halonnesus was sat cross-legged bouncing his little daughter on his knee, arms wrapped around her. His wife was dabbing at their son's face with a linen square. Opposite them, widows, dressed in black, were weaving. One of them appeared to be sharing a private joke. She slapped her thigh and a mischievous chuckle drifted over to him. A little nearer, some of the newcomers – Xandros couldn't even recall where they were from – were gambling with bone counters. Amongst their group were some Myrinians, all resentments forgotten. Their weapons lay in a little pile nearby. There were similar scenes all along the beach: men sharing the watch around campfires, united against a common foe.

He glanced at the Argonauts. Some of them must surely have seen out more than seventy winters and yet they were drinking like youths at their first wedding. Their jokes were coarse and their language would have made sailors in their prime blush. He wouldn't have wanted to fight alongside any other men – not if he'd scoured the Archipelagos for the pick of young spears.

It was only an hour or so previously when Idas had first encountered his son. The permanent scowl on Khalkeus' face had lifted as Idas' eyes had snapped back to him. Neither had said anything for a few seconds before Idas extended his hand. 'Fate has a sense of humour. Seems I *am* a father after all.'

Khalkeus looked at it suspiciously until it was withdrawn. 'I had a mother but a father?' He shook his head. 'No.'

Xandros had experienced a sliver of guilt as he looked on, recalling Hypsipyle's warning not to provoke the past. Idas' face twitched.

'And where *is* your mother?'

A pause. 'Buried her five years ago.'

'Ah,' said Idas softly. 'I'm sorry.'

And it looked like he meant it, so Xandros was grateful for another old Argonaut blustering over, bumping into him without spilling a drop of his own wine. Xandros felt like a bull had just butted his arm and found himself looking at the one called Butes. The man's features marked him out as a wrestler or boxer. His calcified brows looked so heavy they forced his eyes half shut.

'So *you're* the one responsible for dragging a bunch of old men from their homes, are you, boy?'

'I tried.'

'You succeeded; take a look around you. We're not shades!' he muttered. 'Not yet, at least.'

'Then an Olympian must have found you, and I'm grateful he did.'

'Pah!' said Idas. 'If he was the Messenger then I'm the Thunderer. Some lackey of Jason's, wasn't it?' Idas mistook the look of surprise on Xandros' face for confusion. 'You know, boy, your grandfather? And, Poseidon's shrivelled sack, do you look like him!'

'And look over there, by the cresset. That was the one I saw first, on the beach. Soon as I clapped eyes on him, I knew.' Butes chuckled. 'Meleager, but dragged backwards through a hedge. Extraordinary!'

Then they had moved on, making sport of guessing which of their comrades had fathered whom. He noticed them stop by the flame-haired Erythros, 'You, lad, look at me,' said Butes gruffly.

Erythros looked startled.

'What d'you think, Idas? Tell me who you see?'

They looked at each other and laughed. 'Happy! He loved a good red-head, did Theseus.'

But the main reason for Xandros' sense of contentment was that Teodora had returned. She looked tired, strained, said she would describe what had happened later. When Xandros had gone to embrace her, she kept him at arm's length.

'Later!' She laughed. 'After I've had a bath. I've just walked ten miles and I'm filthy!'

'Go inside, then. Auge will fill one more quickly if you ask her – you know she hates me!'

He watched her go, pulling her damp *chiton* from her skin and tutting at the sensation, and felt his heart swell with pride and love. Caeneus passed her with a theatrical bow. He had been helping instruct some of the inexperienced youths with their swordplay, and now he joined Xandros, drying his face with a towel. He pushed the wet hair from his face and put his hands on his hips. 'I'll own that I never thought it possible, lad. All this.' He added, after a few moments, 'A rough-looking bunch, aren't they?'

'They are,' agreed Xandros, 'but given what we face, would you have them any other way?'

'No, I suppose not.'

Xandros gave Caeneus a beaker of wine. 'There's not much left, so you'd better take it. That lot have nearly cleaned us out.' There was a roar from the Argonauts and they clinked cups, oblivious. 'Have you told them you're Polyphemus' son yet?'

Caeneus didn't get a chance to answer. One of the Argonauts, a bear of a man, distinguished by the mane of grey hair that stubbornly retained some streaks of black, slipped away from the others and approached Xandros.

'A quiet word, young man.'

Xandros nodded to Caeneus and drew away to one of the less crowded spots of the square. 'You were the helmsman, weren't you, on *Argo*? Ancaeus?'

'A long time ago. Do you see that boy, there?'

Xandros glanced at the lad. He had noticed him enter the citadel behind the helmsman, rubbing his dark eyes. 'I see him.'

'He's my charge now but if I was to get knocked off my perch... Well, I'd want someone else to look after him.' Ancaeus looked at him intently and Xandros divined the line of his thought.

'Here?'

'Right here.'

At no point had he framed it as a question, Xandros noticed. 'He would be looked after,' he said, not knowing by whom.

Ancaeus grunted in satisfaction but then frowned at something beyond Xandros. A figure of presence was at that moment passing under the arch to the citadel. Cloak trailing behind him, long white hair brushed back, he looked around the square. He had a leather bag slung over one shoulder and a bow over the other. The ambient chatter faded as people watched him but he ignored them. Then, spotting somebody, he approached. It only took Xandros a moment to identify him. The Argonauts fell silent and they all turned towards him.

XIV

Orpheus

I must say, it was not the scene I was expecting – given the severity of their situation – but this was no bad thing. Indeed, it was stubborn and noble and brave. If I close my eyes, which are failing along with my health, I can see it as clearly in my mind as if it was only yesterday. There was a gaiety to the square, festooned as it was in garlands and lamps, filled with refugees from neighbouring islands as well as the Lemnians themselves. A stranger might even have imagined he had arrived during the *Hephaistia*, for which festival the island was well known. And this is how I will always remember it, for I have not been back since and I don't suppose that I ever shall.

It took me a short while to locate them but, even though age had me well in its sure grip – I was beyond my sixtieth year by then – I was still taller than most men and could see over the knots of people. It was the racket they were making that drew my attention. Old warriors are the same the world over when, lost in reminiscing, their wine cups become swords gripped by fingers that were once strong; and those men were always louder than most. I had hoped to surprise them, perhaps even grasp one of them by his shoulders to test his reaction, but they spotted me as I was a short distance away. The looks on their faces! It still moistens my eyes, years later, when I consider the horrors of what was to follow.

Comradeship is an exalted form of love.

Love enters by the eyes and it also leaves by the eyes. Love can be fickle; can sprout jealousies like no Greek herb on earth; can fade. Comradeship transcends it, and I should know, because it eased the agony of a broken heart in a way that nothing else ever did.

It was Butes who turned first, and their bawdy jokes fell silent as their eyes turned to me. I could spot that old warrior's ears in a crowd of hundreds, because I pulled an oar on a bench behind him for many months. He did a double take and his eyes narrowed. The rest of them saw his expression change, for a moment doubtless sensing trouble. Despite the passing of all those years, the looks in their dear, grizzled faces convinced me they could still give a good account of themselves, if ever the situation demanded. And as the gods know, never were the demands so great.

Butes fairly leaped off his stool and crushed me in his embrace. '*Orpheus!* Orpheus! Orpheus!'

XV

Xandros looked on as those old warriors almost fell over each other to get to the bard, embracing him – and each other – and crying like babies. Orpheus staggered back in the press, complaining that they would make him drop his lyre.

All around them, people stopped what they were doing to watch the curious spectacle. His name passed through the citadel like a gentle breeze.

'Orpheus? *That* Orpheus?'

People drifted over towards the Argonauts, although they kept a respectful distance.

'Play something for us, old man,' said Butes, wiping his eyes, 'something from the old times.'

'Let him have a drink first!' growled Idas.

'Wine! Some wine over here for the finest bard in the world!'

A cup was poured for Orpheus and space made for him, whilst the Argonauts fired question after question at him.

'Poor old man can't get a breath,' muttered Caeneus, looking on.

Then they all turned towards Xandros. 'This young man is the reason.'

He would remember the reappraising looks those old heroes gave him – Idas even winked at him – before they resumed their conversation. He dearly wished Teodora was there to share the moment.

'Orpheus?' asked Xandros. 'Is it ready? Your song?' The bard turned to look at him with knowing eyes.

'What song?' asked Peleus, whose question was seconded with curious murmurs.

'Yes, young man. It is ready.'

XVI

Darkness had descended upon Lemnos but the square was aglow with lamps. The few watchmen posted along the beach warmed themselves by their fires and looked up to the starlit vault when they first heard it, floating down from the citadel of Myrine.

'Didn't I raise you with any manners? Bring the man some lights!' said the fisherman Laodon to his young son. 'He can't be expected to play in the dark!'

The boy dutifully gathered some more lights while Orpheus twisted the lyre's pegs this way and that, occasionally strumming the strings and humming to attune them. Absorbed in the task, he smiled briefly at the boy as he set down the clay lamps.

Then the boy struggled over with a stool. Orpheus stopped tuning the lyre and turned a frown upon him. 'Never used one, never will. But thank you.'

'Good lad,' said Laodon, when he returned, ruffling his son's hair affectionately.

When Orpheus was ready, he nodded towards Xandros, and an expectant hush settled upon the square.

He tipped back his head, as if waiting for his muse, and then his fingers flickered across the lyre strings like silvered olive leaves in a breeze. Here, finally, Xandros would have his questions answered. He looked on, mesmerised – like all the onlookers, even the Argonauts, who knew – by the plaintive notes and the rich urgency of Orpheus' voice.

In Thessaly, beside the glittering sea, once dwelt a folk called the Minyae.

There lived a boy, born to the rulers of this northern kingdom, whose father's throne was usurped within hours of his son's birth. Through a daring feat of trickery, the boy was smuggled from the palace under the pretence he had been still-born.

Raised on the wooded slopes of Mount Pelion by a centaur, Cheiron (Idas and Butes sniggered at this), *he came down to the plains twenty years later to claim his birthright from the usurper king Pelias.*

In him, the Mother of the Gods saw a greater purpose. Her altar had once been defiled by the blood of a suppliant, who clung to its milky marble, slain by an arrogant young prince called Pelias. And Pelias it was who now usurped the throne of Aeson.

Forced to accept an impossible challenge to prove his worth, young Jason – for so he was called – recruited forty brave warriors from all around the Archipelagos to retrieve a magical Golden Fleece from a powerful kingdom at the ends of the earth: Colchis ruled by King Aeetes.

Xandros listened, spellbound by the tale Orpheus was spinning of his family. He glanced frequently at the Argonauts, fascinated by their reaction. Gone was the rowdiness, replaced by a curious intensity. A stillness. Whilst Ancaeus' boy, Atukhos, went around with his wineskin, the Argonauts extended their cups with a wink. Telamon ruffled his hair, making the boy's head move like a rag doll's.

When Orpheus reached the island of Lemnos, there was a cheer and he took a break whilst the islanders filled their cups and raised a toast, filling their cups again. Xandros heard someone whisper that the wine had almost run dry.

Then they fell quiet once more and Orpheus struck his lyre, transporting the listeners to a distant kingdom.

And there royally are the guests honoured in his fair hall,
feasted in lamp-lit splendour. Laden with gifts, Argo *lowers sail,*
upon a desolate beach that night blown back by terrible squall.
Attacked in the dark, a fearful fight, only to see by the fires, frail
in dying light, the face of their host Cyzicus.

'A bad business,' muttered Peleus. 'Very bad.'

On they sail, losing Herakles and his squire, lured by beautiful water nymphs, until they reach the land of vicious King Amycus and his Bebrykes.

A fight to the death there must there be, yet in each stout heart no thought to flee.
Pollux steps forth, Zeus-born, tho' not for this foe is vict'ry forsworn.
Slight in stature the Dioskouri are: champions both. Fair Greece rings their fame far.

Pollux's fists are a blur. Finding his range, he names the body parts he will next strike. Tiring of the game, he delivers a blow so powerful it crushes Amycus' skull, and the Argonauts fair slaughter his band of bullies and thieves.

There was a roar from the Argonauts and even Orpheus hesitated, though his frown was full of good humour.

Caeneus leaned towards Xandros. 'Ever heard of him?'

'I have. And his twin, Castor. How old must they be? Sixty? They could claim half those years from here.'

'The light is dim. Here's your woman.'

Xandros turned to see her approach from Hypsipyle's home. She wore a simple cream stole and her still-damp hair was clasped high on her head. It made his heart pound and he drew her close, kissing her head and smelling rosemary.

Her eyes flashed. 'Orpheus is here!'

'He has them in his thrall.'

The Argonauts row on up the Straits to the hilltop kingdom of blind old King Phineus.

Trembling and pale is he, and on the tables lay a royal feast most glorious indeed. Then says the king:

'Sight these eyes need not to see, o guests, with what pity my state disgusts thee. But, I pray, be still and watch me eat and you shall know with what ambrosia the gods tease me.'

And now, indeed, Ocean's dread daughters do the Greeks behold: the deadly Harpies on thumping wings descend. From foulsome mouths such a shriek, talon sharp, rends the air. But swifter than North Winds fly Zetes and Kalais, and in their wake inspired, the Minyae strike a more fearful air with sword upon shield until, struck, beaten true from the plateau they yield.

Ancaeus raised his cup as Orpheus sang of Clashing Rocks, uprooted from the seabed, that narrowly missed crunching *Argo* to kindling.

The drinking began anew, but still they were silent as Orpheus sang. Xandros closed his eyes and filled his lungs with the fragrant night air, drinking deep of it all. The warmth of the company; the music; the long-yearned-for stories of his illustrious grandfather; the hushed chirruping of cicadas and even a few tree frogs; the camaraderie of the Argonauts and the islanders, even Caeneus, Creoboros and especially his love of Teodora. There was an unspoken sense of finality to it all. Rovers' ships had been sighted. Lemnos was – it seemed – one of only two islands whose sands were yet to be ploughed by their prows. He felt warm fingers clasp his and opened his eyes. Teodora was giving him a knowing look: he could swear she read his thoughts.

Argo *has reached the land of Colchis and Jason yokes fire-breathing bulls, plated in bronze, lathered in a protective lotion the Colchian princess Medea has given to him...*

Xandros noticed the strange effect mention of this woman's name exerted upon the Argonauts. The shared looks, the slight tightening of knuckles and pinched features. Nobody drank; indeed, cups moved from lips until such time as it was deemed safe to drink again.

King Aeetes, furious at the Argonauts' success, summons an army of Sirakian warriors – skeletons, sprung from the black, rich earth of Colchis – against Jason and his men in the crowded halls of his palace. The Sirakians have never been defeated – CAN never be defeated, the story goes. The fighting is vicious. Men slip on wine and blood and are struck as they scramble to their feet. The matter hangs in the balance until Butes, the champion wrestler, turns the tide and the Sirakians are routed as they flee...

This episode unleashed the loudest cheer from the Argonauts and, in turn, the onlookers broke into applause, making even Orpheus falter.

Led by Medea, Jason enters the sacred Grove of Ares and takes the Golden Fleece from an ancient oak tree, protected by a huge, unsleeping serpent, drugged by a potion she has made for him.

With trumpets blaring and crews mustering in pursuit, the Argonauts flee along the Phasis river, swirling in mist, sinking a Colchian vessel and disappearing into the night before they run aground. Here they find the bones of Prometheus, picked clean where they were shackled by vultures that they had seen tearing his flesh on the way in....

Xandros noted how the boy Atukhos shuddered at this grisly scene and Ancaeus planted a meaty hand upon his shoulder.

Here, Medea the witch dismembers her mortally wounded cousin to slow her pursuing brethren, for the Colchians must bury their dead whole.

Xandros listened intently, open-mouthed, as Orpheus recounted how the Argonauts narrowly escaped the pursuing Colchians – and Death itself – when they were engulfed by a storm in the open sea, and how they drifted ashore, battered and haggard, to the very shores at which they had landed weeks earlier, populated by the Hut-Dwellers.

...and they would have been betrayed to the pursuers but Medea performs a miraculous feat in turning an unborn baby inside

her mother's womb and delivering her safely to the astonished villagers, then purifying them in a Shining.

As the outraged Colchians torch entire villages in their frantic search for the raiders, the Argonauts seek refuge on the lonely island of Aeaea, home of Circe the witch, aunt of Medea...

Xandros saw Ancaeus frown and whisper something to Idas. 'Aeaea sounds better than Cyanida,' Idas muttered, which seemed to satisfy Ancaeus.

Upon the verdant shore, eyeing them land 'midst many collared beasts, by prowling lion and wolf encircled, the deathless sorceress.

Telamon's shoulders heaved up and down and his wheezing laughter drew some wry smiles from the Argonauts. 'The bard's laying it on a little thick,' observed Ancaeus to the startled boy Atukhos.

And along a creaking corridor she passed,
And reached her dark oakpannelled hall at last,
where with potions and herbs and chants her spell she cast.

At the mention of Circe's magic, the lamp-lit square fell silent, mesmerised by Orpheus' haunting melody and his ageless fingers caressing the lyre strings. Xandros heard the sucking of air – he heard it from his own lungs, too – as Circe drugged the Argonauts with poisoned wine and summoned the Colchians with a brilliant flash of light.

Only by dousing them in seawater can Jason wake them from their sweet slumber and rouse them to fight, though the drugs have leached the strength from their limbs. Fiercely do they defend the beachhead against the enemy, swarming from their ships, seething with indignant rage, erratic though their spear casts, slings and arrows are. Down goes Euphemus, the finest athlete in Greece, screaming at the Argonauts to retreat to the slope to make their last stand.

And there they would have fallen, back to back, until brave Ancaeus and faithful Oileus, golden-haired Theseus and youthful Dascylius return from scouting to scythe through the hordes like a sickle through wheat...

Hearing Oileus' name made Teodora stiffen. She had suspected there was more to her grandfather than she had been led to believe and Orpheus' voice, soaring with the drama of that battle, confirmed it.

It was clear by the way the Argonauts' eyes fell to the floor that they felt their losses still. And then, for the first time, Xandros saw the façade of bravado slip to reveal the grey vulnerabilities of their age, etched in deep lines on their faces.

Xandros didn't even notice the youth's quiet approach and the gentle tap upon his shoulder, making him start. It was one of the lookouts, younger even than him.

Argo *is passing the Clashing Rocks again, now firmly rooted to the seabed, exactly as Phineus had foretold.*

'Lights, lord, from ships,' whispered the lookout. 'Distant pinpricks but they've passed now.'

From the corner of his eye, he caught the expectant faces turning to him. Though the news broke the spell of Orpheus' singing and quickened his heart, Xandros nodded, thanking the lookout, whose own attention flickered towards the bard. When Xandros dismissed him, the youth seemed reluctant to leave.

From high on Olympus, the Great Mother sees Argo *being hunted down by Trojan ships at the mouth of the Hellespont straits. The Argonauts are flagging – for even their stout hearts are exhausted. Within touching distance of the home waters of the Archipelagos, their oars weaken with every stroke and Trojan arrows begin to rain down all around them.*

Xandros filled his lungs with cooling air and looked to the heavens. The moon, her edges clipped, hung heavy over the sea, stealing the light from the stars. He knew sea raiders often struck when the moon's horns were full – it made navigation far easier, after all – but tonight would not be the night. The gods would grant them a day's grace; he could feel it in the music, which had seeped into the very marrow of his bones.

As they wait for the winds – and their luck – to change, the Argonauts are surrounded by soldiers of the island's king and marched inland to his majestic, crumbling palace. Minos is cunning and paranoid and cruel, and rules over the Kretes through fear, cunning and magic. The priestesses of Megalonisi are powerful and have the ear of great Poseidon, who is no friend of the Argonauts. But, for now, the rules of guest friendship hold, and the house arrest is lightly applied.

He asks, 'Won't you tarry? Stay, work with me,

'Help drive the accursed rovers from the sea?'

Jason cannot.

His business is with one man, not a fleet, though he wishes Minos no harm. Outraged, all pretence of hospitality slips and the sentence is passed. The Argonauts may only leave the island should Jason defeat his champion, Talos, in single combat.

Enter the man. The Olympians themselves would shudder to see the bronze-clad warrior who swaggers towards them through the king's chamber like a Titan reborn.

Asks Minos, with a smirk, 'Won't you reconsider?'

Jason says, 'No.'

That evening, the debates and recriminations are hot but they all know that, should dawn's light find them still in the palace, they will never leave...

Xandros and Teodora put their arms around each other and hugged tight, allowing themselves to become lost once more in Orpheus' music. He was singing now of the battle with Talos, and how – with the aid of Medea's magic – the Argonauts were able to attack his heel, from which gushed his life-giving ichor.

The younger boys and girls in the square recoiled at the details but it delighted their parents: the underdog overcoming insuperable odds seemed apposite.

There was a changing of the watch. Those coming off duty hurried into the square whilst those taking their turn were reluctant to yield even an inch. Xandros knew better than to insist upon it.

The Argonauts are in headlong flight across the Archipelagos when they pass a remote islet, drawn by a thin plume of smoke and the sweet song of a lyre. When they draw near, three beautiful nymphs fly from a rocky headland, swooping and soaring around the bow post and the stern, drawing the sailors from their benches.

Entranced by their song, Butes of Athens falls overboard and must be rescued by Jason and Idas of Arene. Just then, a southern wind bellies the sail, preventing the Sirens from luring more men to a watery grave...

Butes looked aghast but the Argonauts were delighted, slapping their crewmate around the shoulders. Idas leaned in and whispered, 'Cheer up, man: you've just become famous!' and the Athenian's beetling eyebrows softened.

And then Argo's *prow ploughs into Iolkan waters, late one rainswept evening. The Argonauts hatch their plan under cover of darkness and set out the following day, their hearts set on bloody vengeance. In the gaily lit halls of the usurper king Pelias, battle is joined, and the matter hangs in the balance until the Great Goddess herself, clad in a war helmet and bearing a gold-gilt spear, scatters the defenders blocking the doorway, allowing the Argonauts to spill into the king's room.*

Pelias is amazed to see Jason and his men alive, and is speechless as the Golden Fleece is spread before his feet, its fibres glittering in the hearth flames. But then a sly grin spreads across his lips and he summons his queen into the hall.

'The throne is ever more firmly in my possession,' says he, 'for your blood is hers, and in her womb grows a king who will unite both houses!'

And Jason's mother reaches out for her long-lost son with arms that yearn to hold him, whilst his hands seek only his sword.

'There is another way!' says faithful Oileus. 'Sheathe your blade!'

Too late! For, seizing the moment, Pelias runs through his former guard as he steps in front of Jason. 'You traitor!' he hisses. The hall rings with Jason's anguish and its floor, thirsty still for blood, echoes his cries. Maddened by rage, Jason drives the usurper past the eyes of his retainers hard against the frescoed wall, where the tip of his father's sword bursts from Pelias' back and into the plaster.

Her revenge complete, Hera's eyes flash in approval and then she is gone, and the light in the halls dims. Witnesses to this hell, survivors of every strange evil from here to the ends of the world, those men of Argo *forge their brotherhood of bronze, a bond that no man nor beast alive can ever hope to sunder.*

May the Muses smile brightly upon any man who, faced with such unconquerable odds, nevertheless steps forth into the fray. For that man will be forever blessed and, so long as his fellow man possesses a voice, he shall never be forgotten.

The final chord of Orpheus' lyre lingered for a moment in the cool night air and then yielded to the distant hush of the sea. No one wanted to sully the moment by clapping until Xandros put his hands together. Then the whole square erupted with applause and cheering. For a moment, Orpheus was lost in a sea of people clamouring to thank him, to bless him or merely to have his eyes settle upon them for just a moment. The islanders had wanted a salve for their worries and, in the form of the bard, they had been gifted a god.

And now they began to clamour for the other Argonauts.

'Up! Up! Up!' came the chants. Idas looked to Butes, and Butes from him to the Spartan twins and finally to Ancaeus. They nodded in unison and stood gingerly, with many a click and sigh.

The square broke into uproar and the Argonauts joined hands and raised each other's arms aloft, accepting the adulation but never more keenly feeling the loss of fallen comrades and absent friends.

'Xandros?' He had not noticed that Teodora had slipped away but now she was back, and her face looked grave. 'You must be quick.' They slipped through the happy faces, dodging the animated islanders until they arrived at Hypsipyle's courtyard. She was stooped over Euneus, whose face was as pale as the moon. Her handmaid Auge was stirring a tisane and looked up as Xandros and Teodora entered the courtyard. For once, she gave him a look that was something other than peevish; it might even have been pity.

'Come see your father, Xandros,' croaked Hypsipyle. 'He was calling for you just now.'

Euneus was sitting propped up in a chair, with an old woollen blanket draped over his knees. He looked pale and drawn, and even the additional layers of clothing couldn't disguise how thin his body had become.

Xandros crouched beside him, offering his hand. Euneus took it in his own and gave it a gentle squeeze. It was cold and dry. 'Your friend, the bard.' He licked his lips and Auge offered him a little of the brew. Some of the liquid dribbled down his chin. 'He sings like a nightingale.'

'I'm glad you liked it, Father.'

'To my shame… I knew none of it. My father and his men – Pelias; *Argo*, their sufferings – none of it.' To Xandros' surprise, a single tear breached his father's eye and trickled down his cheek. He realised at that moment that he had never seen his father cry; never seen him lose control of his emotions at all, in fact. 'And now, when it's too late, I wish I did.' Xandros felt his hand being squeezed, with the force of a wren landing upon a sprig of olive. 'You were right to wonder; I was wrong. All this time, wrong.'

The force of his sudden coughing rattled the frail bones in his chest, nearly making Xandros topple over. When he brought it back under control, Euneus asked for another sip of the infusion and closed his eyes. For a few moments, Xandros wondered if he had already slipped away but then he opened them once more. 'Seeing all these people, preparing to fight together, makes me proud, Xandros. Proud.'

This time, when his eyes closed, they remained so. They watched him draw his final breath and exhale a long, wistful sigh.

Tucked into one corner of the village square, the keening wail that rose within the courtyard was lost to the hum of laughter and conversation without. Stood just outside, leaning on the wall, Caeneus was the only one to have heard. Creoboros joined him and for once did not bare his teeth. Instead, he reared on his hind legs, pawing at the gate and whimpering.

'He'll come back soon,' soothed Caeneus, scratching behind his ears.

Sometime later, the door opened and the handmaid Auge appeared, flinching when she saw Caeneus and the dog hard by.

'He wants you inside.'

Caeneus had seen death before but the sight of the king laid out with a blanket exerted a sobering effect upon him. Xandros raised his head as he entered like it was filled with lead but he made a good show of wearing his grief with dignity, in spite of the redness of his eyes. Teodora let her arm slide from his shoulders and raised her chin.

'Nobody out there must hear of this, not tonight. They need to fill their hearts with as much happiness and joy in each other's company as they can. Do you understand?'

Caeneus said nothing for a moment, struck by the young man's subtle transformation. He nodded. 'I do.'

XVII

Dawn broke upon the beach of Myrine with the promise of a cloudless day. The wail of a single trumpet startled those who had not managed to stay awake for the duration of the last watch, and they snatched up their weapons on confused and unsteady legs, staring out towards the blood-red horizon but seeing no ships.

Then they noticed the procession making its way from the citadel. At the front of the bier went Xandros and Moxos, with Alektruon, Khalkeus and Hektor carrying the rear. Hypsipyle cut a forlorn figure at the front, clad all in black, stooped and frail. Behind the bier came the entire town, followed by every other man, woman and child who had fled to the island in recent days, including the Argonauts and young Atukhos, trailing after Ancaeus.

Xandros' eulogy was brief but heartfelt. He found that by focusing upon the distant huer's hut and imagining himself inside, secluded and invisible, he could get through it without succumbing to an unmanly sobbing that might make the onlookers doubt their new leader. He talked of his father's devotion to duty and the sacrifices he had made at home for the wellbeing of others. All of this he could say without any sense he was telling untruths, though all the while he wondered – in light of his father's final words – what life might have been like.

Would you live it again, Papa, given the choice? And would you be a loving father and I a doting son?

Then it was over. Xandros was given a burning torch, which he passed to Hypsipyle, and accepted one himself. He looked at his grandmother, whose face was a waxy mask of grief. She could barely meet his eyes so he lit the pyre first, and she followed, drawing a veil over her eyes.

The flames were slow in taking but when they licked the treated logs with a muted rumble, Xandros looked to the heavens, sensing something in the ether. A black kite was circling the beach and a gull called out a warning, somewhere out of view. The faintest wisp of a cloud passed over the trees lining the backshore and the sea whispered behind him. Life was continuing, regardless. He wondered how the sky would look on his last day on earth.

'Beacon!'

Xandros almost smiled at the sense of inevitability. *Of course there was!* As one, eyes turned towards the source of the faint cry. Then the trumpet sounded a long, mournful wail. In his fearful haste, the lookout had forgotten to sound the alarm first. It hardly mattered, thought Xandros. At least they had – barely – managed to complete the ceremony. He turned towards the bier, now ablaze in earnest.

Look over me, Father, wherever you are, and send us such help as you can.

'Take up your positions!' called Xandros. *'Women and children back to the citadel!'*

He turned to see Hypsipyle. If it was at all possible, grief seemed to have aged her in the space of an hour. 'Remember who you are, Xandros, and make me proud.' Her thin lips were pressed tightly together but she could not suppress the emotions in those shrewd, bloodshot old eyes of hers. He embraced her tightly and was shocked at just how thin she was; it was a wonder she had the strength to rise each morning.

'Strength and courage, Nanna. I love you.'

Had he ever told her this before? Something about the power of uttering the words, and the way they registered upon her face, suggested not in living memory.

'I love you too, Xandros.'

She smiled sadly at him, summoned some inner reserve of strength and turned, helped away by Auge, who gave him a curious look. He had no time to reflect upon it. Chaos threatened to break upon the beach.

He gently caught one woman by the shoulder who was trembling as she gathered her young daughters. 'Calm,' he said to her, looking her in the eye. 'Your girls will learn from you today and they will live a long life!'

She looked right through him but she nodded and took them away. Others he coaxed back into order as they made for the path, with a word of reassurance here or a stern rebuke there. Inevitably, there was panic but the absence of ships on the immediate horizon prevented a stampede. Whilst the women and children made their way up the slope, boys struggled to wheel handcarts bearing pile upon pile of flatbreads against the human tide. Makeshift ovens had been busy throughout much of the night and the granaries were almost bare but none on the beach would go hungry that morning.

As the beach emptied of non-combatants, the defenders began to get themselves into a semblance of order. Euneus' former guards appeared at his shoulder, and it seemed perverse that he should give them any orders.

'Suggestions, gentlemen?' he asked brightly.

Moxos' hands were on his hips as he scanned the beach. 'More archers in that gap, between Athens and Argos,' he said, pointing to a spot three-quarters around the bay. 'If we fold, it can't be from the middle.'

Which sounded to Xandros like the extreme left of the defences was expendable. Of course, this isn't what he meant, he reminded himself, but this was where the young slingers had taken up position so any errant shots from the novices might not do more harm to the islanders than the pirates.

'Agreed.'

Moxos nodded. 'Then I'll take a handful from elsewhere.'

Xandros watched him walk away, bare-footed. The man was utterly unflappable but carried his private grief about with him. He wondered if he and Euneus had ever buried their differences before he fell ill.

From the corner of his eye, Xandros glimpsed a knot of men making their way from the citadel and he grinned. The Argonauts had fetched their antique-looking armour and were now marching to battle. He heard a wolf whistle from somewhere behind him but there was nothing pointed in it. Orpheus' song the previous evening had put to bed any lingering doubts about the men, despite their spindly legs and grey hair.

And then another group of men emerged, and everyone fell silent. The bright morning light flashed off their bronze greaves, the polished rims of their black shields and their spear tips. The muscles above their knees, which their linen corselets exposed, was thick and solid, and the Myrmidons marched with the confident air of men whose business was fighting and killing. Peleus and Telamon led them down and, for a few moments, the years melted from them.

Xandros had only met them briefly, and in repose they seemed affable enough men if a little proud and aloof, which was understandable enough, given their orders to sail far from home. But as the twenty now formed up before Xandros, and their helmets drew his gaze to their hard, dark eyes, it struck him how fortunate they were to have them.

'Where do you want them?' growled Peleus.

Xandros looked at him in astonishment. If the man was reluctant to ask the question of another man, an unproven one at that, nothing about his expression suggested so.

'The position of honour, here on the right. Thessaly.'

Peleus gave him an intense look before surveying the beach. 'You'll need us nearer the centre but the honour we'll gladly take.' He turned to his men and barked his commands at them and they responded immediately. Peleus was about to join them but then approached Xandros and laid a strong hand upon his shoulder. 'A word of advice from an old hand. The day may be a long one, so spare your voice. When there are women and children and their homes behind them, men will never give up fighting, with or without your commands. Always remember that.' He winked at him and joined his men.

The horn blared from the huer's hut, and someone shouted, *'Ships! I see ships!'*

They all turned towards the horizon. And there they were: three... four... seven galleys, rounding the headland, half a mile distant. The sight made Xandros' stomach crawl. Even in his worst nightmares he had never imagined so many raiders descending upon them.

Courage, Xandros...

He was about to murmur in response but realised that no man or woman alongside him had spoken.

'Sound the horn!' he yelled. One of the Lemnians fetched it – it was still hanging by a nail on a tree – and the whole beach came alive at the mournful note, like an ants' nest prodded by children. He turned to Teodora. 'You know what I am about to ask you?'

'Don't even think about it. My place is here!'

And she meant it. He nodded, hating the idea of her being wounded but seeing no time to debate the matter. 'Nothing rash, then.'

Xandros turned to his father's men and they all set off around the bay, checking on the defences from Thessaly to Argos one more time. The crescent of sand stretched for several hundred yards with a little under seven hundred men to defend it. He had positioned and repositioned the thick hurdles of brush and thorn a dozen times before he was happy with them. At the far end of the bay, they foreshortened the line by twenty yards, no more, and it was anybody's guess for how long they would prove useful, but it was vital to deny the raiders a foothold for as long as possible. They passed the point just short of Athens, halfway along the beach, where a line of spare spears, javelins and a cache of arrows marked a secondary defensive point, should it become necessary. Some archers from an outlying hamlet were testing their strings as they passed.

'I hope you shoot better than you play music,' said Khalkeus, frowning.

'Oh, it'll be sweet enough, you'll see.' The man who replied was cheerful and stocky with a corona of dirty grey hair around a shiny bald patch. Xandros liked him immediately.

Moxos leaned towards him. 'They need more support. If they get picked off...'

Xandros looked over the water. The boats hadn't made much progress and had since sprouted oars. There was still time. He looked around him: support wasn't something he had much of. Then he caught the Argonauts sauntering over and Xandros noticed another figure amongst them. Orpheus had swapped his lyre for a bow.

'Those old foxes read my mind,' muttered Moxos.

They carried on along the beach, dropping words of encouragement and reassurance here and there. By the time they reached Argos at the end of the bay, the volume of chatter had dropped to a few quiet comments, and it was clear that Fear was stretching its bony fingers. The eldest of the youths, flame-haired Erythros, was doing his best to keep up the spirit of his slingers, and with them was a selection of other men armed with spears, a handful of bows, swords, cudgels and even rocks. Xandros gave Moxos a look, and the old warrior smiled back at him, but he could sense it was a brittle one.

The boys were wide-eyed and pale. 'How are they faring, Erythros?'

'Some of them are naturals,' he said quietly. 'They could probably do with a bit longer though, my lord.'

'What better way to learn quickly than this.' He turned to the boys. 'I've released a few good shots and I want to say this. Never underestimate the damage they can do and the fear a whistling pebble can raise!' They smiled at this. 'Erythros here has Theseus' blood in his veins. He is a prodigy so listen to him.' Xandros saw the youth blushing from the corner of his eye. 'Take your time and don't empty your pouches in vain. Make every rock count.'

'Don't allow yourself to get cut off,' said Alektruon. They all turned to him. He was a man of few words but something about the scene had touched even his hard heart.

'We won't; don't worry.'

Alektruon gave a curt nod and looked at Xandros expectantly. The galleys would soon be in range.

XVIII

Braziers burned like beacons all along the beach behind the hurdles of wood that had been extended a long way along the foreshore, and everywhere was the pungent scent of freshly pressed olives, warming in the sun. It seemed inconceivable that such a homely smell could possibly presage slaughter. The ships were just two bowshots distant now. Euneus marched along the beach dropping a reassuring greeting here or final instructions there but he could sense the councillors alongside him becoming restive. The time had come to take up positions.

He had never known a fear like it. He had heard old warriors talk about fighting, the trembling of knees or of one's throat and stomach being gripped and squeezed by a cold fist, such that even swallowing is an ordeal. He experienced all of this and more. He bit down hard upon it and stared out over the sea.

At first, there was just the lapping of waves and the soughing of the trees behind him. An offshore breeze had arisen quite suddenly, as if a god had joined the Lemnians and was making the raiders toil hard against his breath for every stroke. They could hear their helmsmen calling the count, firing their courage and, last of all, their oars churning the water and the *hoom* of the raiders' voices.

Those crouched behind the hurdles of wood were under orders not to peer around them but, all along the beach, these men now bristled and it took their more disciplined comrades to yank their tunics to draw them back. It was anyone's guess what the Sea Peoples were thinking when they beheld the scores of islanders ready to resist them. The boats looked like standard *pentekonters*, meaning there would soon be four hundred warriors, give or take, jumping overboard and rushing the beach.

In those final few minutes, whilst the raiders heaved on their oars, he tried to distract himself from his nerves by counting the defenders. He doubted it was something the heroes of old would ever have done. He turned now to the Argonauts. The Spartan twins were sharing a skin of water and Pollux tossed it behind him. He caught Xandros' gaze and winked at him. The man's coolness was the balm he needed.

Xandros made it to one hundred and nineteen before he heard the first blood-curdling yell and the succession of splashes as the raiders threw themselves into the water. It was the headdresses that first caught his eyes, crowned by thick plumes of feathers; similar to those he had seen in Mycenae.

Had Medea come to avenge her deceit?

They thrashed through the shallows, eyes flaring above the rims of their shields: a horde of thick, broad moustaches and long hair that flowed beyond their shoulders. Lean and hungry. They were heading straight for Athens. They wanted to break the centre. Either side of the first, two more prows hissed into the sand, disgorging score after score of pirates, whooping and roaring to fire their spirits.

'Now!' yelled Xandros. *'Now!'*

The beach purred with the first volley of arrows. As many collected flesh as wood, burrowing into exposed sides, splintering ribs, puncturing lungs. Many were already choking on their own blood before the brine did the rest. Raiders from the stern, last to jump off, had to nudge their corpses aside with their hips as they waded to the beach. Most were themselves floating face down before the fourth and fifth galleys ran aground. A handful of the first line of raiders made it ashore before staggering to their knees and falling within touching distance of the defenders, caught by the enfilade.

Xandros watched one of them breathe his last, propped like a man in prayer by three arrow shafts.

'Spare your arrows! Spare... Your... Arrows!' Moxos stalked behind the archers. *'Arrow a man, dolts!'*

A sixth ship ran aground towards Argos where the defences looked less vigorous. It bore no resemblance to the others and sported a filthy sail but its men were jumping off even before she juddered to a halt.

The time had come. Xandros shouted, *'Light them up!'*

He could tell the defenders were itching to set the hurdles alight. Soaked in oil, the flames took hold more or less instantly, fanned by the offshore breeze. The sight was greeted with a roar of defiance. More defenders stepped into the gaps, unleashing rocks and javelins and more arrows.

It worked, for a while.

The sudden rush of flames and appearance of yet more spirited defenders checked the assault and along most of the beach the wave of raiders faltered. However, a pocket of warriors had formed a shield wall between Athens and Thessaly, covered by some fire from the seventh ship which now drew near. The first few arrows fell short but one drilled into the foot of a Lemnian boy, making him shriek pitiably and hop about until he was dragged back.

'For'ard!' roared Peleus.

Xandros looked on in awe as the Myrmidons tipped their helmets forward. They wasted no breath with yells or hollering. Instead, to his astonishment, they hummed like a swarm of wasps, perfectly in tune, and spread into a crescent that bristled with gleaming spears. Seeing what was happening, the shield wall broke and the raiders charged, stumbling a little as they fought upslope. Spears darted out like striking snakes and the *crack* of first contact made Xandros grimace. A Myrmidon fell rigid to the sand by Peleus' pale, thin legs and the death of their comrade struck them with a blood lust. Now they emptied their lungs in a killing frenzy. Some leaped back, the better to plunge their spears at the pirates; others used brute force to barge and stamp them into range, roaring with each strike. Peleus alone brandished his sword with a ferocity that his own son Achilles would have feared.

Not an attacker was still standing after the third minute and now the Myrmidons recoiled and heaved with the effort, forming a bridgehead around their fallen comrade.

XIX

Orpheus

I had seen good men fall and die before, too often. On the banks of a distant river, the mighty Ister, I had seen my friend – a fellow Argonaut – cut down alongside me by vicious, stinking initiates dressed like wolves. His name was Dascylius and he shouldn't have been there. He was a young tribesman – a prodigious linguist and a fine archer – and we had promised to return him to his loving family. I watched the light fade from his eyes and the colour drain from his cheeks as he panted his last, calling for his mother. There were more, too many more, and now I watched another Argonaut slip away.

Telamon, it was true, had lived a long, eventful life. In his day, he was a ferocious warrior but he was thirty years beyond his prime.

I was stood alongside Xandros, and the boy was making a good fist of directing the defence of the island. In the moments after Telamon fell, a pocket of raiders had gained a hold of a section of beach and others had formed behind them. On such successes do battles sometimes turn. He led a charge and was as good a spearman as many young bucks. On his left was Meleager's son Moxos – almost as fierce as his father, and how I wished a prime Meleager was with us on that beach! – and his right, two other Myrinians, I forget which. Beside his master, impelled by some infernal frenzy and bloodlust, was Xandros' dog – a creature from Hades. It was quite the most extraordinary thing I had seen on a battlefield. I let fly only a pair of arrows, one good, one wide and, seeing how the matter would soon turn in our favour there, not least because of the fear of that frothing creature, I hurried to Telamon's side.

The Myrmidons, dripping with sweat and gore, had formed a defensive wall – those men were the most professional soldiers I have ever seen – whilst another tried to staunch Telamon's wound. Grim-faced Peleus had tossed aside his helmet and was dribbling water into his brother's mouth, shouting at him to keep awake. I can still see Telamon's eyelids fluttering like butterflies, fighting for the light (do men in their final seconds really see anything, I wonder?).

Peleus stared right through me as I dropped to my knees and fumbled to retrieve some salve or other, but Telamon – looking grey and ancient in the throes of death – was well beyond such things. Peleus rocked him back and forth like a new-born, and Telamon died in his brother's arms.

What does a man say in such circumstances?

I am sorry; he was a good man? He died a beautiful death, like the warrior he was?

I had praise-sung the lives of countless men – some not worth the expenditure of breath – but there was nothing beautiful in it and I had no words. I reached across and put my arm upon Peleus' shoulder. He sniffed and tolerated it for a few moments before shrugging it off and standing to give his orders. When the fighting was done, he would be cremated, and Peleus alongside him, if it came to it.

If. How I still remember that word!

XX

Xandros' first kill was almost his last. At the moment he checked a thrust with his spear and plunged his own overarm – as he was taught – towards the raider's neck, it was as if he was in another state; as though a god was controlling his limbs. But with the feeling of the spear tip encountering flesh – and no amount of training could replicate that or the dull groan of pain it unleashed – he became a callow youth once more, looking a dying man in the eyes.

It was the flashing of a bronze spear, so close he fancied he could see the imperfections of its casting, that schooled him. He thrust at the man brandishing it – a man twice his age, he now saw – and moved. As he was taught. Another spear felled the attacker and from the tail of his eye, he saw Khalkeus – with teeth gritted and spittle flecking his lips.

There was a sibilant sucking of breath and Xandros wondered if he might be hearing voices. In the din all around him, the yells and the clash and crack of wood and bronze, and the *thwip* of bowstrings, he was aware of another man hard by and was astonished to glimpse the Argonaut Idas himself alongside his son.

'Good! Good, my lad!'

To Xandros, the old man was either unnervingly brave or utterly reckless to be commenting as he fought but the maniacal glee on Khalkeus' face told him they suffered the same affliction. The pair morphed into a human threshing machine.

They drove the raiders back into the oozing sand by the shore. Those who didn't stumble over their fallen comrades felt their feet being sucked into the beach and were not standing for long. All along the waterfront, in an almost unbroken line, lay the bodies of fallen Sea Peoples, gently nudged this way and that by the breakers. Some still crawled or moaned in pain and they were allowed to suffer.

Xandros backed away and looked about him. The Argonauts fighting at Athens were still hard at it, where the fighting still raged. Through the billowing smoke and crackling flames, it was difficult to see further along the crescent bay.

He turned to Moxos, Caeneus and Alektruon. The latter's blade was at that moment being withdrawn from a fallen raider who twitched and stiffened.

'We go.'

Teodora hurried to meet them bearing a pair of bloated waterskins. She was sheened in sweat and smoke but her eyes were bright with purpose. 'Drink, my love.'

Xandros tipped back his helmet and took a good gulp, not filling his belly, as he had been taught. He handed it back to her and gave her a look that he hoped imparted his feelings. When the others had slaked their thirst, she moved on.

He passed between his father's still-burning pyre and a flaming hurdle. The furnace heat and dull roar, momentarily blinded to the screams and yells and crack of weapons, the presence of his father and the sickly stench of burning flesh, made Xandros feel he had drifted into Hades. He sought the reassuring presence of the grim-faced Lemnians and Caeneus to his left, and saw – at least – that they were feeling something similar.

They had passed through. Xandros recognised Ancaeus' broad back. He had overheard him grumble about an axe the previous evening but, feet planted into the sand like an oak, shield and spear raised, it seemed impossible he could yield, with or without it. He hurried to join him, and noticed a few Giourans and Laodon from Halonnesus fighting bravely, and Xandros saw how it was being played. Ancaeus, the immoveable helmsman, was the mainstay whilst others curved from him like the horns of a bull and before them, in the killing zone, lay a pile of dead. Moxos joined the helmsman and, without the need for words, they all advanced, driving back the raiders inexorably towards the waterfront.

It was grisly work. Passing beneath the shield rim with every step, the dead and dying, some unrecognisable with their wounds. Xandros saw one corpse – his face a mask of black blood – twitch to life and drive his shivered spear into the groin of a man (was he from Halonnesus?) as he stepped over him. The shriek of shock and pain turned Xandros' stomach to water. With one swipe of his sword, Caeneus near beheaded the rover and there was no care for the dead thereafter. Already hacked bodies were given another stripe for good measure.

Xandros didn't notice the sand become cooler or change colour. Not until the first man was thrashing in the sea did he realise the ground they had claimed. Facing imminent death, the raiders redoubled their attack with a frenzy born of desperation. Islanders fell with them. Xandros' shield arm became numb and his lungs were aflame. Slow to react, he felt a spear tip burn his arm, inches from his heart.

In a flashing moment of clarity, he recalled being ambushed by the bandit in the darkness of Mycenae, and the debilitating pain when he was bowled over.

Too close to strike with his own spear, Xandros stamped at the knee he saw straightening, feeling the crack of blown cartilage. He willed himself to sweep his shield around into the man's helmet but his arm would not respond. Unseen, another spear did his work for him. From the tail of his eye, he saw one of the Spartan twins. Pollux's face, so animated in repose, was curiously calm in the fray.

Xandros heard Caeneus cackle beside him. 'By the gods, these old men are crack warriors!'

Within an hour, it was all over.

Pockets of men fought on but not for long. Some threw down their weapons but few were spared. All along the bay, men dropped to their knees and tossed aside their helmets, or threw off their cuirasses and staggered into the few stretches of sea that were clear of boats or floating bodies. Too shattered to speak, the cheering came late. From aching lungs, it sounded more like the wounded bellow of a boar. All around was a scene from the depths of a rancid nightmare: men writhing and groaning and twitching; blood that leaked from hundreds of bodies, leaving dark smears upon the golden sand. When the paean had been sung, it was the cawing of birds that Xandros heard first.

And then came the onset of shock. Alongside Xandros, Moxos tipped back his helmet and wiped his face. 'It always happens. Don't fight it.'

Xandros heard the words but his mind was fogged and he wondered why he was telling him this. Then he noticed that his knees were quivering.

'Drop to one knee, it helps. *Water!*'

All around him, men slumped to the sand or gazed absently at the boats, nudged this way and that by the breakers, or the flames that still consumed the hurdles, fading now.

He didn't want her to see him like this but she seemed to understand. Whilst the quivering of his limbs subsided, it looked like he was genuflecting towards some deity of the sea. He felt the warmth of her hand on his back. 'Drink a little,' she whispered. He didn't resist. Creoboros sat down beside him, whimpering.

Xandros closed his eyes, trying to process all that had happened in the space of a morning: that life would never be the same again was obvious but people would be looking to him now and he would need to prove himself worthy. Filling his lungs, he got to his feet. A knot of men was watching him, encrusted with the indescribable grime of battle. 'We tend to the wounded and raise a pyre to the gods of Lemnos. Anything on those boats we can use, especially food, we'll take it.'

'And their bodies?'

Like Xandros, Hektor's arm had been cut deep. He looked pale. A bird gave a long, keening whistle and Xandros looked up to see a pair of kites gliding over the beach. 'Carrion for the birds.'

The men grunted their assent and set about their duties whilst Xandros made for the sea. Now that the numbness was fading, his arm throbbed and he looked at the rent in his tunic. The wound would turn bad if he wasn't careful and Eriopis – he cursed his lack of foresight in not securing some – had left him with none of her mountain herbs. He passed the Myrmidons, humming a dirge for one of their fallen, and Peleus turned in his direction, looking clean through him with reddened eyes. Creoboros stopped at the water's edge and barked at Xandros, and it was then he noticed the drying blood on the dog's chest. He bent down to examine it and saw the cut.

'Forgive me,' he whispered. Sensing what was coming, Creoboros took a step backwards but Xandros still managed to rub some seawater over the wound. It made the dog yelp and wheel away. 'You were the bravest amongst us! See: I'm doing it too, come on!'

Xandros waded into the sea, ignoring the raider floating face down and the dark hair fanning out over the water. He knew the brine would sting but the pain took his breath away, and when he rubbed the water into the wound, he thought he would pass out. Creoboros paddled over to him. 'Good boy,' he gasped. 'I think that's enough.'

XXI

By the time they had laid out the dead along the backshore – Xandros had stopped counting beyond the first hundred – and mourned them, joined by many of the women from the citadel, and the last of the wailing had faded into the soughing of the leaves, morning had passed into afternoon.

Most of the elation at repulsing the attackers had faded by the time they had begun to strip the corpses of anything useful or valuable. By the time they had finished, the sight and stench of death began to sicken them. Xandros watched the women and children, brothers, sisters and who knew what relations bowing low over the dead, weeping or just gazing, numb, at the breakers washing the shore.

Enough, he thought. *Enough, now.*

He approached his father's smouldering pyre, hoping for some indication of what he should do next but the few lambent tongues of flame offered him nothing. Caeneus appeared at his elbow and when they clasped hands, Xandros gasped in pain.

'You're hurt?'

'It's nothing.'

Caeneus' eyes, he could see, retained some of the horror and exhilaration. 'You know, I think Fate played a hand in bringing you to the mainland. I'd not have missed this for all the gold in Argos.' When Xandros didn't reply, his eyes refocused a little. 'You won a good victory here, boy!'

'Then why does it feel like a defeat?'

'People are exhausted.' Caeneus looked around him. 'That's all.'

'Then we should feed them.'

XXII

Xandros led his cow, Whitefoot, up the slope towards the citadel, occasionally touching her back with a switch whenever she faltered. He wondered then, as he always did, whether she might have any inkling of what was to come. She was not the grandest-looking beast that he had ever seen sacrificed – her ribs were picked out in the slanting light – but stocks had dwindled badly in recent weeks and needs must. As he passed under the arch, excitable children darted about, giggling at the prospect of food and dance. For the first time that day, there were smiles and some laughter, though he also noticed the black clothes of mourning scattered about the square.

Though he knew it must be him, he hated every second of the sacrifice. He had always been told to look the victim in the eye as its vital light faded to capture the essence of its soul and show it respect as it left its mortal body. In her eyes, he saw only betrayal and it made him shudder. He captured enough of the gushing blood in a bronze bowl, gathering plenty more besides over his arms and tunic, adding to the dried crust of battle.

The heifer slumped to the ground. For an underfed animal, she did not buckle easily. He hoped there was some significance to it.

'To the gods of Lemnos. To Hephaistos, the Thunderer and the Lord of the Sea, and to all you Gods of the Earth,' he intoned as the blood drilled into the dusty earth, 'accept our grateful thanks and our eternal reverence.'

He let the other councillors set about the rest – they knew the procedure well enough – whilst he set about cleaning himself with water that Teodora had drawn from the well.

They embraced and they kissed. He noticed the boy Erythros

hovering nearby – he had lost a few of his boys on the beach and it had rattled him badly – and Xandros now drew him in.

'There will be a time for mourning, my friend, and a time for reflecting. But for now, eat and drink because you were amongst the bravest of us, and you made the island proud.'

Erythros sniffed and wiped his eyes, and then the tears flowed and Xandros felt the boy's chest heaving up and down.

XXIII

Orpheus

Many years ago – a lifetime before – I had stood in that very square watching feasting, as I watched it again now. Myrine was the same but it was different, and much the same could be said of the people now drinking and celebrating within it. I looked upon the last surviving Argonauts, my dear comrades and friends, and saw the change from just the previous evening. By the gods, though they raised cups and boasted gamely, and though they had washed the filth from their skin and had changed clothes, how depleted they looked!

Only Peleus didn't join them.

If I only close my eyes, I can still see the grizzled old warrior, leaning heavy upon the walls, gazing out over the beach. I knew what drew his eyes. Though there was a multitude of pyres burning all along the backshore by then behind the charred patches left by the hurdles, the Myrmidons had cremated Telamon at the very edge of the stretch of beach they had called 'Thessaly' and his lonely pyre smouldered still. Next to Peleus sat the little clay pot into which he would scoop his brother's cool ashes. That, at least, was his wish.

Ancaeus approached him, resting a mighty hand upon his back, but Peleus didn't so much as flinch. I closed my eyes in sadness and moved away.

XXIV

Under the westering sun, as the wine began to flow anew – they had found casks of it on the raiders' ships, though some of it was on the turn – the smiles returned to Myrine. Toast after toast was raised to the glorious fallen dead and it was the young girls, as so often, who were the first to dance, and their merriment proved infectious.

Xandros accepted the thanks and adulation as if in a dream, and the happy faces – young and old – blurred into a confusing mass that would one day, when the wine flasks were set aside, morph into memory then myth. He felt a sudden and crushing exhaustion that made his limbs heavy and his mind, which had never been engaged on so many fronts, fogged.

Do you want to build the hurdles up again? Do you think they'll return?

There isn't much oil left – maybe a single vat. How much do you want us to press? Do you even need any more?

Why hadn't the Moudrians shown up? How are you going to punish them? This from a long-standing family friend, this day a widow. Her raw grief and trembling lips stirred the embers of Xandros' anger and resentment. He had recently entertained the same thought and his blood had warmed at the prospect.

We need more linen, for bandages. Does old man Manolis' wife still make it?

What will you do with the newcomers? I would save it for the council but I've caught you in passing. They can't stay here forever; we'll run out of livestock...

That dog is evil. Can you make it stop snarling at the children?

Did those old men really sail on the Argo*?*

Where is Hilarion?

He only cared for the comments of a few, however, and when Moxos approached him his eyes focused a little, though he only heard some of his words.

'...and bids you inside with the rest of them.'

Catching Xandros' confusion, he smiled. 'Do you want me to repeat that?'

Xandros rubbed his face. 'I'm sorry.'

'I said, your grandmother wants to speak to you, and us.' Moxos thumbed over his shoulder. 'And our old relatives over there. In her halls.'

Even though it wasn't yet dusk, the old palace *megaron* was dark and silent. 'Queen Hypsipyle will join you soon,' Auge pronounced archly as Xandros entered.

Queen.

It was deliberate, of course – Auge wore her slavery morosely – but Xandros let it pass. To many now shuffling in behind him, Hypsipyle *was* still queen, at least in their memories.

'Light the hearth.' Auge gave him a sharp look and his eyes left her in no doubt about how it was going to be. 'Then light some lamps. It shouldn't feel like a tomb in here.'

She sagged her shoulders and set about her duties.

'I never set a foot in here, all those years ago...' Idas leaned upon his spear – Xandros noticed that he kept a firm grip of it even when there was no enemy to hand – favouring the leg that hadn't been deadened in the fighting. The Argonaut from Arene craned his neck up to look at the charred upper floor.

'Even when the fire took hold up there, that oak tree wasn't so much as scorched. Not a single branch.' Khalkeus cleared his throat. Fighting alongside his father had felt... good; right, somehow. 'Leads some to believe it's favoured by the Thunderer.'

'Is that so...?'

The click of a walking stick made them turn towards the stooped figure now approaching. 'By some, he means me. The only reason these halls didn't burn down is because of the rains that followed the lightning strike.'

'They give with one hand and take with the other.' Idas sneered. 'Sounds like those wretched Olympians, all right.'

She cocked her head to the side and approached him. 'You still live, don't you?'

'Only because of this, lady.' He tapped the butt of his spear against a flagstone.

'Yes, I remember you.' She fixed him with her shrewd dark eyes and, to Xandros' surprise, her lips straightened. 'Idas of Arene. You always were a thorn in Jason's side, weren't you? Not so much as that young boy, though – the dark-haired one. What was his name?' She screwed her eyes shut.

'Acastus?'

Pollux was about to speak but Xandros had beaten him to it.

'Acastus, yes that's it.'

'I met him in Iolkos.'

'Iolkos?' Ancaeus recoiled. 'The snake was driven out – we all watched it – him and his mother!'

'He was there,' confirmed Xandros.

Butes growled. 'The roach still lives whilst better men lie beneath the ground!'

'No.' Xandros shook his head. 'There had been unrest – the place was crumbling and his people starving – and there was an earthquake, the evening after I went to ask for help. I saw it with my own eyes. They turned on him; burned his palace to the ground.'

'I think I've lived too long,' murmured Ancaeus. They filled the *megaron* with their dark mutterings.

'Enough of this. I didn't invite you here to make these halls any gloomier. I wanted to thank you myself and, I confess, to see you all again. There was bitterness and rancour when you left these shores, all those years ago. No, don't let your heads fall, I am speaking the truth now. All that is passed.' Hypsipyle dabbed her eyes. 'And I am glad. You returned and you helped save Lemnos and, for that alone, you will always be remembered here.'

In the deep silence, Auge lit the lamps with a taper whilst the hearth flames began to take hold of the kindling. Creoboros padded around her for a moment, sniffing her suspiciously, before dropping onto his forepaws with a snort and curling up into a wakeful sleep.

'It was this boy.' Idas pointed his spear at Xandros. 'He was responsible for dragging our tired old carcasses out here. Thank him. And I saw him, down on the beach. He can fight a bit, just like his grandfather.' The sneer returned. 'Though Idas of Arene would never have allowed himself to be scratched like that.'

'No,' Pollux snorted, 'nor would he have been rimmed with a shield like you. His footwork's better.'

'Ares' balls, you speak horseshit even for a Spartan!'

The laughter lit up the room and, when Auge returned with a jug of wine, heavily mixed with water, so did the conversation. Hypsipyle put on a good show of repressing her pain for her son as she shared a few fond words with each of the Argonauts, though Xandros saw in her tired, grief-stricken eyes that it was brimming. Peleus was there, too. When she planted her walking stick on the floor and looked up at him and he down at her, there was a mutual recognition of loss. It was too much for Peleus and the grizzled warrior sobbed into his hands. Hypsipyle extended a gnarled hand and stroked his arm as if he were a new-born, and the simple gesture moved them all deeply.

He acquiesced for a few minutes before bowing a little and moving to the veranda at the far end of the *megaron*, preferring to be alone once more with his sorrow.

Orpheus

And then she came to me: Orpheus.

For a man who had witnessed a thousand sorrows and joys, the nobility of that woman and the stubborn flicker of vital light in those bewrinkled old eyes moved me profoundly.

'I wondered if I might ever get the chance,' she said quietly, 'to share a great secret...'

'I believe now might be such a time.'

A mischievous look creased her face. 'Forty summers ago, when you reprobates first showed on this shore, us women met in the old *agora*, out there. There was a vote. There was a vote to decide what we should do with you all. Did you know, the overwhelming vote was to slaughter you in your tents?'

I must confess, the bluntness with which Hypsipyle delivered that startling news left me at a loss for words. I must have stammered for a response but she continued.

'This is because of what we suffered in the years before at the hands of our men… Ah…' she brushed the digression aside '…but we didn't want to suffer like that again so we voted.'

I cleared my throat. 'And what prevented it?'

Those dark eyes looked deep into my soul. 'You did.'

'Me?'

'Yes, you. I heard your voice, and your lyre music, drifting up from the beach, and I knew then we shouldn't do it. It would have been like drawing a knife upon Apollo himself.'

'Then thank you,' I said with a laugh, 'for not trying to kill us.'

'And I suppose I can thank you now…' she frowned '…for setting that boy (she was referring to Xandros, of course) on his way, though I don't mind saying I cursed you at the time. He is the man of the house now. Because of your kindness, he has earned much of the respect he will need for that duty.' Her face softened again as I tipped my head. 'It is good to see you again, Orpheus, bard of bards, and an honour.'

Never one for overdoing it, she turned away and exchanged a few more pleasantries before turning once more for her private apartments.

I watched her go and experienced the oddest sensation. It was as if a door had closed upon my life, and a great darkness lifted momentarily revealing a long corridor, along which I noticed that many more such doors were closed than remained ajar. I shook my head and rejoined my comrades.

XXV

By the time they left Hypsipyle's halls, darkness had fallen and the drinking and singing began in earnest. Xandros watched Pollux, egged on by his brother, take to the centre of the square and perform his Spartan dance to a brisk, traditional tune from Orpheus' lyre. Though his pirouettes had lost something of their snap, he had the assurance of a master, leaping and sweeping to the click of his fingers and, when he had finished, the applause became an uproar.

Teodora had laced her fingers with Xandros' as they watched and leaned to him when it faded. 'Your grandmother has told me where there is some of last summer's wine.'

Xandros gave her his cup with a wink and she left for Hypsipyle's house. When she returned, she couldn't locate Xandros. Threading her way through the revellers, she spilt much of the cold, pale wine until she saw a little knot of people, by the wall that looked upon the beach.

She forced her way between Caeneus, Moxos and an agitated Creoboros to see Xandros slumped on a chair, head lolling upon his chest. Caeneus, at that moment pinching his earlobes, looked up at her in concern.

'He suddenly went all white and had a turn…'

'Xandros! *Xandros*, look at me!'

'Does he have the affliction?'

'Get him some water!'

Caeneus grunted and stood. 'He shouldn't stay out here.'

'Here, let me help you.'

With some difficulty, Moxos managed to hoist Xandros over his shoulder and the little group made for Hypsipyle's halls. Caeneus mimed a drinking gesture at anyone who turned to look, which was greeted with cheers and raised cups. They set him down on a stone bench in the cool of Hypsipyle's courtyard, and Teodora tried to tip some water into his lips…

Xandros felt himself pitch forwards onto his hands and knees, feeling the sand oozing through his fingers. Alongside him, frothing brine eddied around the pommel of his sword and, though he willed himself to reach for it and get back upon his feet, he was too exhausted. His body felt feverish, his limbs had grown heavy.

Then he caught sight of it, dead ahead. A fishing skiff and the single oarsman in his tatty hat. Against a gentle breeze, his filthy tunic clung to his spare frame with every pull of the oar. Over the soft hiss of breakers, he heard singing, if such a hideous croak could be so called.

But this time, another noise drifted over to him, from somewhere far behind. A hazy but somehow familiar voice.

With great difficulty, Xandros raised his head to meet the oncoming boat just as the oars were feathered and now skimmed along the water. The man's back stiffened and the singing stopped. Xandros knew what was coming; knew he couldn't resist. Amidst the rotting flesh that yet clung to the skeletal face, the sightless eyes smiled at him.

Xandros suddenly stirred with a soft moan and prised open his eyes to see the concerned expressions of his friends.

'You're back!' Caeneus nudged Teodora. 'Didn't I tell you the lad couldn't handle his drink!'

But Teodora knew differently. 'What happened, my love?'

He took a long pull of water and wiped his mouth. 'They're coming.'

'They're not! Not if you're talking about these raiders. They've had their fill of Lemnos, let me tell you.' Caeneus looked at Moxos for support but he didn't look so convinced.

Xandros shook his head. 'I only wish you were right. I want to tell everyone out there to go home to their beds.'

The hum of singing and laughter filled the courtyard. 'I wouldn't, if I were you. Not if you want to keep their respect, not after a daydream.'

XXVI

Xandros woke before dawn after a fitful sleep. Beside him, Teodora stirred but did not wake so he dressed quickly and quietly before closing the door gently behind him.

He watched dawn breaking over Lemnos sat next to his father's ashes. Had he not marked the spot with a little cairn of rocks, such was the number of cremations it would have been impossible to locate them. Nobody else was about. There had been no watches set and nobody yet stirred in the encampment of refugees. Doubtless most of them had thick heads this morning.

Eventually, overwhelmed by the cloying stench of charred flesh and hair that rose from the ashes, he got up and walked along the waterfront but the experience was far from relaxing. The bodies of the raiders had begun to bloat and discolour in an almost unbroken line. Where they had gained some of the beach and pressed the defenders hard, they lay in groups and their attitudes in death said much about the last moments of their lives. Here, a pair still propping each other up, slumped back-to-back on the sand, arrows protruding from their bellies. There, a lank-haired, shrewish-looking man with his mottled fingers gripping a shivered spear shaft embedded in his side. Scores more still floated in the shallows. Nudged back and forth by the breakers, their skulls made soft *thunks* as they struck the hulls of their ships.

As he reached the far end of the bay, Argos, he disturbed a pair of kites and a huge gull pecking at a body. Erythros and his boys had felled a few men nearby and he wondered if this was one of them. The sight of the sharp beaks plucking at the flesh made his stomach crawl and he began to regret his decision not to burn them.

He decided he would summon the council.

Striding back towards Myrine, he noticed a great figure stepping onto the beach behind him, drinking from a gourd. Deep in thought, it took Xandros a moment to place him. Ancaeus, *Argo*'s helmsman.

'Couldn't sleep?'

'Something like that,' replied Xandros.

Ancaeus took another pull of water. 'You did well, laddie.'

'Thank you.' He turned to the waterfront. 'Though I wish I'd burned them. The raiders.'

'They'll stink by midday.'

'Which is why I'm going to get help.'

Ancaeus nodded and pushed back his thick grey hair. 'We'll give you a hand before we leave.'

'You're *going*?'

'Well of course we are!' Ancaeus gave him a look. 'How long did you think we'd stay?'

'I… I hadn't really thought on it. Until we can be sure the threat has passed, I suppose.'

'Then we'd be here forever. We leave today. I've heard talk of lots of these people doing the same.'

The thought appalled Xandros, though he knew plenty in Myrine would rejoice to hear it. 'I think there will be more boats. In the next few days, even.'

'And what makes you say that?'

'A feeling; a strong one. Is there anything we can do to make you stay?'

Ancaeus shook his head and he could see his mind was resolute. 'We're old. We want to get back to our own hearths. A tent is no place for a man of my age; you'll know what I mean, one day.' Ancaeus gargled some water then spat to the side. 'When you've gathered some men, let me know.'

Xandros watched him turn back for his tent, grave doubts swilling within his stomach.

XXVII

It was a bitterly unpopular decision but the prospect of putrefying corpses and the miasma of restless souls swung it, however reluctantly. Barely twenty men set out for the beach, rags in their tunic pockets to dull the stench. By the time they had piled the first few bodies on top of each other, the number of helpers had doubled, Ancaeus, Castor, Pollux, Butes and Idas amongst them, chuntering and cursing like everybody else.

It took several hours to gather enough wood for the fires and, by the time the corpses were ablaze, midday was long past. As Ancaeus had suggested might happen, a few tents had been taken down and one of the Sea Peoples' boats had been requisitioned to ship some families to the mainland. The heated dispute over the boat prompted others to lay claim to the remaining ships. Xandros claimed one for Myrine and none openly disputed it.

He posted a watchman in the huer's hut and made arrangements for replacements every hour until sundown, before returning to the citadel.

'Any more visions?' asked Teodora as she dipped a husk of bread in olive oil that afternoon. The square was much more subdued than the previous evening, even though it was the hour when most people finished their siesta.

Xandros shook his head. 'Caeneus wants his gold before he leaves and the Argonauts are preparing to embark tomorrow.'

She glanced over his shoulder as she chewed the bread. The old warriors had taken over the benches reserved for the councillors since their arrival, unknowing or uncaring of the offence it had caused. Idas was at that moment passing a wine flagon to Butes.

'You will miss them, won't you?'

'I just wish they'd stay a little longer.' He shrugged. 'Actually, I had hoped they might decide to live here permanently.'

'Really?'

'Why not? They seem to belong here.'

Teodora tucked her hair inside her headscarf. 'They'll want to see out their remaining days on their farms, watching the sun set over their olive and almond groves.'

'That almost sounds poetic.'

She smiled. 'It's what one of them said.'

'I can't imagine them doing that. They'd get restless.'

'I wouldn't,' she murmured. Xandros noticed her features tense a little.

'Nor me, as long as I had you.'

Teodora leaned back and filled her lungs with the golden afternoon air. The time was surely right. 'Xandros, listen to me. There's something I need to say...'

The mournful wail of a distant trumpet silenced her and, though plenty seemed deaf to it, the Argonauts' heads all snapped around. Xandros stood and looked towards the huer's hut, catching the glint of sun on the copper instrument.

'Stay here.'

'You know I won't.'

He swept up his weapons and hurried past the Argonauts across the square. He heard one of them gasp a little as men do with stiff joints, and another muttered something about the gods and their sense of timing. When he reached the arch and looked east towards Moudros, he noticed the fire beacon had been lit. It gave him a most peculiar feeling: fear, for sure, but a sense of sadness and inevitability.

Moxos had joined him, fastening his cuirass at the side. 'Anything?'

Xandros gazed out over the water beyond the bay. The sun glittered, laughing upon the sea. He shook his head.

'Then we have some time, young man. Shall we?'

They headed down the path and a second signal from the trumpet drew more people from their tents. Xandros could sense the panic. Men hugged their wives and kissed their children before sending them towards the safety of the citadel. Others turned this way and that in confusion or denial.

'How do you want to play this one out?' asked Moxos.

Xandros' eyes swept the beach. If he had been clever, he could have used the burning bodies in the same way he had used the hurdles on the previous day. The grisly sight and smell might have been particularly effective. As it was, the bodies were burning low along the furthest corner of the backshore, where they posed an advantage to nobody. 'The same as yesterday. We need caches of weapons. Moxos, Hektor, Khalkeus… Can you make sure? Where's Alektruon?'

'He's there, behind you. *Alek!* Come with us.'

They set off towards the tents, hollering at the menfolk to ready their arrows and javelins. By now, there was a stream of women and children heading back towards the path to Myrine, looking terrified and confused. It seemed a cruel blow, after all they had endured.

'My lord, I'm here. Where do you want me?'

'Erythros.' He gripped him by the shoulders and the boy's eyes were bright with trepidation and excitement. 'If you can harry them from the side with your slingers. But don't get cut off. Whatever you do, you must avoid that, so not as far around the bay this time. Between Argos and Athens. Fall back upon us if you need to.'

Erythros looked towards the sight of his stand and looked back upon Xandros. 'The gods be with you!'

'And you, Erythros. Remember: don't get cut off!'

Xandros watched him jog away. A boat had already left earlier in the day and more than one hundred defenders – perhaps as many as two – were now ash and smoke. There was no way they could stretch their defences around the bay…

He glanced over at the galleys bobbing in the shallows. 'We burn the boats.'

'That would not be popular,' said Moxos. 'You saw the way these people were fighting over them. How else will they be able to leave?'

'They won't.'

He sprinted along the beach and cupped his hands around his

mouth. *'Anyone not engaged, we move these boats! Gather firewood and move these boats!'*

Orpheus

I was with Butes and Idas when Xandros suddenly took off down that beach.

'The boy's mad if he thinks we're going to do that,' growled Butes. 'I won't do it.'

'They're not the last ships in the world, old friend. I think I see what he has in mind.'

He turned his beetling brow upon me and stomped off with a huff.

XXVIII

Moudros

Ekhinos had been absently gazing out across the burnished sea when he saw the vessels passing by. Plenty of merchantmen would pull into Moudros Bay. Though the anchorage was, admittedly, not quite as good as at Myrine, it was safe. Traders had told him so, when he was young and he watched them unload their exotic wares and the seas were safer.

But those were not big-bellied goods ships.

Somewhere along the bay, a bell rang out, followed by another and then another. He hurried inside to find his father, who was already gathering up his weapons from the *megaron*.

'We leave now,' said his father without looking at him. 'There's a muster in the square and we're going to lead it.'

'We are going to *help*?'

Plouteos screwed up his face at his son as if he were witless. 'Of course we're going to help.'

XXIX

Xandros everywhere met with resistance or blind eyes being turned upon him until a few of the elders from amongst the refugees stopped him.

'Then how are we supposed to return home?'

'You have to live to do that!'

'It's madness! The raiders may not even come!'

'Then the kindling can be removed! *Just do it!*'

Xandros sidestepped them and hurried to the furthest ship, which was already abeam of the shore. The sight of him struggling to inch it along the bay, alone, drew pity and exasperation in equal measure. A few joined him and then a dozen men, hands splayed along the hull, were shoving her through the shallows towards Argos. Sweat was running freely down Xandros' back by the time they had wedged the second galley, bow to stern, behind the first. Two dozen other men had removed their armour and had waded out to retrieve boats or shove their prows from the sand, where they had become wedged. Others now gathered what meagre bundles of wood they could, for all of the low-hanging branches from trees within a hundred yards had been stripped for the hurdles and pyres. Olive oil was in even shorter supply; they had barely scraped enough to fill a small *pithos* jar for each boat.

By the time they had finished, the sun was westering and an expectant silence had fallen upon the bay. Six of the seven pirate vessels now formed an unbroken chain from the rocky promontory of the huer's hut for a distance of perhaps one hundred yards. One had been spared, along with a few of the other vessels, which had brought the desperate and the needy to Lemnos.

The sweat had long since dried upon their skin but the sudden onshore breeze caused goosebumps, and it seemed a particularly bad omen that the wind that had been so favourable in their defence yesterday had turned against them today.

The short, sharp blast from the huer's hut shattered their hopes that night would follow a peaceful evening. All along the beach, spears bristled. A few minutes later, they snaked around the headland, line astern.

One, two, three... Xandros mouthed the numbers as they appeared, not stopping until he had reached six.

They had dispatched as many before, more, even, but the defenders were tired and sore and disheartened. They bore injuries that had not had time to heal. They had hugged their loved ones for a second time and it seemed inevitable that there would be a third. Even if they lived to see such a moment.

Xandros took a deep breath, composing himself. *'The boats!'* he shouted. *'Light them up! Light them up now!'*

A single fire had been lit by the boats, to which they had continually added precious branches. Some of the torches, dipped in oil, failed to light or, when they did, fizzled out before their bearers reached the boats. Xandros shared a look with Moxos but the warrior shook his head.

By the time they were a bowshot distant, most of the ships were ablaze but even allowing for the compression of available beachhead, the defenders still seemed rather thin. *Had they really lost so many people?*

The boats did not slow as they approached the beach. In fact, to Xandros it seemed their oar strokes became even more urgent. Seeing the burning boats, no doubt, their helmsmen nudged their course towards the centre of the beach and all along towards Thessaly, where the Myrmidons, only one lighter than the previous day, stood ready to make them pay.

The thump of oars and the *hoom* of men firing their courage, and the jarring impact of prows against soft sand took the defenders aback, even though they were expecting it. Xandros noticed the bow post carved like birds and the helmets: bronze discs pincered by bronze horns. And then they were jumping overboard, shields raised.

'Now!'

It wasn't Xandros' order but it was a good one. The first volley of arrows and, a split second later, stone shots rattled against men and wood. Raiders dropped once more into the shallows but, lacking the intensity of the previous day, a dozen made it ashore. Xandros saw Erythros' sling whirling frenziedly and, for the first few minutes, the assault in his section faltered. The Argonauts lowered their helmets and raised their shields and, alongside them, the Myrmidons hummed and advanced.

XXX

Orpheus

It was clear the spirited response had caught the raiders a little by surprise. In fact, not a man from the first boat made it more than ten paces before he crumpled or was forced backwards.

But, by the gods, could those pirates shoot! Covered by more and more shields, their archers popped up, unleashing their arrows with such deadly accuracy that they had dropped a score or more in the first few minutes. In that time, I had half emptied a quiver that wasn't full to begin with. Only a few barbs had found their mark and two of those had struck bowmen, yet still they sprouted from those galleys until it became clear they contained more than fifty oarsmen: in some even women and children. It was a wonder they hadn't capsized.

Amidst the shouting and cursing, I heard Moxos – son of the Argonaut – pounding across the sand and I turned to see him hurling a javelin at a distance of no more than fifteen paces. It shivered right through the neck of a man who wasn't even looking at him. Death claimed him so suddenly that I swear the man's expression didn't even change.

It is one thing to hear fireside tales of fighting to the death, even to see it at such a distance that it is impossible to say whether a man has brown eyes or blue. But that day, under a golden evening sun, we came face to face with an enemy that was driven by the most compelling force man can experience. *Desperation.* They were ready to disembowel us just so they could occupy Lemnos, seize its possessions – however meagre – and force themselves upon the island's women. I could even smell the sharp tang of their sweat as they grunted and bludgeoned and stumbled about on the warm, yielding sand in their hunger to drive us from that beach.

To those who haven't experienced it, who burn for some desperate glory, let me say this. The shouting of battle isn't the din of a sporting contest, such as occur at funeral games or festivals, when the crowd yells and bellows the names of their favoured athlete or curses another. The shrieking and yelling comes first but this is just the firing of courage and anybody who has been in battle, which scalds lungs and numbs limbs in moments, knows the futility of expending precious energy by shouting.

Instead, the sound of battle is the cacophony of breathlessness, panting, groaning and growling, the crack of wood and the clatter of metal. There are screams of pain, it is true, but in my experience there are more cries of 'mother' or despairing calls for loved ones. These from the ones who have received a mortal wound. Those killed outright die in silence: even the fall of their bodies is lost to the din.

All around me, men were dying. Mostly, there was no great glory to it, especially those who had flinched and turned their backs. I saw Idas, thrusting his spear over his shield, as I had seen him do countless times in another age, and the years seemed to roll away. He was a braggart but his tough life had given him good reason to be and, by now well into his seventh decade, his spear was an extension of his arm, and I doubt there was a handful of men on earth who could match him. Hard on his shoulder, his great friend Butes was flagging. Amidst a flurry of arms and legs and weapons, two small fronts collided with a great crack then drew apart.

I nocked another arrow and made a half turn to my right, sensing a greater threat from the third boat. I took a deep breath and tried to steady my trembling hand whilst I chose a target.

The target chose itself: a youth, levelling a bow. Had I seen this before my arrow was already fitted, I don't doubt that I would have panicked and sent it wide or even fumbled it altogether. Still holding my breath, I paused a beat and then released. The string grazed my cheek as it whipped past but my technique was old and true. I watched the shaft all along its short journey, in fascination and revulsion, as the bronze head shattered that youth's front teeth and buried itself in his mouth. It sat him down and, as the moment of shock evaporated, the image of him thrashing about in the shallows as he tried to pluck it from his throat haunted me for years. It took him an age to die.

It was ludicrous folly, I know, but I wanted to shout about what I had done, preventing a death as surely as night follows day, hoping that somebody had witnessed it. The shame I feel in admitting this is faint indeed now but it started a fateful turn of events. Idas and Butes sidled over to me, shields raised, and were forced to yell to make themselves heard.

'Leave this beach now! Get up that citadel and watch!'

Butes nodded with a grimace. I noticed his crabbing movements and the gash across his thigh.

'No!' I shouted. 'My place is here!'

Without warning, they stepped in front of me and, touching shields, began to backpedal towards the citadel. There was an almighty thud and Idas' shield reverberated alarmingly. I saw the head of a javelin had pierced the board and its hide a few inches. He gasped and it was enough to know that such a brave man had been rattled.

I thought they might bowl me over but, once they felt me yield, they slowed their pace. *'Go, Orpheus, leave!'*

The ferocity of their words made me flinch.

'Why?' I cried.

The pair shared the briefest of looks but it contained enough to fill a poem in itself. 'Because we want to be remembered, man. We all do.' Idas glanced over his shoulder at me. 'And you may be the greatest bard but you're a lousy archer.'

I stumbled onto my backside, and it hurt because we were at that part of the beach that yields to the path. Between their hips, I could see the battle raging. It was far from safe here but there was no immediate threat, apart from a stray arrow. I struggled to my feet and retrieved my bow, numb with shock and indecision.

'You want me to join the women and children?'

'You've earned a peaceful death,' rumbled Butes, 'far from here. You more than most. There's no shame in it. Remember us, old friend, if we fall.'

Tears breached my lids and I could no longer rein them in. Had I known this was how it might end, I doubted at that moment I would have rendered young Xandros any help at all, all those weeks ago.

'Go,' said Idas firmly. 'It's getting serious down there.' He reached out and clasped me by the shoulder. To my astonishment, they kissed me on either cheek. 'We love you, Orpheus. Remember us.'

They plunged back down the beach.

XXXI

'Help us!'

It was a cry of pure desperation and it came from Erythros.

Xandros lowered his spear, trying to locate the boy, but the wind had shifted and plumes of acrid smoke billowed back upon the defenders. His strategy was unravelling. The Myrinians, he noticed, had started to backtrack into the gaps, coughing as the smog began to take effect. Away from the worst of it, the Myrmidons had begun to drive the attackers back towards their boats. The bronze discs flashed and twitched as they stepped back and Xandros once more looked for the boy. He caught a glimpse of him, his head uncovered, his body hideously exposed. He sprinted behind the shield wall that was being raised and, legs pumping over the soft sand, arrived at his little band with no air in his lungs.

'Get behind me!' A stray arrow nearly ended Xandros' life then and there. It whistled past his nose with a blurred hiss.

Erythros backpedalled as he loaded a pebble.

'Get behind me now!'

There was only a handful of his boys still standing. Most of them lay still, having long since bled out, though one still tugged weakly at an arrow's shaft. It was a pathetic sight and, had he been nearer, Xandros might have put him out of his misery.

Erythros set his feet and whirled that sling of his with desperation riven on his features. Xandros got to him just as he released his shot. The noise the pebble made as it struck bone set his teeth on edge. Its target was helmetless, ruddy-faced, and he dropped to the sand as if his legs had turned to water. He fell at the very same moment one of the Lemnian lads gathered an arrow in his belly. It landed with a hollow clop.

'Move!'

Erythros yielded, stumbling after Xandros, seeking the protection of his shield. The defenders now formed an irregular line, from Athens to Thessaly. It held but it looked precarious. Xandros looked about him but the caches of arrows and javelins had been used up, and still the raiders fired, encouraged by their women and elders who leaned over the rails of their boats. Every so often, another defender would drop, screaming in mortal pain, and Xandros knew there would be a massacre once there were sufficient gaps in the defenders' line.

He was about to bellow the command to charge when a warrior of monstrous size emerged from the rear lines of the pirates, followed by a stocky man whose garb marked him out as some chieftain or other. The warrior was head and shoulders taller than the largest man Xandros had ever seen, and almost as wide again. He shoved his men aside and flicked his spear towards the sand, whereupon the bows in their lines were lowered immediately.

The titan removed his helmet and ran his fingers through his long, black hair. Even at a distance of thirty yards, Xandros could sense the unearthly power emanating from him. He now grinned at them, enjoying the awed silence.

'One man beat me, these people we go home. Yes?'

His voice sounded like it had emerged from a cavern deep in the earth. It was met with a stony silence. Then, one after the other, people turned to Xandros. Alongside him, Creoboros began to leap and bark. Next to him, Erythros slipped a stone from his little bag, the biggest and smoothest that remained, and pressed it into the sling's pouch. Xandros saw what he was doing and put out a restraining arm.

'I must be the one.'

'Forget it,' said Moxos. 'You're not facing that.'

'Someone take the *kuna* down with an arrow.'

'There's no honour in that.'

Another voice jeered. 'Nor is there in needless death!'

Ancaeus watched the scene unfold with a sinking heart. He had met the man before – Huliat, he thought his name was – and some small part of him had known that he would meet him again. He turned to look up at the walls of Myrine. It was too far distant to pick out faces but he knew Atukhos would be there, looking down upon him.

'Let me through.'

Castor and Pollux gave him a double take and grabbed him by either elbow. 'Don't be a fool!' hissed Pollux. 'He's bigger than Herakles!'

'I wish I had my axe.' He shrugged them off and stepped in front of the shields into the no-man's land of churned sand and blood. The defenders fell silent. Huliat watched Ancaeus in curiosity and his prominent brow creased as recognition dawned upon him. 'What is this? I am not to fight an old man!'

He turned and silenced the laughter behind him with a glare, and Ancaeus knew he had his one chance. He charged the titan and stepped outside of the spear levelled against him. Then he felt himself being bodychecked – as if he had run into a stone wall – and the spear somehow missed its mark. The truth was, two days of fighting had sapped his strength. He lumbered over the sand, regaining his balance.

'Give me my axe. Make it a fair fight.'

The grin became a rictus and Huliat lowered his voice. 'Is at bottom of the sea, where it sinks with our people.'

The weak planking Ancaeus had fitted back in Gytheon had slipped his memory. He disliked spears but it hardly mattered now; he had not swung that axe in anger for many years. Adjusting his grip, he made a sudden lunge at the champion, twisting his wrist at the last moment so that it would not so easily be checked. Huliat's spear clacked against his own, rattling the old bones of his arm, but he held fast and the spear tip opened up a deep cut. Ancaeus kept his footing and thundered past until he was in the clear. Huliat looked at the wound contemptuously and advanced, feinting towards Ancaeus' groin before flicking his spear towards his heart. It scored a clean rent in his tunic and left a perfect welt up his chest, making him rock backwards in agony.

Then he heard his name being called, high-pitched. From the tail of his eye, he saw Atukhos running over the sand towards him. 'Get him *away*!' he roared.

He heard the swish of the spear, as thick as a weaver's rod, and felt it cleave him beneath his ear. In his last sliver of consciousness, he heard the scream of the boy but, of the heavy fall to the sand, he felt nothing.

Atukhos squirmed free of the grip of a Lemnian, slipped through the front rank to roars of protest and fell to his knees at Ancaeus' face. He sobbed whilst he tried to clear away the blood that sprang from the black valley in the steersman's neck. He was aware of the great shadow that now fell upon him but he didn't care. When he sensed he was close enough, Atukhos sprang to his feet and rained his fists upon the giant's thigh, screaming boyish curses at him, smearing his skin with Ancaeus' blood.

Other raiders now hurried out to lay rough hands upon him, dragging him from Huliat. The titan swiped at one of them, knocking him senseless and picked the other up by his tunic so that he found himself looking into the swirling darkness of the champion's eyes. Huliat stank of stale sweat and the raider could hear the rasp of warm air in his nostrils. Then he tossed him aside like a rag doll, and the impact of the sand stole the breath from the raider's lungs.

Huliat jabbed his finger at his men and he knew by their expressions he had their attention. 'This boy, you *leave*!'

He turned to him now and knelt before him, and even then he was a head taller than Atukhos. Through the tears, Huliat saw the fire in the boy's eyes, and it stirred something in the dregs of his own memory.

Life is a series of cycles, his father had once told him, *and the only question is how many you are allotted.* He knew something of the lad's thoughts, what he was feeling, and the greatest of these was loneliness.

'Go now, boy,' he whispered, 'and live bravely like your father.'

Your father.

Ancaeus, 'The Bear', was everything his own father had never managed to be.

Father.

He felt the weight of that sacred word crushing some part of his spirit, uttered for the first time by the very man who had killed him. Just then, he noticed the golden ring on Ancaeus' little finger, which still curled around the spear. He blinked whilst his mind raced. It felt wrong taking it from him but what if the pirates got their hands on it? Without looking at the ogre who had killed Ancaeus, he prised the finger from the spear and began to twist the ring free. The sudden slap of a meaty hand on the spear shaft made him flinch and his eyes darted fearfully to the champion, whose whole face creased in a frown. The warrior batted Atukhos' hand away and tugged unceremoniously at the ring, making the boy gasp. He took Atukhos' wrist and pressed the ring into his trembling palm.

'Now go.'

Atukhos rose warily, not quite believing he wasn't being tricked but the warrior's gaze seemed somehow distant; pained even. He turned and stumbled along the sand, lost in his waking nightmare.

XXXII

Orpheus

The wailing that arose from the citadel might have wakened the dead. I wanted no part of it and took myself away to a quieter stretch, away from the entrance, whilst what I had just witnessed sank in.

Had the epithet 'Bravest amongst us' been overused? Possibly. But those men lived by a different code of honour than people today, and I never saw the likes again. Ancaeus was not the greatest steersman – that honour must surely go to Tiphys – nor was he the finest man-at-arms aboard *Argo*, though he pushed the others close with his axe. But his was the greatest heart I had ever known.

While that behemoth strode through his own ranks, the few remaining Argonauts went to collect their comrade's body unchallenged. They carried it between them with as much dignity as they could muster, though Ancaeus was a very big man, and deposited him somewhere out of my view before returning to the lines, utterly deflated. I yearned to call to them, to spare them the inevitable. This was not their fight. The gods knew they had earned their rest. As they trudged back, they glanced up at the citadel and I fancy their eyes found me.

I became aware of a stirring amongst the onlookers and turned to see them pointing towards the east. I shielded my eyes to see what it was they had seen. A column of men was snaking towards Myrine through the parched valley that gave to the inner island. It did not look like many – certainly less than one hundred – but it might have been enough to turn the tide. Some of the women began to cheer and scream and I silenced them with a sharp rebuke.

'If they are to help, their arrival needs to be a *surprise*!'

Well, my theory was at least sound enough, I thought. I received a few looks and turned back to the fighting, for the lines had closed once more and the din of battle drifted up to the walls. And then, from the corner of my right eye, I saw something out on the water. A sail.

I glanced at the huer's hut on the opposite headland but could see no activity: doubtless the man posted there had since joined the fray. This gave me the most wretched feeling of helplessness. Would those men on the beach even benefit from a warning? They would surely see for themselves what was happening. I peered over the wall and saw that there was space between the few vessels of the defenders, tucked into the stretch of Thessaly, where the newcomer might run ashore. That way, the defence would be turned from the rear.

Yes, they needed to know.

I was just about to join the throng of onlookers to demand a horn – there were few instruments I couldn't play by then – and glanced back at the ship to see the owl emblem bellying in the onshore breeze. I had of course been to Athens many times and could recognise it anywhere. A few hundred yards from the beach, the sail was trimmed a little and I could see in my mind's eye the pilot weighing up his options. He would surely know that the soldiers with their backs to the citadel were the defenders. A warning served no purpose. The sharper the surprise those magnificent Athenians could bring to bear, the better.

To the east, the column of reinforcements was less than half a mile distant and, by the looks of things, forcing the pace. I closed my eyes and looked to the heavens. In the warmth of the slanting light, I fancied that Lady Hera had once more smiled upon us.

XXXIII

Xandros' throat was aflame and his body had begun to quiver with fatigue. The fighting had descended into a series of tired, disjointed sallies and, in the ensuing clash, spears were thrust and blades flashed and hacked. Men would drop. Some were dragged clear; most were left where they fell. Teodora was one of a few water carriers who braved the fighting. Though her mouth burned with thirst, she would only wet her lips before running this way and that as men dropped out of the line and fell to their knees, barely able to raise a hand.

It was the older men who suffered the most, men whose best days were long behind them, such that it seemed to become a battle of youthful attrition. Yet, though they dropped back frequently for water, the Argonauts held the line.

As they tipped back their heads, Teodora was overcome with pity, though her tears were disguised by the sweat that flowed freely from her brow. It seemed scarcely possible that men so old could perform such feats. In the raking sun, she became familiar with every wrinkle, every scar, the hue of their haunted eyes as they looked through her. Peleus was the oldest amongst them but there was something unquenchable about his desire to avenge his brother. She noticed how his beard was flecked with a mist of blood and, when he opened his mouth, his teeth were coated in it. He gargled and spat a brief crimson fountain before rejoining the line.

There was not a part of Xandros' body that was not doused in sweat and blood or dusted with sand. Yet still, impelled by some dreadful, irresistible force, the lines drew together. He could tell by the gasping and the panting, the expressions racked by horror and exhaustion, that the raiders were shattered too.

He had seen Loukios fall in the first clash after the champion had despatched the Argonaut Ancaeus. Xandros hated the youth, it was true, but he had died bravely, and a few friends with him too. His father, a hill farmer, had dragged his body clear, wailing with wild grief and he could still be heard somewhere behind. Xandros staggered out of the line to get a view of how things looked, throwing aside his shivered spear and withdrawing his sword. *Jason*'s sword. The mere act of moving his eyeballs made pain flare in their sockets and he was forced to twist his torso around.

The left was hardest pressed and was starting to bow. The fishermen and carpenters from Gioura and Halonnesus had vowed to fight with honour and, by the gods, they were doing that, though they were ill-suited for this sort of work. To the right, the Myrmidons had almost turned the line single-handedly, but another ship had disgorged some more soldiers – Xandros had not seen it arrive if indeed it was a newcomer – and the reinforcements had pressed them back. The Myrmidons had lost five or six men, and the ants emblazoned upon their shields stared up at the sky in a defiant pile.

The line held but the thread was slender. Were there two hundred men still defending Lemnos? That there were more raiders was clear.

And then he saw the sail. His foggy mind failed to register the significance of the owl and he assumed another pirate galley had arrived to finish them off. At least it would be swift: maybe even painless. It wasn't until the hiss and thud of the first few arrows that he understood. The galley crept along the shore, bristling with archers and spearmen, making her list starboard.

'Athenians!' yelled Moxos.

Demophon and his old-fashioned sense of honour would save them. It made Xandros' heart burst with pride.

It took a few minutes for the pirates to respond, precious minutes in which dozens fell, groaning and writhing, unable to reach the shafts burrowed into their backs. Some of the elderly and infirm that had played no part in the fighting now hobbled over to raise shields with which to cover their men. At first, it was clear the Athenians wanted no part in wasting their arrows on such easy targets but, as the protective carapace strengthened, they picked a few of the men off. The missiles the raiders returned were a motley assortment of stones, spent arrows and javelins, and these did little to blunt the withering bronze fire. But those shields… Around just a handful of these, they established a second front and nearly every Athenian arrow that fizzed harmlessly into the sand was turned against them.

'One more push!' bellowed Xandros, feeling his exhaustion lift. *'One more!'*

'Back! Back!' came the chant. *'Back! Back! Back!'*

It began to work. The left held and, led by Laodon the fisherman, one eye swimming in his own blood, gained a few yards. Sensing a turning of the tide, none dropped out now, willing to expend every last drop of their souls to fold the raiders in upon themselves. Wily old Peleus had seen what was happening. 'Now!' he screamed at the Myrmidons. *'Now! Now!'*

The warriors responded magnificently, tucking their shoulders into the boards of their shields, emptying their lungs in a frenzied burst of spearing. The line of pirates started to bow.

'Moudros!' someone croaked. 'They came!'

Xandros caught the dull glint of helmets emerging from the long shadows cast by the trees along the backshore. It didn't surprise him that Plouteos' bore an elaborate clump of colourful feathers. Ekhinos strode next to him, followed by a few other faces Xandros vaguely recognised as he dared glance at them. He caught the flash of shock; their eyes darting around the carnage before them.

'Now!' Xandros wheezed.

The Moudrians waited.

'Wretches!' Khalkeus had dropped back and now fell to his knees as dehydration sapped him. He planted the butt of his spear in the sand to steady himself. 'Cowards!'

Xandros saw their hesitancy and took it for fear. *'Courage!'* He staggered towards the Moudrians, unable to draw the breath for any more words. When he tried to raise his sword to point towards the enemy, his arms barely responded. *'For Lemnos!'*

Ekhinos licked his lips and adjusted the grip of his spear, setting himself. He looked at his father and then at the levy behind him, sixty or seventy strong. 'Well then? Why wait?'

Creoboros, caked in dried blood and sand, began to tremble and snarl. A yelp of dismay made Xandros turn to see a body slip to the sand and another warrior cover him. It took a moment for him to recognise him.

Hektor, one of Euneus' most trusted men. He sensed that the surge was fading.

'Help us!'

From Xandros' parched mouth and lungs, his words were barely a whisper. The loss of his voice induced a surge of panic.

'Courage!' yelled Ekhinos, plunging forwards.

Creoboros bristled then pounced upon the nomarch's son before he had taken his third step.

'No!' gasped Xandros, lunging at the dog but his fingertips only grazed his body. On hands and knees, Xandros looked on in vain as Creoboros sank his teeth into Ekhinos' throat, bowling him over with the force of his leap.

The Moudrians charged.

Unsighted, Creoboros did not release his jaws even when Plouteos' sword plunged into his ribs. Only when the nomarch heaved him off his son did he hobble away with a whimper and breathe his last as he licked his deep wound. Dumbstruck, Xandros willed himself to rise but his legs would not respond. Only when he felt the savage kick in his own ribs did it register that they had been betrayed. The pain bent him double and he blacked out for a moment and, when his hazed eyes sprang open once more, the world had changed.

He saw Moxos twisting in disbelief, parrying weakly at the spear thrust at his side. Caeneus, too, earning far more gold than he had been given in his gallant defence. A few feet from Xandros, Khalkeus turned the first Moudrian spear but the second punched through his cuirass and he toppled over, teeth gritted and eyes screwed shut.

The sand reverberated with the thump of desperate feet. The defenders, bewildered, turning this way and that, were cut down at will. Xandros felt a shadow fall upon him and tensed himself for the brief flare of pain but looked up to see instead Caeneus, hollow-eyed with exhaustion, struggling to drag Xandros to his feet.

Somehow, he rose, gripping the mercenary's tunic, leaning heavily upon him, feeling the pounding of his heart. Caeneus brandished his broken rapier. He thrust it at a face, plastered with sweat and dark hair, through which dark eyes flared. Xandros heard Caeneus' winded grunt, felt him buckle, but it was the attacker who slipped from view.

Moxos, the only man on Lemnos to have fought before the walls of Troy, went down tall in the onslaught, selling his life dear, and all around him, like trees uprooted in a storm, the line collapsed. Xandros watched it with a bone-weary detachment. Like a bladder pierced by a needle, he felt the strength ebb from Caeneus' body. He heard him sigh as they both sank to the beach and he realised, when they had settled into the long shadows that now raked across the sand, that Caeneus was gripping him by the wrist.

Tears breached his eyelids and they stung. He wiped his eyes but only succeeded in making them burn, and he realised he must watch his final moments through a blurry, gritty film. He could not scream for water for he had no voice. And if he did have a voice, who would come to his aid?

Teodora?

He looked down and noticed that his tunic was black with glistening blood and that he was panting for breath. He raised a weak hand and cried her name but no sound emerged. There was no hurt, in a physical sense, only relief. The pain that now burrowed into every cell of his being was the quiet understanding that, amidst the fading uproar, he would never again lay loving eyes upon her.

Teodora.

XXXIV

Orpheus

It took me many years before I was able to let my mind settle upon the infernal visions of that late evening. In the meantime, every time my thoughts drifted back towards Lemnos, I would grit my teeth and, with a supreme effort, divert them. It is no surprise that, despite my advanced years, there followed a period of the most intense travel, despite the manifest dangers of the sea. I sought solace in far-flung places and I did not rest. I did not dare.

But I will tell you now, stranger, what I saw.

I saw the essence of courage and brotherhood. I saw Love and it made me weep, as it makes me weep now. This is how I have chosen to remember that day.

Summer was waning by then – it was late in the Month of Ploughing – and the sun was sinking fast. The fighting was reduced to pockets of broken, lacerated men, drawing back to back, striving to fend off death for a few moments longer. Some sought the protection of bodies, piled in front like a palisade. Others drew to the higher ground of the dunes that concealed the charred bones of men slaughtered on that beach generations before. Even at a distance, I recognised that dear boy Xandros. As the intentions of those treacherous Moudrians became clear, I recalled – the first time I met him – what he said about 'Red', who seemed to be the manifestation of some youthful rage he once struggled to control. What those struggles might have been before I met him, I can only conjecture, as all storytellers must. Red's memory came to the fore now. I gripped the walls of the old citadel and willed him to respond.

Now! Now is the time for your anger!

But he was broken by exhaustion. He had fought like the warrior perhaps his father was and certainly his grandfather but, as he stumbled towards those perfidious islanders, I saw just a child, raising his arms for help. His dog, loyal, indomitable Creoboros (I confess I never warmed to him until that moment), sniffed treachery doubtless before even seeing those men emerge from the shadows.

There was an eclipse of the sun, only months following these events. Most folk believed that the world was about to end, the fools. I had myself spoken to temple priests in Egypt about phenomena such as these and the possibility of such an event in our lifetime, so I knew what was happening. It was that eerie dusk during a sunlit day that left its impression, and the way it silenced nature. The birds and the dogs sensed it before anyone, or anything, and I credit Creoboros with scenting the tension in the air the moment he set eyes upon the boy called 'Sea Urchin'.

I do not think, as some speculated in the desperate flight from that citadel, that the dog's attack swung the Moudrians against Myrine. That was surely predetermined and the beast was merely striking the first blow. Against that dog, Ekhinos stood no chance. Though his father Plouteos was slain minutes later – and I firmly believe it was at the spear tip of Idas of Arene – the tide had turned.

But, Xandros. Stated simply, he was a boy troubled by his solitude. That voyage – his Odyssey, if you will – drew the man from within. He departed with a stammer, returned with his voice and died leading hundreds, and what is this if not a lesson to us all?

Naturally, my eyes were also drawn towards my friends and, amidst the wailing and screaming hard by, and the more distant clash of arms, I tried to focus my attention upon them, as I had sworn to do. There is no doubt the arrival of that valiant Athenian, Demophon (whose bravery is still celebrated today in their god-favoured city), and his crew almost claimed the day. Had that band of Moudrians done as honour demanded, it surely would have.

But Huliat, who had been watching the fighting aloof, arms folded, now bestirred himself. I did not at first pay him much attention but when the first brand flashed across my peripheral vision, snuffed by the sea, I had to. He lit two or three more stakes from the few pyres that still burned and sauntered towards the shore, hurling them at the galley. The second landed on the deck and, whilst it may have injured some, the third and fourth struck the centre of the sail. The fabric caught alight at once. Though the crew tried to extinguish it, more torches were thrown and they must abandon it for their lives. Most jumped overboard but they were as vulnerable as the Sea Peoples themselves had been and it was a grim business to cover those few short yards to join the islanders.

It was the Myrmidons and, at their head, Peleus, who strove to cover them and this was to be their last and most glorious act. I doubt there were still ten of them standing by then and they fell to a man, each taking a raider down with him. One of those Thessalians had lost his shield and I watched him drag a man down with his bare hands. Peleus himself may have been the last of them and, knowing his pig-headed, cold courage, I rather think he was. I can still see the Athenians – led by Demophon – snatching up those ant-faced shields and earning their protection, though the honour was not long theirs.

Truly, it saddens me that that race of flint-hard warriors, the Myrmidons, hasn't been praise-sung more. If I had more years at my disposal…

And what of the others? What of Castor and Pollux, those inseparable Spartan twins? What of Idas and Butes? What of my pledge?

Let me tell you this, stranger. Commit it to heart and wish that you never must face it for, in war, it is as if the earth yawns open and discloses a seeping, suppurating wound. War is blood and cloven flesh and unspeakable pain. It is grown men shrieking for their mothers as they claw at the air in their final breaths.

It is confusion.

I wish I could say I can recall every detail of those four Argonauts', my dear friends' final moments, but I cannot.

It is surely enough to know that not a single man who took the beach against those pirates was left standing. Not one. They fought with courage and they died with honour. All of them. Let that speak for itself and be satisfied. Do details matter so?

Of all the unspeakable horrors that day unleashed, the fate of young Teodora fills me with the most guilt and sorrow. I have said that not a single man was left standing, and this is true, but two girls were. Both had done as much as anyone else to keep those defenders upright, and their resilience and bravery were something to behold. It was easy to identify Teodora, working like a honeybee, and she did not deserve the cruel luck the Spinners wove.

She had been with Xandros not moments before the arrival of the Moudrians before hurrying to the waterfront to tend to a pair of Myrmidons who had been injured in quick succession. Perhaps, seeing the late arrivals to the field, she had believed the matter settled. So intent was she on staunching a wound and dressing another that her back was turned when Creoboros pounced and it was still turned when young Xandros and his mercenary friend Caeneus received their mortal wounds. Were the gods more merciful, they would have forced her head towards her lover sooner.

But the gods had abandoned us by then.

By the time she became aware of something amiss, it was too late. I could hear her piercing scream from Myrine's walls. She reached them both – here was the smallest mercy – and cradled them on her lap for a few moments before three or four of those Moudrians dragged her away; her and the other water carrier, whose name I later learned to be Melli.

I couldn't bear to look.

The sun was setting. We in the citadel knew we had to leave, and leave quickly, before the roving eyes of those godless men fell upon easier plunder. I had no mind to lead them. It was no business of mine where those fugitives went, after all, but then my eyes fell upon Ancaeus' boy, Atukhos. He was sat alone with his back to a wall and his knees drawn up, and the mournful look upon his dirty face would have drawn pity from a lump of wood.

I said to him, 'You, boy, get up! You are coming with me.'

He looked up at me like a stray whelp finding a new owner but I had no time for consolations. My lyre was in Hypsipyle's courtyard and it was there we hurried through the dusk-filled square. I was about to leave again when I caught a glimpse of a frail spectre in the hall, staring at us both. It made me flinch, despite all I had seen that day.

'Orpheus,' it croaked.

My heart took a moment to return from my mouth. 'My lady,' I gasped. 'Come with us!'

'Don't be a fool.' She hobbled into the half-light of the porch. 'Is it over, then?'

'It is.' Curse my vanity, lest she think me a coward, I added, 'They sent me from the battle, to tell the tale.'

I could feel those shrewd eyes reading my mind. 'I am glad they did.'

'Come with us.'

'My place is here.' She glanced at Atukhos, who was staring at her with his dark eyes. 'Tell me one thing before you leave. Was it with honour?'

Some screams now rose above the general pandemonium in the square. I was anxious to be away. 'More than most, my lady, and there was no coward soul out there. Only heroes.' I swallowed hard. 'It was a thing for the ages.'

It was enough, I could see. She wiped a tear from her eye with a crooked finger and raised her chin. Right there, the years fell away to that day I first laid eyes upon her, the proud queen of Lemnos. 'You must go but not that way. There is a sally port at the far end of the square, concealed by a hurdle of brush. Take it. Be sure the boy gets free but they cannot all go.' She placed a hand on her heart and I believe it nearly gave out at that very moment. She was breathy when she next spoke. 'The drop is sheer and they are too loud. Go. Go whilst the light is still faint and fare well, Orpheus. You have earned this.'

I clasped her hands, and her skin was as cold and dry as an autumn leaf. 'Thank you, Queen,' I said, for truly she was once more, though her reign would be brief and difficult.

Mesmerised by her, I had to half drag the boy out of the courtyard, and we were out of the gate without looking back. Panic whipped through the *agora* like a mountain wind. I could sense the raiders approaching. Their blood would be up and some of them would have enough spite left in them for wine and women. I looked about me. Those gripped by hysteria I ignored, for they would get us all caught, but then I noticed an elderly couple and some children, only a little older than Atukhos, and I hurried over to them.

They understood the manner of my approach and I, for my part, appreciated their good sense. When they asked if they could bring others, I snapped that they need be quick, for I would not wait. Two women, clearly widows, were coaxed over, trembling and pale, and another, tight-lipped and dignified. One of them said they were from Halonnesus but it made no odds to me if they said they were from Colchis or Cyanida. Cutting across that square, my nerves shredding by the second, I could not at first locate that wretched sally port.

Atukhos did.

He pointed to a little kink in the circuit wall. It was a simple but clever means of introducing a gap that could easily be concealed by the thicket hurdle that we now hauled away with no great difficulty, to a little breath of cool night air.

'Be sure to slide it back,' I said testily, in no mind for pleasantry, before ducking under the little corbelled arch and stepping onto what felt like the lip of a chasm. In the solid embrace of that citadel, I had no impression of how high above the sea we were but looking out over that sheer drop, it was only too clear. The rock-cut shelf was no doubt safe enough in daylight but the sun had set, leaving only pink striations above the horizon, and the moon was veiled behind us. A stiff breeze made it cold as well as precarious. I could just make out the track that hugged the walls and snaked away around the rocky contour of the hill and down into blackness. It was wide enough for two men at a pinch so I made sure Atukhos kept contact with the bedrock with his right hand.

The little escape party had been well chosen for there were no histrionics – only a sharp breath behind me, no doubt at the sight of the drop – but progress was painfully slow. There was not a word of complaint from Atukhos and his fortitude impressed me. It took my mind off our situation to reflect upon what Ancaeus had told us about him, though it was brief. The poor wretch had put up with much hardship in his short life and this was all grist to his millstone. I hoped one of the women behind us would take care of him.

We made it, with great relief, onto the lower reaches of the hill and could now hear the raiders, faintly, on the beach. When the track petered out altogether in a fragrant olive grove, and Myrine and its farmstead was now between us and the sea, I gathered our little band together and looked back. Torchlights pricked the waterfront and there were a few campfires, and all seemed peaceful. Much as it had forty years earlier, no doubt, when the Argonauts first hove to.

'*Look!*' one of the women whispered as we started moving again through the night chorus of crickets. She was pointing towards the slope to the citadel. There were a few torches on the way up: perhaps more already in the square. It had been a close-run thing for us, that was clear, and the serenity was deceptive. It didn't bear thinking about what was happening up there: I only hoped that those dogs showed some clemency towards Hypsipyle. I doubted they would.

What else is there to say about the flight from that town?

It was not without incident. A short while later, whilst we trudged on in silence, each lost in their thoughts, there was a stifled scream and I cursed the woman who made it. She was called Ana and was the only Myrinian amongst us. In fairness, she had been dignified throughout and had good reason to be scared.

The silhouette had loomed out of the darkness quite suddenly, swaying from the branches of an oak. I stepped in front of Atukhos. As much as he had been exposed to in his young life, there was no reason to add a hanging to his nightmares.

'Close your eyes,' I told him. He did so with a sullen nod. There were fearful groans and tears but, again, their resilience held. I noticed a little milking stool, tipped on its side next to an oilcloth and a smashed wine flagon. The fellow had taken his own life; that much was clear.

I took out the knife I had in my few possessions, balancing on that rickety stool.

'Move away!'

When I heard their shuffling feet, I cut him down and he landed with a weighty thump. There was an intake of breath. 'It's Hilarion!' said Ana.

I had seen the bloated face and blackened tongue, protruding from his mouth as if he had choked upon a catfish, and had no wish for a second look.

'Who is Hilarion?' I said, ushering the group away.

For a few moments, she didn't answer. 'One of the council of Euneus' men. He had turned traitor, so they said.'

Then he deserved his ignominious death.

We made it to the bay of Moudros just as dawn was breaking. Quite how those old souls made it, I will never know: they might easily have given up. My foolhardy plan proved effective. There had been grumbles that it was madness to make for the harbour of the island's bitter enemies though, naturally, I disagreed. Whoever the men their treacherous leaders had mustered and dispatched to Myrine, they were a long way away by now. Those who remained were likely to be people who wanted no part in the matter. And so it proved. I was able to barter safe passage on a skiff and a merchantman for less gold than I had in my possession. There was pity in their faces and the fare was reasonable.

The skiff was mine. The others could go where they liked.

I have never cared much for people who proclaim themselves to have no regrets in the course of a life of any length: they are either singularly unimaginative or self-deceiving liars. Saying goodbye to that wide-eyed boy is one of my greatest. Something about him drew affection from the coldest of souls but my wish to depart alone was not because I did not like him. I reasoned I was old and my life was ill-suited to surrogate fatherhood. Ana gladly opened her arms to him and, before he went, he opened his little fist and showed me what he had been clenching so tightly. 'A ring,' he said.

'I can see that. Whose is it?'

He looked at me in confusion. 'Ancaeus' of course.'

My disapproving frown softened when I recalled the scene on the beach. Though his back had been to me, I now understood what had transpired. 'Ah,' I said. 'And now you must guard it for seventy years before you pass it on. Do you think you can manage that?'

He thought about it and nodded.

'Good boy.' I reached out for his hand but he flung himself against my legs and clasped them tight. I ruffled his hair and felt my heart quicken, and I was grateful when Ana gently prised him from me. He turned back just once before stepping onto the boarding ramp and, damn my sentimental eyes, it was all I could do not to rub them. That time would come, soon enough.

My brief guardianship left me aware of something I had never had and all the more wistful for its absence. It reminded me of Eurydice. Heed me, stranger, when I say that only one thing endures the holocaust of memory, and this is love.

I never saw Atukhos again. I often wonder what became of him but I think he would have made something of himself. A good little heart beat beneath his breast, and what is more important than this? I have seen the wealthiest of men living unhappily in miserable splendour because they lacked that one vital spark that we all crave.

As for the rogues of the *Salamander*, I only saw them twice again in the next eleven or twelve years. The spring following events in Lemnos, I paid them for a sea crossing to the island of Thasos from Thrace, where I had spent a difficult winter. They spoke with grudging respect of Xandros and, when I told them of his grisly fate, their condolences were sincere enough. The young lookout Glaux looked particularly affected by it.

Many years later, I heard my name being called on a quayside in Cyprus. My performances were rather briefer by this time and I was less able to travel. I had been on that island from autumn to spring.

'Orpheus! Hey, Orpheus, don't you recognise me?'

A bronzed, lean and gaudily bedecked figure swaggered towards me. Behind him was a crew of bare-chested toughs, and it seemed most of them bore at least two blades. I looked from them back to him and admitted I had no idea who he was. Were it not for him calling my name, I confess I thought I might have been robbed then and there, in broad daylight.

The man's face fell like a sulking child. 'It's me, Glaux!'

I murmured my apologies and muttered something about my poor eyesight, but he appeared not to have heard for he immediately introduced me to his crew. I recognised none of them but, over their shoulders, I could see the *Salamander* was much as she ever was.

Some of them were half-impressed by meeting the Thracian bard; most clearly were not. They chewed on their mastic and fidgeted like men keen to be on their way.

'Where is the captain?' I asked.

'He's here!' he declared with a shifty grin. 'It's me now!' I don't recall much else that he said: it was clear that he had fallen in with the sea raiders.

'It was well met, Orpheus,' he said as his crew began to drift off. 'We're on our way to the rich land of the pharaohs and that's where we'll settle. There are no harbours in the Archipelagos big enough for all our ships!'

He fairly bounded away, with his face flushed. I watched the *Salamander* slip her cables and sail away over the horizon under a flawless sky, albeit not out of any affection for that young braggart. Instead, it was like watching another door slowly closing on one's life. As it happened, that same door slammed shut upon Glaux and his men. Many people speak of the battle at the Nile Delta as the greatest and most ferociously fought of all time, and I have heard nothing to give the lie to this. Rameses III knew well what was coming and he lay in wait for that unholy armada of Sea Peoples. His archers and chariots cut them to ribbons on land whilst the raiders' ships were forced ashore. Despite his own losses, Rameses was wise enough to allow most of the surviving pirates to settle in the fertile lands at the edge of his dominion and, almost at a stroke, solve the problems that had plagued the seas and the coasts for two generations.

In connection with this, there is one more story that I must share before I depart, and it concerns the champion called Huliat. Many years later, when I was travelling through the ancient lands of the Levant, I stopped in a little village of baked bricks and palm trees by the sea, not far from the city of Joppa. I was hosted by a garrulous couple, who told me a curious tale about a recent skirmish between the people of Philistia and their neighbours to the east, the Canaanites. The matter was settled, so the story went, by single combat. The Philistines had amongst their number a proud champion of quite extraordinary size; as tall as six cubits according to some. Nobody wanted to face him and thus entire battles were decided without the clash of a single sword. So when a Canaanite boy stepped forwards, the Philistine roared with laughter and refused to raise his spear against such a diminutive opponent.

But the Canaanites had the last laugh, for the boy was an accomplished slinger and felled him with a single shot between the eyes. I took them aback, I think, by the eagerness with which I sought his name.

'"Huliat", which in our language is "Goliath". It means "Lion Man".'

Goliath.

For the death of my friend Ancaeus, I was glad he was brought down in such a manner. Though she took her time, Nemesis eventually caught up with his Hubris. In that moment, I began to wonder whether the gods had abandoned us after all.

And with that, my friend, for such you now are, I must lay down my lyre for I am tired and the days grow short.

Farewell.

XXXV

In a bay, tucked within the opposite recesses of the Archipelagos, lay the shell of a mouldering galley. The wild-haired man who now approached it, clutching a little bundle under his arm, paced his way around it, murmuring anecdotes and chuckling sadly at all that it had witnessed with him. He wondered how many men still drew breath who could relive any of the memories. He tutted at the exposed ribs of the hull and patted them consolingly. Noticing one of the few remaining patches of black paint, curling free of the faded eye by the prow, he leaned over and prodded it with a gnarled finger. It slid away altogether and fluttered to the sand. The sight induced a wave of sadness far more urgent than he was prepared for and he sniffed, muttering in annoyance with himself.

Dusk was encroaching and he noticed a peculiar tautness to the evening. He realised that the birds were quiet and the cicadas had fallen silent. Even the lap of the waves against the shore seemed distant. He turned on his heels, looking around him, sensing a presence.

Did he hear a whisper or was it the soughing of trees in the gentle breeze?

As he was about to lower himself onto his favoured patch of sand by the bow of the ship, he caught a glimpse of a man whom he had not seen in many years walking towards him. He wore a felt cap that showed his greying temples and a sweat-stained tunic. As he approached, he bustled with restless energy, and he twirled a shipwright's axe in his right hand. He pointed to a spot just above where the old man was now stood and turned towards someone unseen.

'You see that?' the shipwright growled.

'I see it,' came a familiar voice from out of the encroaching darkness.

'It covers a little wedge cut from a sacred oak within the holy shrine at Dodona. She'll speak to you when you don't know what's in your own heart. Listen to her.'

The old man looked on as the shipwright wiped the sweat from his brow and buried his axe into the space where once there was the trunk of an olive tree.

'And now, I'm done.'

'Thank you!' the voice called after the shipwright. 'She's beautiful.'

'She is,' he said, without looking back. 'The finest ship ever made.' Then the shipwright vanished and the tension in the air eased a little. Birds began to trill their evensong and the cicadas screeched in search of a mate.

There was a time when he would have been terrified by such an apparition but these days, apart from snakes, which still turned him cold, he was too old to be scared by anything. He eased himself to the sand with a grimace and let the words he had just heard run through his mind. He recognised the voice of the one speaking to the shipwright without any difficulty. He recognised it because it was his own.

In truth, no oracle had ever spoken to him through the sacred oaken section or, for that matter, any other part of the galley, but it didn't matter. *Argo* had accomplished her impossible task and outlived nearly all of those who had sailed aboard her. He reached up and patted the prow.

The finest ship ever made.

On that point, Jason agreed with Argus. She was.

He unwrapped the little bundle, which contained a husk of bread and a little wooden horse with wheels. Spinning the wheels absently, he wondered why he had brought it this evening but, feeling unbidden tears stinging his eyes, he put it on his lap. Taking a bite from the bread, he looked out over the bay of Iolkos. The moon hung heavy over the water and began to spill its light as darkness fell. The days were drawing short and he would soon need to bring his cloak for the evenings.

A sudden wind picked up and it caught him by surprise. It brought with it a sense of melancholy so crushingly profound that he wondered if his lungs were collapsing. Had he not, after all, witnessed his beloved helmsman Tiphys suffer a similar fate?

And then he knew.

He knew that the best of them and the last of them had perished. He knew with a final certainty that they had died defending the boy who carried Jason's own blood in his veins. The world he had once known and the life he had once cherished were at an end. He tossed away the half-eaten bread and clutched at the tender hands, the long-absent hands, that had once held the same little horse he now held, and closed his eyes.

The groan sharpened to a dull crack but he experienced a moment of serenity. As the rotten bow post tottered upon the last few fragments of wood directly above him, the breeze stiffened and nudged it. It gained speed as it swung from on high and struck him in his temple with a dull thump.

Agata found him early the following morning under grey skies, disturbing a gull that hopped away with his husk of bread. Jason lay on his side under *Argo*'s broken prow like a slumbering child, clutching his wooden horse tight against his chest.

He had been a cantankerous, difficult man at times but, underneath it all, a sad and sometimes kindly heart had beaten. She wept for him and mumbled a prayer of deliverance. When she was ready, she got up and dried her eyes. The bones of Jason's mother and father lay cold in the family tomb at Dimini and none in Iolkos – what remained of it – would turn such a weight of soil without gold.

With a leaden heart, she crossed the pine-strewn beach towards the forlorn city.

At that very moment, a fishing skiff drifted into a bay at the tip of the Perachora peninsula. Huddled against the chill of early morning were two passengers, who fell silent as the fisherman took the last few strokes before hauling the oars inboard with a double *clunk*. The skiff scraped against the beach and the fisherman splashed into the shallows to help them disembark, brushing down the tips of his magnificent moustache and straightening his back, which clicked in protest.

One of the passengers removed her hood and pressed a polished stone of jasper into his palm. 'Wait here. We will only be a few minutes.'

'My lady,' said the fisherman. He had never seen Greek women with such startling green eyes. He watched them cross the beach then climb the track up the rocky hillside, wondering who on earth they were and what they wanted in this desolate place. The locals never came here; it was haunted.

Medea found the ancient path that led through a patch of scrub to a little stone enclosure, overgrown and silent, and Eriopis followed. Medea closed her eyes before stepping inside. The twin cairns were in good order and the undergrowth behind had been recently cut back. She embraced each in turn, only prising herself away with great reluctance.

'My darlings, I told you your mother would return, did I not?' Medea retrieved a linen square from her sleeve and dabbed her eyes. 'You would have been thirty tomorrow but you will be forever eight.'

Behind her, Eriopis saw her mother become rigid then bend down to retrieve something from the ground beneath the cairns. 'What is it?' she asked.

'Look.'

Eriopis took them from Medea and looked closely at them: olivewood boats with sweeping keels and graceful prows. One of them looked like it had since been repaired. Though little patches of mildew had penetrated the wax coating, it was clear that they had been carved by a highly skilled hand. 'Did Jason make these?'

Tears flowed freely down Medea's cheeks but she managed a dry laugh and sniffed. 'No. Jason was many things but he was no craftsman, unlike a few of his men. Put them back now, my love. It is enough to know they have been remembered and respects have been paid here.' She closed her eyes and laid a hand on either cairn whilst whispering a prayer in the Colchian tongue. 'Sleep in peace, my darlings.'

When she had finished, she dipped her head and left the enclosure. Eriopis watched her pass and experienced a wash of sadness. Her mother looked stooped and grey, as if events in recent weeks had added many years to her life. They had both remarked on the journey here that it felt like an age had passed, and they hoped they would both find some peace in the lands far to the east of this spot. The long journey would be worth it but the nights were drawing in. They must not linger.

They made their way to the path and the bay where the fisherman was waiting. He looked up at them and flattened his moustache with a smile.

EPILOGUE

Katharsis

Athens, 480 BC

The bard finished his tale and his words faded into the fragrant night. There was a ripple of applause and he gratefully accepted a cup of wine to slake his thirst.

'Do you think, sir, that we will be victorious, should they strike this month?'

The bard turned to see a sandy-haired boy, not yet a youth, looking up at him. He had seen such wide-eyed innocence in almost every town and dusty village he had ever visited but never so earnestly nor eloquently expressed.

'These pirates that you told us about. Well… They killed everyone, didn't they? Do you think the same thing will happen again? Do you think we could possibly prevail?'

The bard looked about him but could see no sign of any who might be the boy's parents, though plenty on their way to leave the square now waited expectantly for the answer.

'Do I think we could prevail?' The bard stroked his beard ruminatively. 'Well now, let me think.'

He had considered this very question many times every day, every month of this past year and had always arrived at the same answer. Of course not. The Persian horde, even allowing for the inevitable conflation of rumour, was innumerable. But was the raw truth what they wanted to hear that balmy evening? No. A hundred times, no.

He was about to offer some bland, encouraging response when he took in the people around him, framed by pine and olive as timeless as the earth itself. They were upright and proud. Even the elderly seemed to transform before his eyes, straightening and casting aside their walking sticks. Some of these folk in their twilight years would have been men in their prime when the last tyrant was ejected from Athens, over three decades previously. Perhaps a handful had witnessed it. Maybe someone in this very square had even laid hands on Hippias himself.

'You listen to me, my boy, and listen well. Look around you. What do you see?'

Dutifully, the boy turned on his heels. He shrugged. 'I see people.'

'People, yes,' said the bard, raising his finger, 'but not just any people. Survivors! For the Sea Peoples cannot possibly have extinguished everyone, can they? Our ancestors have met pain and suffering, desperation and hardship many times over in the distant past. They have stood at the same crossroads as you and doubted what to do next, fearing they might take the wrong road and find Hades. And yet here these people are now, despite it all.' He tapped the side of his head and smiled, as he began to believe the power of his own words. 'Come what may, my boy, we will prevail.'

Glossary

agora	the ancient Greek market square
chiton	a long woollen tunic
dioskouroi	twin sons of Zeus (here used in affectionate jest)
eidolon	a spirit image of a living or dead person
himation	an outer garment worn over the left shoulder
katharsis	ritual cleansing of emotions or spirit
kleos	everlasting glory
krater	a mixing bowl for wine
kuna	a term of abuse
lawagetas	second highest dignitary after the *wanax*, likely an army leader
ma Dia!	an expression of surprise, meaning (roughly) 'By God!'
megaron	the main hall of a palace
nomarch	a governor of a community, similar to a mayor
palaestra	an exercise area
pentekonter	a fifty-oared galley
phantasma	a spectre
phthisis	a non-specific wasting disease such as tuberculosis
pithos	a measuring jar
polis	an ancient Greek 'city state'
propylon	the front gate of a building
pyxis	a box for jewellery

stele (plural *stelai*)	a grave-marker, usually a stone slab
thes (plural *thetes)*	the lowest strata of Greek society; the peasantry
tholos	a tomb with a domed chamber
wanax	a 'king', the central figure of authority in Greek societies
xenia	ritualised guest-friendship or hospitality

Months

There is no simple Bronze Age equivalent for our Gregorian calendar but it is possible to identify certain clues from the so-called 'Linear B' inscriptions that have survived from this era. For example, two months (probably linked to festivals) are attested in Linear B tablets from the palace at Pylos: the *pakijanijojo* and the *powowitojo*. The latter has been interpreted as the sailing month. I have also referred to agricultural duties inscribed upon the 'Gezer calendar', inscribed in Canaanite and probably dating to the end of the Bronze Age. The activities it mentions, albeit in a different part of the Mediterranean basin, correlate to our knowledge of seasonal produce in Greece both then and now. I am also indebted to the work of Dr Emily Hauser, whose calendar in her novel *For the Winner* blends the Linear B evidence with Hesiod's didactic poem from the Archaic Period, *Works and Days*.

January	The Month of Poseidon
February	The Month of New Wine
March	The Month of Sowing
April	The Month of Sailing
May	The Month of Barley
June	The Month of Roses
July	The Month of Threshing Wheat
August	The Month of the Grape Harvest
September	The Month of Ploughing
October	The Month of Rains
November	The Month of Gathering
December	The Month of the Goddess

Historical Note

In 2001, I was with friends in a pub in Westminster in the early evening following the Remembrance Day parade at the Cenotaph. A sizeable group of smartly uniformed veterans – none of whom appeared to be under sixty – was finding its voice in one corner of the venue. They were quite loud, very proud but causing not a whit of trouble. I glanced over when their singing faltered, sensing a confrontation. A couple of much younger drinkers had dared to interrupt them, suggesting, I suppose, that they take their reunion elsewhere. I recall those old soldiers rising to a man, crimson-faced, medals bristling as they straightened their backs. They didn't breathe a word: they didn't need to. The fearsome looks on those decorated old warriors (I think from the Parachute Regiment, though the colour of their berets eludes me) was enough to send the dissenters packing. This projection of brotherhood was the inspiration behind the annual gathering of the Argonauts at the tip of the Perachora peninsula.

Whilst there is, of course, no trace in the surviving stories of any of Jason's brothers-in-arms rallying to the island's defence, we should not scoff at the thought of a sexagenarian – or, for that matter, even a septuagenarian – still being capable of wielding a spear in the ancient world. There is, after all, plenty of evidence that a Roman soldier must still be capable of twenty-mile route marches at the end of his twenty-five-year career, and the general Gaius Marius was still fighting right up to his death in his late sixties. He may well have been exceptional but so, surely, were the Argonauts, and theirs was a tough, unforgiving world.

Following these men has been the most wonderful – and often

frustrating – privilege, and the length of this note hopefully gives some impression of the range of issues I have encountered during the previous few years. Through the trilogy, the data available for constructing a plausible and semi-realistic story steadily diminished to the point of becoming almost a Will-o'-the wisp. Until some definitive evidence comes to light (and what would that look like anyway?), the so-called 'Bronze Age Collapse' will remain one of the greatest unknowns in world history, certainly in proportion to its impact upon European and Near Eastern civilisations. This is both a blessing and a curse to a novelist. Whereas the likes of Pindar and Apollonius, amongst other writers, left us with substantial material for the outward leg of *Argo*'s voyage and some rather more fanciful stuff for the return, reconstructing the period following the Trojan War is rather like groping in the dark through the crumbling ruins of a Mycenaean palace.

And this is precisely where Professor Michael B. Cosmopoulos came riding over the horizon. His recent lecture ('Homer and the Mycenaeans: The Mycenaean City of Iklaina and the Iliad'), hosted online by the British School at Athens, peeled back the layers of Homer and enabled a fleeting but brilliant glimpse of late Mycenaean society. Referencing Pierre Nora's *Between Memory and History: Les Lieux de Mémoire* (University of California, 1989), Cosmopoulos offered a compelling demonstration of how the 'storied landscape' of ancient ruins, as carriers of local memories, can help shape oral tradition. In the hands of an expert bard like Orpheus, that shaping could have a profound effect upon successive generations of storytellers.

The vital work of American scholars Albert Lord and Milman Parry in the first half of the twentieth century, in preserving and studying thousands of hours of Slavic poetry, proved that epics as long as the *Iliad* and the *Odyssey*, could be composed and performed by highly-accomplished, and often illiterate, bards. The most skilful and versatile professional they encountered, Avdo Međedović, was able to deliver over the course of five days a poem, *The Wedding of Smailagić Meho*, that ran to 13,000 lines. Međedović boasted he knew even longer poems. To anybody interested in this astonishing (and, sadly, almost extinct) art, I would highly recommend the first half of Albert Lord's *The Singer of Tales* (Harvard University Press, 1960), particularly the section on the three stages of bardic composition. The ability of Homer to layer and nuance the *Odyssey* through embedded narratives is an astonishing human achievement considering it was composed without any recourse to writing. Struggling for even a sense of this layering is hard enough with all the benefits of a word processor.

We should remember that the *Iliad* and *Odyssey* were not the only epic poems in circulation. Whilst the story of Xandros is entirely fictional, his father Euneus – the son of Jason and Hypsipyle – is referenced in numerous sources, including Homer (in the *Iliad*, for instance, Euneus reprovisions the Greek fleet with a vast quantity of Lemnian wine).

Interestingly, the work of Professor Alessandro Della Seta (American Journal of Archaeology, 1927) suggests the remnants of a Mycenaean civilisation on Lemnos into the Iron Age, when the Aegean had not seen the boats of the Sea Peoples for more than 200 years. This stubbornness, and the importance of Hypsipyle to Jason's story, only confirmed for me that the last stand must be set on the island. I therefore felt sufficiently justified by the island's rich heritage – both literary and archaeological – to populate it with a free hand.

Of the large cast in *Hades*, I will single out only two. Firstly, Orestes. Anybody familiar with the post-war history of Greece will know something of the bloody turmoil caused by the Nazi invasion and withdrawal, and the subsequent struggles for ascendancy by feuding partisan groups. In some ways, Orestes is an amalgam of Late Bronze Age and twentieth-century bandit leader and small island Classical tyrant, driven by opportunism and blinded by bitterness. Physically, however, I have based him closely upon human remains discovered during the excavation of Grave Circle B at Mycenae in 1951. These skeletons were initially examined by archaeologist Dr J. Lawrence Angel, and their skulls were revisited in 1986/7 by a team led by noted experts in facial reconstruction Dr Jonathan Prag and Richard Neave. The facial similarities suggest ties of kinship stretching across several generations of the Mycenaean elite but it is the grisly damage to the bones that really draws attention. Skull Z59, according to Dr Angel, 'belonged to a man of perhaps fifty with a long face and an arthritic shoulder, a battle-scarred and formidable old warrior'. At some point in his life, he sustained a significant injury above his left eyebrow which, though apparently not fatal, would have left his skull with a visible indentation. Although the bones in the shaft graves predate Orestes by at least a couple of centuries, Z59's age at death – and the tell-tale signs of a very tough life – made him an irresistible candidate for the son of Agamemnon.

Secondly, a note on Huliat. Biblical scholars with vastly more knowledge than me will be quick to point out that King David's rule of the united kingdom of Israel and Judah rightly belongs to the eleventh century BC, so I have stretched poetic license some way beyond breaking point by including his old adversary in this story. However, other scholars such as Finkelstein and Silberman have adopted a freer interpretation of David's life (*The Bible Unearthed*, Free Press, 2001) that also suited my purpose. Author Malcolm Gladwell makes a fascinating argument for Goliath suffering from the medical condition of acromegaly (see his short, sharp TED talk from 2013) and, if this was true, he would be in the same company as wrestler Andre the Giant and world's tallest ever man, Robert Pershing Wadlow.

Most commentators agree that, of the Sea Peoples named upon Rameses III's funerary monument at Medinet Habu, the Peleset are likely the Philistines, and the material culture of the Philistines certainly bears a close resemblance to Mycenaean style. The literature on these shadowy sea rovers is vast and opinions differ widely as to their geographical origins no less than it does about the circumstances that drove people to take to the seas in the first place. That some Mycenaean Greeks joined them is beyond reasonable doubt, as is their defeat by Rameses III, and it is their depiction by the Egyptians that we can thank for much of what we do know about them. Therefore I felt fully justified in having Huliat/Goliath's origins somewhere in the Archipelagos, and, moreover, it is readily accepted that single combat between champions was sometimes the means of settling wider disputes. Who is to say that the Sea Peoples did not boast such a warrior amongst them? For a general overview of these rovers, the Mycenaeans and the ancient world in general, I restate my love of Michael Wood's timeless series *In Search of The Trojan War* and would also highly recommend Dan Davis' excellent history-based YouTube channel. I have drunk a lot of coffee watching these documentaries and podcasts over the past few years.

Finally, a good portion of Orpheus' final song is inspired by the poem published in 1867 by the multi-talented William Morris, *The Life and Death of Jason*. I lack all of the skills required to arrange it in dactylic hexameter, the metre of Homeric epic, but the lines (for the most part) at least fall within the correct range of syllables. For any artistic offence caused by these verses, please take it up with me, not him!

Mark Knowles
August 2023

ACKNOWLEDGEMENTS

If ever there was an iceberg that refused to melt in contact with Hades – *this* Hades, at any rate – it was editor Greg Rees. He has been a cool, calm head throughout my early struggles with this manuscript, and I am immensely grateful for his good humour, common sense and bardic wisdom. Copyeditor Helena Newton's extraordinarily keen eye and memory have, once more, saved me from a few blushes and I owe her, as well as every other contributing member of the Head of Zeus/Bloomsbury team my very grateful thanks.

I was very fortunate in the course of researching this novel to visit Mycenae, and was luckier still to stay at the fantastic hotel La Petite Planete, a short walk from the site. It was there I met the owners Vasiliki and Greg and was received with the most wonderful Greek hospitality. Greg is a first-rate artisan and Vasiliki is a descendant of the venerable lady who first opened her doors to banker-turned-archaeologist Heinrich Schliemann and his entourage in the early 1870s. Her knowledge of – and passion for – Mycenae's history is profound, and flows through generations of her family. She was the first to tell me about the valley to the west of the citadel and the partially overgrown tholos tombs, somewhat off the beaten track, that no school textbook had ever mentioned. One of these, aptly called The Tomb of Orestes, features in *Hades*. I returned earlier this year with over thirty school pupils and staff, all of whom were deeply touched by the owners' warmth and generosity.

A big thank you to Niall MacDonald for introducing me to Tennyson's *Ulysses*. I only knew the famous last line but, when hearing about the premise to *Hades*, he flawlessly recited the whole thing! It struck me how much this poem resonated with the Argonauts' desire for one last adventure, and I kept the sentiments at the front of my mind during the various edits.

Thanks also to Angie Snelling for showing me the Huer's Hut in Newquay and explaining its use. It really appealed to add another Bronze Age link between Cornwall and Greece!

Even as I write these notes, in the courtyard of an idyllic French watermill at the end of a family holiday (I doubt I will ever get to repeat these words!), I can hear my two children playing indoors. It reminds me of those many occasions in the past few years that I have been present, without being *fully* present, in their company. It's only fitting, therefore, that Lara and Max – and my wife Rachael – receive the final thank you for their boundless love and forbearance. I promise I will make it up to you.

About the Author

Mark Knowles took degrees in Classics and Management Studies at Downing College, Cambridge. After a decade working as a frontline officer and supervisor within the Metropolitan Police Service, he became Head of Classics at a school in Harrogate. He is a particular fan of experimental archaeology and rowed on the reconstructed ancient Athenian trireme *Olympias* during its last sea trials in Greece in 1994.

Follow Mark on @mark77knowles and markknowles.info.